doctor and he was the second of six children. ... ...
at Oak Park, a Chicago suburb.

In 1917 Hemingway joined the Kansas City *Star* as a cub reporter. The following year he volunteered to work as an ambulance driver on the Italian front where he was badly wounded but twice decorated for his services. He returned to America in 1919 and married in 1921. In 1922 he reported on the Greco-Turkish war, then two years later resigned from journalism to devote himself to fiction. He settled in Paris where he renewed his earlier friendship with such fellow-American expatriates as Ezra Pound and Gertrude Stein. Their encouragement and criticism were to play a valuable part in the formation of his style.

Hemingway's first two published works were *Three Stories and Ten Poems* and *In Our Time*, but it was the satirical novel, *The Torrents of Spring*, which established his name more widely. His international reputation was firmly secured by his next three books: *Fiesta*, *Men Without Women* and *A Farewell to Arms*.

He was passionately involved with bullfighting, big-game hunting and deep-sea fishing, and his writing reflected this. He visited Spain during the Civil War and described his experiences in the bestseller, *For Whom the Bell Tolls*.

His direct and deceptively simple style of writing spawned generations of imitators but no equals. Recognition of his position in contemporary literature came in 1954 when he was awarded the Nobel Prize for Literature, following the publication of *The Old Man and the Sea*.

Ernest Hemingway died in 1961.

By the same author

Novels
The Torrents of Spring
Fiesta
A Farewell to Arms
To Have and Have Not
For Whom the Bell Tolls
Across the River and Into the Trees
The Old Man and the Sea
Islands in the Stream
The Garden of Eden
True at First light

Stories
Men Without Women
Winner Take Nothing
The Snows of Kilimanjaro

General
Death in the Afternoon
Green Hills of Africa
A Moveable Feast
The Dangerous Summer

Drama
The Fifth Column

Collected Works
The Essential Hemingway
By-Line

THE FIRST FORTY-NINE STORIES

Ernest Hemingway

arrow books

Published by Arrow Books in 2004

21

Copyright © Hemingway Foreign Rights Trust 1939

First published in Great Britain in 1944 by
Jonathan Cape

Arrow Books
Random House, 20 Vauxhall Bridge Road,
London, SW1V 2SA

www.randomhouse.co.uk

Addresses for companies within The Random House Group Limited can be
found at: www.randomhouse.co.uk/offices.htm

The Random House Group Limited Reg. No. 954009

A CIP catalogue record for this book
is available from the British Library

ISBN 9780099339212

The Random House Group Limited supports The Forest Stewardship
Council (FSC), the leading international forest certification organisation. All
our titles that are printed on Greenpeace approved FSC certified paper carry
the FSC logo. Our paper procurement policy can be found at
www.randomhouse.co.uk/environment

Mixed Sources
Product group from well-managed
forests and other controlled sources
www.fsc.org Cert no. TT-COC-002139
© 1996 Forest Stewardship Council

Typeset by SX Composing DTP, Rayleigh, Essex
Printed in the UK by CPI Bookmarque, Croydon, CR0 4TD

Preface

The first four stories are the last ones I have written. The others follow in the order in which they were originally published.

The first one I wrote was Up in Michigan, written in Paris in 1921. The last was Old Man at the Bridge cabled from Barcelona in April of 1938.

Beside The Fifth Column, I wrote The Killers, Today Is Friday, Ten Indians, part of The Sun Also Rises and the first third of To Have and Have Not in Madrid. It was always a good place for working. So was Paris, and so were Key West, Florida, in the cool months; the ranch, near Cooke City, Mountain; Kansas City; Chicago; Toronto; and Havana, Cuba.

Some other places were not so good but maybe we were not so good when we were in them.

There are many kinds of stories in this book. I hope that you will find some that you like. Reading them over, the ones I liked the best, outside of those that have achieved some notoriety so that school teachers include them in story collections that their pupils have to buy in story courses, and you are always faintly embarrassed to read them and wonder whether you really wrote them or did you maybe hear them somewhere, are The Short Happy Life of Francis Macomber, In Another Country, Hills Like White Elephants, A Way You'll Never Be, The Snows of Kilimanjaro, A Clean Well-Lighted Place, and a story called The Light of the World which nobody else ever liked. There are some others too. Because if you did not like them you would not publish them.

In going where you have to go, and doing what you have to do, and seeing what you have to see, you dull and blunt the instrument you write with. But I would rather have it bent and dull and know I had to put it on the grindstone again and hammer it into shape and put a whetstone to it, and know that I had something to write about, than to have it bright and shining and nothing to say, or smooth and well-oiled in the closet, but unused.

Now it is necessary to get to the grindstone again. I would like to live long enough to write three more novels and twenty-five more stories. I know some pretty good ones.

ERNEST HEMINGWAY

Contents

The Short Stories of Ernest Hemingway

The Short Happy Life of
Francis Macomber

It was now lunch time and they were all sitting under the double green fly of the dining tent pretending that nothing had happened.

'Will you have lime juice or lemon squash?' Macomber asked.

'I'll have a gimlet,' Robert Wilson told him.

'I'll have a gimlet too. I need something,' Macomber's wife said.

'I suppose it's the thing to do,' Macomber agreed. 'Tell him to make three gimlets.'

The mess boy had started them already, lifting the bottles out of the canvas cooling bags that sweated wet in the wind that blew through the trees that shaded the tents.

'What had I ought to give them?' Macomber asked.

'A quid would be plenty,' Wilson told him. 'You don't want to spoil them.'

'Will the headman distribute it?'

'Absolutely.'

Francis Macomber had, half an hour before, been carried to his tent from the edge of the camp in triumph on the arms and shoulders of the cook, the personal boys, the skinner and the porters. The gun-bearers had taken no part in the demonstration. When the native boys put him down at the door of his tent, he had shaken all their hands, received their congratulations, and then gone into the tent and sat on the bed until his wife came in. She did not speak to him when she came in and he left the tent at once to wash his face and hands in the portable wash basin outside and go over to the

3

dining tent to sit in a comfortable canvas chair in the breeze and the shade.

'You've got your lion,' Robert Wilson said to him, 'and a damned fine one too.'

Mrs Macomber looked at Wilson quickly. She was an extremely handsome and well-kept woman of the beauty and social position which had, five years before, commanded five thousand dollars as the price of endorsing, with photographs, a beauty product which she had never used. She had been married to Francis Macomber for eleven years.

'He is a good lion, isn't he?' Macomber said. His wife looked at him now. She looked at both these men as though she had never seen them before.

One, Wilson, the white hunter, she knew she had never truly seen before. He was about middle height with sandy hair, a stubby moustache, a very red face and extremely cold blue eyes with faint white wrinkles at the corners that grooved merrily when he smiled. He smiled at her now and she looked away from his face at the way his shoulders sloped in the loose tunic he wore with the four big cartridges held in loops where the left breast pocket should have been, at his big brown hands, his old slacks, his very dirty boots and back to his red face again. She noticed where the baked red of his face stopped in a white line that marked the circle left by his Stetson hat that hung now from one of the pegs of the tent pole.

'Well, here's to the lion,' Robert Wilson said. He smiled at her again and, not smiling, she looked curiously at her husband.

Francis Macomber was very tall, very well built if you did not mind that length of bone, dark, his hair cropped like an oarsman, rather thin-lipped, and was considered handsome. He was dressed in the same sort of safari clothes that Wilson wore except that his were new, he was thirty-five years old, kept himself very fit, was good at court games, had a number of big-game fishing records, and had just shown himself, very publicly, to be a coward.

'Here's to the lion,' he said. 'I can't ever thank you for what you did.'

Margaret, his wife, looked away from him and back to Wilson.

'Let's not talk about the lion,' she said.

Wilson looked over at her without smiling and now she smiled at him.

'It's been a very strange day,' she said. 'Hadn't you ought to put your hat on even under the canvas at noon? You told me that, you know.'

'Might put it on,' said Wilson.

'You know you have a very red face, Mr Wilson,' she told him and smiled again.

'Drink,' said Wilson.

'I don't think so,' she said. 'Francis drinks a great deal, but his face is never red.'

'It's red today,' Macomber tried a joke.

'No,' said Margaret. 'It's mine that's red today. But Mr Wilson's is always red.'

'Must be racial,' said Wilson. 'I say, you wouldn't like to drop my beauty as a topic, would you?'

'I've just started on it.'

'Let's chuck it,' said Wilson.

'Conversation is going to be so difficult,' Margaret said.

'Don't be silly, Margot,' her husband said.

'No difficulty,' Wilson said. 'Got a damn fine lion.'

Margot looked at them both and they both saw that she was going to cry. Wilson had seen it coming for a long time and he dreaded it. Macomber was past dreading it.

'I wish it hadn't happened. Oh, I wish it hadn't happened,' she said and started for her tent. She made no noise of crying but they could see that her shoulders were shaking under the rose-colored, sun-proofed shirt she wore.

'Women upset,' said Wilson to the tall man. 'Amounts to nothing. Strain on the nerves and one thing'n another.'

'No,' said Macomber. 'I suppose that I rate that for the rest of my life now.'

'Nonsense. Let's have a spot of the giant killer,' said Wilson. 'Forget the whole thing. Nothing to it anyway.'

'We might try,' said Macomber. 'I won't forget what you did for me though.'

'Nothing,' said Wilson. 'All nonsense.'

So they sat there in the shade where the camp was pitched under some wide-topped acacia trees with a boulder-strewn cliff behind them, and a stretch of grass that ran to the bank of a boulder-filled stream in front with forest beyond it, and drank their just-cool lime drinks and avoided one another's eyes while the boys set the table for lunch. Wilson could tell that the boys all knew about it now and when he saw Macomber's personal boy looking curiously at his master while he was putting dishes on the table he snapped at him in Swahili. The boy turned away with his face blank.

'What were you telling him?' Macomber asked.

'Nothing. Told him to look alive or I'd see he got about fifteen of the best.'

'What's that? Lashes?'

'It's quite illegal,' Wilson said. 'You're supposed to fine them.'

'Do you still have them whipped?'

'Oh, yes. They could raise a row if they chose to complain. But they don't. They prefer it to the fines.'

'How strange!' said Macomber.

'Not strange, really,' Wilson said. 'Which would you rather do? Take a good birching or lose your pay?'

Then he felt embarrassed at asking it and before Macomber could answer he went on, 'We all take a beating every day, you know, one way or another.'

This was no better. 'Good God,' he thought. 'I am a diplomat, aren't I?'

'Yes, we take a beating,' said Macomber, still not looking at him. 'I'm awfully sorry about that lion business. It doesn't have to go any further, does it? I mean no one will hear about it, will they?'

'You mean will I tell it at the Mathaiga Club?' Wilson looked at him now coldly. He had not expected this. So he's a bloody four-letter man as well as a bloody coward, he thought. I rather liked him too until today. But how is one to know about an American?

'No,' said Wilson. 'I'm a professional hunter. We never talk about our clients. You can be quite easy on that. It's supposed to be bad form to ask us not to talk though.'

He had decided now that to break would be much easier. He would eat, then, by himself and could read a book with his meals. They would eat by themselves. He would see them

6

through the safari on a very formal basis – what was it the French called it? Distinguished consideration – and it would be a damn sight easier than having to go through this emotional trash. He'd insult him and make a good clean break. Then he could read a book with his meals and he'd still be drinking their whisky. That was the phrase for it when a safari went bad. You ran into another white hunter and you asked, 'How is everything going?' and he answered, 'Oh, I'm still drinking their whiskey,' and you knew everything had gone to pot.

'I'm sorry,' Macomber said and looked at him with his American face that would stay adolescent until it became middle-aged, and Wilson noted his crew-cropped hair, fine eyes only faintly shifty, good nose, thin lips and handsome jaw. 'I'm sorry I didn't realize that. There are lots of things I don't know.'

So what could he do, Wilson thought. He was all ready to break it off quickly and neatly and here the beggar was apologizing after he had just insulted him. He made one more attempt. 'Don't worry about me talking,' he said. 'I have a living to make. You know in Africa no woman ever misses her lion and no white man ever bolts.'

'I bolted like a rabbit,' Macomber said.

Now what in hell were you going to do about a man who talked like that, Wilson wondered.

Wilson looked at Macomber with his flat, blue, machine-gunner's eyes and the other smiled back at him. He had a pleasant smile if you did not notice how his eyes showed when he was hurt.

'Maybe I can fix it up on buffalo,' he said. 'We're after them next, aren't we?'

'In the morning if you like,' Wilson told him. Perhaps he had been wrong. This was certainly the way to take it. You most certainly could not tell a damned thing about an American. He was all for Macomber again. If you could forget the morning. But, of course, you couldn't. The morning had been about as bad as they come.

'Here comes the Memsahib,' he said. She was walking over from her tent looking refreshed and cheerful and quite lovely. She had a very perfect oval face, so perfect that you expected

7

her to be stupid. But she wasn't stupid, Wilson thought, no, not stupid.

'How is the beautiful red-faced Mr Wilson? Are you feeling better, Francis, my pearl?'

'Oh, much,' said Macomber.

'I've dropped the whole thing,' she said, sitting down at the table. 'What importance is there to whether Francis is any good at killing lions? That's not his trade. That's Mr Wilson's trade. Mr Wilson is really very impressive killing anything. You do kill anything, don't you?'

'Oh, anything,' said Wilson. 'Simply anything.' They are, he thought, the hardest in the world; the hardest, the cruelest, the most predatory and the most attractive and their men have softened or gone to pieces nervously as they have hardened. Or is it that they pick men they can handle? They can't know that much at the age they marry, he thought. He was grateful that he had gone through his education on American women before now because this was a very attractive one.

'We're going after buff in the morning,' he told her.

'I'm coming,' she said.

'No, you're not.'

'Oh, yes, I am. Mayn't I, Francis?'

'Why not stay in camp?'

'Not for anything,' she said. 'I wouldn't miss something like today for anything.'

When she left, Wilson was thinking, when she went off to cry, she seemed a hell of a fine woman. She seemed to understand, to realize, to be hurt for him and for herself and to know how things really stood. She is away for twenty minutes and now she is back, simply enamelled in that American female cruelty. They are the damnedest women. Really the damnedest.

'We'll put on another show for you tomorrow,' Francis Macomber said.

'You're not coming,' Wilson said.

'You're very mistaken,' she told him. 'And I want *so* to see you perform again. You were lovely this morning. That is if blowing things' heads off is lovely.'

'Here's the lunch,' said Wilson. 'You're very merry, aren't you?'

8

'Why not? I didn't come out here to be dull.'

'Well, it hasn't been dull,' Wilson said. He could see the boulders in the river and the high bank beyond with the trees and he remembered the morning.

'Oh, no,' she said. 'It's been charming. And tomorrow. You don't know how I look forward to tomorrow.'

'That's eland he's offering you,' Wilson said.

'They're the big cowy things that jump like hares, aren't they?'

'I suppose that describes them,' Wilson said.

'It's very good meat,' Macomber said.

'Did you shoot it, Francis?' she asked.

'Yes.'

'They're not dangerous, are they?'

'Only if they fall on you,' Wilson told her.

'I'm so glad.'

'Why not let up on the bitchery just a little, Margot,' Macomber said, cutting the eland steak and putting some mashed potato, gravy and carrot on the down-turned fork that tined through the piece of meat.

'I suppose I could,' she said, 'since you put it so prettily.'

'Tonight we'll have champagne for the lion,' Wilson said. 'It's a bit too hot at noon.'

'Oh, the lion,' Margot said. 'I'd forgotten the lion!'

So, Robert Wilson thought to himself, she *is* giving him a ride, isn't she? Or do you suppose that's her idea of putting up a good show? How should a woman act when she discovers her husband is a bloody coward? She's damned cruel but they're all cruel. They govern, of course, and to govern one has to be cruel sometimes. Still, I've seen enough of their damn terrorism.

'Have some more eland,' he said to her politely.

That afternoon, late, Wilson and Macomber went out in the motor car with the native driver and the two gun-bearers. Mrs Macomber stayed in the camp. It was too hot to go out, she said, and she was going with them in the early morning. As they drove off Wilson saw her standing under the big tree looking pretty rather than beautiful in her faintly rosy khaki, her dark brown hair drawn back off her forehead and gathered in a knot low on her neck, her face as fresh, he thought, as though she were in England. She waved to them as the car went off through the swale of high grass and curved through the trees into the small hills of orchard bush.

In the orchard bush they found a herd of impala, and leaving the car they stalked one old ram with long, widespread horns and Macomber killed it with a very creditable shot that knocked the buck down at a good two hundred yards and sent the herd off bounding wildly and leaping over one another's backs in long, leg-drawn-up leaps as unbelievable and as floating as those one makes sometimes in dreams.

'That was a good shot,' Wilson said. 'They're a small target.'

'Is it a worth-while head?' Macomber asked.

'It's excellent,' Wilson told him. 'You shoot like that and you'll have no trouble.'

'Do you think we'll find buffalo tomorrow?'

'There's a good chance of it. They feed out early in the morning and with luck we may catch them in the open.'

'I'd like to clear away that lion business,' Macomber said. 'It's not very pleasant to have your wife see you do something like that.'

I should think it would be even more unpleasant to do it, Wilson thought, wife or no wife, or to talk about it having done it. But he said, 'I wouldn't think about that any more. Anyone could be upset by his first lion. That's all over.'

But that night after dinner and a whisky and soda by the fire before going to bed, as Francis Macomber lay on his cot with the mosquito bar over him and listened to the night noises it was not all over. It was neither all over nor was it beginning. It was there exactly as it happened with some parts of it indelibly emphasized and he was miserably ashamed of it. But more than shame he felt cold, hollow fear in him. The fear was still there like a cold slimy hollow in all the emptiness where once his confidence had been and it made him feel sick. It was still there with him now.

It had started the night before when he had awakened and heard the lion roaring somewhere up along the river. It was a deep sound and at the end there were sort of coughing grunts that made him seem just outside the tent, and when Francis Macomber woke in the night to hear it he was afraid. He could hear his wife breathing quietly, asleep. There was no one to tell he was afraid, nor to be afraid with him, and, lying alone, he did not know the Somali proverb that says a brave man is always frightened three times by a lion; when he first sees his track, when he first hears him roar and when he first confronts him. Then while they were eating breakfast by lantern light out in the dining tent, before the sun was up, the lion roared again and Francis thought he was just at the edge of camp.

'Sounds like an old-timer,' Robert Wilson said, looking up from his kippers and coffee. 'Listen to him cough.'

'Is he very close?'

'A mile or so up the stream.'

'Will we see him?'

'We'll have a look.'

'Does his roaring carry that far? It sounds as though he were right in camp.'

'Carries a hell of a long way,' said Robert Wilson. 'It's strange the way it carries. Hope he's a shootable cat. The boys said there was a very big one about here.'

'If I get a shot, where should I hit him?' Macomber asked, 'to stop him?'

'In the shoulders,' Wilson said. 'In the neck if you can make it. Shoot for bone. Break him down.'

'I hope I can place it properly,' Macomber said.

'You shoot very well,' Wilson told him. 'Take your time. Make sure of him. The first one in is the one that counts.'

'What range will it be?'

'Can't tell. Lion has something to say about that. Don't shoot unless it's close enough so you can make sure.'

'At under a hundred yards?' Macomber asked.

Wilson looked at him quickly.

'Hundred's about right. Might have to take him a bit under. Shouldn't chance a shot at much over that. A hundred's a decent range. You can hit him wherever you want at that. Here comes the Memsahib.'

'Good morning,' she said. 'Are we going after that lion?'

'As soon as you deal with your breakfast,' Wilson said. 'How are you feeling?'

'Marvelous,' she said. 'I'm very excited.'

11

'I'll just go and see that everything is ready.' Wilson went off. As he left the lion roared again.

'Noisy beggar,' Wilson said. 'We'll put a stop to that.'

'What's the matter, Francis?' his wife asked him.

'Nothing,' Macomber said.

'Yes, there is,' she said. 'What are you upset about?'

'Nothing,' he said.

'Tell me,' she looked at him. 'Don't you feel well?'

'It's that damned roaring,' he said. 'It's been going on all night, you know.'

'Why didn't you wake me?' she said. 'I'd love to have heard it.'

'I've got to kill the damned thing,' Macomber said, miserably.

'Well, that's what you're out here for, isn't it?'

'Yes. But I'm nervous. Hearing the thing roar gets on my nerves.'

'Well then, as Wilson said, kill him and stop his roaring.'

'Yes, darling,' said Francis Macomber. 'It sounds easy, doesn't it?'

'You're not afraid, are you?'

'Of course not. But I'm nervous from hearing him roar all night.'

'You'll kill him marvelously,' she said. 'I know you will. I'm awfully anxious to see it.'

'Finish your breakfast and we'll be starting.'

'It's not light yet,' she said. 'This is a ridiculous hour.'

Just then the lion roared in a deep-chested moaning, suddenly guttural, ascending vibration that seemed to shake the air and ended in a sigh and a heavy, deep-chested grunt.

'He sounds almost here,' Macomber's wife said.

'My God,' said Macomber. 'I hate that damned noise.'

'It's very impressive.'

'Impressive. It's frightful.'

Robert Wilson came up then carrying his short, ugly, shockingly big-bored .505 Gibbs and grinning.

'Come on,' he said. 'Your gun-bearer has your Springfield and the big gun. Everything's in the car. Have you solids?'

'Yes.'

'I'm ready,' Mrs Macomber said.

12

'Must make him stop that racket,' Wilson said. 'You get in front. The Memsahib can sit back here with me.'

They climbed into the motor car and, in the gray first daylight, moved off up the river through the trees. Macomber opened the breech of his rifle and saw he had metal-cased bullets, shut the bolt and put the rifle on safety. He saw his hand was trembling. He felt in his pocket for more cartridges and moved his fingers over the cartridges in the loops of his tunic front. He turned back to where Wilson sat in the rear seat of the doorless, box-bodied motor car beside his wife, them both grinning with excitement, and Wilson leaned forward and whispered.

'See the birds dropping. Means the old boy has left his kill.'

On the far bank of the stream Macomber could see, above the trees, vultures circling and plummeting down.

'Chances are he'll come to drink along here,' Wilson whispered. 'Before he goes to lay up. Keep an eye out.'

They were driving slowly along the high bank of the stream which here cut deeply to its boulder-filled bed, and they wound in and out through big trees as they drove. Macomber was watching the opposite bank when he felt Wilson take hold of his arm. The car stopped.

'There he is,' he heard the whisper. 'Ahead and to the right. Get out and take him. He's a marvelous lion.'

Macomber saw the lion now. He was standing almost broadside, his great head up and turned toward them. The early morning breeze that blew toward them was just stirring his dark mane, and the lion looked huge, silhouetted on the rise of bank in the gray morning light, his shoulders heavy, his barrel of a body bulking smoothly.

'How far is he?' asked Macomber, raising his rifle.

'About seventy-five. Get out and take him.'

'Why not shoot from where I am?'

'You don't shoot them from cars,' he heard Wilson saying in his ear. 'Get out. He's not going to stay there all day.'

Macomber stepped out of the curved opening at the side of the front seat, onto the step and down on to the ground. The lion still stood looking majestically and coolly toward this object that his eyes only showed in silhouette, bulking like some super-rhino. There was no man smell carried toward him

13

and he watched the object, moving his great head a little from side to side. Then watching the object, not afraid, but hesitating before going down the bank to drink with such a thing opposite him, he saw a man figure detach itself from it and he turned his heavy head and swung away toward the cover of the trees as he heard a cracking crash and felt the slam of a .30–06 220-grain solid bullet that bit his flank and ripped in sudden hot scalding nausea through his stomach. He trotted, heavy, big-footed, swinging wounded full-bellied, through the trees toward the tall grass and cover, and the crash came again to go past him ripping the air apart. Then it crashed again and he felt the blow as it hit his lower ribs and ripped on through, blood sudden hot and frothy in his mouth, and he galloped toward the high grass where he could crouch and not be seen and make them bring the crashing thing close enough so he could make a rush and get the man that held it.

Macomber had not thought how the lion felt as he got out of the car. He only knew his hands were shaking and as he walked away from the car it was almost impossible for him to make his legs move. They were stiff in the thighs, but he could feel the muscles fluttering. He raised the rifle, sighted on the junction of the lion's head and shoulders and pulled the trigger. Nothing happened though he pulled until he thought his finger would break. Then he knew he had the safety on and as he lowered the rifle to move the safety over he moved another frozen pace forward, and the lion seeing his silhouette now clear of the silhouette of the car, turned and started off at a trot, and, as Macomber fired, he heard a whunk that meant the bullet was home; but the lion kept on going. Macomber shot again and everyone saw the bullet throw a spout of dirt beyond the trotting lion. He shot again, remembering to lower his aim, and they all heard the bullet hit, and the lion went into a gallop and was in the tall grass before he had the bolt pushed forward.

Macomber stood there feeling sick at his stomach, his hands that held the Springfield still cocked, shaking, and his wife and Robert Wilson were standing by him. Beside him too were the gun-bearers chattering in Wakamba.

'I hit him,' Macomber said. 'I hit him twice.'

'You gut-shot him and you hit him somewhere forward,'

14

Wilson said without enthusiasm. The gun-bearers looked very grave. They were silent now.

'You may have killed him,' Wilson went on. 'We'll have to wait a while before we go in to find out.'

'What do you mean?'

'Let him get sick before we follow him up.'

'Oh,' said Macomber.

'He's a hell of a fine lion,' Wilson said cheerfully. 'He's gotten into a bad place though.'

'Why is it bad?'

'Can't see him until you're on him.'

'Oh,' said Macomber.

'Come on,' said Wilson. 'The Memsahib can stay here in the car. We'll go to have a look at the blood spur.'

'Stay here, Margot,' Macomber said to his wife. His mouth was very dry and it was hard for him to talk.

'Why?' she asked.

'Wilson says to.'

'We're going to have a look,' Wilson said. 'You stay here. You can see even better from here.'

'All right.'

Wilson spoke in Swahili to the driver. He nodded and said, 'Yes, Bwana.'

Then they went down the steep bank and across the stream, climbing over and around the boulders and up the other bank, pulling up by some projecting roots, and along it until they found where the lion had been trotting when Macomber first shot. There was dark blood on the short grass that the gun-bearers pointed out with grass stems, and that ran away behind the river bank trees.

'What do we do?' asked Macomber.

'Not much choice,' said Wilson. 'We can't bring the car over. Bank's too steep. We'll let him stiffen up a bit and then you and I'll go in and have a look for him.'

'Can't we set the grass on fire?' Macomber asked.

'Too green.'

'Can't we send beaters?'

Wilson looked at him appraisingly. 'Of course we can,' he said. 'But it's just a touch murderous. You see we know the

15

lion's wounded. You can drive an unwounded lion – he'll move on ahead of a noise – but a wounded lion's going to charge. You can't see him until you're right on him. He'll make himself perfectly flat in cover you wouldn't think would hide a hare. You can't very well send boys in there to that sort of a show. Somebody's bound to get mauled.'

'What about the gun-bearers?'

'Oh, they'll go with us. It's their *shauri*. You see, they signed on for it. They don't look too happy though, do they?'

'I don't want to go in there,' said Macomber. It was out before he knew he'd said it.

'Neither do I,' said Wilson very cheerily. 'Really no choice though.' Then, as an afterthought, he glanced at Macomber and saw suddenly how he was trembling and the pitiful look on his face.

'You don't have to go in, of course,' he said. 'That's what I'm hired for, you know. That's why I'm so expensive.'

'You mean you'd go in by yourself? Why not leave him there?'

Robert Wilson, whose entire occupation had been with the lion and the problem he presented, and who had not been thinking about Macomber except to note that he was rather windy, suddenly felt as though he had opened the wrong door in a hotel and seen something shameful.

'What do you mean?'

'Why not just leave him?'

'You mean pretend to ourselves he hasn't been hit?'

'No. Just drop it.'

'It isn't done.'

'Why not?'

'For one thing, he's certain to be suffering. For another, someone else might run onto him.'

'I see.'

'But you don't have to have anything to do with it.'

'I'd like to,' Macomber said. 'I'm just scared, you know.'

'I'll go ahead when we go in,' Wilson said, 'with Kongoni tracking. You keep behind me and a little to one side. Chances are we'll hear him growl. If we see him we'll both shoot. Don't worry about anything. I'll keep you backed up. As a matter of fact, you know, perhaps you'd better not go. It might be much better. Why don't you go over and join the Memsahib while I just get it over with?'

'No, I want to go.'

'All right,' said Wilson.' But don't go in if you don't want to. This is my *shauri* now, you know.'

'I want to go,' said Macomber.

They sat under a tree and smoked.

'Want to go back and speak to the Memsahib while we're waiting?' Wilson asked.

'No.'

'I'll just step back and tell her to be patient.'

'Good,' said Macomber. He sat there, sweating under his arms, his mouth dry, his stomach hollow feeling, wanting to find courage to tell Wilson to go on and finish off the lion without him. He could not know that Wilson was furious because he had not noticed the state he was in earlier and sent him back to his wife. While he sat there Wilson came up. 'I have your big gun,' he said. 'Take it. We've given him time, I think. Come on.'

Macomber took the big gun and Wilson said:

'Keep behind me and about five yards to the right and do exactly as I tell you.' Then he spoke in Swahili to the two gun-bearers who looked the picture of gloom.

'Let's go,' he said.

'Could I have a drink of water?' Macomber asked. Wilson spoke to the older gun-bearer, who wore a canteen on his belt, and the man unbuckled it, unscrewed the top and handed it to Macomber, who took it noticing how heavy it seemed and how hairy and shoddy the felt covering was in his hand. He raised it to drink and looked ahead at the high grass with the flat-topped trees behind it. A breeze was blowing toward them and the grass rippled gently in the wind. He looked at the gun-bearer and he could see the gun-bearer was suffering too with fear.

Thirty-five yards into the grass the big lion lay flattened out along the ground. His ears were back and his only movement was a slight twitching up and down of his long, black-tufted tail. He had turned at bay as soon as he had reached this cover and he was sick with the wound through his full belly, and weakening with the wound through his lungs that brought a

17

thin foamy red to his mouth each time he breathed. His flanks were wet and hot and flies were on the little openings the solid bullets had made in his tawny hide, and his big yellow eyes, narrowed with hate, looking straight ahead, only blinking when the pain came as he breathed, and his claws dug in the soft baked earth. All of him, pain, sickness, hatred and all of his remaining strength, was tightening into an absolute concentration for a rush. He could hear the men talking and he waited, gathering all of himself into this preparation for a charge as soon as the men would come into the grass. As he heard their voices his tail stiffened to twitch up and down, and, as they came into the edge of the grass, he made a coughing grunt and charged.

Kongoni, the old gun-bearer, in the lead watching the blood spoor, Wilson watching the grass for any movement, his big gun ready, the second gun-bearer looking ahead and listening, Macomber close to Wilson, his rifle cocked, they had just moved into the grass when Macomber heard the blood-choked coughing grunt, and saw the swishing rush in the grass. The next thing he knew he was running; running wildly, in panic in the open, running toward the stream.

He heard the *ca-ra-wong!* of Wilson's big rifle, and again in a second crashing *ca-ra-wong!* and turning saw the lion, horrible-looking now, with half his head seeming to be gone, crawling toward Wilson in the edge of the tall grass while the red-faced man worked the bolt on the short ugly rifle and aimed carefully as another blasting *ca-ra-wong!* came from the muzzle, and the crawling, heavy, yellow bulk of the lion stiffened and the huge, mutilated head slid forward and Macomber, standing by himself in the clearing where he had run, holding a loaded rifle, while two black men and a white man looked back at him in contempt, knew the lion was dead. He came toward Wilson, his tallness all seeming a naked reproach, and Wilson looked at him and said:

'Want to take pictures?'

'No,' he said.

That was all anyone had said until they reached the motor car. Then Wilson had said:

'Hell of a fine lion. Boys will skin him out. We might as well stay here in the shade.'

Macomber's wife had not looked at him nor he at her and he

18

had sat by her in the back seat with Wilson sitting in the front seat. Once he had reached over and taken his wife's hand without looking at her and she had removed her hand from his. Looking across the stream to where the gun-bearers were skinning out the lion he could see that she had been able to see the whole thing. While they sat there his wife had reached forward and put her hand on Wilson's shoulder. He turned and she had leaned forward over the low seat and kissed him on the mouth.

'Oh, I say,' said Wilson, going redder than his natural baked color.

'Mr Robert Wilson,' she said. 'The beautifully red-faced Mr Robert Wilson.'

Then she sat down beside Macomber again and looked away across the stream to where the lion lay, with uplifted, white-muscled, tendon-marked naked forearms, and white bloating belly, as the black men fleshed away the skin. Finally the gun-bearers brought the skin over, wet and heavy, and climbed in behind with it, rolling it up before they got in, and the motor car started. No one had said anything more until they were back in camp.

That was the story of the lion. Macomber did not know how the lion had felt before he started his rush, nor during it when the unbelievable smash of the .505 with a muzzle velocity of two tons had hit him in the mouth, nor what kept him coming after that, when the second ripping crash had smashed his hind quarters and he had come crawling on toward the crashing, blasting thing that had destroyed him. Wilson knew something about it and only expressed it by saying, 'Damned fine lion,' but Macomber did not know how Wilson felt about things either. He did not know how his wife felt except that she was through with him.

His wife had been through with him before but it never lasted. He was very wealthy, and would be much wealthier, and he knew she would not leave him ever now. That was one of the few things he really knew. He knew about that, about motor cycles – that was earliest – about motor cars, about duck-shooting, about fishing, trout, salmon and big sea, about sex in books, many books, too many books, about all court games, about dogs, not much about horses, about hanging on to his money, about most of the other things his world dealt in, and about his wife not leaving him. His wife had been a great beauty and she was still a great beauty in Africa, but she was not a great enough beauty any more at home to be able to leave him and better herself and she knew it and he knew it. She had missed the chance to leave him and he knew it. If he had been better with women she would probably have started to worry about his getting another new, beautiful wife; but she knew too much about him to worry about him either. Also, he had always had a great tolerance which seemed the nicest thing about him if it were not the most sinister.

All in all they were known as a comparatively happily married couple, one of those whose disruption is often rumored but never occurs, and as the society columnist put it, they were adding more than a spice of *adventure* to their much envied and ever-enduring *Romance* by a *Safari* in what was known as *Darkest Africa* until the Martin Johnsons lighted it on so many silver screens where they were pursuing *Old Simba* the lion, the buffalo, *Tembo* the elephant and as well collecting specimens for the Museum of Natural History. This same columnist had reported them *on the verge* at least three times in the past and they had been. But they always made it up. They had a sound basis of union. Margot was too beautiful for Macomber to divorce her and Macomber had too much money for Margot ever to leave him.

It was now about three o'clock in the morning and Francis Macomber, who had been asleep a little while after he had stopped thinking about the lion, wakened and then slept again, woke suddenly, frightened in a dream of the bloody-headed lion standing over him, and listening while his heart pounded, he realized that his wife was not in the other cot in the tent. He lay awake with that knowledge for two hours.

At the end of that time his wife came into the tent, lifted her mosquito bar and crawled cosily into bed.

'Where have you been?' Macomber asked in the darkness.

'Hello,' she said. 'Are you awake?'

'Where have you been?'

'I just went out to get a breath of air.'

'You did, like hell.'

'What do you want me to say, darling?'

'Where have you been?'

'Out to get a breath of air.'

'That's a new name for it. You *are* a bitch.'

'Well, you're a coward.'

'All right,' he said. 'What of it?'

'Nothing as far as I'm concerned. But please let's not talk, darling, because I'm very sleepy.'

'You think that I'll take anything.'

'I know you will, sweet.'

'Well, I won't.'

'Please, darling, let's not talk. I'm so very sleepy.'

'There wasn't going to be any of that. You promised there wouldn't be.'

'Well, there is now,' she said sweetly.

'You said if we made this trip there would be none of that. You promised.'

'Yes, darling. That's the way I meant it to be. But the trip was spoiled yesterday. We don't have to talk about it, do we?'

'You don't wait long when you have an advantage, do you?'

'Please, let's not talk. I'm so sleepy, darling.'

'I'm going to talk.'

'Don't mind me then, because I'm going to sleep.' And she did.

At breakfast they were all three at the table before daylight and Francis Macomber found that, of all the many men that he had hated, he hated Robert Wilson the most.

'Sleep well?' Wilson asked in his throaty voice, filling a pipe. 'Did you?'

'Topping,' the white hunter told him.

You bastard, thought Macomber, you insolent bastard.

So she woke him when she came in, Wilson thought, looking at them both with his flat, cold eyes. Well, why doesn't he keep his wife where she belongs? What does he think I am, a bloody plaster saint? Let him keep her where she belongs. It's his own fault.

'Do you think we'll find buffalo?' Margot asked, pushing away a dish of apricots.

'Chance of it,' Wilson said and smiled at her. 'Why don't you stay in camp?'

'Not for anything,' she told him.

'Why not order her to stay in camp?' Wilson said to Macomber.

'You order her,' said Macomber coldly.

'Let's not have any ordering, nor,' turning to Macomber, 'any silliness, Francis,' Margot said quite pleasantly.

'Are you ready to start?' Macomber asked.

'Any time,' Wilson told him. 'Do you want the Memsahib to go?'

'Does it make any difference whether I do or not?'

The hell with it, thought Robert Wilson. The utter complete hell with it. So this is what it's going to be like. Well, this is what it's going to be like then.

'Makes no difference,' he said.

'You're sure you wouldn't like to stay in camp with her yourself and let me go out and hunt the buffalo?' Macomber asked.

'Can't do that,' said Wilson. 'Wouldn't talk rot if I were you.'

'I'm not talking rot. I'm disgusted.'

'Bad word, disgusted.'

'Francis, will you please try to speak sensibly!' his wife said.

'I speak too damned sensibly,' Macomber said. 'Did you ever eat such filthy food?'

'Something wrong with the food?' asked Wilson quietly.

'No more than with everything else.'

'I'd pull yourself together, laddybuck,' Wilson said very quietly. 'There's a boy waits at table that understands a little English.'

'The hell with him.'

Wilson stood up and puffing on his pipe strolled away, speaking a few words in Swahili to one of the gun-bearers who was standing waiting for him. Macomber and his wife sat on at the table. He was staring at his coffee cup.

'If you make a scene I'll leave you, darling,' Margot said quietly.

'No, you won't.'

'You can try it and see.'

'You won't leave me.'

'No,' she said. 'I won't leave you and you'll behave yourself.'

'Behave myself? That's a way to talk. Behave myself.'

'Yes. Behave yourself.'

'Why don't *you* try behaving?'

'I've tried it so long. So very long.'

'I hate that red-faced swine,' Macomber said. 'I loathe the sight of him.'

'He's really *very* nice.'

'Oh, *shut up*,' Macomber almost shouted. Just then the car came up and stopped in front of the dining tent and the driver and the two gun-bearers got out. Wilson walked over and looked at the husband and wife sitting there at the table.

'Going shooting?' he asked.

'Yes,' said Macomber, standing up. 'Yes.'

'Better bring a woolly. It will be cool in the car,' Wilson said.

'I'll get my leather jacket,' Margot said.

'The boy has it,' Wilson told her. He climbed into the front with the driver and Francis Macomber and his wife sat, not speaking, in the back seat.

Hope the silly beggar doesn't take a notion to blow the back of my head off, Wilson thought to himself. Women *are* a nuisance on safari.

The car was grinding down to cross the river at a pebbly ford in the gray daylight and then climbed, angling up the steep bank, where Wilson had ordered a way shovelled out the day before so they could reach the parklike wooded rolling country on the far side.

It was a good morning, Wilson thought. There was a heavy dew and as the wheels went through the grass and low bushes he could smell the odor of the crushed fronds. It was an odor like verbena and he liked this early morning smell of the dew, the crushed bracken and the look of the tree trunks showing black through the early morning mist, as the car made its way through the untracked, parklike country. He had put the two in the back seat out of his mind now and was thinking about buffalo. The buffalo that he was after stayed in the daytime in a thick swamp where it was impossible to get a shot, but in the night they fed out into an open stretch of country and if he could come between them and their swamp with the car, Macomber would

23

have a good chance at them in the open. He did not want to hunt buff with Macomber in thick cover. He did not want to hunt buff or anything else with Macomber at all, but he was a professional hunter and he had hunted with some rare ones in his time. If they got buff today there would only be rhino to come and the poor man would have gone through his dangerous game and things might pick up. He'd have nothing more to do with the woman and Macomber would get over that too. He must have gone through plenty of that before by the look of things. Poor beggar. He must have a way of getting over it. Well, it was the poor sod's own bloody fault.

He, Robert Wilson, carried a double size cot on safari to accommodate any windfalls he might receive. He had hunted for a certain clientele, the international fast, sporting set, where the women did not feel they were getting their money's worth unless they had shared that cot with the white hunter. He despised them when he was away from them although he liked some of them well enough at the time, but he made his living by them; and their standards were his standards as long as they were hiring him.

They were his standards in all except the shooting. He had his own standards about the killing and they could live up to them or get someone else to hunt them. He knew, too, that they all respected him for this. This Macomber was an odd one though. Damned if he wasn't. Now the wife. Hell, the wife. Yes, the wife. Mm, the wife. Well, he'd dropped all that. He looked around at them. Macomber sat grim and furious. Margot smiled at him. She looked younger today, more innocent and fresher and not so professionally beautiful. What's in her heart God knows, Wilson thought. She hadn't talked much last night. At that it was a pleasure to see her.

The motor car climbed up a slight rise and went on through the trees and then out into a grassy prairie-like opening and kept in the shelter of the trees along the edge, the driver going slowly and Wilson looking carefully out across the prairie and all along its far side. He stopped the car and studied the opening with his field glasses. Then he motioned the driver to go on and the car moved slowly along, the driver avoiding wart-hog holes and driving around the mud castles ants had built. Then,

looking across the opening, Wilson suddenly turned and said,
'By God, there they are!'

And looking where he pointed, while the car jumped forward and Wilson spoke in rapid Swahili to the driver, Macomber saw three huge black animals looking almost cylindrical in their long heaviness, like big black tank cars, moving at a gallop across the far edge of the open prairie. They moved at a stiff-necked, stiff-bodied gallop and he could see the upswept wide black horns on their heads as they galloped heads out; the heads not moving.

'They're three old bulls,' Wilson said. 'We'll cut them off before they get to the swamp.'

The car was going a wild forty-five miles an hour across the open and as Macomber watched, the buffalo got bigger and bigger until he could see the gray, hairless, scabby look of one huge bull and how his neck was a part of his shoulders and the shiny black of his horns as he galloped a little behind the others that were strung out in that steady plunging gait; and then, the car swaying as though it had just jumped a road, they drew up close and he could see the plunging hugeness of the bull, and the dust in his sparsely haired hide, the wide boss of horn and his outstretched, wide-nostrilled muzzle, and he was raising his rifle when Wilson shouted, 'Not from the car, you fool!' and he had no fear, only hatred of Wilson, while the brakes clamped on and the car skidded, plowing sideways to an almost stop and Wilson was out on one side and he on the other, stumbling as his feet hit the still speeding-by of the earth, and then he was shooting at the bull as he moved away, hearing the bullets whunk into him, emptying his rifle at him as he moved steadily away, finally remembering to get his shots forward into the shoulder, and as he fumbled to re-load, he saw the bull was down. Down on his knees, his big head tossing, and seeing the other two still galloping he shot at the leader and hit him. He shot again and missed and he heard the *ca-ra-wonging* roar as Wilson shot and saw the leading bull slide forward on to his nose.

'Get that other,' Wilson said. 'Now you're shooting!'

But the other bull was moving steadily at the same gallop and he missed, throwing a spout of dirt, and Wilson missed and the dust rose in a cloud and Wilson shouted, 'Come on. He's too far!' and grabbed his arm and they were in the car again,

25

Macomber and Wilson hanging on the sides and rocketing swayingly over the uneven ground, drawing up on the steady, plunging, heavy-necked, straight-moving gallop of the bull.

They were behind him and Macomber was filling his rifle, dropping shells on to the ground, jamming it, clearing the jam, then they were almost up with the bull when Wilson yelled 'Stop,' and the car skidded so that it almost swung over and Macomber fell forward on to his feet, slammed his bolt forward and fired as far forward as he could aim into the galloping, rounded black back, aimed and shot again, then again, then again, and the bullets, all of them hitting, had no effect on the buffalo that he could see. Then Wilson shot, the roar deafening him, and he could see the bull stagger. Macomber shot again, aiming carefully, and down he came, on to his knees.

'All right,' Wilson said. 'Nice work. That's the three.'

Macomber felt a drunken elation.

'How many times did you shoot?' he asked.

'Just three,' Wilson said. 'You killed the first bull. The biggest one. I helped you finish the other two. Afraid they might have got into cover. You had them killed. I was just mopping up a little. You shot damn well.'

'Let's go to the car,' said Macomber. 'I want a drink.'

'Got to finish off that buff first,' Wilson told him. The buffalo was on his knees and he jerked his head furiously and bellowed in pig-eyed, roaring rage as they came toward him.

'Watch he doesn't get up,' Wilson said. Then, 'Get a little broadside and take him in the neck just behind the ear.'

Macomber aimed carefully at the centre of the huge, jerking, rage-driven neck and shot. At the shot the head dropped forward.

'That does it,' said Wilson. 'Got the spine. They're a hell of a looking thing, aren't they?'

'Let's get the drink,' said Macomber. In his life he had never felt so good.

In the car Macomber's wife sat very white faced. 'You were marvelous, darling,' she said to Macomber. 'What a ride.'

'Was it rough?' Wilson asked.

'It was frightful. I've never been more frightened in my life.'

'Let's all have a drink,' Macomber said.

'By all means,' said Wilson. 'Give it to the Memsahib.' She drank the neat whisky from the flask and shuddered a little when she swallowed. She handed the flask to Macomber who handed it to Wilson.

'It was frightfully exciting,' she said. 'It's given me a dreadful headache. I didn't know you were allowed to shoot them from cars though.'

'No one shot from cars,' said Wilson coldly.

'I mean chase them from cars.'

'Wouldn't ordinarily,' Wilson said. 'Seemed sporting enough to me though while we were doing it. Taking more chance driving that way across a plain full of holes and one thing and another than hunting on foot. Buffalo could have charged us each time we shot if he liked. Gave him every chance. Wouldn't mention it to anyone though. It's illegal if that's what you mean.'

'It seemed very unfair to me,' Margo said, 'chasing those big helpless things in a motor car.'

'Did it?' said Wilson.

'What would happen if they heard about that in Nairobi?'

'I'd lose my license for one thing. Other unpleasantnesses,' Wilson said, taking a drink from the flask. 'I'd be out of business.'

'Really?'

'Yes, really.'

'Well,' said Macomber, and he smiled for the first time all day, 'Now she has something on you.'

'You have such a pretty way of putting things, Francis,' Margot Macomber said. Wilson looked at them both. If a four-letter man marries a five-letter woman, he was thinking, what number of letters would their children be? What he said was, 'We lost a gun-bearer. Did you notice it?'

'My God, no,' Macomber said.

'Here he comes,' Wilson said. 'He's all right. He must have fallen off when we left the first bull.'

Approaching them was the middle-aged gun-bearer, limping along in his knitted cap, khaki tunic, shorts and rubber sandals, gloomy-faced and disgusted looking. As he came up he called out to Wilson in Swahili and they all saw the change in the white hunter's face.

'What does he say?' asked Margot.

'He says the first bull got up and went into the bush,' Wilson said with no expression in his voice.

'Oh,' said Macomber blankly.

'Then it's going to be just like the lion,' said Margot, full of anticipation.

'It's not going to be a damned bit like the lion,' Wilson told her. 'Did you want another drink, Macomber?'

'Thanks, yes,' Macomber said. He expected the feeling he had had about the lion to come back but it did not. For the first time in his life he really felt wholly without fear. Instead of fear he had a feeling of definite elation.

'We'll go and have a look at the second bull,' Wilson said. 'I'll tell the driver to put the car in the shade.'

'What are you going to do?' asked Margot Macomber.

'Take a look at the buff,' Wilson said.

'I'll come.'

'Come along.'

The three of them walked over to where the second buffalo bulked blackly in the open, head forward on the grass, the massive horns swung wide.

'He's a very good head,' Wilson said. 'That's close to a fifty-inch spread.'

Macomber was looking at him with delight.

'He's hateful looking,' said Margot. 'Can't we go into the shade?'

'Of course,' Wilson said. 'Look,' he said to Macomber, and pointed. 'See that patch of bush?'

'Yes.'

'That's where the first bull went in. The gun-bearer said when he fell off the bull was down. He was watching us helling along and the other two buff galloping. When he looked up there was the bull up and looking at him. Gun-bearer ran like hell and the bull went off slowly into that bush.'

'Can we go in after him now?' asked Macomber eagerly.

Wilson looked at him appraisingly. Damned if this isn't a strange one, he thought. Yesterday he's scared sick and today he's a ruddy fire-eater.

'No, we'll give him a while.'

'Let's please go into the shade,' Margot said. Her face was white and she looked ill.

They made their way to the car where it stood under a single wide-spreading tree and all climbed in.

'Chances are he's dead in there,' Wilson remarked. 'After a little we'll have a look.'

Macomber felt a wild unreasonable happiness that he had never known before.

'By God, that was a chase,' he said. 'I've never felt any such feeling. Wasn't it marvelous, Margot?'

'I hated it.'

'Why?'

'I hated it,' she said bitterly. 'I loathed it.'

'You know I don't think I'd be afraid of anything again,' Macomber said to Wilson. 'Something happened in me after we first saw the buff and started after him. Like a dam bursting. It was pure excitement.'

'Cleans out your liver,' said Wilson. 'Damn funny things happen to people.'

Macomber's face was shining. 'You know, something did happen to me,' he said, 'I feel absolutely different.'

His wife said nothing and eyed him strangely. She was sitting far back in the seat and Macomber was sitting forward talking to Wilson who turned sideways talking over the back of the front seat.

'You know, I'd like to try another lion,' Macomber said. 'I'm not really afraid of them now. After all, what can they do to you?'

'That's it,' said Wilson. 'Worst one can do is kill you. How does it go? Shakespeare. Damned good. See if I can remember. Oh, damned good. Used to quote it to myself at one time. Let's see. "By my troth, I care not; a man can die but once; we owe God a death and let it go which way it will, he that dies this year is quit for the next." Damned fine, eh?'

He was very embarrassed, having brought out this thing he had lived by, but he had seen men come of age before and it always moved him. It was not a matter of their twenty-first birthday.

It had taken a strange chance of hunting, a sudden precipitation into action without opportunity for worrying beforehand, to bring this about with Macomber, but regardless of how it had happened it had most certainly happened. Look at the beggar now, Wilson thought. It's that some of them stay little boys so long, Wilson thought. Sometimes all their lives. Their figures stay boyish when they're fifty. The great American boy-men. Damned strange people. But he liked this Macomber now. Damned strange fellow. Probably meant the end of cuckoldry too. Well, that would be a damned good thing. Damned good thing. Beggar had probably been afraid all his life. Don't know what started it. But over now. Hadn't had time to be afraid with the buff. That and being angry too. Motor car too. Motor cars made it familiar. Be a damn fire-eater now. He'd seen it in the war work the same way. More of a change than any loss of virginity. Fear gone like an operation. Something else grew in its place. Main thing a man had. Made him into a man. Women knew it too. No bloody fear.

From the far corner of the seat Margaret Macomber looked at the two of them. There was no change in Wilson. She saw Wilson as she had seen him the day before when she had first realized what his great talent was. But she saw the change in Francis Macomber now.

'Do you have that feeling of happiness about what's going to happen?' Macomber asked, still exploring his new wealth.

'You're not supposed to mention it,' Wilson said, looking in the other's face. 'Much more fashionable to say you're scared. Mind you, you'll be scared too, plenty of times.'

'But you *have* a feeling of happiness about action to come?'

'Yes,' said Wilson. 'There's that. Doesn't do to talk too much about all this. Talk the whole thing away. No pleasure in anything if you mouth it up too much.'

'You're both talking rot,' said Margot. 'Just because you've chased some helpless animals in a motor car you talk like heroes.'

'Sorry,' said Wilson. 'I have been gassing too much.' She's worried about it already, he thought.

'If you don't know what we're talking about why not keep out of it?' Macomber asked his wife.

'You've gotten awfully brave, awfully suddenly,' his wife said contemptuously, but her contempt was not secure. She was very afraid of something.

Macomber laughed, a very natural hearty laugh. 'You know *I have*,' he said. 'I really have.'

'Isn't it sort of late?' Margot said bitterly. Because she had done the best she could for many years back and the way they were together now was no one person's fault.

'Not for me,' said Macomber.

Margot said nothing but sat back in the corner of the seat.

'Do you think we've given him time enough?' Macomber asked Wilson cheerfully.

'We might have a look,' Wilson said. 'Have you any solids left?'

'The gun-bearer has some.'

Wilson called in Swahili and the older gun-bearer, who was skinning out one of the heads, straightened up, pulled a box of solids out of his pocket and brought them over to Macomber, who filled his magazine and put the remaining shells in his pocket.

'You might as well shoot the Springfield,' Wilson said. 'You're used to it. We'll leave the Mannlicher in the car with the Memsahib. Your gun-bearer can carry your heavy gun. I've this damned cannon. Now let me tell you about them.' He had saved this until the last because he did not want to worry Macomber. 'When a buff comes he comes with his head high and thrust straight out. The boss of the horns covers any sort of a brain shot. The only shot is straight into the nose. The only other shot is into his chest or, if you're to one side, into the neck or the shoulders. After they've been hit once they take a hell of a lot of killing. Don't try anything fancy. Take the easiest shot there is. They've finished skinning out that head now. Should we get started?'

He called to the gun-bearers, who came up wiping their hands, and the older one got into the back.

'I'll only take Kongoni,' Wilson said. 'The other can watch to keep the birds away.'

As the car moved slowly across the open space toward the island of brushy trees that ran in a tongue of foliage along a dry water course that cut the open swale, Macomber felt his heart pounding and his mouth was dry again, but it was excitement, not fear.

'Here's where he went in,' Wilson said. Then to the gun-bearer in Swahili, 'Take the blood spur.'

The car was parallel to the patch of bush. Macomber, Wilson and the gun-bearer got down. Macomber, looking back, saw his wife, with the rifle by her side, looking at him. He waved to her and she did not wave back.

The brush was very thick ahead and the ground was dry. The middle-aged gun-bearer was sweating heavily and Wilson had his hat down over his eyes and his red neck showed just ahead of Macomber. Suddenly the gun-bearer said something in Swahili to Wilson and ran forward.

'He's dead in there,' Wilson said. 'Good work,' and he turned to grip Macomber's hand and as they shook hands, grinning at each other, the gun-bearer shouted wildly and they saw him coming out of the bush sideways, fast as a crab, and the bull coming, nose out, mouth tight closed, blood dripping, massive head straight out, coming in a charge, his little pig eyes bloodshot as he looked at them. Wilson, who was ahead, was kneeling shooting, and Macomber, as he fired, unhearing his shot in the roaring of Wilson's gun, saw fragments like slate burst from the huge boss of the horns, and the head jerked, he shot again at the wide nostrils and saw the horns jolt again and fragments fly, and he did not see Wilson now and, aiming carefully, shot again with the buffalo's huge bulk almost on him and his rifle almost level with the on-coming head, nose out, and he could see the little wicked eyes and the head started to lower and he felt a sudden white-hot, blinding flash explode inside his head and that was all he ever felt.

Wilson had ducked to one side to get in a shoulder shot. Macomber had stood solid and shot for the nose, shooting a touch high each time and hitting the heavy horns, splintering and chipping them like hitting a slate roof, and Mrs Macomber, in the car, had shot at the buffalo with the 6.5 Mannlicher as it seemed about to gore Macomber and had hit her husband about two inches up and a little to one side of the base of his skull.

Francis Macomber lay now, face down, not two yards from

where the buffalo lay on his side and his wife knelt over him with Wilson beside her.

'I wouldn't turn him over,' Wilson said.

The woman was crying hysterically.

'I'd get back in the car,' Wilson said. 'Where's the rifle?'

She shook her head, her face contorted. The gun-bearer picked up the rifle.

'Leave it as it is,' said Wilson. Then, 'Go get Abdulla so that he may witness the manner of the accident.'

He knelt down, took a handkerchief from his pocket, and spread it over Francis Macomber's crew-cropped head where it lay. The blood sank into the dry, loose earth.

Wilson stood up and saw the buffalo on his side, his legs out, his thinly-haired belly crawling with ticks. 'Hell of a good bull,' his brain registered automatically. 'A good fifty inches, or better. Better.' He called to the driver and told him to spread a blanket over the body and stay by it. Then he walked over to the motor car where the woman sat crying in the corner.

'That was a pretty thing to do,' he said in a toneless voice. 'He *would* have left you too.'

'Stop it,' she said.

'Of course it's an accident,' he said. 'I know that.'

'Stop it,' she said.

'Don't worry,' he said. 'There will be a certain amount of unpleasantness but I will have some photographs taken that will be very useful at the inquest. There's the testimony of the gun-bearers and the driver too. You're perfectly all right.'

'Stop it,' she said.

'There's a hell of a lot to be done,' he said. 'And I'll have to send a truck off to the lake to wireless for a plane to take the three of us into Nairobi. Why didn't you poison him? That's what they do in England.'

'Stop it. Stop it. Stop it,' the woman cried.

Wilson looked at her with his flat blue eyes.

'I'm through now,' he said. 'I was a little angry. I'd begun to like your husband.'

'Oh, please stop it,' she said. 'Please, please stop it.'

'That's better,' Wilson said. 'Please is much better. Now I'll stop.'

33

The Capital of the World

Madrid is full of boys named Paco, which is the diminutive of the name Francisco, and there is a Madrid joke about a father who came to Madrid and inserted an advertisement in the personal columns of *El Liberal* which said: PACO MEET ME AT HOTEL MONTANA NOON TUESDAY ALL IS FORGIVEN PAPA and how a sqaudron of Guardia Civil had to be called out to disperse the eight hundred young men who answered the advertisement. But this Paco, who waited on table at the Pension Luarca, had no father to forgive him, nor anything for the father to forgive. He had two older sisters who were chambermaids at the Luarca, who had gotten their place through coming from the same small village as a former Luarca chambermaid who had proven hardworking and honest and hence given her village and its products a good name; and these sisters had paid his way on the auto-bus to Madrid and gotten him his job as an apprentice waiter. He came from a village in a part of Extramadura where conditions were incredibly primitive, food scarce, and comforts unknown and he had worked hard ever since he could remember.

He was a well built boy with very black, rather curly hair, good teeth and a skin that his sisters envied, and he had a ready and unpuzzled smile. He was fast on his feet and did his work well and he loved his sisters, who seemed beautiful and sophisticated; he loved Madrid, which was still an unbelievable place, and he loved his work which, done under bright lights, with clean linen, the wearing of evening clothes, and abundant food in the kitchen, seemed romantically beautiful.

There were from eight to a dozen other people who lived at the Luarca and ate in the dining room but for Paco, the youngest of the three waiters who served at table, the only ones who really existed were the bull fighters.

Second-rate matadors lived at that pension because the address in the Calle San Jeronimo was good, the food was excellent and the room and board was cheap. It is necessary for a bull fighter to give the appearance, if not of prosperity, at least of respectability, since decorum and dignity rank above courage as the virtues most highly prized in Spain, and bull fighters stayed at the Luarca until their last pesetas were gone. There is no record of any bull fighter having left the Luarca for a better or more expensive hotel; second-rate bull fighters never became first rate; but the descent from the Luarca was swift since any one could stay there who was making anything at all and a bill was never presented to a guest unasked until the woman who ran the place knew that the case was hopeless.

At this time there were three full matadors living at the Luarca as well as two very good picadors, and one excellent banderillero. The Luarca was luxury for the picadors and the banderilleros who, with their families in Seville, required lodging in Madrid during the Spring season; but they were well paid and in the fixed employ of fighters who were heavily contracted during the coming season and three of these subalterns would probably make much more apiece than any of the three matadors. Of the three matadors one was ill and trying to conceal it; one had passed his short vogue as a novelty; and the third was a coward.

The coward had at one time, until he had received a peculiarly atrocious horn wound in the lower abdomen at the start of his first season as a full matador, been exceptionally brave and remarkably skillful and he still had many of the hearty mannerisms of his days of success. He was jovial to excess and laughed constantly with and without provocation. He had, when successful, been very addicted to practical jokes but he had given them up now. They took an assurance that he did not feel. This matador had an intelligent, very open face and he carried himself with much style.

The matador who was ill was careful never to show it and

was meticulous about eating a little of all the dishes that were presented at the table. He had a great many handkerchiefs which he laundered himself in his room, and, lately, he had been selling his fighting suits. He had sold one, cheaply, before Christmas and another in the first week of April. They had been very expensive suits, had always been well kept and he had one more. Before he had become ill he had been a very promising, even a sensational, fighter and, while he himself could not read, he had clippings which said that in his debut in Madrid he had been better than Belmonte. He ate alone at a small table and looked up very little.

The matador who had once been a novelty was very short and brown and very dignified. He also ate alone at a separate table and he smiled very rarely and never laughed. He came from Valladolid, where the people are extremely serious, and he was a capable matador; but his style had become old-fashioned before he had ever succeeded in endearing himself to the public through his virtues, which were courage and a calm capability, and his name on a poster would draw no one to a bull ring. His novelty had been that he was so short that he could barely see over the bull's withers, but there were other short fighters, and he had never succeeded in imposing himself on the public's fancy.

Of the picadors one was a thin, hawk-faced, gray-haired man, lightly built but with legs and arms like iron, who always wore cattle-men's boots under his trousers, drank too much every evening and gazed amorously at any woman in the pension. The other was huge, dark, brown-faced, good-looking, with black hair like an Indian and enormous hands. Both were great picadors although the first was reputed to have lost much of his ability through drink and dissipation, and the second was said to be too headstrong and quarrelsome to stay with any matador more than a single season.

The banderillero was middle-aged, gray, cat-quick in spite of his years and, sitting at the table he looked a moderately prosperous business man. His legs were still good for this season, and when they should go he was intelligent and experienced enough to keep regularly employed for a long time. The difference would be that when his speed of foot would be gone he would always be frightened where now he was assured and calm in the ring and out of it.

On this evening every one had left the dining room except the hawk-faced picador who drank too much, the birthmarked-faced auctioneer of watches at the fairs and festivals of Spain, who also drank too much, and two priests from Galicia who were sitting at a corner table and drinking if not too much certainly enough. At that time wine was included in the price of the room and board at the Luarca and the waiters had just brought fresh bottles of Valdepeñas to the tables of the auctioneer, then to the picador and, finally, to the two priests.

The three waiters stood at the end of the room. It was the rule of the house that they should all remain on duty until the diners whose tables they were responsible for should all have left, but the one who served the table of the two priests had an appointment to go to an Anarcho-Syndicalist meeting and Paco had agreed to take over his table for him.

Upstairs the matador who was ill was lying face down on his bed alone. The matador who was no longer a novelty was sitting looking out of his window preparatory to walking out to the café. The matador who was a coward had the older sister of Paco in his room with him, and was trying to get her to do something which she was laughingly refusing to do. This matador was saying 'Come on, little savage.'

'No,' said the sister. 'Why should I?'

'For a favor.'

'You've eaten and now you want me for dessert.'

'Just once. What harm can it do?'

'Leave me alone. Leave me alone, I tell you.'

'It is a very little thing to do.'

'Leave me alone, I tell you.'

Down in the dining room the tallest of the waiters, who was overdue at the meeting, said, 'Look at those black pigs drink.'

'That's no way to speak,' said the second waiter. 'They are decent clients. They do not drink too much.'

'For me it is a good way to speak,' said the tall one. 'They are the two curses of Spain, the bulls and the priests.'

'Certainly not the individual bull and the individual priest,' said the second waiter.

'Yes,' said the tall waiter. 'Only through the individual can you attack the class. It is necessary to kill the individual bull and the individual priest. All of them. Then there are no more.'

'Save it for the meeting,' said the other waiter.

'Look at the barbarity of Madrid,' said the tall waiter. 'It is now half-past eleven o'clock and these are still guzzling.'

'They only started to eat at ten,' said the other waiter. 'As you know there are many dishes. That wine is cheap and these have paid for it. It is not a strong wine.'

'How can there be solidarity of workers with fools like you?' asked the tall waiter.

'Look,' said the second waiter who was a man of fifty. 'I have worked all my life. In all that remains of my life I must work. I have no complaints against work. To work is normal.'

'Yes, but the lack of work kills.'

'I have always worked,' said the older waiter. 'Go on to the meeting. There is no necessity to stay.'

'You are a good comrade,' said the tall waiter. 'But you lack all ideology.'

'*Mejor si me falta eso que el otro*,' said the older waiter (meaning it is better to lack that than work). 'Go on to the *mitin*.'

Paco had said nothing. He did not yet understand politics but it always gave him a thrill to hear the tall waiter speak of the necessity for killing the priests and the Guardia Civil. The tall waiter represented to him revolution and revolution also was romantic. He himself would like to be a good catholic, a revolutionary, and have a steady job like this, while, at the same time, being a bullfighter.

'Go on to the meeting, Ignacio,' he said. 'I will respond for your work.'

'The two of us,' said the older waiter.

'There isn't enough, for one,' said Paco. 'Go on to the meeting.'

'*Pues, me voy*,' said the tall waiter. 'And thanks.'

In the meantime, upstairs, the sister of Paco had gotten out of the embrace of the matador as skillfully as a wrestler

38

breaking a hold and said, now angry, 'These are the hungry people. A failed bullfighter. With your ton-load of fear. If you have so much of that, use it in the ring.'

'That is the way a whore talks.'

'A whore is also a woman, but I am not a whore.'

'You'll be one.'

'Not through you.'

'Leave me,' said the matador who, now, repulsed and refused, felt the nakedness of his cowardice returning.

'Leave you? What hasn't left you?' said the sister. 'Don't you want me to make up the bed? I'm paid to do that.'

'Leave me,' said the matador, his broad good-looking face wrinkled into a contortion that was like crying. 'You whore. You dirty little whore.'

'Matador,' she said, shutting the door. 'My matador.'

Inside the room the matador sat on the bed. His face still had the contortion which, in the ring, he made into a constant smile which frightened those people in the first rows of seats who knew what they were watching. 'And this,' he was saying aloud. 'And this. And this.'

He could remember when he had been good and it had only been three years before. He could remember the weight of the heavy gold-brocaded fighting jacket on his shoulders on that hot afternoon in May when his voice had still been the same in the ring as in the café, and how he sighted along the point-dipping blade at the place in the top of the shoulders where it was dusty in the short-haired black hump of muscle above the wide, wood-knocking, splintered-tipped horns that lowered as he went in to kill, and how the sword pushed in as easy as into a mound of stiff butter with the palm of his hand pushing the pommel, his left arm crossed low, his left shoulder forward, his weight on his left leg, and then his weight wasn't on his leg. His weight was on his lower belly and as the bull raised his head the horn was out of sight in him and he swung over on it twice before they pulled him off it. So now when he went in to kill, and it was seldom, he could not look at the horns and what did any whore know about what he went through before he fought? And what had they been through that laughed at him? They were all whores and they knew what they could do with it.

Down in the dining room the picador sat looking at the priests. If there were women in the room he stared at them. If there were no women he would stare with enjoyment at a foreigner, *un inglés,* but lacking women or strangers, he now stared with enjoyment and insolence at the two priests. While he stared the birth-marked auctioneer rose and folding his napkin went out, leaving over half the wine in the last bottle he had ordered. If his accounts had been paid up at the Luarca he would have finished the bottle.

The two priests did not stare back at the picador. One of them was saying, 'It is ten days since I have been here waiting to see him and all day I sit in the ante-chamber and he will not receive me.'

'What is there to do?'

'Nothing. What can one do? One cannot go against authority.'

'I have been here for two weeks and nothing. I wait and they will not see me.'

'We are from the abandoned country. When the money runs out we can return.'

'To the abandoned country? What does Madrid care about Galicia? We are a poor province.'

'One understands the action of our brother Basilio.'

'Still I have no real confidence in the integrity of Basilio Alvarez.'

'Madrid is where one learns to understand. Madrid kills Spain.'

'If they would simply see one and refuse.'

'No. You must be broken and worn out by waiting.'

'Well, we shall see. I can wait as well as another.'

At this moment the picador got to his feet, walked over to the priests' table and stood, gray-headed and hawk-faced, staring at them and smiling.

'A torero,' said one priest to the other.

'And a good one,' said the picador and walked out of the dining room, gray-jacketed, trim-waisted, bow-legged, in tight breeches over his high-heeled cattleman's boots that clicked on the floor as he swaggered quite steadily, smiling to himself. He lived in a small, tight, professional world of personal efficiency, nightly alcoholic triumph, and insolence. Now he lit a cigar and tilting his hat at an angle in the hallway went out to the café.

The priests left immediately after the picador, hurriedly conscious of being the last people in the dining room, and there was no one in the room now but Paco and the middle-aged waiter. They cleared the tables and carried the bottles into the kitchen.

In the kitchen was the boy who washed the dishes. He was three years older than Paco and was very cynical and bitter.

'Take this,' the middle-aged waiter said, and poured out a glass of Valdepeñas and handed it to him.

'Why not?' the boy took the glass.

'Tu, Paco?' the older waiter asked.

'Thank you,' said Paco. The three of them drank.

'I will be going,' said the middle-aged waiter.

'Good night,' they told him.

He went out and they were alone. Paco took a napkin one of the priests had used and standing straight, his heels planted, lowered the napkin and with head following the movements swung his arms in the motion of a slow weeping veronica. He turned and advancing his right foot slightly, made the second pass, gained a little terrain on the imaginary bull and made a third pass, slow, perfectly timed and suave, then gathered the napkin to his waist and swung his hips away from the bull in a media-veronica.

The dishwasher, whose name was Enrique, watched him critically and sneeringly.

'How is the bull?' he said.

'Very brave,' said Paco. 'Look.'

Standing slim and straight he made four more perfect passes, smooth, elegant and graceful.

'And the bull?' asked Enrique standing against the sink, holding his wine glass and wearing his apron.

'Still has lots of gas,' said Paco.

'You make me sick,' said Enrique.

'Why?'

'Look.'

Enrique removed his apron and citing the imaginary bull he

41

sculptured four perfect, languid gypsy veronicas and ended up with a rebolera that made the apron swing in a stiff arc past the bull's nose as he walked away from him.

'Look at that,' he said. 'And I wash dishes.'

'Why?'

'Fear,' said Enrique. *'Miedo.* The same fear you would have in a ring with a bull.'

'No,' said Paco. 'I wouldn't be afraid.'

'Leche!' said Enrique. 'Every one is afraid. But a torero can control his fear so that he can work the bull. I went in an amateur fight and I was so afraid I couldn't keep from running. Every one thought it was very funny. So would you be afraid. If it wasn't for fear every bootblack in Spain would be a bullfighter. You, a country boy, would be frightened worse than I was.'

'No,' said Paco.

He had done it too many times in his imagination. Too many times he had seen the horns, seen the bull's wet muzzle, the ear twitching, then the head go down and the charge, the hoofs thudding and the hot bull pass him as he swung the cape, to re-charge as he swung the cape again, then again, and again, and again, to end winding the bull around him in his great media-veronica, and walk swingingly away, with bull hairs caught in the gold ornaments of his jacket from the close passes; the bull standing hypnotized and the crowd applauding. No, he would not be afraid. Others, yes. Not he. He knew he would not be afraid. Even if he ever was afraid he knew that he could do it anyway. He had confidence. 'I wouldn't be afraid,' he said.

Enrique said, *'Leche,'* again.

Then he said, 'If we should try it?'

'How?'

'Look,' said Enrique. 'You think of the bull but you do not think of the horns. The bull has such force that the horns rip like a knife, they stab like a bayonet, and they kill like a club. Look,' he opened a table drawer and took out two meat knives. 'I will bind these to the legs of a chair. Then I will play bull for you with the chair held before my head. The knives are the horns. If you make those passes then they mean something.'

42

'Lend me your apron,' said Paco. 'We'll do it in the dining room.'

'No,' said Enrique, suddenly not bitter. 'Don't do it, Paco.'

'Yes,' said Paco. 'I'm not afraid.'

'You will be when you see the knives come.'

'We'll see,' said Paco. 'Give me the apron.'

At this time, while Enrique was binding the two heavy-bladed razor-sharp meat knives fast to the legs of the chair with two soiled napkins holding the half of each knife, wrapping them tight and then knotting them, the two chambermaids, Paco's sisters, were on their way to the cinema to see Greta Garbo in *Anna Christie*. Of the two priests, one was sitting in his underwear reading his breviary and the other was wearing a nightshirt and saying the rosary. All the bullfighters except the one who was ill had made their evening appearance at the Café Fornos, where the big, dark-haired picador was playing billiards, the short, serious matador was sitting at a crowded table before a coffee and milk, along with the middle-aged banderillero and other serious workmen.

The drinking, gray-headed picador was sitting with a glass of cazalas brandy before him staring with pleasure at a table where the matador whose courage was gone was with another matador who had renounced the sword to become a banderillero again, and two very houseworn-looking prostitutes.

The auctioneer stood on the street corner talking with friends. The tall waiter was at the Anarcho-Syndicalist meeting waiting for an opportunity to speak. The middle aged waiter was seated on the terrace of the Café Alvarez drinking a small beer. The woman who owned the Luarca was already asleep in her bed, where she lay on her back with the bolster between her legs; big, fat, honest, clean, easy-going, very religious and never having ceased to miss or pray daily for her husband, dead now, twenty years. In his room, alone, the matador who was ill lay face down on his bed with his mouth against a handkerchief.

Now, in the deserted dining room, Enrique tied the last knot in the napkins that bound the knives to the chair legs and lifted the chair. He pointed the legs with the knives on them forward and held the chair over his head with the two knives pointing straight ahead, one on each side of his head.

'It's heavy,' he said. 'Look, Paco. It is very dangerous. Don't do it.' He was sweating.

Paco stood facing him, holding the apron spread, holding a fold of it bunched in each hand, thumbs up, first finger down, spread to catch the eye of the bull.

'Charge straight,' he said. 'Turn like a bull. Charge as many times as you want.'

'How will you know when to cut the pass?' asked Enrique. 'It's better to do three and then a media.'

'All right,' said Paco. 'But come straight. Huh, torito! Come on, little bull!'

Running with head down Enrique came toward him and Paco swung the apron just ahead of the knife blade as it passed close in front of his belly and as it went by it was, to him, the real horn, white-tipped, black, smooth, and as Enrique passed him and turned to rush again it was the hot, blood-flanked mass of the bull that thudded by, then turned like a cat and came again as he swung the cape slowly. Then the bull turned and came again and, as he watched the onrushing point, he stepped his left foot two inches too far forward and the knife did not pass, but had slipped in as easily as into a wineskin and there was a hot scalding rush above and around the sudden inner rigidity of steel and Enrique shouting. 'Ay! Ay! Let me get it out! Let me get it out!' and Paco slipped forward on the chair, the apron cape still held, Enrique puffing on the chair as the knife turned in him, in him, Paco.

The knife was out now and he sat on the floor in the widening warm pool.

'Put the napkin over it. Hold it!' said Enrique. 'Hold it tight. I will run for the doctor. You must hold in the hemorrhage.'

'There should be a rubber cup,' said Paco. He had seen that used in the ring.

'I came straight,' said Enrique, crying. 'All I wanted was to show the danger.'

'Don't worry,' said Paco, his voice sounding far away. 'But bring the doctor.'

In the ring they lifted you and carried you, running with you, to the operating room. If the femoral artery emptied itself before you reached there they called the priest.

'Advise one of the priests,' said Paco, holding the napkin tight against his lower abdomen. He could not believe that this had happened to him.

But Enrique was running down the Carrera San Jeromino to the all-night first-aid station and Paco was alone, first sitting up, then huddled over, then slumped on the floor, until it was over, feeling his life go out of him as dirty water empties from a bathtub when the plug is drawn. He was frightened and he felt faint and he tried to say an act of contrition and he remembered how it started but before he had said, as fast as he could, 'Oh, my God, I am heartily sorry for having offended Thee who art worthy of all my love and I firmly resolve . . .' he felt too faint and he was lying face down on the floor and it was over very quickly. A severed femoral artery empties itself faster than you can believe.

As the doctor from the first-aid station came up the stairs accompanied by a policeman who held on to Enrique by the arm, the two sisters of Paco were still in the moving picture palace of the Gran Via, where they were intensely disappointed in the Greta Garbo film, which showed the great star in miserable low surroundings when they had been accustomed to see her surrounded by great luxury and brilliance. The audience disliked the film thoroughly and were protesting by whistling and stamping their feet. All the other people from the hotel were doing almost what they had been doing when the accident happened, except that the two priests had finished their devotions and were preparing for sleep, and the gray-haired picador had moved his drink over to the table with the two houseworn prostitutes. A little later he went out of the café with one of them. It was the one for whom the matador who had lost his nerve had been buying drinks.

The boy Paco had never known about any of this nor about what all these people would be doing on the next day and on other days to come. He had no idea how they really lived nor how they ended. He did not even realize they ended. He died, as the Spanish phrase has it, full of illusions. He had not had

45

time in his life to lose any of them, nor even, at the end, to complete an act of contrition.

He had not even had time to be disappointed in the Garbo picture which disappointed all Madrid for a week.

The Snows of Kilimanjaro

Kilimanjaro is a snow covered mountain 19,710 feet high, and is said to be the highest mountain in Africa. Its western summit is called 'Ngàje Ngài', the House of God. Close to the western summit there is the dried and frozen carcass of a leopard. No one has explained what the leopard was seeking at that altitude.

'The marvelous thing is that it's painless,' he said. 'That's how you know when it starts.'

'Is it really?'

'Absolutely. I'm awfully sorry about the odor, though. That must bother you.'

'Don't! Please don't.'

'Look at them,' he said. 'Now is it sight or is it scent that brings them like that?'

The cot the man lay on was in the wide shade of a mimosa tree and as he looked out past the shade on to the glare of the plain there were three of the big birds squatted obscenely, while in the sky a dozen more sailed, making quick-moving shadows as they passed.

'They've been there since the day the truck broke down,' he said. 'Today's the first time any have lit on the ground. I watched the way they sailed very carefully at first in case I ever wanted to use them in a story. That's funny now.'

'I wish you wouldn't,' she said.

'I'm only talking,' he said. 'It's much easier if I talk. But I don't want to bother you.'

'You know it doesn't bother me,' she said. 'It's that I've

47

gotten so very nervous not being able to do anything. I think we might make it as easy as we can until the plane comes.'

'Or until the plane doesn't come.'

'Please tell me what I can do. There must be something I can do.'

'You can take the leg off and that might stop it, though I doubt it. Or you can shoot me. You're a good shot now. I taught you to shoot didn't I?'

'Please don't talk that way. Couldn't I read to you?'

'Read what?'

'Anything in the book bag that we haven't read.'

'I can't listen to it,' he said. 'Talking is the easiest. We quarrel and that makes the time pass.'

'I don't quarrel. I never want to quarrel. Let's not quarrel any more. No matter how nervous we get. Maybe they will be back with another truck today. Maybe the plane will come.'

'I don't want to move,' the man said. 'There is no sense in moving now except to make it easier for you.'

'That's cowardly.'

'Can't you let a man die as comfortably as he can without calling him names? What's the use of slanging me?'

'You're not going to die.'

'Don't be silly. I'm dying now. Ask those bastards.' He looked over to where the huge, filthy birds sat, their naked head sunk in the hunched feathers. A fourth planed down, to run quick-legged and then waddle slowly towards the others.

'They are around every camp. You never notice them. You can't die if you don't give up.'

'Where did you read that? You're such a bloody fool.'

'You might think about someone else.'

'For Christ's sake,' he said, 'that's been my trade.'

He lay then and was quiet for a while and looked across the heat shimmer of the plain to the edge of the bush. There were a few Tommies that showed minute and white against the yellow and, far off, he saw a herd of zebra, white against the green of the bush. This was a pleasant camp under big trees against a hill, with good water, and close by, a nearly dry water hole where sand grouse flighted in the mornings.

'Wouldn't you like me to read?' she asked. She was sitting on

48

a canvas chair beside his cot. 'There's a breeze coming up.'

'No thanks.'

'Maybe the truck will come.'

'I don't give a damn about the truck.'

'I do.'

'You give a damn about so many things that I don't.'

'Not so many, Harry.'

'What about a drink?'

'It's supposed to be bad for you. It said in Black's to avoid all alcohol. You shouldn't drink.'

'Molo!' he shouted.

'Yes, Bwana.'

'Bring whiskey-soda.'

'Yes, Bwana.'

'You shouldn't,' she said. 'That's what I mean by giving up. It says it's bad for you. I know it's bad for you.'

'No,' he said. 'It's good for me.'

So now it was all over, he thought. So now he would never have a chance to finish it. So this was the way it ended in a bickering over a drink. Since the gangrene started in his right leg he had no pain and with the pain the horror had gone and all he felt now was a great tiredness and anger that this was the end of it. For this, that now was coming, he had very little curiosity. For years it had obsessed him; but now it meant nothing in itself. It was strange how easy being tired enough made it.

Now he would never write the things that he had saved to write until he knew enough to write them well. Well, he would not have to fail at trying to write them either. Maybe you could never write them, and that was why you put them off and delayed the starting. Well, he would never know, now.

'I wish we'd never come,' the woman said. She was looking at him holding the glass and biting her lip. 'You never would have gotten anything like this in Paris. You always said you loved Paris. We could have stayed in Paris or gone anywhere. I'd have gone anywhere. I said I'd go anywhere you wanted. If you wanted to shoot we could have gone shooting in Hungary and been comfortable.'

'Your bloody money,' he said.

'That's not fair,' she said. 'It was always yours as much as mine. I left everything and I went wherever you wanted to go and I've done what you wanted to do. But I wish we'd never come here.'

'You said you loved it.'

'I did when you were all right. But now I hate it. I don't see why that had to happen to your leg. What have we done to have that happen to us?'

'I suppose what I did was to forget to put iodine on it when I first scratched it. Then I didn't pay any attention to it because I never infect. Then, later, when it got bad, it was probably using that weak carbolic solution when the other antiseptics ran out that paralyzed the minute blood vessels and started the gangrene.' He looked at her, 'What else?'

'I don't mean that.'

'If we would have hired a good mechanic instead of a half-baked kikuyu driver, he would have checked the oil and never burned out that bearing in the truck.'

'I don't mean that.'

'If you hadn't left your own people, your goddamned Old Westbury, Saratoga, Palm Beach people to take me on –'

'Why, I loved you. That's not fair. I love you now. I'll always love you. Don't you love me?'

'No,' said the man. 'I don't think so. I never have.'

'Harry, what are you saying? You're out of your head.'

'No. I haven't any head to go out of.'

'Don't drink that,' she said. 'Darling, please don't drink that. We have to do everything we can.'

'You do it,' he said. 'I'm tired.'

Now in his mind he saw a railway station at Karagatch and he was standing with his pack and that was the headlight of the Simplon–Orient cutting the dark now and he was leaving Thrace then after the retreat. That was one of the things he had saved to write, with, in the morning at breakfast, looking out the window and seeing snow on the mountains in Bulgaria and Nansen's Secretary asking the old man if it were snow and the old man looking at it and saying, No, that's not snow. It's too early for snow. And the Secretary repeating to the other girls, No, you see.

50

It's not snow and them all saying, It's not snow we were mistaken. But it was snow all right and he sent them on into it when he evolved exchange of populations. And it was snow they tramped along in until they died that winter.

It was snow too that fell all Christmas week that year up in the Gauertal, that year they lived in the woodcutter's house with the big square porcelain stove that filled half the room, and they slept on mattresses filled with beech leaves, the time the deserter came with his feet bloody in the snow. He said the police were right behind him and they gave him woolen socks and held the gendarmes talking until the tracks had drifted over.

In Schrunz, on Christmas day, the snow was so bright it hurt your eyes when you looked out from the weinstube and saw everyone coming home from church. That was where they walked up the sleigh-smoothed urine-yellowed road along the river with the steep pine hills, skis heavy on the shoulder, and where they ran that great run down the glacier above the Madlener-haus, the snow as smooth to see as cake frosting and as light as powder and he remembered the noiseless rush the speed made as you dropped down like a bird.

They were snow-bound a week in the Madlener-haus that time in the blizzard playing cards in the smoke by the lantern light and the stakes were higher all the time as Herr Lent lost more. Finally he lost it all. Everything, the skischule money and all the season's profit and then his capital. He could see him with his long nose, picking up the cards and then opening, 'Sans Voir'. There was always gambling then. When there was no snow you gambled and when there was too much you gambled. He thought of all the time in his life he had spent gambling.

But he had never written a line of that, nor of that cold, bright Christmas day with the mountains showing across the plain that Johnson had flown across the lines to bomb the Austrian officers' leave train, machine-gunning them as they scattered and ran. He remembered Johnson afterward coming into the mess and starting to tell about it. And how quiet it got and then somebody saying: 'You bloody murderous bastard.'

They were the same Austrians they killed then that he skied with later. No not the same. Hans, that he skied with all that year, had been in the Kaiser-Jägers and when they went hunting hares *together up the little valley above the saw-mill they had talked of the fighting on Pasubio and of the attack on Pertica and Asalone and he had never written a word of that. Nor of Monte Corno, nor the Siete Commum, nor of Arsiedo.*

How many winters had he lived in the Voralberg and the Arlberg? It was four and then he remembered the man who had the fox to sell when they had walked into Bludenz, that time to buy presents, and the cherry-pip taste of the good kirsch, the fast-slipping rush of running powder-snow on crust, singing 'Hi! Ho! said Rolly!' as you ran down the last stretch to the steep drop, taking it straight, then running the orchard in three turns and out across the ditch and on to the icy road behind the inn. Knocking your bindings loose, kicking the skis free and leaning them up against the wooden wall of the inn, the lamplight coming from the window, where inside, in the smokey, new-wine smelling warmth, they were playing the accordion.

'Where did we stay in Paris?' he asked the woman who was sitting by him in a canvas chair, now, in Africa.

'At the Crillon. You know that.'

'Why do I know that?'

'That's where we always stayed.'

'No. Not always.'

'There and at the Pavillion Henri-Quatre in St Germain. You said you loved it there.'

'Love is a dunghill,' said Harry. 'And I'm the cock that gets on it to crow.'

'If you have to go away,' she said, 'is it absolutely necessary to kill off everything you leave behind? I mean do you have to take away everything? Do you have to kill your horse, and your wife and burn your saddle and your armour?'

'Yes,' he said. 'Your damned money was my armor. My Swift and my Armor.'

'Don't.'

'All right. I'll stop that. I don't want to hurt you.'

'It's a little bit late now.'

'All right then. I'll go on hurting you. It's more amusing. The only thing I ever really liked to do with you I can't do now.'

'No, that's not true. You liked to do many things and everything you wanted to do I did.'

'Oh, for Christ sake stop bragging, will you?'

He looked at her and saw her crying.

'Listen,' he said. 'Do you think that it is fun to do this? I don't know why I'm doing it. It's trying to kill to keep yourself alive, I imagine. I was all right when we started talking. I didn't mean to start this, and now I'm crazy as a coot and being as cruel to you as I can be. Don't pay any attention, darling, to what I say. I love you, really. You know I love you. I've never loved anyone else the way I love you.'

He slipped into the familiar lie he made his bread and butter by.

'You're sweet to me.'

'You bitch,' he said. 'You rich bitch. That's poetry. I'm full of poetry now. Rot and poetry. Rotten poetry.'

'Stop it. Harry, why do you have to turn into a devil now?'

'I don't like to leave anything,' the man said. 'I don't like to leave things behind.'

It was evening now and he had been asleep. The sun was gone behind the hill and there was a shadow all across the plain and the small animals were feeding close to camp; quick dropping heads and switching tails, he watched them keeping well out away from the bush now. The birds no longer waited on the ground. They were all perched heavily in a tree. There were many more of them. His personal boy was sitting by the bed.

'Memsahib's gone to shoot,' the boy said. 'Does Bwana want?'

'Nothing.'

She had gone to kill a piece of meat and, knowing how he liked to watch the game, she had gone well away so she would not disturb this little pocket of the plain that he could see. She was always thoughtful, he thought. On anything she knew about, or had read, or what she had ever heard.

It was not her fault that when he went to her he was already over. How could a woman know that you meant nothing that you said; that you spoke only from habit and to be comfortable? After he no longer meant what he said, his lies were more successful with women than when he had told them the truth.

It was not so much that he lied as that there was no truth to tell. He had had his life and it was over and then he went on living it again with different people and more money, with the best of the same places, and some new ones.

You kept from thinking and it was all marvelous. You were equipped with good insides so that you did not go to pieces that way, the way most of them had, and you made an attitude that you cared nothing for the work you used to do, now that you could no longer do it. But, in yourself, you said that you would write about people; about the very rich; that you were really not of them but a spy in their country; that you would leave it and write of it and for once it would be written by someone who knew what he was writing of. But he would never do it, because each day of not writing, of comfort, of being that which he despised, dulled his ability and softened his will to work so that, finally, he did no work at all. The people he knew now were all much more comfortable when he did not work. Africa was where he had been happiest in the good time of his life, so he had come out here to start again. They had made this safari with the minimum of comfort. There was no hardship; but there was no luxury and he had thought that he could get back into training that way. That in some way he could work the fat off his soul the way a fighter went into the mountains to work and train in order to burn it out of his body.

She had liked it. She said she loved it. She loved anything that was exciting, that involved a change of scene, where there were new people and where things were pleasant. And he had felt the illusion of returning strength of will to work. Now if this was how it ended, and he knew it was, he must not turn like some snake biting itself because its back was broken. It wasn't this woman's fault. If it had not been she it would have been another. If he lived by a lie he should try to die by it. He heard a shot beyond the hill.

She shot very well, this good, this rich bitch, this kindly caretaker and destroyer of his talent. Nonsense. He had destroyed his talent himself. Why should he blame this woman because she kept him well? He had destroyed his talent by not using it, by betrayals of himself and what he believed in, by drinking so much that he blunted the edge of his perceptions, by laziness, by sloth, and by snobbery, by pride and by prejudice, by hook and by crook. What was this? A catalogue of old books? What was his talent anyway? It was a talent all right but instead of using it, he had traded on it. It was never what he had done, but always what he could do. And he had chosen to make his living with something else instead of a pen or a pencil. It was strange, too, wasn't it, that when he fell in love with another woman, that woman should always have more money than the last one? But when he no longer was in love, when he was only lying, as to this woman, now, who had the most money of all, who had all the money there was, who had had a husband and children, who had taken lovers and been dissatisfied with them, and who loved him dearly as a writer, as a man, as a companion and as a proud possession; it was strange that when he did not love her at all and was lying, that he should be able to give her more for her money than when he had really loved.

We must all be cut out for what we do, he thought. However you make your living is where your talent lies. He had sold vitality, in one form or another, all his life and when your affections are not too involved you give much better value for the money. He had found that out but he would never write that, now, either. No, he would not write that, although it was well worth writing.

Now she came in sight, walking across the open toward the camp. She was wearing jodhpurs and carrying her rifle. The two boys had a Tommie slung and they were coming along behind her. She was still a good-looking woman, he thought, and she had a pleasant body. She had a great talent and appreciation for the bed, she was not pretty, but he liked her face, she read enormously, liked to ride and shoot and, certainly, she drank too much. Her husband had died when she was still a comparatively young woman and for a while she had devoted herself to her two just-grown children, who did not need her and were embarrassed at having her about, to her stable of horses, to books, and to bottles. She liked to read in the evening before dinner and she drank Scotch and soda while she read. By dinner she was fairly drunk and after a bottle of wine at dinner she was usually drunk enough to sleep.

That was before the lovers. After she had the lovers she did not drink so much because she did not have to be drunk to sleep. But the lovers bored her. She had been married to a man who never bored her and these people bored her very much.

Then one of her two children was killed in a plane crash and after that was over she did not want the lovers, and drink being no anaesthetic she had to make another life. Suddenly, she had been acutely frightened of being alone. But she wanted someone that she respected with her.

It had begun very simply. She liked what he wrote and she had always envied the life he led. She thought he did exactly what he wanted to. The steps by which she had acquired him and the way in which she had finally fallen in love with him were all part of a regular progression in which she had built herself a new life and he had traded away what remained of his old life.

He had traded it for security, for comfort too, there was no denying that, and for what else? He did not know. She would have bought him anything he wanted. He knew that. She was a damned nice woman too. He would as soon be in bed with her as anyone; rather with her, because she was richer, because she was very pleasant and appreciative and because she never made scenes. And now this life that she had built again was coming to a term because he had not used iodine two weeks ago when a thorn had scratched his knee as they moved forward trying to photograph a herd of waterbuck standing, their heads up, peering while their nostrils searched the air, their ears spread wide to hear the first noise that would send them rushing into the bush. They had bolted, too, before he got the picture.

Here she came now.

He turned his head on the cot to look toward her. 'Hello,' he said.

'I shot a Tommy ram,' she told him. 'He'll make you good broth and I'll have them mash some potatoes with the Klim. How do you feel?'

'Much better.'

'Isn't that lovely? You know I thought perhaps you would. You were sleeping when I left.'

'I had a good sleep. Did you walk far?'

'No. Just around the hill. I made quite a good shot on the Tommy.'

'You shoot marvelously, you know.'

'I love it. I've loved Africa. Really. If *you're* all right it's the most fun that I've ever had. You don't know the fun it's been to shoot with you. I've loved the country.'

'I love it too.'

'Darling, you don't know how marvelous it is to see you feeling better. I couldn't stand it when you felt that way. You won't talk to me like that again, will you? Promise me?'

'No,' he said. 'I don't remember what I said.'

'You don't have to destroy me. Do you? I'm only a middle-aged woman who loves you and wants to do what you want to do. I've been destroyed two or three times already. You wouldn't want to destroy me again, would you?'

'I'd like to destroy you a few times in bed,' he said.

'Yes. That's the good destruction. That's the way we're made to be destroyed. The plane will be here tomorrow.'

'How do you know?'

'I'm sure. It's bound to come. The boys have the wood all ready and the grass to make the smudge. I went down and looked at it again today. There's plenty of room to land and we have the smudges ready at both ends.'

'What makes you think it will come tomorrow?'

'I'm sure it will. It's overdue now. Then, in town, they will fix up your leg and then we will have some good destruction. Not that dreadful talking kind.'

'Should we have a drink? The sun is down.'

'Do you think you should?'

'I'm having one.'

'We'll have one together. *Molo, letti dui whiskey-soda!*' she called.

'You'd better put on your mosquito boots,' he told her.

'I'll wait till I bathe . . . .'

While it grew dark they drank and just before it was dark and

57

there was no longer enough light to shoot, a hyena crossed the open on his way around the hill.

'That bastard crosses there every night,' the man said. 'Every night for two weeks.'

'He's the one makes the noise at night. I don't mind it. They're a filthy animal though.'

Drinking together, with no pain now except the discomfort of lying in the one position, the boys lighting a fire, its shadow jumping on the tents, he could feel the return of acquiescence in this life of pleasant surrender. She *was* very good to him. He had been cruel and unjust in the afternoon. She was a fine woman, marvelous really. And just then it occurred to him that he was going to die.

It came with a rush; not as a rush of water nor of wind; but of a sudden evil-smelling emptiness and the odd thing was that the hyena slipped lightly along the edge of it.

'What is it, Harry?' she asked him.

'Nothing,' he said. 'You had better move over to the other side. To windward.'

'Did Molo change the dressing?'

'Yes. I'm just using the boric now.'

'How do you feel?'

'A little wobbly.'

'I'm going in to bathe,' she said. 'I'll be right out. I'll eat with you and then we'll put the cot in.'

So, he said to himself, we did well to stop the quarreling. He had never quarreled much with this woman, while with the women that he loved he had quarreled so much they had finally, always, with the corrosion of the quarreling, killed what they had together. He had loved too much, demanded too much, and he wore it all out.

He thought about alone in Constantinople that time, having quarrelled in Paris before he had gone out. He had whored the whole time and then, when that was over, and he had failed to kill his loneliness, but only made it worse, he had written her, the first one, the one who left him, a letter telling her how he had never been able to kill it ... How when he thought he saw her outside the Regence *one time it made him go all faint and sick inside, and* that he would follow a woman who looked like her in some way, along the Boulevard, afraid to see it was not she, afraid to lose the feeling it gave him. How everyone he had slept with had only made him miss her more. How what she had done could never matter since he knew he could not cure himself of loving her. He wrote this letter at the Club, cold sober, and mailed it to New York asking her to write him at the office in Paris. That seemed safe. And that night missing her so much made him feel hollow sick inside, he wandered up past Taxim's, picked a girl up and took her out to supper. He had gone to a place to dance with her afterward, she danced badly, and left her for a hot Armenian slut, that swung her belly against him so it almost scalded. He took her away from a British gunner subaltern after a row. The gunner asked him outside and they fought in the street on the cobbles in the dark. He'd hit him twice, hard, on the side of the jaw and when he didn't go down he knew he was in for a fight. The gunner hit him in the body, then beside his eye. He swung with his left again and landed and the gunner fell on him and grabbed his coat and tore the sleeve off and he clubbed him twice behind the ear and then smashed him with his right as he pushed him away. When the gunner went down his head hit first and he ran with the girl because they heard the M.P.s coming. They got into a taxi and drove out to Rimmily Hissa along the Bosphorus, and around, and back in the cool night and went to bed and she felt as over-ripe as she looked but smooth, rose-petal, syrupy, smooth-bellied, big-breasted and needed no pillow under her buttocks, and he left her before she was awake and looking blowzy enough in the first daylight and turned up at the Pera Palace with a black eye, carrying his coat because one sleeve was missing.

That same night he left for Anatolia and he remembered, later on that trip, riding all day through fields of poppies that they raised for opium and how strange it made you feel, finally, and all the distances seemed wrong, to where they had made the attack with the newly arrived Constantine officers, that did not know a goddamned thing, and the artillery had fired into the troops and the British observer had cried like a child.

That was the day he'd first seen dead men wearing white ballet skirts and upturned shoes with pompoms on them. The Turks had come steadily and lumpily and he had seen the skirted men *running and the officers shooting into them and running then themselves and he and the British observer had run too until his lungs ached and his mouth was full of the taste of pennies and they stopped behind some rocks and there were the Turks coming as lumpily as ever. Later he had seen the things that he could never think of and later still he had seen much worse. So when he got back to Paris that time he could not talk about it or stand to have it mentioned. And there in the café as he passed was that American poet with a pile of saucers in front of him and a stupid look on his potato face talking about the Dada movement with a Roumanian who said his name was Tristan Tzara, who always wore a monocle and had a headache, and, back at the apartment with his wife that now he loved again, the quarrel all over, the madness all over, glad to be home, the office sent his mail up to the flat. So then the letter in answer to the one he'd written came in on a platter one morning and when he saw the handwriting he went cold all over and tried to slip the letter underneath another. But his wife said, 'Who is that letter from, dear?' and that was the end of the beginning of that.*

He remembered the good times with them all, and the quarrels. They always picked the finest places to have quarrels. And why had they always quarrelled when he was feeling best? He had never written any of that because, at first, he never wanted to hurt anyone and then it seemed as though there was enough to write without it. But he had always thought that he would write it finally. There was so much to write. He had seen the world change; not just the events; although he had seen many of them and had watched the people, but he had seen the subtler change and he could remember how the people were at different times. He had been in it and he had watched it and it was his duty to write of it; but now he never would.

'How do you feel?' she said. She had come out from the tent now after her bath.

'All right.'

'Could you eat now?' He saw Molo behind her with the folding table and the other boy with the dishes.

'I want to write,' he said.

'You ought to take some broth to keep your strength up.'

'I'm going to die tonight,' he said. 'I don't need my strength up.'

'Don't be melodramatic, Harry, please,' she said.

'Why don't you use your nose? I'm rotted half way up my thigh now. What the hell should I fool with broth for? Molo, bring whiskey-soda.'

'Please take the broth,' she said gently.

'All right.'

The broth was too hot. He had to hold it in the cup until it cooled enough to take it and then he just got it down without gagging.

'You're a fine woman,' he said. 'Don't pay any attention to me.'

She looked at him with her well-known, well-loved face from *Spur* and *Town and Country*, only a little the worse for drink, only a little the worse for bed, but *Town and Country* never showed those good breasts and those useful thighs and those lightly small-of-back-caressing hands, and as he looked and saw her well-known pleasant smile, he felt death come again. This time there was no rush. It was a puff, as of a wind that makes a candle flicker and the flame go tall.

'They can bring my net out later and hang it from the tree and build the fire up. I'm not going in the tent tonight. It's not worth moving. It's a clear night. There won't be any rain.'

So this was how you died, in whispers that you did not hear. Well, there would be no more quarrelling. He could promise that. The one experience that he had never had he was not going to spoil now. He probably would. You spoiled everything. But perhaps he wouldn't.

'You can't take dictation, can you?'

'I never learned,' she told him.

'That's all right.'

There wasn't time, of course, although it seemed as though it telescoped so that you might put it all into one paragraph if you could get it right.

There was a log house, chinked white with mortar, on a hill above the lake. There was a bell on a pole by the door to call the people in to meals. Behind the house were fields and behind the fields was the timber. A line of lombardy poplars ran from the house to the dock. Other poplars ran along the point. A road went up to the hills along the edge of the timber and along that road he picked blackberries. Then that log house was burned down and all the guns that had been on deer foot racks above the open fire place were burned and afterward their barrels, with the lead melted in the magazines, and the stocks burned away, lay out on the heap of ashes that were used to make lye for the big iron soap kettles, and you asked Grandfather if you could have them to play with, and he said, no. You see they were his guns and he never bought any others. Nor did he hunt any more. The house was rebuilt in the same place out of lumber now and painted white and from its porch you saw the poplars and the lake beyond; but there were never any more guns. The barrels of the guns that had hung on the deer feet on the wall of the log house lay out there on the heap of ashes and no one ever touched them.

In the Black Forest, after the war, we rented a trout stream and there were two ways to walk it. One was down the valley from Triberg and around the valley road in the shade of the trees that bordered the white road, and then up a side road that went up through the hills, past many small farms, with the big Schwarzwald houses, until that road crossed the stream. That was where our fishing began.

The other way was to climb steeply up to the edge of the woods and then go across the top of the hills through the pine woods, and then out to the edge of a meadow and down across this meadow to the bridge. There were birches along the stream and it was not big, but narrow, clear and fast, with pools where it had cut under the roots of the birches. At the Hotel in Triberg the proprietor had a fine season. It was very pleasant and we were all great friends. The next year came the inflation and the money he had made the year before was not enough to buy supplies to open the hotel and he hanged himself.

You could dictate that, but you could not dictate the Place Contrescarpe where the flower sellers dyed their flowers in the street and the dye ran over the paving where the autobus started and the old men and the women, always drunk on wine and bad marc; and the children with their noses running in the cold; the smell of dirty sweat and poverty and drunkenness at the Café des

Amateurs and the whores at the Bal Musette they lived above. The Concierge who entertained the trooper of the Garde Republicaine in her loge, his horse-hair-plumed helmet on a chair. The locataire across the hall whose husband was a bicycle racer and her joy that morning at the Crémerie when she had opened L'Auto and seen where he placed third in Paris-Tours, his first big race. She had blushed and laughed and then gone upstairs crying with the yellow sporting paper in her hand. The husband of the woman who ran the Bal Musette drove a taxi and when he, Harry, had to take an early plane the husband knocked upon the door to wake him and they each drank a glass of white wine at the zinc of the bar before they started. He knew his neighbors in that quarter then because they all were poor.

Around the Place there were two kinds: the drunkards and the sportifs. The drunkards killed their poverty that way; the sportifs took it out in exercise. They were the descendants of the Communards and it was no struggle for them to know their politics. They knew who had shot their fathers, their relatives, their brothers, and their friends when the Versailles troops came in and took the town after the Commune and executed anyone they could catch with calloused hands, or who wore a cap, or carried any other sign he was a working man. And in that poverty, and in that quarter across the street from a Boucherie Chevaline and a wine co-operative he had written the start of all he was to do. There never was another part of Paris that he loved like that, the sprawling trees, the old white plastered houses painted brown below, the long green of the autobus in that round square, the purple flower dye upon the paving, the sudden drop down the hill of the rue Cardinal Lemoine to the River, and the other way the narrow crowded world of the rue Mouffetard. The street that ran up toward the Pantheon and the other that he always took with the bicycle, the only asphalted street in all that quarter, smooth under the tires, with the high narrow houses and the cheap tall hotel where Paul Verlaine had died. There were only two rooms in the apartments where they lived and he had a room on the top floor of that hotel that cost him sixty francs a month where he did his writing, and from it he could see the roofs and chimney pots and all the hills of Paris.

From the apartment you could only see the wood and coal

man's place. He sold wine, too, bad wine. The golden horse's head
outside the Boucherie Chevaline where the carcasses hung yellow
gold and red in the open window, and the green painted co-
operative where they bought their wine; good wine and cheap. The
rest was plaster walls and the windows of the neighbors. The
neighbors who, at night, when someone lay drunk in the street,
moaning and groaning in typical French ivresse *that you were*
propaganded to believe did not exist, would open their windows
and then the murmur of talk.

'Where is the policeman? When you don't want him the bugger
is always there. He's sleeping with some concierge. Get the Agent.'
Till someone threw a bucket of water from a window and the
moaning stopped. 'What's that? Water. Ah, that's intelligent.'
And the windows shutting. Marie, his femme de ménage,
protesting against the eight-hour day saying, 'If a husband works
until six he only gets a little drunk on the way home and does not
waste too much. If he works only until five he is drunk every night
and one has no money. It is the wife of the working man who
suffers from this shortening of hours.'

'Wouldn't you like some more broth?' the woman asked him
now.

'No, thank you very much. It is awfully good.'

'Cry just a little.'

'I would like a whiskey-soda.'

'It's not good for you.'

'No. It's bad for me. Cole Porter wrote the words and the
music. This knowledge that you're going mad for me.'

'You know I like you to drink.'

'Oh yes. Only it's bad for me.'

When she goes, he thought. I'll have all I want. Not all I
want but all there is. Ayee he was tired. Too tired. He was
going to sleep a little while. He lay still and death was not
there. It must have gone around another street. It went in
pairs, on bicycles, and moved absolutely silently on the
pavements.

No, he had never written about Paris. Not the Paris that he cared
about. But what about the rest that he had never written?

What about the ranch and the silvered gray of the sage brush, the quick, clear water in the irrigation ditches, and the heavy green of the alfalfa. The trail went up into the hills and the cattle in the summer were shy as deer. The bawling and the steady noise and slow moving mass raising dust as you brought them down in the fall. And behind the mountains, the clear sharpness of the peak in the evening light and, riding down along the trail in the moonlight, bright across the valley. Now he remembered coming down through the timber in the dark holding the horse's tail when you could not see and all the stories that he meant to write.

About the half-wit chore boy who was left at the ranch that time and told not to let anyone get any hay, and that old bastard from the Forks who had beaten the boy when he had worked for him stopping to get some feed. The boy refusing and the old man saying he would beat him again. The boy got the rifle from the kitchen and shot him when he tried to come into the barn and when they came back to the ranch he'd been dead a week, frozen in the corral, and the dogs had eaten part of him. But what was left you packed on a sled wrapped in a blanket and roped on and you got the boy to help you haul it, and the two of you took it out over the road on skis, and sixty miles down to town to turn the boy over. He having no idea that he would be arrested. Thinking he had done his duty and that you were his friend and he would be rewarded. He'd helped to haul the old man in so everybody could know how bad the old man had been and how he'd tried to steal some feed that didn't belong to him, and when the sheriff put the handcuffs on the boy he couldn't believe it. Then he started to cry. That was one story he had saved to write. He knew at least twenty good stories from out there and he had never written one. Why?

'You tell them why,' he said.
  'Why what, dear?'
  'Why nothing.'
  She didn't drink so much, now, since she had him. But if he lived he would never write about her, he knew that now. Nor about any of them. The rich were dull and they drank too much, or they played too much backgammon. They were dull and they were repetitious. He remembered poor Julian and his romantic awe of them and how he had started a story once that

65

began, 'The very rich are different from you and me.' And how someone had said to Julian, Yes, they have more money. But that was not humorous to Julian. He thought they were a special glamorous race and when he found they weren't it wrecked him just as much as any other thing that wrecked him.

He had been contemptuous of those who wrecked. You did not have to like it because you understood it. He could beat anything, he thought, because nothing could hurt him if he did not care.

All right. Now he would not care for death. One thing he had always dreaded was the pain. He could stand pain as well as any man, until it went on too long, and wore him out, but here he had something that had hurt frightfully and just when he had felt it breaking him, the pain had stopped.

He remembered long ago when Williamson, the bombing officer, had been hit by a stick bomb someone in a German patrol had thrown as he was coming in through the wire that night and, screaming, had begged everyone to kill him. He was a fat man, very brave, and a good officer, although addicted to fantastic shows. But that night he was caught in the wire, with a flare lighting him up and his bowels spilled out into the wire, so when they brought him in, alive, they had to cut him loose. Shoot me, Harry. For Christ sake shoot me. They had had an argument one time about our Lord never sending you anything you could not bear and someone's theory had been that meant that at a certain time the pain passed you out automatically. But he had always remembered Williamson, that night. Nothing passed out Williamson until he gave him all his morphine tablets that he had always saved to use himself and then they did not work right away.

Still this now, that he had, was very easy; and if it was no worse as it went on there was nothing to worry about. Except that he would rather be in better company.

He thought a little about the company that he would like to have.

No, he thought, when everything you do, you do too long, and do too late, you can't expect to find the people still there.

The people all are gone. The party's over and you are with your hostess now.

I'm getting bored with dying as with everything else, he thought.

'It's a bore,' he said out loud.

'What is, my dear?'

'Anything you do too bloody long.'

He looked at her face between him and the fire. She was leaning back in the chair and the firelight shone on her pleasantly lined face and he could see that she was sleepy. He heard the hyena make a noise just outside the range of the fire.

'I've been writing,' he said. 'But I got tired.'

'Do you think you will be able to sleep?'

'Pretty sure. Why don't you turn in?'

'I like to sit here with you.'

'Do you feel anything strange?' he asked her.

'No. Just a little sleepy.'

'I do,' he said.

He had just felt death come by again.

'You know the only thing I've never lost is curiosity,' he said to her.

'You've never lost anything. You're the most complete man I've ever known.'

'Christ,' he said. 'How little a woman knows. What is that? Your intuition?'

Because, just then, death had come and rested its head on the foot of the cot and he could smell its breath.

'Never believe any of that about a scythe and a skull,' he told her. 'It can be two bicycle policemen as easily, or be a bird. Or it can have a wide snout like a hyena.'

It had moved up on him now, but it had no shape any more. It simply occupied space.

'Tell it to go away.'

It did not go away but moved a little closer.

'You've got a hell of a breath,' he told it. 'You stinking bastard.'

It moved up closer to him still and now he could not speak to it, and when it saw he could not speak it came a little closer, and now he tried to send it away without speaking, but it

67

moved in on him so its weight was all upon his chest, and while it crouched there and he could not move, or speak, he heard the woman say, 'Bwana is asleep now. Take the cot up very gently and carry it into the tent.'

He could not speak to tell her to make it go away and it crouched now, heavier, so he could not breathe. And then, while they lifted the cot, suddenly it was all right and the weight went from his chest.

It was morning and had been morning for some time and he heard the plane. It showed very tiny and then made a wide circle and the boys ran out and lit the fires, using kerosene, and piled on grass so there were two big smudges at each end of the level place and the morning breeze blew them toward the camp and the plane circled twice more, low this time, and then glided down and levelled off and landed smoothly and, coming walking toward him, was old Compton in slacks, a tweed jacket and a brown felt hat.

'What's the matter, old cock?' Compton said.

'Bad leg,' he told him. 'Will you have some breakfast?'

'Thanks. I'll just have some tea. It's the Puss Moth you know. I won't be able to take the Memsahib. There's only room for one. Your lorry is on the way.'

Helen had taken Compton aside and was speaking to him. Compton came back more cheery than ever.

'We'll get you right in,' he said. 'I'll be back for the Mem. Now I'm afraid I'll have to stop at Arusha to refuel. We'd better get going.'

'What about the tea?'

'I don't really care about it you know.'

The boys had picked up the cot and carried it around the green tents and down along the rock and out on to the plain and along past the smudges that were burning brightly now, the grass all consumed, and the wind fanning the fire, to the little plane. It was difficult getting him in, but once he lay back in the leather seat, and the leg was stuck straight out to one side of the seat where Compton sat. Compton started the motor and got in. He waved to Helen and to the boys and, as the clatter moved into the old familiar roar, they swung

68

around with Compie watching for wart-hog holes and roared, bumping, along the stretch between the fires and with the last bump rose and he saw them all standing below, waving, and the camp beside the hill, flattening now, and the plain spreading, clumps of trees, and the bush flattening, while the game trails ran now smoothly to the dry waterholes, and there was a new water that he had never known of. The zebra, small rounded backs now, and the wildebeeste, big-headed dots seeming to climb as they moved in long fingers across the plain, now scattering as the shadow came toward them, they were tiny now, and the movement had no gallop, and the plain as far as you could see, gray-yellow now and ahead old Compie's tweed back and the brown felt hat. Then they were over the first hills and the wildebeeste were trailing up them, and then they were over mountains with sudden depths of green-rising forest and the solid bamboo slopes, and then the heavy forest again, sculptured into peaks and hollows until they crossed, and hills sloped down and then another plain, hot now, and purple brown, bumpy with heat and Compie looking back to see how he was riding. Then there were other mountains dark ahead.

And then instead of going on to Arusha they turned left, he evidently figured that they had the gas, and looking down he saw a pink sifting cloud, moving over the ground, and in the air, like the first snow in a blizzard, that comes from nowhere, and he knew the locusts were coming up from the South. Then they began to climb and they were going to the East it seemed, and then it darkened and they were in a storm, the rain so thick it seemed like flying through a waterfall, and then they were out and Compie turned his head and grinned and pointed and there, ahead, all he could see, as wide as all the world, great, high, and unbelievably white in the sun, was the square top of Kilimanjaro. And then he knew that there was where he was going.

Just then the hyena stopped whimpering in the night and started to make a strange, human, almost crying sound. The woman heard it and stirred uneasily. She did not wake. In her dream she was at the house on Long Island and it was the night before her daughter's début. Somehow her father was there and he had been very rude. Then the noise the hyena made was so loud she woke and for a moment she did not know where she was and she was very afraid. Then she took a flashlight and shone it on the other cot that they had carried in after Harry had gone to sleep. She could see his bulk under the mosquito bar but somehow he had gotten his leg out and it hung down alongside the cot. The dressings had all come down and she could not look at it.

'Molo,' she called, 'Molo! Molo!'

Then she said, 'Harry, Harry!' Then her voice rising, 'Harry! Please, Oh Harry!'

There was no answer and she could not hear him breathing.

Outside the tent the hyena made the same strange noise that had awakened her. But she did not hear him for the beating of her heart.

Old Man at the Bridge

An old man with steel rimmed spectacles and very dusty clothes sat by the side of the road. There was a pontoon bridge across the river and carts, trucks, and men, women and children were crossing it. The mule-drawn carts staggered up the steep bank from the bridge with soldiers helping push against the spokes of the wheels. The trucks ground up and away heading out of it all and the peasants plodded along in the ankle deep dust. But the old man sat there without moving. He was too tired to go any farther.

It was my business to cross the bridge, explore the bridge-head beyond and find out to what point the enemy had advanced. I did this and returned over the bridge. There were not so many carts now and very few people on foot, but the old man was still there.

'Where do you come from?' I asked him.

'From San Carlos,' he said, and smiled.

That was his native town and so it gave him pleasure to mention it and he smiled.

'I was taking care of animals,' he explained.

'Oh,' I said, not quite understanding.

'Yes,' he said, 'I stayed, you see, taking care of animals. I was the last one to leave the town of San Carlos.'

He did not look like a shepherd nor a herdsman and I looked at his black dusty clothes and his gray dusty face and his steel rimmed spectacles and said, 'What animals were they?'

'Various animals,' he said, and shook his head. 'I had to leave them.'

I was watching the bridge and the African looking country of the Ebro Delta and wondering how long now it would be before we would see the enemy, and listening all the while for the first noises that would signal that ever mysterious event called contact, and the old man still sat there.

'What animals were they?' I asked.

'There were three animals altogether,' he explained. 'There were two goats and a cat and then there were four pairs of pigeons.'

'And you had to leave them?' I asked.

'Yes. Because of the artillery. The captain told me to go because of the artillery.'

'And you have no family?' I asked, watching the far end of the bridge where a few last carts were hurrying down the slope of the bank.

'No,' he said, 'only the animals I stated. The cat, of course, will be all right. A cat can look out for itself, but I cannot think what will become of the others.'

'What politics have you?' I asked.

'I am without politics,' he said. 'I am seventy-six years old. I have come twelve kilometers now and I think now I can go no further.'

'This is not a good place to stop,' I said. 'If you can make it, there are trucks up the road where it forks for Tortosa.'

'I will wait a while,' he said, 'and then I will go. Where do the trucks go?'

'Towards Barcelona,' I told him.

'I know no one in that direction,' he said, 'but thank you very much. Thank you again very much.'

He looked at me very blankly and tiredly, then said, having to share his worry with some one, 'The cat will be all right, I am sure. There is no need to be unquiet about the cat. But the others. Now what do you think about the others?'

'Why they'll probably come through all right.'

'You think so?'

'Why not?' I said, watching the far bank where now there were no carts.

'But what will they do under the artillery when I was told to leave because of the artillery?'

72

'Did you leave the dove cage unlocked?' I asked.

'Yes.'

'Then they'll fly.'

'Yes, certainly they'll fly. But the others. It's better not to think about the others,' he said.

'If you are rested I would go,' I urged. 'Get up and try to walk now.'

'Thank you,' he said and got to his feet, swayed from side to side and then sat down backwards in the dust.

'I was taking care of animals,' he said dully, but no longer to me. 'I was only taking care of animals.'

There was nothing to do about him. It was Easter Sunday and the Fascists were advancing toward the Ebro. It was a gray overcast day with a low ceiling so their planes were not up. That and the fact that cats know how to look after themselves was all the good luck that old man would ever have.

Up in Michigan

Jim Gilmore came to Hortons Bay from Canada. He bought the blacksmith shop from old man Horton. Jim was short and dark with big moustaches and big hands. He was a good horseshoer and did not look much like a blacksmith even with his leather apron on. He lived upstairs above the blacksmith shop and took his meals at D. J. Smith's.

Liz Coates worked for Smith's. Mrs Smith, who was a very large clean woman, said Liz Coates was the neatest girl she'd ever seen. Liz had good legs and always wore clean gingham aprons and Jim noticed that her hair was always neat behind. He liked her face because it was so jolly but he never thought about her.

Liz liked Jim very much. She liked it the way he walked over from the shop and often went to the kitchen door to watch for him to start down the road. She liked it about his moustache. She liked it about how white his teeth were when he smiled. She liked it very much that he didn't look like a blacksmith. She liked it how much D. J. Smith and Mrs Smith liked Jim. One day she found that she liked it the way the hair was black on his arms and how white they were above the tanned line when he washed up in the washbasin outside the house. Liking that made her feel funny.

Hortons Bay, the town, was only five houses on the main road between Boyne City and Charlevoix. There was the general store and the post office with a high false front and maybe a wagon hitched out in front, Smith's house, Stroud's house, Dilworth's house, Horton's house and Van Hoosen's

74

house. The houses were in a big grove of elm trees and the road was very sandy. There was farming country and timber each way up the road. Up the road a ways was the Methodist church and down the road the other direction was the township school. The blacksmith shop was painted red and faced the school.

A steep sandy road ran down the hill to the bay through the timber. From Smith's back door you could look out across the woods that ran down to the lake and across the bay. It was very beautiful in the spring and summer, the bay blue and bright and usually whitecaps on the lake out beyond the point from the breeze blowing from Charlevoix and Lake Michigan. From Smith's back door Liz could see ore barges way out in the lake going toward Boyne City. When she looked at them they didn't seem to be moving at all but if she went in and dried some more dishes and then came out again they would be out of sight beyond the point.

All the time now Liz was thinking about Jim Gilmore. He didn't seem to notice her much. He talked about the shop to D. J. Smith and about the Republican Party and James G. Blaine. In the evenings he read *The Toledo Blade* and the Grand Rapids paper by the lamp in the front room or went out spearing fish in the bay with a jacklight from D. J. Smith. In the fall he and Smith and Charley Wyman took a wagon and tent, grub, axes, their rifles and two dogs and went on a trip to the pine plains beyond Vanderbilt deer hunting. Liz and Mrs Smith were cooking for four days for them before they started. Liz wanted to make something special for Jim to take but she didn't finally because she was afraid to ask Mrs Smith for the eggs and flour and afraid if she bought them Mrs Smith would catch her cooking. It would have been all right with Mrs Smith but Liz was afraid.

All the time Jim was gone on the deer-hunting trip Liz thought about him. It was awful while he was gone. She couldn't sleep well from thinking about him but she discovered it was fun to think about him too. If she let herself go it was better. The night before they were due to come back she didn't sleep at all, that is she didn't think she slept because it was all mixed up in a dream about not sleeping and really not sleeping. When she saw the wagon coming down the road she felt weak and sick sort of inside. She couldn't wait till she saw Jim and it seemed as though everything would be all right when he came. The wagon stopped outside under the high elm and Mrs Smith and Liz went out. All the men had beards and there were three deer in the back of the wagon, their thin legs sticking stiff over the edge of the wagon box. Mrs Smith kissed D. J. and he hugged her. Jim said 'Hello, Liz,' and grinned. Liz hadn't known just what would happen when Jim got back but she was sure it would be something. Nothing had happened. The men were just home, that was all. Jim pulled the burlap sacks off the deer and Liz looked at them. One was a big buck. It was stiff and hard to lift out of the wagon.

'Did you shoot it, Jim?' Liz asked.

'Yeah. Ain't it a beauty?' Jim got it on to his back to carry into the smokehouse.

That night Charley Wyman stayed to supper at Smith's. It was too late to get back to Charlevoix. The men washed up and waited in the front room for supper.

'Ain't there something left in that crock, Jimmy?' D. J. Smith asked, and Jim went out to the wagon in the barn and fetched in the jug of whiskey the men had taken hunting with them. It was a four-gallon jug and there was quite a little slopped back and forth in the bottom. Jim took a long pull on his way back to the house. It was hard to lift such a big jug up to drink out of it. Some of the whiskey ran down on his shirt front. The two men smiled when Jim came in with the jug. D. J. Smith sent for glasses and Liz brought them. D. J. poured out three big shots.

'Well, here's looking at you, D. J.,' said Charley Wyman.

'That damn big buck, Jimmy,' said D. J.

'Here's all the ones we missed, D. J.,' said Jim, and downed his liquor.

'Tastes good to a man.'

'Nothing like it at this time of year for what ails you.'

'How about another, boys?'

'Here's how, D. J.'

'Down the creek, boys.'

'Here's to next year.'

Jim began to feel great. He loved the taste and the feel of whiskey. He was glad to be back to a comfortable bed and warm food and the shop. He had another drink. The men came in to supper feeling hilarious but acting very respectable. Liz sat at the table after she put on the food and ate with the family. It was a good dinner. The men ate seriously. After supper they went into the front room again and Liz cleaned off with Mrs Smith. Then Mrs Smith went upstairs and pretty soon Smith came out and went upstairs too. Jim and Charley were still in the front room. Liz was sitting in the kitchen next to the stove pretending to read a book and thinking about Jim. She didn't want to go to bed yet because she knew Jim would be coming out and she wanted to see him as he went out so she could take the way he looked up to bed with her.

She was thinking about him hard and then Jim came out. His eyes were shining and his hair was a little rumpled. Liz looked down at her book. Jim came over back of her chair and stood there and she could feel him breathing and then he put his arms around her. Her breasts felt plump and firm and the nipples were erect under his hands. Liz was terribly frightened, no one had ever touched her, but she thought, 'He's come to me finally. He's really come.'

She held herself stiff because she was so frightened and did not know anything else to do and then Jim held her tight against the chair and kissed her. It was such a sharp, aching, hurting feeling that she thought she couldn't stand it. She felt Jim right through the back of the chair and she couldn't stand it and then something clicked inside of her and the feeling was warmer and softer. Jim held her tight hard against the chair and she wanted it now and Jim whispered, 'Come on for a walk.'

Liz took her coat off the peg on the kitchen wall and they went out the door. Jim had his arm around her and every little way they stopped and pressed against each other and Jim kissed her. There was no moon and they walked ankle-deep in the sandy road through the trees down to the dock and the warehouse on the bay. The water was lapping in the piles and the point was dark across the bay. It was cold but Liz was hot all over from being with Jim. They sat down in the shelter of the warehouse and Jim pulled Liz close to him. She was frightened. One of Jim's hands went inside her dress and stroked over her breast and the other hand was in her lap. She was very frightened and didn't know how he was going to go about things but she snuggled close to him. Then the hand that felt so big in her lap went away and was on her leg and started to move up it.

'Don't, Jim,' Liz said. Jim slid the hand further up.

'You mustn't.' Neither Jim nor Jim's big hand paid any attention to her.

The boards were hard. Jim had her dress up and was trying to do something to her. She was frightened but she wanted it. She had to have it but it frightened her.

'You mustn't do it, Jim. You mustn't.'

'I got to. I'm going to. You know we got to.'

'No, we haven't, Jim. We ain't got to. Oh, it isn't right. Oh, it's so big and it hurts so. You can't. Oh, Jim. Jim. Oh.'

The hemlock planks of the docks were hard and splintery and cold and Jim was heavy on her and he had hurt her. Liz pushed him, she was so uncomfortable and cramped. Jim was asleep. He wouldn't move. She worked out from under him and sat up and straightened her skirt and coat and tried to do something with her hair. Jim was sleeping with his mouth a little open. Liz leaned over and kissed him on the cheek. He was still asleep. She lifted his head a little and shook it. He rolled his head over and swallowed. Liz started to cry. She walked over to the edge of the dock and looked down to the water. There was a mist coming up from the bay. She was cold and miserable and everything felt gone. She walked back to where Jim was lying and shook him once to make sure. She was crying.

'Jim,' she said. 'Jim. Please, Jim.'

Jim stirred and curled a little tighter. Liz took off her coat and leaned over and covered him with it. She tucked it around him neatly and carefully. Then she walked across the dock and up the steep sandy road to go to bed. A cold mist was coming up through the woods from the bay.

On the Quai at Smyrna

The strange thing was, he said, how they screamed every night at midnight. I do not know why they screamed at that time. We were in the harbor and they were all on the pier and at midnight they started screaming. We used to turn the search-light on them to quiet them. That always did the trick. We'd run the searchlight up and down over them two or three times and they stopped it. One time I was senior officer on the pier and a Turkish officer came up to me in a frightful rage because one of our sailors had been most insulting to him. So I told him the fellow would be sent on ship and be most severely punished. I asked him to point him out. So he pointed out a gunner's mate, most inoffensive chap. Said he'd been most frightfully and repeatedly insulting; talking to me through an interpreter. I couldn't imagine how the gunner's mate knew enough Turkish to be insulting. I called him over and said, 'And just in case you should have spoken to any Turkish officers.'

'I haven't spoken to any of them, sir.'

'I'm quite certain of it,' I said, 'but you'd best go on board ship and not come ashore again for the rest of the day.'

Then I told the Turk the man was being sent on board ship and would be most severely dealt with. Oh most rigorously. He felt topping about it. Great friends we were.

The worst, he said, were the women with dead babies. You couldn't get the women to give up their dead babies. They'd have babies dead for six days. Wouldn't give them up. Nothing you could do about it. Had to take them away finally. Then

79

there was an old lady, most extraordinary case. I told it to a doctor and he said I was lying. We were clearing them off the pier, had to clear off the dead ones, and this old woman was lying on a sort of litter. They said, 'Will you have a look at her, sir?' So I had a look at her and just then she died and went absolutely stiff. Her legs drew up and she drew up from the waist and went quite rigid. Exactly as though she had been dead over night. She was quite dead and absolutely rigid. I told a medical chap about it and he told me it was impossible.

They were all out there on the pier and it wasn't at all like an earthquake or that sort of thing because they never knew about the Turk. They never knew what the old Turk would do. You remember when they ordered us not to come in to take off any more? I had the wind up when we came in that morning. He had any amount of batteries and could have blown us clean out of the water. We were going to come in, run close along the pier, let go the front and rear anchors and then shell the Turkish quarter of the town. They would have blown us out of water but we would have blown the town simply to hell. They just fired a few blank charges at us as we came in. Kemal came down and sacked the Turkish commander. For exceeding his authority or some such thing. He got a bit above himself. It would have been the hell of a mess.

You remember the harbor. There were plenty of nice things floating around in it. That was the only time in my life I got so I dreamed about things. You didn't mind the women who were having babies as you did those with the dead ones. They had them all right. Surprising how few of them died. You just covered them over with something and let them go to it. They'd always pick out the darkest places in the hold to have them. None of them minded anything once they got off the pier.

The Greeks were nice chaps too. When they evacuated they had all their baggage animals they couldn't take off with them so they just broke their forelegs and dumped them into the shallow water. All those mules with their forelegs broken pushed over into the shallow water. It was all a pleasant business. My word, yes, a most pleasant business.

Chapter I

Everybody was drunk. The whole battery was drunk going along the road in the dark. We were going to the Champagne. The lieutenant kept riding his horse out into the fields and saying to him, 'I'm drunk, I tell you, mon vieux. Oh, I am so soused.' We went along the road all night in the dark and the adjutant kept riding up alongside my kitchen and saying, 'You must put it out. It is dangerous. It will be observed.' We were fifty kilometers from the front but the adjutant worried about the fire in my kitchen. It was funny going along that road. That was when I was a kitchen corporal.

Indian Camp

At the lake shore there was another rowboat drawn up. The two Indians stood waiting.

Nick and his father got in the stern of the boat and the Indians shoved it off and one of them got in to row. Uncle George sat in the stern of the camp rowboat. The young Indian shoved the camp boat off and got in to row Uncle George.

The two boats started off in the dark. Nick heard the oar locks of the other boat quite a way ahead of them in the mist. The Indians rowed with quick choppy strokes. Nick lay back with his father's arm around him. It was cold on the water. The Indian who was rowing them was working very hard, but the other boat moved further ahead in the mist all the time.

'Where are we going, Dad?' Nick asked.

'Over to the Indian camp. There is an Indian lady very sick.'

'Oh,' said Nick.

Across the bay they found the other boat beached. Uncle George was smoking a cigar in the dark. The young Indian pulled the boat way up the beach. Uncle George gave both the Indians cigars.

They walked up from the beach through a meadow that was soaking wet with dew, following the young Indian who carried a lantern. Then they went into the woods and followed a trail that led to the logging road that ran back into the hills. It was much lighter on the logging road as the timber was cut away on both sides. The young Indian stopped and blew out his lantern and they all walked on along the road.

They came around a bend and a dog came out barking.

Ahead were the lights of the shanties where the Indian bark-peelers lived. More dogs rushed out at them. The two Indians sent them back to the shanties. In the shanty nearest the road there was a light in the window. An old woman stood in the doorway holding a lamp.

Inside on a wooden bunk lay a young Indian woman. She had been trying to have her baby for two days. All the old women in the camp had been helping her. The men had moved off up the road to sit in the dark and smoke out of range of the noise she made. She screamed just as Nick and the two Indians followed his father and Uncle George into the shanty. She lay in the lower bunk, very big under a quilt. Her head was turned to one side. In the upper bunk was her husband. He had cut his foot very badly with an ax three days before. He was smoking a pipe. The room smelled very bad.

Nick's father ordered some water to be put on the stove, and while it was heating he spoke to Nick.

'This lady is going to have a baby, Nick,' he said.

'I know,' said Nick.

'You don't know,' said his father. 'Listen to me. What she is going through is called being in labor. The baby wants to be born and she wants it to be born. All her muscles are trying to get the baby born. That is what is happening when she screams.'

'I see,' Nick said.

Just then the woman cried out.

'Oh, Daddy, can't you give her something to make her stop screaming?' asked Nick.

'No. I haven't any anaesthetic,' his father said. 'But her screams are not important. I don't hear them because they are not important.'

The husband in the upper bunk rolled over against the wall.

The woman in the kitchen motioned to the doctor that the water was hot. Nick's father went into the kitchen and poured about half of the water out of the big kettle into a basin. Into the water left in the kettle he put several things he unwrapped from a handkerchief.

'Those must boil,' he said, and began to scrub his hands in the basin of hot water with a cake of soap he had brought from the camp. Nick watched his father's hands scrubbing each

84

other with the soap. While his father washed his hands very carefully and thoroughly, he talked.

'You see, Nick, babies are supposed to be born head first but sometimes they're not. When they're not they make a lot of trouble for everybody. Maybe I'll have to operate on this lady. We'll know in a little while.'

When he was satisfied with his hands he went in and went to work.

'Pull back that quilt, will you, George?' he said. 'I'd rather not touch it.'

Later when he started to operate Uncle George and three Indian men held the woman still. She bit Uncle George on the arm and Uncle George said, 'Damn squaw bitch!' and the young Indian who had rowed Uncle George over laughed at him. Nick held the basin for his father. It all took a long time.

His father picked the baby up and slapped it to make it breathe and handed it to the old woman.

'See, it's a boy, Nick,' he said. 'How do you like being an interne?'

Nick said, 'All right.' He was looking away so as not to see what his father was doing.

'There. That gets it,' said his father and put something into the basin.

Nick didn't look at it.

'Now,' his father said, 'there's some stitches to put in. You can watch this or not, Nick, just as you like. I'm going to sew up the incision I made.'

Nick did not watch. His curiosity had been gone for a long time.

His father finished and stood up. Uncle George and the three Indian men stood up. Nick put the basin out in the kitchen.

Uncle George looked at his arm. The young Indian smiled reminiscently.

'I'll put some peroxide on that, George,' the doctor said.

He bent over the Indian woman. She was quiet now and her eyes were closed. She looked very pale. She did not know what had become of the baby or anything.

'I'll be back in the morning,' the doctor said, standing up.

85

'The nurse should be here from St Ignace by noon and she'll bring everything we need.'

He was feeling exalted and talkative as football players are in the dressing room after a game.

'That's one for the medical journal, George,' he said. 'Doing a Caesarian with a jack-knife and sewing it up with nine-foot, tapered gut leaders.'

Uncle George was standing against the wall, looking at his arm.

'Oh, you're a great man, all right,' he said.

'Ought to have a look at the proud father. They're usually the worst sufferers in these little affairs,' the doctor said. 'I must say he took it all pretty quietly.'

He pulled back the blanket from the Indian's head. His hand came away wet. He mounted on the edge of the lower bunk with the lamp in one hand and looked in. The Indian lay with his face toward the wall. His throat had been cut from ear to ear. The blood had flowed down into a pool where his body sagged the bunk. His head rested on his left arm. The open razor lay, edge up, in the blankets.

'Take Nick out of the shanty, George,' the doctor said.

There was no need of that. Nick, standing in the door of the kitchen, had a good view of the upper bunk when his father, the lamp in one hand, tipped the Indian's head back.

It was just beginning to be daylight when they walked along the logging road back toward the lake.

'I'm terribly sorry I brought you along, Nickie,' said his father, all his post-operative exhilaration gone. 'It was an awful mess to put you through.'

'Do ladies always have such a hard time having babies?' Nick asked.

'No, that was very, very exceptional.'

'Why did he kill himself, Daddy?'

'I don't know, Nick. He couldn't stand things, I guess.'

'Do many men kill themselves, Daddy?'

'Not very many, Nick.'

'Do many women?'

'Hardly ever.'

'Don't they ever?'

'Oh, yes. They do sometimes.'

'Daddy?'

'Yes.'

'Where did Uncle George go?'

'He'll turn up all right.'

'Is dying hard, Daddy?'

'No, I think it's pretty easy, Nick. It all depends.'

They were seated in the boat, Nick in the stern, his father rowing. The sun was coming up over the hills. A bass jumped, making a circle in the water. Nick trailed his hand in the water. It felt warm in the sharp chill of the morning.

In the early morning on the lake sitting in the stern of the boat with his father rowing, he felt quite sure that he would never die.

Chapter II

Minarets stuck up in the rain out of Adrianople across the mud flats. The carts were jammed for thirty miles along the Karagatch road. Water buffalo and cattle were hauling carts through the mud. There was no end and no beginning. Just carts loaded with everything they owned. The old men and women, soaked through, walked along keeping the cattle moving. The Maritza was running yellow almost up to the bridge. Carts were jammed solid on the bridge with camels bobbing along through them. Greek cavalry herded along the procession. Women and children were in the carts, crouched with mattresses, mirrors, sewing machines, bundles. There was a woman having a baby with a young girl holding a blanket over her and crying. Scared sick looking at it. It rained all through the evacuation.

The Doctor and the Doctor's Wife

Dick Boulton came from the Indian camp to cut up logs for Nick's father. He brought his son Eddy, and another Indian named Billy Tabeshaw with him. They came in through the back gate out of the woods, Eddy carrying the long cross-cut saw. It flopped over his shoulder and made a musical sound as he walked. Billy Tabeshaw carried two big cant-hooks. Dick had three axes under his arm.

He turned and shut the gate. The others went on ahead of him down to the lake shore where the logs were buried in the sand.

The logs had been lost from the big log booms that were towed down the lake to the mill by the steamer *Magic*. They had drifted up on to the beach and if nothing were done about them sooner or later the crew of the *Magic* would come along the shore in a rowboat, spot the logs, drive an iron spike with a ring on it into the end of each one and then tow them out into the lake to make a new boom. But the lumbermen might never come for them because a few logs were not worth the price of a crew to gather them. If no one came for them they would be left to waterlog and rot on the beach.

Nick's father always assumed that this was what would happen, and hired the Indians to come down from the camp and cut the logs up with the cross-cut saw and split them with a wedge to make cord wood and chunks for the open fireplace. Dick Boulton walked around past the cottage down to the lake. There were four big beech logs lying almost buried in the sand. Eddy hung the saw up by one of its handles in the crotch of a tree. Dick put the three axes down on the little dock. Dick was a half-breed and many of the farmers around the lake believed he was really a white man. He was very lazy but a great worker once he was started. He took a plug of tobacco out of his pocket, bit off a chew and spoke in Ojibway to Eddy and Billy Tabeshaw.

They sunk the ends of their cant-hooks into one of the logs and swung against it to loosen it in the sand. They swung their weight against the shafts of the cant-hooks. The log moved in the sand. Dick Boulton turned to Nick's father.

'Well, Doc,' he said, 'that's a nice lot of timber you've stolen.'

'Don't talk that way, Dick,' the doctor said. 'It's drift-wood.'

Eddy and Billy Tabeshaw had rocked the log out of the wet sand and rolled it toward the water.

'Put it right in,' Dick Boulton shouted.

'What are you doing that for?' asked the doctor.

'Wash it off. Clean off the sand on account of the saw. I want to see who it belongs to,' Dick said.

The log was just awash in the lake. Eddy and Billy Tabeshaw leaned on their cant-hooks sweating in the sun. Dick kneeled down in the sand and looked at the mark of the scaler's hammer in the wood at the end of the log.

'It belongs to White and McNally,' he said, standing up and brushing off his trousers knees.

The doctor was very uncomfortable.

'You'd better not saw it up, then, Dick,' he said, shortly.

'Don't get huffy, Doc,' said Dick. 'Don't get huffy. I don't care who you steal from. It's none of my business.'

'If you think the logs are stolen, leave them alone and take your tools back to the camp,' the doctor said. His face was red.

'Don't go off at half cock, Doc,' Dick said. He spat tobacco juice on the log. It slid off, thinning in the water. 'You know they're stolen as well as I do. It don't make any difference to me.'

'All right. If you think the logs are stolen, take your stuff and get out.'

'Now, Doc –'

'Take your stuff and get out.'

'Listen, Doc.'

'If you call me Doc once again, I'll knock your eye teeth down your throat.'

'Oh, no, you won't, Doc.'

Dick Boulton looked at the doctor. Dick was a big man. He knew how big a man he was. He liked to get into fights. He was happy. Eddy and Billy Tabeshaw leaned on their cant-hooks and looked at the doctor. The doctor chewed the beard on his lower lip and looked at Dick Boulton. Then he turned away and walked up the hill to the cottage. They could see from his back how angry he was. They all watched him walk up the hill and go inside the cottage.

Dick said something in Ojibway. Eddy laughed but Billy Tabeshaw looked very serious. He did not understand English but he had sweat all the time the row was going on. He was fat with only a few hairs of moustache like a Chinaman. He picked up the two cant-hooks. Dick picked up the axes and Eddy took the saw down from the tree. They started off and walked up past the cottage and out the back gate into the woods. Dick left the gate open. Billy Tabeshaw went back and fastened it. They were gone through the woods.

In the cottage the doctor, sitting on the bed in his room, saw a pile of medical journals on the floor by the bureau. They were still in their wrappers unopened. It irritated him.

'Aren't you going back to work, dear?' asked the doctor's wife from the room where she was lying with the blinds drawn.

'No!'

'Was anything the matter?'

'I had a row with Dick Boulton.'

'Oh,' said his wife. 'I hope you didn't lose your temper, Henry.'

'No,' said the doctor.

'Remember, that he who ruleth his spirit is greater than he that taketh a city,' said his wife. She was a Christian Scientist. Her Bible, her copy of *Science and Health* and her *Quarterly* were on a table beside her bed in the darkened room.

Her husband did not answer. He was sitting on his bed now, cleaning a shotgun. He pushed the magazine full of the heavy yellow shells and pumped them out again. They were scattered on the bed.

'Henry,' his wife called. Then paused a moment. 'Henry!'

'Yes,' the doctor said.

'You didn't say anything to Boulton to anger him, did you?'

'No,' said the doctor.

'What was the trouble about, dear?'

'Nothing much.'

'Tell me, Henry. Please don't try and keep anything from me. What was the trouble about?'

'Well, Dick owes me a lot of money for pulling his squaw through pneumonia and I guess he wanted a row so he wouldn't have to take it out in work.'

His wife was silent. The doctor wiped his gun carefully with a rag. He pushed the shells back in against the spring of the magazine. He sat with the gun on his knees. He was very fond of it. Then he heard his wife's voice from the darkened room.

'Dear, I don't think, I really don't think that anyone would really do a thing like that.'

'No?' said the doctor.

'No. I can't believe that anyone would do a thing of that sort intentionally.'

The doctor stood up and put the shotgun in the corner behind the dresser.

'Are you going out, dear?' his wife said.

'I think I'll go for a walk,' the doctor said.

'If you see Nick, dear, will you tell him his mother wants to see him?' his wife said.

The doctor went out on the porch. The screen door slammed behind him. He heard his wife catch her breath when the door slammed.

'Sorry,' he said, outside her window with the blinds drawn.

'It's all right, dear,' she said.

He walked in the heat out the gate and along the path into the hemlock woods. It was cool in the woods even on such a hot day. He found Nick sitting with his back against a tree, reading.

'Your mother wants you to come and see her,' the doctor said.

'I want to go with you,' Nick said.

His father looked down at him.

'All right. Come on, then,' his father said. 'Give me the book, I'll put it in my pocket.'

'I know where there's black squirrels, Daddy,' Nick said.

'All right,' said his father. 'Let's go there.'

Chapter III

We were in a garden in Mons. Young Buckley came in with his patrol from across the river. The first German I saw climbed over the garden wall. We waited till he got one leg over and then potted him. He had so much equipment on and looked awfully surprised and fell down into the garden. Then three more came over further down the wall. We shot them. They all came just like that.

The End of Something

In the old days Hortons Bay was a lumbering town. No one who lived in it was out of sound of the big saws in the mill by the lake. Then one year there were no more logs to make lumber. The lumber schooners came into the bay and were loaded with the cut of the mill that stood stacked in the yard. All the piles of lumber were carried away. The big mill building had all its machinery that was removable taken out and hoisted on board one of the schooners by the men who had worked in the mill. The schooner moved out of the bay toward the open lake carrying the two great saws, the travelling carriage that hurled the logs against the revolving, circular saws and all the rollers, wheels, belts and iron piled on a hull-deep load of lumber. Its open hold covered with canvas and lashed tight, the sails of the schooner filled and it moved out into the open lake, carrying with it everything that had made the mill a mill and Hortons Bay a town.

The one-storey bunk houses, the eating-house, the company store, the mill offices, and the big mill itself stood deserted in the acres of sawdust that covered the swampy meadow by the shore of the bay.

Then years later there was nothing of the mill left except the broken white limestone of its foundations showing through the swampy second growth as Nick and Marjorie rowed along the shore. They were trolling along the edge of the channel-bank where the bottom dropped off suddenly from sandy shallows to twelve feet of dark water. They were trolling on their way to the point to set night lines for rainbow trout.

'There's our old ruin, Nick,' Marjorie said.

Nick, rowing, looked at the white stone in the green trees.

'There it is,' he said.

'Can you remember when it was a mill?' Marjorie asked.

'I can just remember,' Nick said.

'It seems more like a castle,' Marjorie said.

Nick said nothing. They rowed on out of sight of the mill, following the shore line. Then Nick cut across the bay.

'They aren't striking,' he said.

'No,' Marjorie said. She was intent on the rod all the time they trolled, even when she talked. She loved to fish. She loved to fish with Nick.

Close beside the boat a big trout broke the surface of the water. Nick pulled hard on one oar so the boat would turn and the bait spinning far behind would pass where the trout was feeding. As the trout's back came up out of the water the minnows jumped wildly. They sprinkled the surface like a handful of shot thrown into the water. Another trout broke water, feeding on the other side of the boat.

'They're feeding,' Marjorie said.

'But they won't strike,' Nick said.

He rowed the boat around to troll past both the feeding fish, then headed it for the point. Marjorie did not reel in until the boat touched the shore.

They pulled the boat up the beach and Nick lifted out a pail of live perch. The perch swam in the water in the pail. Nick caught three of them with his hands and cut their heads off and skinned them while Marjorie chased with her hands in the bucket, finally caught a perch, cut its head off and skinned it. Nick looked at her fish.

'You don't want to take the ventral fin out,' he said. 'It'll be all right for bait but it's better with the ventral fin in.'

He hooked each of the skinned perch through the tail. There were two hooks attached to a leader on each rod. Then Marjorie rowed the boat out over the channel-bank, holding the line in her teeth, and looking toward Nick, who stood on the shore holding the rod and letting the line run out from the reel.

'That's about right,' he called.

100

'Should I let it drop?' Marjorie called back, holding the line in her hand.

'Sure. Let it go.' Marjorie dropped the line overboard and watched the baits go down through the water.

She came in with the boat and ran the second line out the same way. Each time Nick set a heavy slab of driftwood across the butt of the rod to hold it solid and propped it up at an angle with a small slab. He reeled in the slack line so the line ran taut out to where the bait rested on the sandy floor of the channel and set the click on the reel. When a trout, feeding on the bottom, took the bait it would run with it, taking line out of the reel in a rush and making the reel sing with the click on.

Marjorie rowed up the point a little way so she would not disturb the line. She pulled hard on the oars and the boat went way up the beach. Little waves came in with it. Marjorie stepped out of the boat and Nick pulled the boat high up the beach.

'What's the matter, Nick?' Marjorie asked.

'I don't know,' Nick said, getting wood for a fire.

They made a fire with driftwood. Marjorie went to the boat and brought a blanket. The evening breeze blew the smoke toward the point, so Marjorie spread the blanket out between the fire and the lake.

Marjorie sat on the blanket with her back to the fire and waited for Nick. He came over and sat down beside her on the blanket. In back of them was the close second-growth timber of the point and in front was the bay with the mouth of Hortons Creek. It was not quite dark. The fire-light went as far as the water. They could both see the two steel rods at an angle over the dark water. The fire glinted on the reels.

Marjorie unpacked the basket of supper.

'I don't feel like eating,' said Nick.

'Come on and eat, Nick.'

'All right.'

They ate without talking, and watched the two rods and the fire-light in the water.

'There's going to be a moon tonight,' said Nick. He looked across the bay to the hills that were beginning to sharpen

101

against the sky. Beyond the hills he knew the moon was coming up.

'I know it,' Marjorie said happily.

'You know everything,' Nick said.

'Oh, Nick, please cut it out! Please, please don't be that way!'

'I can't help it,' Nick said. 'You do. You know everything. That's the trouble. You know you do.'

Marjorie did not say anything.

'I've taught you everything. You know you do. What don't you know, anyway?'

'Oh, shut up,' Marjorie said. 'There comes the moon.'

They sat on the blanket without touching each other and watched the moon rise.

'You don't have to talk silly,' Marjorie said. 'What's really the matter?'

'I don't know.'

'Of course you know.'

'No I don't.'

'Go on and say it.'

Nick looked on at the moon, coming up over the hills.

'It isn't fun any more.'

He was afraid to look at Marjorie. Then he looked at her. She sat there with her back toward him. He looked at her back. 'It isn't fun any more. Not any of it.'

She didn't say anything. He went on, 'I feel as though everything was gone to hell inside of me. I don't know, Marge. I don't know what to say.'

He looked at her back.

'Isn't love any fun?' Marjorie said.

'No,' Nick said. Marjorie stood up. Nick sat there, his head in his hands.

'I'm going to take the boat,' Marjorie called to him. 'You can walk back around the point.'

'All right,' Nick said. 'I'll push the boat off for you.'

'You don't need to,' she said. She was afloat in the boat on the water with the moonlight on it. Nick went back and lay down with his face in the blanket by the fire. He could hear Marjorie rowing on the water.

102

He lay there for a long time. He lay there while he heard Bill come into the clearing, walking around through the woods. He felt Bill coming up to the fire. Bill didn't touch him, either.

'Did she go all right?' Bill said.

'Oh, yes,' Nick said, lying, his face on the blankets.

'Have a scene?'

'No, there wasn't any scene.'

'How do you feel?'

'Oh, go away, Bill! Go away for a while.'

Bill selected a sandwich from the lunch basket and walked over to have a look at the rods.

Chapter IV

It was a frightfully hot day. We'd jammed an absolutely perfect barricade across the bridge. It was simply priceless. A big old wrought-iron grating from the front of a house. Too heavy to lift and you could shoot through it and they would have to climb over it. It was absolutely topping. They tried to get over it, and we potted them from forty yards. They rushed it, and officers came out alone and worked on it. It was an absolutely perfect obstacle. Their officers were very fine. We were frightfully put out when we heard the flank had gone, and we had to fall back.

The Three-Day Blow

The rain stopped as Nick turned into the road that went up through the orchard. The fruit had been picked and the fall wind blew through the bare trees. Nick stopped and picked up a Wagner apple from beside the road, shiny in the brown grass from the rain. He put the apple in the pocket of his Mackinaw coat.

The road came out of the orchard on to the top of the hill. There was the cottage, the porch bare, smoke coming from the chimney. In back was the garage, the chicken coop and the second-growth timber like a hedge against the woods behind. The big trees swayed far over in the wind as he watched. It was the first of the autumn storms.

As Nick crossed the open field above the orchard the door of the cottage opened and Bill came out. He stood on the porch looking out

'Well, Wemedge,' he said.

'Hey, Bill,' Nick said, coming up the steps.

They stood together looking out across the country, down over the orchard, beyond the road, across the lower fields and the woods of the point to the lake. The wind was blowing straight down the lake. They could see the surf along the Ten Mile point.

'She's blowing,' Nick said.

'She'll blow like that for three days,' Bill said.

'Is your dad in?' Nick said.

'No. He's out with the gun. Come on in.'

Nick went inside the cottage. There was a big fire in the fireplace. The wind made it roar. Bill shut the door.

'Have a drink?' he said.

He went out to the kitchen and came back with two glasses and a pitcher of water. Nick reached the whiskey bottle from the shelf above the fireplace.

'All right?' he said.

'Good,' said Bill.

They sat in front of the fire and drank the Irish whiskey and water.

'It's got a swell, smoky taste,' Nick said, and looked at the fire through the glass.

'That's the peat,' Bill said.

'You can't get peat into liquor,' Nick said.

'That doesn't make any difference,' Bill said.

'You ever seen any peat?' Nick asked.

'No,' said Bill.

'Neither have I,' Nick said.

His shoes, stretched out on the hearth, began to steam in front of the fire.

'Better take your shoes off,' Bill said.

'I haven't got any socks on.'

'Take them off and dry them and I'll get you some,' Bill said. He went upstairs into the loft and Nick heard him walking about overhead. Upstairs was open under the roof and was where Bill and his father and he, Nick, sometimes slept. In back was a dressing room. They moved the cots back out of the rain and covered them with rubber blankets.

Bill came down with a pair of heavy wool socks.

'It's getting too late to go around without socks,' he said.

'I hate to start them again,' Nick said. He pulled the socks on and slumped back in the chair, putting his feet up on the screen in front of the fire.

'You'll dent in the screen,' Bill said. Nick swung his feet over to the side of the fireplace.

'Got anything to read?' he asked.

'Only the paper.'

'What did the Cards do?'

'Dropped a double header to the Giants.'

108

'That ought to cinch it for them.'

'It's a gift,' Bill said. 'As long as McGraw can buy every good player in the league there's nothing to it.'

'He can't buy them all,' Nick said.

'He buys all the ones he wants,' Bill said. 'Or he makes them discontented so they have to trade them to him.'

'Like Heinie Zim,' Nick agreed.

'That bonehead will do him a lot of good.'

Bill stood up.

'He can hit,' Nick offered. The heat from the fire was baking his legs.

'He's a sweet fielder, too,' Bill said. 'But he loses ball games.'

'Maybe that's what McGraw wants him for,' Nick suggested.

'Maybe,' Bill agreed.

'There's always more to it than we know about,' Nick said.

'Of course. But we've got pretty good dope for being so far away.'

'Like how much better you can pick them if you don't see the horses.'

'That's it.'

Bill reached down the whiskey bottle. His big hand went all the way around it. He poured the whiskey into the glass Nick held out.

'How much water?'

'Just the same.'

He sat down on the floor beside Nick's chair.

'It's good when the fall storms come, isn't it?' Nick said.

'It's swell.'

'It's the best time of year,' Nick said.

'Wouldn't it be hell to be in town?' Bill said.

'I'd like to see the World Series,' Nick said.

'Well, they're always in New York or Philadelphia now,' Bill said. 'That doesn't do us any good.'

'I wonder if the Cards will ever win a pennant?'

'Not in our lifetime,' Bill said.

'Gee, they'd go crazy,' Nick said.

'Do you remember when they got going that once before they had the train wreck?'

'Boy!' Nick said, remembering.

Bill reached over to the table under the window for the book that lay there, face down, where he had put it when he went to the door. He held his glass in one hand and the book in the other, leaning back against Nick's chair.

'What are you reading?'

'*Richard Feverel*.'

'I couldn't get into it.'

'It's all right,' Bill said. 'It ain't a bad book, Wemedge.'

'What else have you got I haven't read?' Nick asked.

'Did you read the *Forest Lovers*?'

'Yup. That's the one where they go to bed every night with the naked sword between them.'

'That's a good book, Wemedge.'

'It's a swell book. What I couldn't ever understand was what good the sword would do. It would have to stay edge up all the time because if it went over flat you could roll right over it and it wouldn't make any trouble.'

'It's a symbol,' Bill said.

'Sure,' said Nick, 'but it isn't practical.'

'Did you ever read *Fortitude*?'

'It's fine,' Nick said. 'That's a real book. That's where his old man is after him all the time. Have you got any more by Walpole?'

'*The Dark Forest*,' Bill said. 'It's about Russia.'

'What does he know about Russia?' Nick asked.

'I don't know. You can't ever tell about those guys. Maybe he was there when he was a boy. He's got a lot of dope on it.'

'I'd like to meet him,' Nick said.

'I'd like to meet Chesterton,' Bill said.

'I wish he was here now,' Nick said. 'We'd take him fishing to the 'Voix tomorrow.'

'I wonder if he'd like to go fishing,' Bill said.

'Sure,' said Nick. 'He must be about the best guy there is. Do you remember the *Flying Inn*?'

> ' "If an angel out of heaven
> Gives you something else to drink,
> Thank him for his kind intentions;
> Go and pour them down the sink!" '

'That's right,' said Nick. 'I guess he's a better guy than Walpole.'

'Oh, he's a better guy, all right,' Bill said.

'But Walpole's a better writer.'

'I don't know,' Nick said. 'Chesterton's a classic.'

'Walpole's a classic, too,' Bill insisted.

'I wish we had them both here,' Nick said. 'We'd take them both fishing to the 'Voix tomorrow.'

'Let's get drunk,' Bill said.

'All right,' Nick agreed.

'My old man won't care,' Bill said.

'Are you sure?' said Nick.

'I know it,' Bill said.

'I'm a little drunk now,' Nick said.

'You aren't drunk,' Bill said.

He got up from the floor and reached for the whiskey bottle. Nick held out his glass. His eyes fixed on it while Bill poured.

Bill poured the glass half-full of whiskey.

'Put in your own water,' he said. 'There's just one more shot.'

'Got any more?' Nick asked.

'There's plenty more but dad only likes me to drink what's open.'

'Sure,' said Nick.

'He says opening bottles is what makes drunkards,' Bill explained.

'That's right,' said Nick. He was impressed. He had never thought of that before. He had always thought it was solitary drinking that made drunkards.

'How is your dad?' he asked respectfully.

'He's all right,' Bill said. 'He gets a little wild sometimes.'

'He's a swell guy,' Nick said. He poured water into his glass out of the pitcher. It mixed slowly with the whiskey. There was more whiskey than water.

'You bet your life he is,' Bill said.

'My old man's all right,' Nick said.

'You're damn right he is,' said Bill.

'He claims he's never taken a drink in his life,' Nick said, as though announcing a scientific fact.

'Well, he's a doctor. My old man's a painter. That's different.'

'He's missed a lot,' Nick said sadly.

'You can't tell,' Bill said. 'Everything's got its compensations.'

'He says he's missed a lot himself,' Nick confessed.

'Well, Dad's had a tough time,' Bill said.

'It all evens up,' Nick said.

They sat looking into the fire and thinking of this profound truth.

'I'll get a chunk from the back porch,' Nick said. He had noticed while looking into the fire that the fire was dying down. Also he wished to show he could hold his liquor and be practical. Even if his father had never touched a drop Bill was not going to get him drunk before he himself was drunk.

'Bring one of the big beech chunks,' Bill said. He was also being consciously practical.

Nick came in with the log through the kitchen and in passing knocked a pan off the kitchen table. He laid the log down and picked up the pan. It had contained dried apricots, soaking in water. He carefully picked up all the dried apricots off the floor, some of them had gone under the stove, and put them back in the pan. He dipped some more water on to them from the pail by the table. He felt quite proud of himself. He had been thoroughly practical.

He came in carrying the log and Bill got up from the chair and helped him put it on the fire.

'That's a swell log,' Nick said.

'I'd been saving it for the bad weather,' Bill said. 'A log like that will burn all night.'

'There'll be coals left to start the fire in the morning,' Nick said.

'That's right,' Bill agreed. They were conducting the conversation on a high plane.

'Let's have another drink,' Nick said.

'I think there's another bottle open in the locker,' Bill said.

He kneeled down in the corner in front of the locker and brought out a square-faced bottle.

'It's Scotch,' he said.

'I'll get some more water,' Nick said. He went out into the

kitchen again. He filled the pitcher with the dipper, dipping cold spring water from the pail. On his way back to the living room he passed a mirror in the dining room and looked into it. His face looked strange. He smiled at the face in the mirror and it grinned back at him. He winked at it and went on. It was not his face but it didn't make any difference.

Bill had poured out the drinks.

'That's an awfully big shot,' Nick said.

'Not for us, Wemedge,' Bill said.

'What'll we drink to?' Nick asked, holding up the glass.

'Let's drink to fishing,' Bill said.

'All right,' Nick said. 'Gentlemen, I give you fishing.'

'All fishing,' Bill said. 'Everywhere.'

'Fishing,' Nick said. 'That's what we drink to.'

'It's better than baseball,' Bill said.

'There isn't any comparison,' said Nick. 'How did we ever get talking about baseball?'

'It was a mistake,' Bill said. 'Baseball is a game for louts.'

They drank all that was in their glasses.

'Now let's drink to Chesterton.'

'And Walpole,' Nick interposed.

Nick poured out the liquor. Bill poured in the water. They looked at each other. They felt very fine.

'Gentlemen,' Bill said, 'I give you Chesterton and Walpole.'

'Exactly, gentlemen,' Nick said.

They drank. Bill filled up the glasses. They sat down in the big chairs in front of the fire.

'You were very wise, Wemedge,' Bill said.

'What do you mean?' asked Nick.

'To bust off that Marge business,' Bill said.

'I guess so,' said Nick.

'It was the only thing to do. If you hadn't, by now you'd be back home working trying to get enough money to get married.'

Nick said nothing.

'Once a man's married he's absolutely bitched,' Bill went on. 'He hasn't got anything more. Nothing. Not a damn thing. He's done for. You've seen the guys that get married.'

Nick said nothing.

'You can tell them,' Bill said, 'They get this sort of fat married look. They're done for.'

'Sure,' said Nick.

'It was probably bad busting it off,' Bill said. 'But you always fall for somebody else and then it's all right. Fall for them but don't let them ruin you.'

'Yes,' said Nick.

'If you'd have married her you would have had to marry the whole family. Remember her mother and that guy she married.'

Nick nodded.

'Imagine having them around the house all the time and going to Sunday dinners at their house, and having them over to dinner and telling Marge all the time what to do and how to act.'

Nick sat quiet.

'You came out of it damned well,' Bill said. 'Now she can marry somebody of her own sort and settle down and be happy. You can't mix oil and water and you can't mix that sort of thing any more than if I'd marry Ida that works for Strattons. She'd probably like it, too.'

Nick said nothing. The liquor had all died out of him and left him alone. Bill wasn't there. He wasn't sitting in front of the fire or going fishing tomorrow with Bill and his dad or anything. He wasn't drunk. It was all gone. All he knew was that he had once had Marjorie and that he had lost her. She was gone and he had sent her away. That was all that mattered. He might never see her again. Probably he never would. It was all gone, finished.

'Let's have another drink,' Nick said.

Bill poured it out. Nick splashed in a little water.

'If you'd gone on that way we wouldn't be here now,' Bill said.

That was true. His original plan had been to go down home and get a job. Then he had planned to stay in Charlevoix all winter so he could be near Marge. Now he did not know what he was going to do.

'Probably we wouldn't even be going fishing tomorrow,' Bill said. 'You had the right dope, all right.'

'I couldn't help it,' Nick said.

114

'I know. That's the way it works out,' Bill said.

'All of a sudden everything was over,' Nick said. 'I don't know why it was. I couldn't help it. Just like when the three-day blows come now and rip all the leaves off the trees.'

'Well, it's over. That's the point,' Bill said.

'It was my fault,' Nick said.

'It doesn't make any difference whose fault it was,' Bill said.

'No, I suppose not,' Nick said.

The big thing was that Marjorie was gone and that probably he would never see her again. He had talked to her about how they would go to Italy together and the fun they would have. Places they would be together. It was all gone now.

'So long as it's over that's all that matters,' Bill said. 'I tell you, Wemedge, I was worried while it was going on. You played it right. I understand her mother is sore as hell. She told a lot of people you were engaged.'

'We weren't engaged,' Nick said.

'It was all around that you were.'

'I can't help it,' Nick said. 'We weren't.'

'Weren't you going to get married?' Bill asked.

'Yes. But we weren't engaged,' Nick said.

'What's the difference?' Bill asked judicially.

'I don't know. There's a difference.'

'I don't see it,' said Bill.

'All right,' said Nick. 'Let's get drunk.'

'All right,' Bill said. 'Let's get really drunk.'

'Let's get drunk and then go swimming,' Nick said.

He drank off his glass.

'I'm sorry as hell about her but what could I do?' he said. 'You know what her mother was like!'

'She was terrible,' Bill said.

'All of a sudden it was over,' Nick said. 'I oughtn't to talk about it.'

'You aren't,' Bill said. 'I talked about it and now I'm through. We won't ever speak about it again. You don't want to think about it. You might get back into it again.'

Nick had not thought about that. It had seemed so absolute. That was a thought. That made him feel better.

'Sure,' he said. 'There's always that danger.'

He felt happy now. There was not anything that was irrevocable. He might go into town Saturday night. Today was Thursday.

'There's always a chance,' he said.

'You'll have to watch yourself,' Bill said.

'I'll watch myself,' he said.

He felt happy. Nothing was finished. Nothing was ever lost. He would go into town on Saturday. He felt lighter, as he had felt before Bill started to talk about it. There was always a way out.

'Let's take the guns and go down to the point and look for your dad,' Nick said.

'All right.'

Bill took down the two shotguns from the rack on the wall. He opened a box of shells. Nick put on his Mackinaw coat and his shoes. His shoes were stiff from the drying. He was still quite drunk but his head was clear.

'How do you feel?' Nick asked.

'Swell, I've just got a good edge on.' Bill was buttoning up his sweater.

'There's no use getting drunk.'

'No. We ought to get outdoors.'

They stepped out the door. The wind was blowing a gale.

'The birds will lie right down in the grass with this,' Nick said.

They struck down toward the orchard.

'I saw a woodcock this morning,' Bill said.

'Maybe we'll jump him,' Nick said.

'You can't shoot in this wind,' Bill said.

Outside now the Marge business was no longer so tragic. It was not even very important. The wind blew everything like that away.

'It's coming right off the big lake,' Nick said.

Against the wind they heard the thud of a shotgun.

'That's Dad,' Bill said. 'He's down in the swamp.'

'Let's cut down that way,' Nick said.

'Let's cut across the lower meadow and see if we jump anything,' Bill said.

'All right,' Nick said.

116

None of it was important now. The wind blew it out of his head. Still, he could always go into town Saturday night. It was a good thing to have in reserve.

Chapter V

They shot the six cabinet ministers at half-past six in the morning against the wall of the hospital. There were pools of water in the courtyard. There were wet dead leaves on the paving of the courtyard. It rained hard. All the shutters of the hospital were nailed shut. One of the ministers was sick with typhoid. Two soldiers carried him downstairs and out into the rain. They tried to hold him up against the wall but he sat down in a puddle of water. The other five stood quietly against the wall. Finally the officer told the soldiers it was no good trying to make him stand up. When they fired the first volley he was sitting down in the water with his head on his knees.

The Battler

Nick stood up. He was all right. He looked up the track at the lights of the caboose going out of sight around a curve. There was water on both sides of the track, then tamarack swamp.

He felt his knee. The pants were torn and the skin was barked. His hands were scraped and there were sand and cinders driven up under his nails. He went over to the edge of the track, down the little slope to the water and washed his hands. He washed them carefully in the cold water, getting the dirt out from the nails. He squatted down and bathed his knee.

That lousy crut of a brakeman. He would get him some day. He would know him again. That was a fine way to act.

'Come here, kid,' he said. 'I got something for you.'

He had fallen for it. What a lousy kid thing to have done. They would never suck him in that way again.

'Come here, kid, I got something for you.' Then *wham* and he lit on his hands and knees beside the track.

Nick rubbed his eye. There was a big bump coming up. He would have a black eye, all right. It ached already. That son of a crutting brakeman.

He touched the bump over his eye with his fingers. Oh, well, it was only a black eye. That was all that he had gotten out of it. Cheap at the price. He wished he could see it. Could not see it looking into the water, though. It was dark and he was a long way off from anywhere. He wiped his hands on his trousers and stood up, then climbed the embankment to the rails.

He started up the track. It was well ballasted and made easy walking, sand and gravel packed between the ties, solid

121

walking. The smooth roadbed like a causeway went on ahead through the swamp. Nick walked along. He must get to somewhere.

Nick had swung on to the freight train when it slowed down for the yards outside of Walton Junction. The train, with Nick on it, had passed through Kalkaska as it started to get dark. Now he must be nearly to Mancelona. Three or four miles of swamp. He stepped along the track, walking so he kept on the ballast between the ties, the swamp ghostly in the rising mist. His eye ached and he was hungry. He kept on hiking, putting the miles of track back of him. The swamp was all the same on both sides of the track.

Ahead there was a bridge. Nick crossed it, his boots ringing hollow on the iron. Down below the water showed black between the splits of ties. Nick kicked a loose spike and it dropped into the water. Beyond the bridge were hills. It was high and dark on both sides of the track. Up the track Nick saw a fire.

He came up the track toward the fire carefully. It was off to one side of the track, below the railway embankment. He had only seen the light from it. The track came out through a cut and where the fire was burning the country opened out and fell away into woods. Nick dropped carefully down the embankment and cut into the woods to come up to the fire through the trees. It was a beechwood forest and the fallen beechnut burrs were under his shoes as he walked between the trees. The fire was bright now, just at the edge of the trees. There was a man sitting by it. Nick waited behind the tree and watched. The man looked to be alone. He was sitting there with his head in his hands looking at the fire. Nick stepped out and walked into the firelight.

The man sat there looking into the fire. When Nick stopped quite close to him he did not move.

'Hello!' Nick said.

The man looked up.

'Where did you get the shiner?' he said.

'A brakeman busted me.'

'Off the through freight?'

'Yes.'

'I saw the bastard,' the man said. 'He went through here

122

'bout an hour and a half ago. He was walking the top of the cars slapping his arms and singing.'

'The bastard!'

'It must have made him feel good to bust you,' the man said seriously.

'I'll bust him.'

'Get him with a rock some time when he's going through,' the man advised.

'I'll get him.'

'You're a tough one, aren't you?'

'No,' Nick answered.

'All you kids are tough.'

'You got to be tough,' Nick said.

'That's what I said.'

The man looked at Nick and smiled. In the firelight Nick saw that his face was misshapen. His nose was sunken, his eyes were slits, he had queer-shaped lips. Nick did not perceive all this at once, he only saw the man's face was queerly formed and mutilated. It was like putty in colour. Dead looking in the firelight.

'Don't you like my pan?' the man asked.

Nick was embarrassed.

'Sure,' he said.

'Look here!' the man took off his cap.

He had only one ear. It was thickened and tight against the side of his head. Where the other ear should have been there was a stump.

'Ever see one like that?'

'No,' said Nick. It made him a little sick.

'I could take it,' the man said. 'Don't you think I could take it, kid?'

'You bet!'

'They all bust their hands on me,' the little man said. 'They couldn't hurt me.'

He looked at Nick. 'Sit down,' he said. 'Want to eat?'

'Don't bother,' Nick said. 'I'm going on to the town.'

'Listen!' the man said. 'Call me Ad.'

'Sure!'

'Listen,' the little man said. 'I'm not quite right.'

123

'What's the matter?'

'I'm crazy.'

He put on his cap. Nick felt like laughing.

'You're all right,' he said.

'No, I'm not. I'm crazy. Listen, you ever been crazy?'

'No,' Nick said. 'How does it get you?'

'I don't know,' Ad said. 'When you got it you don't know about it. You know me, don't you?'

'No.'

'I'm Ad Francis.'

'Honest to God?'

'Don't you believe it?'

'Yes.'

Nick knew it must be true.

'You know how I beat them?'

'No.' Nick said.

'My heart's slow. It only beats forty a minute. Feel it.'

Nick hesitated.

'Come on,' the man took hold of his hand. 'Take hold of my wrist. Put your fingers there.'

The little man's wrist was thick and the muscles bulged above the bone. Nick felt the slow pumping under his fingers.

'Got a watch?'

'No.'

'Neither have I,' Ad said. 'It ain't any good if you haven't got a watch.'

Nick dropped his wrist.

'Listen,' Ad Francis said. 'Take ahold again. You count and I'll count up to sixty.'

Feeling the slow hard throb under his fingers Nick started to count. He heard the little man counting slowly, one, two, three, four, five, and on – aloud.

'Sixty,' Ad finished. 'That's a minute. What did you make it?'

'Forty,' Nick said.

'That's right,' Ad said happily. 'She never speeds up.'

A man dropped down the railroad embankment and came across the clearing to the fire.

'Hello, Bugs,' Ad said.

'Hello!' Bugs answered. It was a Negro's voice. Nick knew from the way he walked that he was a Negro. He stood with his back to them bending over the fire. He straightened up.

'This is my pal Bugs,' Ad said. 'He's crazy, too.'

'Glad to meet you,' Bugs said. 'Where you say you're from?'

'Chicago,' Nick said.

'That's a fine town,' the Negro said. 'I didn't catch your name.'

'Adams. Nick Adams.'

'He says he's never been crazy, Bugs,' Ad said.

'He's got a lot coming to him,' the Negro said. He was unwrapping a package by the fire.

'When are we going to eat, Bugs?' the prize-fighter asked.

'Right away.'

'Are you hungry, Nick?'

'Hungry as hell.'

'Hear that, Bugs?'

'I hear most of what goes on.'

'That ain't what I asked you.'

'Yes. I heard what the gentleman said.'

Into a skillet he was laying slices of ham. As the skillet grew hot the grease sputtered and Bugs, crouching on long nigger legs over the fire, turned the ham and broke eggs into the skillet, tipping it from side to side to baste the eggs with the hot fat.

'Will you cut some bread out of that bag, Mister Adams?' Bugs turned from the fire.

'Sure.'

Nick reached in the bag and brought out a loaf of bread. He cut six slices. Ad watched him and leaned forward.

'Let me take your knife, Nick,' he said.

'No, you don't,' the Negro said. 'Hang on to your knife, Mister Adams.'

The prizefighter sat back.

'Will you bring me the bread, Mister Adams?' Bugs asked.

Nick brought it over.

'Do you like to dip your bread in the ham fat?' the Negro asked.

'You bet!'

'Perhaps we'd better wait until later. It's better at the finish of the meal. Here.'

The Negro picked up a slice of ham and laid it on one of the pieces of bread, then slid an egg on top of it.

'Just close that sandwich, will you, please, and give it to Mister Francis.'

Ad took the sandwich and started eating.

'Watch out how that egg runs,' the Negro warned. 'This is for you, Mister Adams. The remainder for myself.'

Nick bit into the sandwich. The Negro was sitting opposite him beside Ad. The hot fried ham and eggs tasted wonderful.

'Mister Adams is right hungry,' the Negro said. The little man whom Nick knew by name as a former champion fighter was silent. He had said nothing since the Negro had spoken about the knife.

'May I offer you a slice of bread dipped right in the hot ham fat?' Bugs said.

'Thanks a lot.'

The little white man looked at Nick.

'Will you have some, Mister Adolph Francis?' Bugs offered from the skillet.

Ad did not answer. He was looking at Nick.

'Mister Francis?' came the nigger's soft voice.

Ad did not answer. He was looking at Nick.

'I spoke to you, Mister Francis,' the nigger said softly.

Ad kept on looking at Nick. He had his cap down over his eyes. Nick felt nervous.

'How the hell do you get that way?' came out from under the cap sharply at Nick.

'Who the hell do you think you are? You're a snotty bastard. You come in here when nobody asks you and eat a man's food and when he asks to borrow a knife you get snotty.'

He glared at Nick, his face was white and his eyes almost out of sight under his cap.

'You're a hot sketch. Who the hell asked you to butt in here?'

'Nobody.'

'You're damn right nobody did. Nobody asked you to stay either. You come in here and act snotty about my face and

126

smoke my cigars and drink my liquor and then talk snotty. Where the hell do you think you get off?'

Nick said nothing. Ad stood up.

'I'll tell you, you yellow-livered Chicago bastard. You're going to get your can knocked off. Do you get that?'

Nick stepped back. The little man came toward him slowly, stepping flat-footed forward, his left foot stepping forward, his right dragging up to it.

'Hit me,' he moved his head. 'Try and hit me.'

'I don't want to hit you.'

'You won't get out of it that way. You're going to take a beating, see? Come on and lead at me.'

'Cut it out,' Nick said.

'All right, then, you bastard.'

The little man looked down at Nick's feet. As he looked down the Negro, who had followed behind him as he moved away from the fire, set himself and tapped him across the base of the skull. He fell forward and Bugs dropped the cloth-wrapped blackjack on the grass. The little man lay there, his face in the grass. The Negro picked him up, his head hanging, and carried him to the fire. His face looked bad, the eyes open. Bugs laid him down gently.

'Will you bring me the water in the bucket, Mister Adams?' he said. 'I'm afraid I hit him just a little hard.'

The Negro splashed water with his hand on the man's face and pulled his ears gently. The eyes closed.

Bugs stood up.

'He's all right,' he said. 'There's nothing to worry about. I'm sorry, Mister Adams.'

'It's all right.' Nick was looking down at the little man. He saw the blackjack on the grass and picked it up. It had a flexible handle and was limber in his hand. It was made of worn black leather with a handkerchief wrapped around the heavy end.

'That's a whalebone handle,' the Negro smiled. 'They don't make them any more. I didn't know how well you could take care of yourself and, anyway, I didn't want you to hurt him or mark him up no more than he is.'

The Negro smiled again.

'You hurt him yourself.'

'I know how to do it. He won't remember nothing of it. I have to do it to change him when he gets that way.'

Nick was still looking down at the little man, lying, his eyes closed in the firelight. Bugs put some wood on the fire.

'Don't worry about him none, Mister Adams. I seen him like this plenty of times before.'

'What made him crazy?' Nick said.

'Oh, a lot of things,' the Negro answered from the fire. 'Would you like a cup of this coffee, Mister Adams?'

He handed Nick the cup and smoothed the coat he had placed under the unconscious man's head.

'He took too many beatings, for one thing,' the Negro sipped the coffee. 'But that just made him sort of simple. Then his sister was his manager and they was always being written up in the papers all about brothers and sisters and how she loved her brother and how he loved his sister, and then they got married in New York and that made a lot of unpleasantness.'

'I remember about it.'

'Sure. Of course they wasn't brother and sister no more than a rabbit, but there was a lot of people didn't like it either way and they commenced to have disagreements, and one day she just went off and never come back.'

He drank the coffee and wiped his lips with the pink palm of his hand.

'He just went crazy. Will you have some more coffee, Mister Adams?'

'Thanks.'

'I seen her a couple of times,' the Negro went on. 'She was an awful good-looking woman. Looked enough like him to be twins. He wouldn't be bad-looking without his face all busted.'

He stopped. The story seemed to be over.

'Where did you meet him?' asked Nick.

'I met him in jail,' the Negro said. 'He was busting people all the time after she went away and they put him in jail. I was in for cuttin' a man.'

He smiled, and went on, soft-voiced:

'Right away I liked him and when I got out I looked him

128

up. He likes to think I'm crazy and I don't mind. I like to be with him and I like seeing the country and I don't have to commit no larceny to do it. I like living like a gentleman.'

'What do you all do?' Nick asked.

'Oh, nothing. Just move around. He's got money.'

'He must have made a lot of money.'

'Sure. He spent all his money, though. Or they took it away from him. She sends him money.'

He poked up the fire.

'She's a mighty fine woman,' he said. 'She looks enough like him to be his own twin.'

The Negro looked over at the little man, lying breathing heavily. His blond hair was down over his forehead. His mutilated face looked childish in repose.

'I can wake him up any time now, Mister Adams. If you don't mind I wish you'd sort of pull out. I don't like to not be hospitable, but it might disturb him back again to see you. I hate to have to thump him and it's the only thing to do when he gets started. I have to sort of keep him away from people. You don't mind, do you Mister Adams? No, don't thank me, Mister Adams. I'd have warned you about him but he seemed to have taken such a liking to you and I thought things were going to be all right. You'll hit a town about two miles up the track. Mancelona they call it. Good-bye. I wish we could ask you to stay the night but it's just out of the question. Would you like to take some of that ham and some bread with you? No? You better take a sandwich,' all this in a low, smooth, polite nigger voice.

'Good. Well, good-bye, Mister Adams. Good-bye and good luck!'

Nick walked away from the fire across the clearing to the railway tracks. Out of the range of the fire he listened. The low soft voice of the Negro was talking. Nick could not hear the words. Then he heard the little man say, 'I got an awful headache, Bugs.'

'You'll feel better, Mister Francis,' the Negro's voice soothed. 'Just you drink a cup of this hot coffee.'

Nick climbed the embankment and started up the track. He found he had a ham sandwich in his hand and put it in his pocket. Looking back from the mounting grade before the track curved into the hills he could see the firelight in the clearing.

Chapter VI

Nick sat against the wall of the church where they had dragged him to be clear of machine-gun fire in the street. Both legs stuck out awkwardly. He had been hit in the spine. His face was sweaty and dirty. The sun shone on his face. The day was very hot. Rinaldi, big backed, his equipment sprawling, lay face downward against the wall. Nick looked straight ahead brilliantly. The pink wall of the house opposite had fallen out from the roof, and an iron bedstead hung twisted toward the street. Two Austrian dead lay in the rubble in the shade of the house. Up the street were other dead. Things were getting forward in the town. It was going well. Stretcher bearers would be along any time now. Nick turned his head and looked down at Rinaldi. 'Senta Rinaldo. Senta. You and me we've made a separate peace.' Rinaldi lay still in the sun, breathing with difficulty. 'We're not patriots.' Nick turned his head away, smiling sweatily. Rinaldi was a disappointing audience.

A Very Short Story

One hot evening in Padua they carried him up on to the roof and he could look out over the top of the town. There were chimney swifts in the sky. After a while it got dark and the searchlights came out. The others went down and took the bottles with them. He and Luz could hear them below on the balcony. Luz sat on the bed. She was cool and fresh in the hot night.

Luz stayed on night duty for three months. They were glad to let her. When they operated on him she prepared him for the operating table; and they had a joke about friend or enema. He went under the anaesthetic holding tight on to himself so he would not blab about anything during the silly, talky time. After he got on crutches he used to take the temperatures so Luz would not have to get up from the bed. There were only a few patients, and they all knew about it. They all liked Luz. As he walked back along the halls he thought of Luz in his bed.

Before he went back to the front they went into the Duomo and prayed. It was dim and quiet, and there were other people praying. They wanted to get married, but there was not enough time for the banns, and neither of them had birth certificates. They felt as though they were married, but they wanted everyone to know about it, and to make it so they could not lose it.

Luz wrote him many letters that he never got until after the armistice. Fifteen came in a bunch to the front and he sorted them by the dates and read them all straight through. They were all about the hospital and how much she loved him and how it was impossible to get along without him and how terrible it was missing him at night.

After the armistice they agreed he should go home to get a job so they might be married. Luz would not come home until he had a good job and could come to New York to meet her. It was understood he would not drink, and he did not want to see his friends or anyone in the States. Only to get a job and be married. On the train from Padua to Milan they quarrelled about her not being willing to come home at once. When they had to say good-bye, in the station at Milan, they kissed good-bye, but were not finished with the quarrel. He felt sick about saying good-bye like that.

He went to America on a boat from Genoa. Luz went back to Pordenone to open a hospital. It was lonely and rainy there, and there was a battalion of arditi quartered in the town. Living in the muddy, rainy town in the winter, the major of the battalion made love to Luz, and she had never known Italians before, and finally wrote to the States that theirs had been only a boy and girl affair. She was sorry, and she knew he would probably not be able to understand, but might some day forgive her, and be grateful to her, and she expected, absolutely unexpectedly, to be married in the spring. She loved him as always, but she realized now it was only a boy and girl love. She hoped he would have a great career, and believed in him absolutely. She knew it was for the best.

The major did not marry her in the spring, or any other time. Luz never got an answer to the letter to Chicago about it. A short time after he contracted gonorrhea from a sales girl in a Loop department store while riding in a taxicab through Lincoln Park.

Chapter VII

While the bombardment was knocking the trench to pieces at Fossalta, he lay very flat and sweated and prayed, 'Oh Jesus Christ, get me out of here. Dear Jesus, please get me out. Christ, please, please, please, Christ. If you'll only keep me from getting killed I'll do anything you say. I believe in you and I'll tell everybody in the world that you are the only thing that matters. Please, please, dear Jesus.' The shelling moved further up the line. We went to work on the trench and in the morning the sun came up and the day was hot and muggy and cheerful and quiet. The next night back at Mestre he did not tell the girl he went upstairs with at the Villa Rossa about Jesus. And he never told anybody.

Soldier's Home

Krebs went to the war from a Methodist college in Kansas. There is a picture which shows him among his fraternity brothers, all of them wearing exactly the same height and style collar. He enlisted in the Marines in 1917 and did not return to the United States until the second division returned from the Rhine in the summer of 1919.

There is a picture which shows him on the Rhine with two German girls and another corporal. Krebs and the corporal look too big for their uniforms. The German girls are not beautiful. The Rhine does not show in the picture.

By the time Krebs returned to his home town in Oklahoma the greeting of heroes was over. He came back much too late. The men from the town who had been drafted had all been welcomed elaborately on their return. There had been a great deal of hysteria. Now the reaction had set in. People seemed to think it was rather ridiculous for Krebs to be getting back so late, years after the war was over.

At first Krebs, who had been at Belleau Wood, Soissons, the Champagne, St Mihiel and in the Argonne did not want to talk about the war at all. Later he felt the need to talk but no one wanted to hear about it. His town had heard too many atrocity stories to be thrilled by actualities. Krebs found that to be listened to at all he had to lie, and after he had done this twice, he, too, had a reaction against the war and against talking about it. A distaste for everything that happened to him in the war set in because of the lies he had told. All of the times that had been able to make him feel cool and clear inside himself

137

when he thought of them; the times so long back when he had done the one thing, the only thing for a man to do, easily and naturally, when he might have done something else, now lost their cool, valuable quality and then were lost themselves.

His lies were quite unimportant lies and consisted in attributing to himself things other men had seen, done or heard of, and stating as facts certain apocryphal incidents familiar to all soldiers. Even his lies were not sensational at the pool room. His acquaintances, who had heard detailed accounts of German women found chained to machine-guns in the Argonne forest and who could not comprehend, or were barred by their patriotism from interest in, any German machine-gunners who were not chained, were not thrilled by his stories.

Krebs acquired the nausea in regard to experience that is the result of untruth or exaggeration, and when he occasionally met another man who had really been a soldier and they talked a few minutes in the dressing room at a dance he fell into the easy pose of the old soldier among other soldiers; that he had been badly, sickeningly frightened all the time. In this way he lost everything.

During this time, it was late summer, he was sleeping late in bed, getting up to walk down town to the library to get a book, eating lunch at home, reading on the front porch until he became bored and then walking down through the town to spend the hottest hours of the day in the cool dark of the pool room. He loved to play pool.

In the evening he practised on his clarinet, strolled down town, read and went to bed. He was still a hero to his two young sisters. His mother would have given him breakfast in bed if he had wanted it. She often came in when he was in bed and asked him to tell her about the war, but her attention always wandered. His father was non-committal.

Before Krebs went away to the war he had never been allowed to drive the family motor car. His father was in the real estate business and always wanted the car to be at his command when he required it to take clients out into the country to show them a piece of farm property. The car always stood outside the First National Bank building where his father had an office on the second floor. Now, after the war, it was still the same car.

Nothing was changed in the town except that the young girls had grown up. But they lived in such a complicated world of already defined alliances and shifting feuds that Krebs did not feel the energy or the courage to break into it. He liked to look at them, though. There were so many good-looking young girls. Most of them had their hair cut short. When he went away only little girls wore their hair like that or girls that were fast. They all wore sweaters and shirt waists with round Dutch collars. It was a pattern. He liked to look at them from the front porch as they walked on the other side of the street. He liked to watch them walking under the shade of the trees. He liked the round Dutch collars above their sweaters. He liked their silk stockings and flat shoes. He liked their bobbed hair and the way they walked.

When he was in town their appeal to him was not very strong. He did not like them when he saw them in the Greek's ice cream parlor. He did not want them themselves really. They were too complicated. There was something else. Vaguely he wanted a girl but he did not want to have to work to get her. He would have liked to have a girl but he did not want to have to spend a long time getting her. He did not want to get into the intrigue and the politics. He did not want to have to do any courting. He did not want to tell any more lies. It wasn't worth it.

He did not want any consequences. He did not want any consequences ever again. He wanted to live along without consequences. Besides he did not really need a girl. The army had taught him that. It was all right to pose as though you had to have a girl. Nearly everybody did that. But it wasn't true. You did not need a girl. That was the funny thing. First a fellow boasted how girls meant nothing to him, that he never thought of them, that they could not touch him. Then a fellow boasted that he could not get along without girls, that he had to have them all the time, that he could not go to sleep without them.

That was all a lie. It was all a lie both ways. You did not need a girl unless you thought about them. He learned that in the army. Then sooner or later you always got one. When you were

139

really ripe for a girl you always got one. You did not have to think about it. Sooner or later it would come. He had learned that in the army.

Now he would have liked a girl if she had come to him and not wanted to talk. But here at home it was all too complicated. He knew he could never go through it all again. It was not worth the trouble. That was the thing about French girls and German girls. There was not all this talking. You couldn't talk much and you did not need to talk. It was simple and you were friends. He thought about France and then he began to think about Germany. On the whole he had liked Germany better. He did not want to leave Germany. He did not want to come home. Still, he had come home. He sat on the front porch.

He liked the girls that were walking along the other side of the street. He liked the look of them much better than the French girls or the German girls. But the world they were in was not the world he was in. He would like to have one of them. But it was not worth it. They were such a nice pattern. He liked the pattern. It was exciting. But he would not go through all the talking. He did not want one badly enough. He liked to look at them all, though. It was not worth it. Not now when things were getting good again.

He sat there on the porch reading a book on the war. It was a history and he was reading about all the engagements he had been in. It was the most interesting reading he had ever done. He wished there were more maps. He looked forward with a good feeling to reading all the really good histories when they would come out with good detail maps. Now he was really learning about the war. He had been a good soldier. That made a difference.

One morning after he had been home about a month his mother came into his bedroom and sat on the bed. She smoothed her apron.

'I had a talk with your father last night, Harold,' she said, 'and he is willing for you to take the car out in the evenings.'

'Yeah?' said Krebs, who was not fully awake. 'Take the car out? Yeah?'

'Yes. Your father has felt for some time that you should be

140

able to take the car out in the evenings whenever you wished but we only talked it over last night.'

'I'll bet you made him,' Krebs said.

'No. It was your father's suggestion that we talk the matter over.'

'Yeah. I'll bet you made him.' Krebs sat up in bed.

'Will you come down to breakfast, Harold?' his mother said.

'As soon as I get my clothes on,' Krebs said.

His mother went out of the room and he could hear her frying something downstairs while he washed, shaved and dressed to go down into the dining-room for breakfast. While he was eating breakfast his sister brought in the mail.

'Well, Hare,' she said. 'You old sleepy-head. What do you ever get up for?'

Krebs looked at her. He liked her. She was his best sister.

'Have you got the paper?' he asked.

She handed him the Kansas City *Star* and he shucked off its brown wrapper and opened it to the sporting page. He folded the *Star* open and propped it against the water pitcher with his cereal dish to steady it, so he could read while he ate.

'Harold,' his mother stood in the kitchen doorway, 'Harold, please don't muss up the paper. Your father can't read his *Star* if it's been mussed.'

'I won't muss it,' Krebs said.

His sister sat down at the table and watched him while he read.

'We're playing indoor over at school this afternoon,' she said. 'I'm going to pitch.'

'Good,' said Krebs. 'How's the old wing?'

'I can pitch better than lots of the boys. I tell them all you taught me. The other girls aren't much good.'

'Yeah?' said Krebs.

'I tell them all you're my beau. Aren't you my beau, Hare?'

'You bet.'

'Couldn't your brother really be your beau just because he's your brother?'

'I don't know.'

'Sure you know. Couldn't you be my beau, Hare, if I was old enough and if you wanted to?'

141

'Sure. You're my girl now.'

'Am I really your girl?'

'Sure.'

'Do you love me?'

'Uh, huh.'

'Will you love me always?'

'Sure.'

'Will you come over and watch me play indoor?'

'Maybe.'

'Aw, Hare, you don't love me. If you loved me, you'd want to come over and watch me play indoor.'

Krebs's mother came into the dining-room from the kitchen. She carried a plate with two fried eggs and some crisp bacon on it and a plate of buckwheat cakes.

'You run along, Helen,' she said. 'I want to talk to Harold.'

She put the eggs and bacon down in front of him and brought in a jug of maple syrup for the buckwheat cakes. Then she sat down across the table from Krebs.

'I wish you'd put down the paper a minute, Harold,' she said.

Krebs took down the paper and folded it.

'Have you decided what you are going to do yet, Harold?' his mother said, taking off her glasses.

'No,' said Krebs.

'Don't you think it's about time?' His mother did not say this in a mean way. She seemed worried.

'I hadn't thought about it,' Krebs said.

'God has some work for everyone to do,' his mother said. 'There can be no idle hands in His Kingdom.'

'I'm not in His Kingdom,' Krebs said.

'We are all of us in His Kingdom.'

Krebs felt embarrassed and resentful as always.

'I've worried about you so much, Harold,' his mother went on. 'I know the temptations you must have been exposed to. I know how weak men are. I know what your own dear grandfather, my own father, told us about the Civil War and I have prayed for you. I pray for you all day long, Harold.'

Krebs looked at the bacon fat hardening on his plate.

'Your father is worried, too,' his mother went on. 'He thinks you have lost your ambition, that you haven't got a definite aim in life. Charley Simmons, who is just your age, has a good job and is going to be married. The boys are all settling down; they're all determined to get somewhere; you can see that boys like Charley Simmons are on their way to being really a credit to the community.'

Krebs said nothing.

'Don't look that way, Harold,' his mother said. 'You know we love you and I want to tell you for your own good how matters stand. Your father does not want to hamper your freedom. He thinks you should be allowed to drive the car. If you want to take some of the nice girls out riding with you, we are only too pleased. We want you to enjoy yourself. But you are going to have to settle down to work, Harold. Your father doesn't care what you start in at. All work is honorable as he says. But you've got to make a start at something. He asked me to speak to you this morning and then you can stop in and see him at his office.'

'Is that all?' Krebs said.

'Yes. Don't you love your mother, dear boy?'

'No,' said Krebs.

His mother looked at him across the table. Her eyes were shiny. She started crying.

'I don't love anybody,' Krebs said.

It wasn't any good. He couldn't tell her, he couldn't make her see it. It was silly to have said it. He had only hurt her. He went over and took hold of her arm. She was crying with her head in her hands.

'I didn't mean it,' he said. 'I was just angry at something. I didn't mean I didn't love you.'

His mother went on crying. Krebs put his arm on her shoulder.

'Can't you believe me, Mother?'

His mother shook her head.

'Please, please, Mother. Please believe me.'

'All right,' his mother said chokily. She looked up at him. 'I believe you, Harold.'

Krebs kissed her hair. She put her face up to him.

'I'm your mother,' she said. 'I held you next to my heart when you were a tiny baby.'

Krebs felt sick and vaguely nauseated.

'I know, Mummy,' he said. 'I'll try and be a good boy for you.'

'Would you kneel and pray with me, Harold?' his mother asked.

They knelt down beside the dining-room table and Krebs's mother prayed.

'Now, you pray, Harold,' she said.

'I can't,' Krebs said.

'Try, Harold.'

'I can't.'

'Do you want me to pray for you?'

'Yes.'

So his mother prayed for him and then they stood up and Krebs kissed his mother and went out of the house. He had tried to keep his life from being complicated. Still, none of it had touched him. He had felt sorry for his mother and she had made him lie. He would go to Kansas City and get a job and she would feel all right about it. There would be one more scene maybe before he got away. He would not go down to his father's office. He would miss that one. He wanted his life to go smoothly. It had just gotten going that way. Well, that was all over now, anyway. He would go over to the schoolyard and watch Helen play indoor baseball.

Chapter VIII

At two o'clock in the morning two Hungarians got into a cigar store at Fifteenth Street and Grand Avenue. Drevitts and Boyle drove up from the Fifteenth Street police station in a Ford. The Hungarians were backing their wagon out of an alley. Boyle shot one off the seat of the wagon and one out of the wagon box. Drevitts got frightened when he found they were both dead. 'Hell, Jimmy,' he said, 'you oughtn't to have done it. There's liable to be a hell of a lot of trouble.'

'They're crooks, ain't they?' said Boyle. 'They're wops, ain't they? Who the hell is going to make any trouble?'

'That's all right maybe this time,' said Drevitts, 'but how did you know they were wops when you bumped them?'

'Wops,' said Boyle, 'I can tell wops a mile off.'

The Revolutionist

In 1919 he was traveling on the railroads in Italy, carrying a square of oilcloth from the headquarters of the party written in indelible pencil and saying here was a comrade who had suffered very much under the Whites in Budapest and requesting comrades to aid him in any way. He used this instead of a ticket. He was very shy and quite young and the train men passed him on from one crew to another. He had no money, and they fed him behind the counter in railway eating houses.

He was delighted with Italy. It was a beautiful country, he said. The people were all kind. He had been in many towns, walked much, and seen many pictures. Giotto, Masaccio, and Piero della Francesca he bought reproductions of and carried them wrapped in a copy of *Avanti*. Mantegna he did not like.

He reported at Bologna, and I took him with me up to the Romagna where it was necessary I go to see a man. We had a good trip together. It was early September and the country was pleasant. He was a Magyar, a very nice boy and very shy. Horthy's men had done some bad things to him. He talked about it a little. In spite of Hungary, he believed altogether in the world revolution.

'But how is the movement going in Italy?' he asked.

'Very badly,' I said.

'But it will go better,' he said. 'You have everything here. It is the one country that everyone is sure of. It will be the starting point of everything.'

I did not say anything.

At Bologna he said good-bye to us to go on the train to Milano and then to Aosta to walk over the pass into Switzerland. I spoke to him about the Mantegnas in Milano. 'No,' he said, very shyly, he did not like Mantegna. I wrote out for him where to eat in Milano and the addresses of comrades. He thanked me very much, but his mind was already looking forward to walking over the pass. He was very eager to walk over the pass while the weather held good. He loved the mountains in the autumn. The last I heard of him the Swiss had him in jail near Sion.

Chapter IX

The first matador got the horn through his sword hand and the crowd hooted him out. The second matador slipped and the bull caught him through the belly and he hung on to the horn with one hand and held the other tight against the place, and the bull rammed him wham against the barrier and the horn came out, and he lay in the sand, and then got up like crazy drunk and tried to slug the men carrying him away and yelled for his sword but he fainted. The kid came out and had to kill five bulls because you can't have more than three matadors, and the last bull he was so tired he could hardly get the sword in. He could hardly lift his arm. He tried five times and the crowd was quiet because it was a good bull and it looked like him or the bull and then he finally made it. He sat down in the sand and puked and they held a cape over him while the crowd hollered and threw things down into the bull ring.

Mr and Mrs Elliot

Mr and Mrs Elliot tried very hard to have a baby. They tried as often as Mrs Elliot could stand it. They tried in Boston after they were married and they tried coming over on the boat. They did not try very often on the boat because Mrs Elliot was quite sick. She was sick and when she was sick she was sick as Southern women are sick. That is women from the Southern part of the United States. Like all Southern women, Mrs Elliot disintegrated very quickly under sea sickness, travelling at night, and getting up too early in the morning. Many of the people on the boat took her for Elliot's mother. Other people who knew they were married believed she was going to have a baby. In reality she was forty years old. Her years had been precipitated suddenly when she started travelling.

She had seemed much younger, in fact she had seemed not to have any age at all, when Elliot had married her after several weeks of making love to her after knowing her for a long time in her tea shop before he had kissed her one evening.

Hubert Elliot was taking postgraduate work in law at Harvard when he was married. He was a poet with an income of nearly ten thousand dollars a year. He wrote very long poems very rapidly. He was twenty-five years old and had never gone to bed with a woman until he married Mrs Elliot. He wanted to keep himself pure so that he could bring to his wife the same purity of mind and body that he expected of her. He called it to himself living straight. He had been in love with various girls before he kissed Mrs Elliot and always told them sooner or later that he had led a clean life. Nearly all the girls

151

lost interest in him. He was shocked and really horrified at the way girls would become engaged to and marry men whom they must know had dragged themselves through the gutter. He once tried to warn a girl he knew against a man of whom he had almost proof that he had been a rotter at college and a very unpleasant incident had resulted.

Mrs Elliot's name was Cornelia. She had taught him to call her Calutina, which was her family nickname in the South. His mother cried when he brought Cornelia home after their marriage but brightened very much when she learned they were going to live abroad.

Cornelia had said, 'You dear sweet boy,' and held him closer than ever when he told her how he had kept himself clean for her. Cornelia was pure too. 'Kiss me again like that,' she said.

Hubert explained to her that he had learned that way of kissing from hearing a fellow tell a story once. He was delighted with his experiment and they developed it as far as possible. Sometimes when they had been kissing together a long time, Cornelia would ask him to tell her again that he had kept himself really straight for her. The declaration always set her off again.

At first Hubert had no idea of marrying Cornelia. He had never thought of her that way. She had been such a good friend of his, and then one day in the little back room of the shop they had been dancing to the gramophone while her girl friend was in the front of the shop and she had looked up into his eyes and he had kissed her. He could never remember just when it was decided that they were to be married. But they were married.

They spent the night of the day they were married in a Boston hotel. They were both disappointed but finally Cornelia went to sleep. Hubert could not sleep and several times went out and walked up and down the corridor of the hotel in his new Jaeger bathrobe that he had bought for his wedding trip. As he walked he saw all the pairs of shoes, small shoes and big shoes, outside the doors of the hotel rooms. This set his heart to pounding and he hurried back to his own room but Cornelia was asleep. He did not like to waken her and soon everything was quite all right and he slept peacefully.

The next day they called on his mother and the next day they sailed for Europe. It was possible to try to have a baby but Cornelia could not attempt it very often although they wanted a baby more than anything else in the world. They landed in Cherbourg and came to Paris. They tried to have a baby in Paris. Then they decided to go to Dijon where there was summer school and where a number of people who crossed on the boat with them had gone. They found there was nothing to do in Dijon. Hubert, however, was writing a great number of poems and Cornelia typed them for him. They were all very long poems. He was very severe about mistakes and would make her re-do an entire page if there was one mistake. She cried a good deal and they tried several times to have a baby before they left Dijon.

They came to Paris and most of their friends from the boat came back too. They were tired of Dijon and anyway would now be able to say that after leaving Harvard or Columbia or Wabash they had studied at the University of Dijon down in the Côte d'Or. Many of them would have preferred to go to Languedoc, Montpellier or Perpignan if there are universities there. But all those places are too far away. Dijon is only four and a half hours from Paris and there is a diner on the train.

So they all sat around the Café du Dôme, avoiding the Rotonde across the street because it is always so full of foreigners, for a few days and then the Elliots rented a château in Touraine through an advertisement in the New York *Herald*. Elliot had a number of friends by now all of whom admired his poetry and Mrs Elliot had prevailed upon him to send over to Boston for her girl friend who had been in the tea shop. Mrs Elliot became much brighter after her girl friend came and they had many good cries together. The girl friend was several years older than Cornelia and called her Honey. She too came from a very old Southern family.

The three of them, with several of Elliot's friends who called him Hubie, went down to the château in Touraine. They found Touraine to be a very flat hot country very much like Kansas. Elliot had nearly enough poems for a book now. He was going to bring it out in Boston and had already sent his check to, and made a contract with, a publisher.

153

In a short time the friends began to drift back to Paris. Touraine had not turned out the way it looked when it started. Soon all the friends had gone off with a rich young and unmarried poet to a seaside resort near Trouville. There they were all very happy.

Elliot kept on at the château in Touraine because he had taken it for all summer. He and Mrs Elliot tried very hard to have a baby in the big hot bedroom on the big, hard bed. Mrs Elliot was learning the touch system on the typewriter, but she found that while it increased the speed it made more mistakes. The girl friend was now typing practically all of the manuscripts. She was very neat and efficient and seemed to enjoy it.

Elliot had taken to drinking white wine and lived apart in his own room. He wrote a good deal of poetry during the night and in the morning looked very exhausted. Mrs Elliot and the girl friend now slept together in the big medieval bed. They had many a good cry together. In the evening they all sat at dinner together in the garden under a plane tree and the hot evening wind blew and Elliot drank white wine and Mrs Elliot and the girl friend made conversation and they were all quite happy.

Chapter X

They whack-whacked the white horse on the legs and he kneed himself up. The picador twisted the stirrups straight and pulled and hauled up into the saddle. The horse's entrails hung down in a blue bunch and swung backward and forward as he began to canter, the monos whacking him on the back of his legs with the rods. He cantered jerkily along the barrera. He stopped stiff and one of the monos held his bridle and walked him forward. The picador kicked in his spurs, leaned forward and shook his lance at the bull. Blood pumped regularly from between the horse's front legs. He was nervously unsteady. The bull could not make up his mind to charge.

Cat in the Rain

There were only two Americans stopping at the hotel. They did not know any of the people they passed on the stairs on their way to and from their room. Their room was on the second floor facing the sea. It also faced the public garden and the war monument. There were big palms and green benches in the public garden. In the good weather there was always an artist with his easel. Artists liked the way the palms grew and the bright colors of the hotels facing the gardens and the sea. Italians came from a long way off to look up at the war monument. It was made of bronze and glistened in the rain. It was raining. The rain dripped from the palm trees. Water stood in pools on the gravel paths. The sea broke in a long line in the rain and slipped back down the beach to come up and break again in a long line in the rain. The motor cars were gone from the square by the war monument. Across the square in the doorway of the café a waiter stood looking out at the empty square.

The American wife stood at the window looking out. Outside right under their window a cat was crouched under one of the dripping green tables. The cat was trying to make herself so compact that she would not be dripped on.

'I'm going down and get that kitty,' the American wife said.

'I'll do it,' her husband offered from the bed.

'No, I'll get it. The poor kitty out trying to keep dry under a table.'

The husband went on reading, lying propped up with the two pillows at the foot of the bed.

'Don't get wet,' he said.

The wife went downstairs and the hotel owner stood up and bowed to her as she passed the office. His desk was at the far end of the office. He was an old man and very tall.

'Il piove,' the wife said. She liked the hotel-keeper.

'Si, si, Signora, brutto tempo. It is very bad weather.'

He stood behind his desk in the far end of the dim room. The wife liked him. She liked the deadly serious way he received any complaints. She liked his dignity. She liked the way he wanted to serve her. She liked the way he felt about being a hotel-keeper. She liked his old, heavy face and big hands.

Liking him she opened the door and looked out. It was raining harder. A man in a rubber cape was crossing the empty square to the café. The cat would be around to the right. Perhaps she could go along under the eaves. As she stood in the doorway an umbrella opened behind her. It was the maid who looked after their room.

'You must not get wet,' she smiled, speaking Italian. Of course, the hotel-keeper had sent her.

With the maid holding the umbrella over her, she walked along the gravel path until she was under their window. The table was there, washed bright green in the rain, but the cat was gone. She was suddenly disappointed. The maid looked up at her.

'Ha perduto qualque cosa, Signora?'

'There was a cat,' said the American girl.

'A cat?'

'Si, il gatto.'

'A cat?' the maid laughed. 'A cat in the rain?'

'Yes,' she said, 'under the table.' Then, 'Oh, I wanted it so much, I wanted a kitty.'

When she talked English the maid's face tightened.

'Come, Signora,' she said. 'We must get back inside. You will be wet.'

'I suppose so,' said the American girl.

They went back along the gravel path and passed in the door. The maid stayed outside to close the umbrella. As the American girl passed the office, the padrone bowed from his desk. Something felt very small and tight inside the girl. The padrone made her feel very small and at the same time really important. She had a momentary feeling of being of supreme importance. She went on up the stairs. She opened the door of the room. George was on the bed, reading.

'Did you get the cat?' he asked, putting the book down.

'It was gone.'

'Wonder where it went to?' he said, resting his eyes from reading.

She sat down on the bed.

'I wanted it so much,' she said. 'I don't know why I wanted it so much. I wanted that poor kitty. It isn't any fun to be a poor kitty out in the rain.'

George was reading again.

She went over and sat in front of the mirror of the dressing table looking at herself with the hand glass. She studied her profile, first one side and then the other. Then she studied the back of her head and her neck.

'Don't you think it would be a good idea if I let my hair grow out?' she asked, looking at her profile again.

George looked up and saw the back of her neck, clipped close like a boy's.

'I like it the way it is.'

'I get so tired of it,' she said. 'I get so tired of looking like a boy.'

George shifted his position in the bed. He hadn't looked away from her since she started to speak.

'You look pretty darn nice,' he said.

She laid the mirror down on the dresser and went over to the window and looked out. It was getting dark.

'I want to pull my hair back tight and smooth and make a big knot at the back that I can feel,' she said. 'I want to have a kitty to sit on my lap and purr when I stroke her.'

'Yeah?' George said from the bed.

'And I want to eat at a table with my own silver and I want candles. And I want it to be spring and I want to brush my hair out in front of a mirror and I want a kitty and I want some new clothes.'

'Oh, shut up and get something to read,' George said. He was reading again.

159

His wife was looking out of the window. It was quite dark now and still raining in the palm trees.

'Anyway, I want a cat,' she said, 'I want a cat. I want a cat now. If I can't have long hair or any fun, I can have a cat.'

George was not listening. He was reading his book. His wife looked out of the window where the light had come on in the square.

Someone knocked at the door.

'Avanti,' George said. He looked up from his book.

In the doorway stood the maid. She held a big tortoiseshell cat pressed tight against her and swung down against her body.

'Excuse me,' she said, 'the padrone asked me to bring this for the Signora.'

Chapter XI

The crowd shouted all the time, and threw pieces of bread down into the bull ring, then cushions and leather wine bottles, keeping up whistling and yelling. Finally the bull was too tired from so much sticking and folded his knees and lay down and one of the cuadrilla *leaned out over his neck and killed him with the* puntillo. *The crowd came over the barrera and around the torero and two men grabbed him and held him and someone cut off his pigtail and was waving it and a kid grabbed it and ran away with it. Afterwards I saw him at the café. He was very short with a brown face and quite drunk and he said: After all, it has happened before like that. I am not really a good bull fighter.*

Out of Season

On the four lire Peduzzi had earned by spading the hotel garden he got quite drunk. He saw the young gentleman coming down the path and spoke to him mysteriously. The young gentleman said he had not eaten but would be ready to go as soon as lunch was finished. Forty minutes or an hour.

At the cantina near the bridge they trusted him for three more grappas because he was so confident and mysterious about his job for the afternoon. It was a windy day with the sun coming out from behind clouds and then going under in sprinkles of rain. A wonderful day for trout fishing.

The young gentleman came out of the hotel and asked him about the rods. Should his wife come behind with the rods? 'Yes,' said Peduzzi, 'let her follow us.' The young gentleman went back into the hotel and spoke to his wife. He and Peduzzi started down the road. The young gentleman had a musette over his shoulder. Peduzzi saw the wife, who looked as young as the young gentleman, and was wearing mountain boots and a blue beret, start out to follow them down the road, carrying the fishing rods, unjointed, one in each hand. Peduzzi didn't like her to be way back there. 'Signorina,' he called, winking at the young gentleman, 'come up here and walk with us. Signora, come up here. Let us all walk together.' Peduzzi wanted them all three to walk down the street of Cortina together.

The wife stayed behind, following rather sullenly. 'Signorina,' Peduzzi called tenderly, 'come up here with us.' The young gentleman looked back and shouted something. The wife stopped lagging behind and walked up.

163

Everyone they met walking through the main street of the town Peduzzi greeted elaborately. Buon' di, Arturo! Tipping his hat. The bank clerk stared at him from the door of the Fascist café. Groups of three and four people standing in front of the shops stared at the three. The workmen in their stone-powdered jackets working on the foundations of the new hotel looked up as they passed. Nobody spoke or gave any sign to them except the town beggar, lean and old, with a spittle thickened beard, who lifted his hat as they passed.

Peduzzi stopped in front of a store with the window full of bottles and brought his empty grappa bottle from an inside pocket of his old military coat. 'A little to drink, some marsala for the Signora, something, something to drink.' He gestured with the bottle. It was a wonderful day. 'Marsala, you like marsala, Signorina? A little marsala?'

The wife stood sullenly. 'You'll have to play up to this,' she said. 'I can't understand a word he says. He's drunk, isn't he?'

The young gentleman appeared not to hear Peduzzi. He was thinking, what in hell makes him say marsala? That's what Max Beerbohm drinks.

'Geld,' Peduzzi said finally, taking hold of the young gentleman's sleeve. 'Lire.' He smiled, reluctant to press the subject but needing to bring the young gentleman into action.

The young gentleman took out his pocketbook and gave him a ten-lira note. Peduzzi went up the steps to the door of the Speciality of Domestic and Foreign Wines shop. It was locked.

'It is closed until two,' someone passing in the street said scornfully. Peduzzi came down the steps. He felt hurt. Never mind, he said, we can get it at the Concordia.

They walked down the road to the Concordia three abreast. On the porch of the Concordia, where the rusty bobsleds were stacked, the young gentleman said, 'Was wollen sie?' Peduzzi handed him the ten-lira note folded over and over. 'Nothing,' he said, 'anything.' He was embarrassed. 'Marsala, maybe. I don't know. Marsala?'

The door of the Concordia shut on the young gentleman and the wife. 'Three marsalas,' said the young gentleman to the girl behind the pastry counter. 'Two, you mean?' she asked. 'No,' he said, 'one for a vecchio.' 'Oh,' she said, 'a vecchio,' and laughed, getting down the bottle. She poured out the three muddy-looking drinks into three glasses. The wife was sitting at a table under the line of newspapers on sticks. The young gentleman put one of the marsalas in front of her. 'You might as well drink it,' he said, 'maybe it'll make you feel better.' She sat and looked at the glass. The young gentleman went outside the door with a glass for Peduzzi but could not see him.

'I don't know where he is,' he said, coming back into the pastry room carrying the glass.

'He wanted a quart of it,' said the wife.

'How much is a quarter litre?' the young gentleman asked the girl.

'Of the bianco? One lira.'

'No, of the marsala. Put these two in, too,' he said, giving her his own glass and the one poured for Peduzzi. She filled the quarter litre wine measure with a funnel. 'A bottle to carry it,' said the young gentleman.

She went to hunt for a bottle. It all amused her.

'I'm sorry you feel so rotten, Tiny,' he said. 'I'm sorry I talked the way I did at lunch. We were both getting at the same thing from different angles.'

'It doesn't make any difference,' she said. 'None of it makes any difference.'

'Are you too cold?' he asked. 'I wish you'd worn another sweater.'

'I've got on three sweaters.'

The girl came in with a very slim brown bottle and poured the marsala into it. The young gentleman paid five lire more. They went out the door. The girl was amused. Peduzzi was walking up and down at the other end out of the wind and holding the rods.

'Come on,' he said, 'I will carry the rods. What difference does it make if anybody sees them? No one will trouble us. No one will make any trouble for me in Cortina. I know them at the municipio. I have been a soldier. Everybody in this town likes me. I sell frogs. What if it is forbidden to fish? Not a thing. Nothing. No trouble. Big trout, I tell you. Lots of them.'

165

They were walking down the hill towards the river. The town was in back of them. The sun had gone under and it was sprinkling rain. 'There,' said Peduzzi, pointing to a girl in the doorway of a house they passed. 'My daughter.'

'His doctor,' the wife said, 'has he got to show us his doctor?'

'He said his daughter,' said the young gentleman.

The girl went into the house as Peduzzi pointed.

They walked down the hill across the fields and then turned to follow the river bank. Peduzzi talked rapidly with much winking and knowingness. As they walked three abreast the wife caught his breath across the wind. Once he nudged her in the ribs. Part of the time he talked in d'Ampezzo dialect and sometimes in Tyroler German dialect. He could not make out which the young gentleman and his wife understood the best so he was being bilingual. But as the young gentleman said, Ja, Ja, Peduzzi decided to talk altogether in Tyroler. The young gentleman and the wife understood nothing.

'Everybody in the town saw us going through with these rods. We're probably being followed by the game police now. I wish we weren't in on this damn thing. This damned old fool is so drunk, too.'

'Of course you haven't got the guts to just go back,' said the wife. 'Of course you have to go on.'

'Why don't you go back? Go on back, Tiny.'

'I'm going to stay with you. If you go to jail we might as well both go.'

They turned sharp down the bank and Peduzzi stood, his coat blowing in the wind, gesturing at the river. It was brown and muddy. Off on the right there was a dump heap.

'Say it to me in Italian,' said the young gentleman.

'Un' mezz' ora. Pù d' un' mezz' ora.'

'He says it's at least a half hour more. Go on back, Tiny. You're cold in this wind anyway. It's a rotten day and we aren't going to have any fun, anyway.'

'All right,' she said, and climbed up the grassy bank.

Peduzzi was down at the river and did not notice her till she was almost out of sight over the crest. 'Frau!' he shouted. 'Frau! Fraülein! You're not going.'

She went on over the crest of the hill.

'She's gone!' said Peduzzi. It shocked him.

He took off the rubber bands that held the rod segments together and commenced to joint up one of the rods.

'But you said it was half an hour further.'

'Oh yes. It is good half an hour down. It is good here, too.'

'Really?'

'Of course. It is good here and good there, too.'

The young gentleman sat down on the bank and jointed up a rod, put on the reel and threaded the line through the guides. He felt uncomfortable and afraid that any minute a gamekeeper or a posse of citizens would come over the bank from the town. He could see the houses of the town and the campanile over the edge of the hill. He opened his leader box. Peduzzi leaned over and dug his flat, hard thumb and forefinger in and tangled the moistened leaders.

'Have you some lead?'

'No.'

'You must have some lead.' Peduzzi was excited. 'You must have piombo. Piombo. A little piombo. Just here. Just above the hook or your bait will float on the water. You must have it. Just a little piombo.'

'Have you got some?'

'No.' He looked through his pockets desperately. Sifting through the cloth dirt in the linings of his inside military pockets. 'I haven't any. We must have piombo.'

'We can't fish then,' said the young gentleman, and unjointed the rod, reeling the line back through the guides. 'We'll get some piombo and fish tomorrow.'

'But listen, caro, you must have piombo. The line will lie flat on the water.' Peduzzi's day was going to pieces before his eyes. 'You must have piombo. A little is enough. Your stuff is all clean and new but you have no lead. I would have brought some. You said you had everything.'

The young gentleman looked at the stream discolored by the melting snow. 'I know,' he said, 'we'll get some piombo and fish tomorrow.'

'At what hour in the morning? Tell me that.'

'At seven.'

The sun came out. It was warm and pleasant. The young gentleman felt revived. He was no longer breaking the law. Sitting on the bank he took the bottle of marsala out of his pocket and passed it to Peduzzi. Peduzzi passed it back. The young gentleman took a drink of it and passed it to Peduzzi again. Peduzzi passed it back again. 'Drink,' he said, 'drink. It's your marsala.' After another short drink the young gentleman handed the bottle over. Peduzzi had been watching it closely. He took the bottle very hurriedly and tipped it up. The gray hairs in the folds of his neck oscillated as he drank, his eyes fixed on the end of the narrow brown bottle. He drank it all. The sun shone while he drank. It was wonderful. This was a great day, after all. A wonderful day.

'Senta, caro! In the morning at seven.' He had called the young gentleman caro several times and nothing had happened. It was good marsala. His eyes glistened. Days like this stretched out ahead. It would begin at seven in the morning.

They started to walk up the hill toward the town. The young gentleman went on ahead. He was quite a way up the hill. Peduzzi called to him.

'Listen, caro, can you let me take five lire for a favor?'

'For today?' asked the young gentleman frowning.

'No, not today. Give it to me today for tomorrow. I will provide everything for tomorrow. Pane, salami, formaggio, good stuff for all of us. You and I and the Signora. Bait for fishing, minnows, not worms only. Perhaps I can get some marsala. All for five lire. Five lire for a favor.'

The young gentleman looked through his pocketbook and took out a two-lira note and two ones.

'Thank you, caro. Thank you,' said Peduzzi, in the tone of one member of the Carleton Club accepting the *Morning Post* from another. This was living. He was through with the hotel garden, breaking up frozen manure with a dung fork. Life was opening out.

'Until seven o'clock then, caro,' he said, slapping the young gentleman on the back. 'Promptly at seven.'

'I may not be going,' said the young gentleman, putting his purse back in his pocket.

'What,' said Peduzzi, 'I will have minnows, Signor. Salami, everything. You and I and the Signora. The three of us.'

'I may not be going,' said the young gentleman, 'very probably not. I will leave word with the padrone at the hotel office.'

Chapter XII

If it happened right down close in front of you, you could see Villalta snarl at the bull and curse him, and when the bull charged he swung back firmly like an oak when the wind hits it, his legs tight together, the muleta trailing and the sword following the curve behind. Then he cursed the bull, flopped the muleta at him, and swung back from the charge, his feet firm, the muleta curving and at each swing the crowd roaring.

When he started to kill it was all in the same rush. The bull looking at him straight in front, hating. He drew out the sword from the folds of the muleta and sighted with the same movement and called to the bull, 'Toro! Toro!' and the bull charged and Villalta charged and just for a moment they became one. Villalta became one with the bull and then it was over. Villalta standing straight and the red hilt of the sword sticking out dully between the bull's shoulders. Villalta, his hand up at the crowd and the bull roaring blood, looking straight at Villalta and his legs caving.

Cross-Country Snow

The funicular car bucked once more and then stopped. It could not go farther, the snow drifted solidly across the track. The gale scouring the exposed surface of the mountain had swept the snow surface into a wind-board crust. Nick, waxing his skis in the baggage car, pushed his boots into the toe irons and shut the clamp tight. He jumped from the car sideways on to the hard wind-board, made a jump turn and crouching and trailing his sticks slipped in a rush down the slope.

On the white below George dipped and rose and dipped out of sight. The rush and the sudden swoop as he dropped down a steep undulation in the mountain side plucked Nick's mind out and left him only the wonderful flying, dropping sensation in his body. He rose to a slight up-run and then the snow seemed to drop out from under him as he went down, down, faster and faster in a rush down the last, long, steep slope. Crouching so he was almost sitting back on his skis, trying to keep the center of gravity low, the snow driving like a sand-storm, he knew the pace was too much. But he held it. He would not let go and spill. Then a patch of soft snow, left in a hollow by the wind, spilled him and he went over and over in a clashing of skis, feeling like a shot rabbit, then stuck, his legs crossed, his skis sticking straight up and his nose and ears jammed full of snow.

George stood a little farther down the slope, knocking the snow from his wind jacket with big slaps.

'You took a beauty, Mike,' he called to Nick. 'That's lousy soft snow. It bagged me the same way.'

'What's it like over the khud?' Nick kicked his skis around as he lay on his back and stood up.

'You've got to keep to your left. It's a good fast drop with a Christy at the bottom on account of a fence.'

'Wait a sec and we'll take it together.'

'No, you come on and go first. I like to see you take the khuds.'

Nick Adams came up past George, big back and blond head still faintly snowy, then his skis started slipping at the edge and he swooped down, hissing in the crystalline powder snow and seeming to float up and drop down as he went up and down the billowing khuds. He held to his left and at the end, as he rushed toward the fence, keeping his knees locked tight together and turning his body like tightening a screw brought his skis sharply around to the right in a smother of snow and slowed into a loss of speed parallel to the hillside and the wire fence.

He looked up the hill. George was coming down in telemark position, kneeling; one leg forward and bent, the other trailing; his sticks hanging like some insect's thin legs, kicking up puffs of snow as they touched the surface and finally the whole kneeling, trailing figure coming around in a beautiful right curve, crouching, the legs forward and back, the body leaning out against the swing, the sticks accenting the curve like points of light, all in a wild cloud of snow.

'I was afraid to Christy,' George said, 'the snow was too deep. You made a beauty.'

'I can't telemark with my leg,' Nick said.

Nick held down the top strand of the wire fence with his ski and George slid over. Nick followed him down to the road. They thrust bent-kneed along the road into a pine forest. The road became polished ice, stained orange and a tobacco yellow from the teams hauling logs. The skiers kept to the stretch of snow along the side. The road dipped sharply to a stream and then ran straight up-hill. Through the woods they could see a long, low-eaved, weather-beaten building. Through the trees it was a faded yellow. Closer the window frames were painted green. The paint was peeling. Nick knocked his clamps loose with one of his ski sticks and kicked off the skis.

'We might as well carry them up here,' he said.

174

He climbed the steep road with the skis on his shoulder, kicking his heel nails into the icy footing. He heard George breathing and kicking in his heels just behind him. They stacked the skis against the side of the inn and slapped the snow off each other's trousers, stamped their boots clean, and went in.

Inside it was quite dark. A big porcelain stove shone in the corner of the room. There was a low ceiling. Smooth benches back of dark, wine-stained tables were along each side of the room. Two Swiss sat over their pipes and two decies of cloudy new wine next to the stove. The boys took off their jackets and sat against the wall on the other side of the stove. A voice in the next room stopped singing and a girl in a blue apron came in through the door to see what they wanted to drink.

'A bottle of Sion,' Nick said. 'Is that all right, Gidge?'

'Sure,' said George. 'You know more about wine than I do. I like any of it.'

The girl went out.

'There's nothing really can touch ski-ing, is there?' Nick said. 'The way it feels when you first drop off on a long run.'

'Huh,' said George. 'It's too swell to talk about.'

The girl brought the wine in and they had trouble with the cork. Nick finally opened it. The girl went out and they heard her singing in German in the next room.

'Those specks of cork in it don't matter,' said Nick.

'I wonder if she's got any cake.'

'Let's find out.'

The girl came in and Nick noticed that her apron covered swellingly her pregnancy. I wonder why I didn't see that when she first came in, he thought.

'What were you singing?' he asked her.

'Opera, German opera.' She did not care to discuss the subject. 'We have some apple strudel if you want it.'

'She isn't so cordial, is she?' said George.

'Oh, well. She doesn't know us and she thought we were going to kid her about her singing, maybe. She's from up where they speak German probably and she's touchy about being here and then she's got that baby coming without being married and she's touchy.'

'How do you know she isn't married?'

'No ring. Hell, no girls get married around here till they're knocked up.'

The door came open and a gang of woodcutters from up the road came in, stamping their boots and steaming in the room. The waitress brought in three litres of new wine for the gang and they sat at the two tables, smoking and quiet, with their hats off, leaning back against the wall or forward on the table. Outside the horses on the wood sledges made an occasional sharp jangle of bells as they tossed their heads.

George and Nick were happy. They were fond of each other. They knew they had the run back home ahead of them.

'When have you got to go back to school?' Nick asked.

'Tonight,' George answered. 'I've got to get the ten-forty from Montreux.'

'I wish you could stick over and we could do the Dent du Lys tomorrow.'

'I got to get educated,' George said. 'Gee, Nick, don't you wish we could just bum together? Take our skis and go on the train to where there was good running and then go on and put up at pubs and go right across the Oberland and up the Valais and all through the Engadine and just take repair kit and extra sweaters and pyjamas in our rucksacks and not give a damn about school or anything.'

'Yes, and go through the Schwartzwald that way. Gee, the swell places.'

'That's where you went fishing last summer isn't it?'

'Yes.'

They ate the strudel and drank the rest of the wine.

George leaned back against the wall and shut his eyes.

'Wine always makes me feel this way,' he said.

'Feel bad?' Nick asked.

'No. I feel good, but funny.'

'I know,' Nick said.

'Sure,' said George.

'Should we have another bottle?' Nick asked.

'Not for me,' George said.

They sat there, Nick leaning his elbows on the table, George slumped back against the wall.

'Is Helen going to have a baby?' George said, coming down to the table from the wall.

'Yes.'

'When?'

'Late next summer.'

'Are you glad?'

'Yes. Now.'

'Will you go back to the States?'

'I guess so.'

'Do you want to?'

'No.'

'Does Helen?'

'No.'

George sat silent. He looked at the empty bottle and the empty glasses.

'It's hell, isn't it?' he said.

'No. Not exactly,' Nick said.

'Why not?'

'I don't know,' Nick said.

'Will you ever go skiing together in the States?' George said.

'I don't know,' said Nick.

'The mountains aren't much,' George said.

'No,' said Nick. 'They're too rocky. There's too much timber and they're too far away.'

'Yes,' said George, 'that's the way it is in California.'

'Yes,' Nick said, 'that's the way it is everywhere I've ever been.'

'Yes,' said George, 'that's the way it is.'

The Swiss got up and paid and went out.

'I wish we were Swiss,' George said.

'They've all got goiter,' said Nick.

'I don't believe it,' George said.

'Neither do I,' said Nick.

They laughed.

'Maybe we'll never go skiing again, Nick,' George said.

'We've got to,' said Nick. 'It isn't worth while if you can't.'

'We'll go, all right,' George said.

'We've got to,' Nick agreed.

'I wish we could make a promise about it,' George said.

Nick stood up. He buckled his wind jacket tight. He leaned over George and picked up the two ski poles from against the wall. He stuck one of the ski poles into the floor.

'There isn't any good in promising,' he said.

They opened the door and went out. It was very cold. The snow had crusted hard. The road ran up the hill into the pine trees.

They took down their skis from where they leaned against the wall in the inn. Nick put on his gloves. George was already started up the road, his skis on his shoulder. Now they would have the run home together.

Chapter XIII

I heard the drums coming down the street and then the fifes and pipes and then they came around the corner, all dancing. The street full of them. Maera saw him and then I saw him. When they stopped the music for the crouch he haunched down in the street with them all and when they started it again he jumped up and went dancing down the street with them. He was drunk all right.

'You go down after him,' said Maera, 'he hates me.'

So I went down and caught up with them and grabbed him while he was crouched down waiting for the music to break loose and said, 'Come on, Luis. For Christ sake, you've got bulls this afternoon.' He didn't listen to me, he was listening so hard for the music to start.

I said, 'Don't be a damn fool, Luis. Come on back to the hotel.'

Then the music started up again and he jumped up and twisted away from me and started dancing. I grabbed his arm and he pulled loose and said, 'Oh, leave me alone. You're not my father.'

I went back to the hotel and Maera was on the balcony looking out to see if I'd be bringing him back. He went inside when he saw me and came downstairs disgusted.

'Well, after all,' I said, 'he's just an ignorant Mexican savage.'

'Yes,' Maera said, 'and who will kill his bulls after he gets cogida?'

'We, I suppose,' I said.

'Yes, we,' said Maera. 'We kill the savages' bulls, and the drunkards' bulls, and the riau-riau dancers' bulls. Yes. We kill them. We kill them all right. Yes. Yes. Yes.'

My Old Man

I guess looking at it, now, my old man was cut out for a fat guy, one of those regular little roly fat guys you see around, but he sure never got that way, except a little towards the last, and then it wasn't his fault, he was riding over the jumps only and he could afford to carry plenty of weight then. I remember the way he'd pull on a rubber shirt over a couple of jerseys and a big sweat shirt over that, and get me to run with him in the forenoon in the hot sun. He'd have, maybe, taken a trial trip with one of Razzo's skins early in the morning after just getting in from Torino at four o'clock in the morning and beating it out to the stables in a cab and then with the dew all over everything and the sun just starting to get going, I'd help him pull off his boots and he'd get into a pair of sneakers and all these sweaters and we'd start out.

'Come on, kid,' he'd say, stepping up and down on his toes in front of the jock's dressing-room, 'let's get moving.'

Then we'd start off jogging around the infield once, maybe, with him ahead, running nice, and then turn out the gate and along one of those roads with all the trees along both sides of them that run out from San Siro. I'd go ahead of him when we hit the road and I could run pretty stout and I'd look around and he'd be jogging easy just behind me and after a while I'd look around again and he'd begun to sweat. Sweating heavy and he'd just be dogging it along with his eyes on my back, but when he'd catch me looking at him he'd grin and say, 'Sweating plenty?' When my old man grinned, nobody could help but grin too. We'd keep right on running out towards the

181

mountains and then my old man would yell, 'Hey, Joe!' and I'd look back and he'd be sitting under a tree with a towel he'd had around his waist wrapped around his neck.

I'd come back and sit down beside him and he'd pull a rope out of his pocket and start skipping rope out in the sun with the sweat pouring off his face and him skipping rope out in the white dust with the rope going cloppetty, cloppetty, clop, clop, clop, and the sun hotter, and him working harder up and down a patch of road. Say, it was a treat to see my old man skip rope, too. He could whirr it fast or lop it slow and fancy. Say, you ought to have seen wops look at us sometimes, when they'd come by, going into town walking along with big white steers hauling the cart. They sure looked as though they thought the old man was nuts. He'd start the rope whirring till they'd stop dead still and watch him, then give the steers a cluck and a poke with the goad and get going again.

When I'd sit watching him working out in the hot sun I sure felt fond of him. He sure was fun and he done his work so hard and he'd finish up with a regular whirring that'd drive the sweat out on his face like water and then sling the rope at the tree and come over and sit down with me and lean back against the tree with the towel and a sweater wrapped around his neck.

'Sure is hell keeping it down, Joe,' he'd say and lean back and shut his eyes and breathe long and deep, 'it ain't like when you're a kid.' Then he'd get up and before he started to cool we'd jog along back to the stables. That's the way it was keeping down to weight. He was worried all the time. Most jocks can just about ride off all they want to. A jock loses about a kilo every time he rides, but my old man was sort of dried out and he couldn't keep down his kilos without all that running.

I remember once at San Siro, Regoli, a little wop, that was riding for Buzoni, came out across the paddock going to the bar for something cool; and flicking his boots with his whip, after he'd just weighed in and my old man had just weighed in too, and came out with the saddle under his arm looking red-faced and tired and too big for his silks and he stood there looking at young Regoli standing up to the outdoors bar, cool and kid-looking, and I said, 'What's the matter, Dad?' 'cause I

182

thought maybe Regoli had bumped him or something and he just looked at Regoli and said, 'Oh, to hell with it,' and went on to the dressing room.

Well, it would have been all right, maybe, if we'd stayed in Milan and ridden at Milan and Torino, 'cause if there ever were any easy courses, it's those two. 'Pianola, Joe,' my old man said when he dismounted in the winning stall after what the wops thought was a hell of a steeplechase. I asked him once. 'This course rides itself. It's the pace you're going at, that makes riding the jumps dangerous, Joe. We ain't going any pace here, and they ain't any really bad jumps either. But it's the pace always – not the jumps – that makes the trouble.'

San Siro was the swellest course I'd ever seen but the old man said it was a dog's life. Going back and forth between Mirafiore and San Siro and riding just about every day in the week with a train ride every other night.

I was nuts about the horses, too. There's something about it, when they come out and go up the track to the post. Sort of dancy and tight looking with the jock keeping a tight hold on them and maybe easing off a little and letting them run a little going up. Then once they were at the barrier it got me worse than anything. Especially at San Siro with that big green infield and the mountains way off and the fat wop starter with his big whip and the jocks fiddling them around and then the barrier snapping up and that bell going off and them all getting off in a bunch and then commencing to string out. You know the way a bunch of skins gets off. If you're up in the stand with a pair of glasses all you see is them plunging off and then that bell goes off and it seems like it rings for a thousand years and then they come sweeping round the turn. There wasn't ever anything like it for me.

But my old man said one day, in the dressing-room, when he was getting into his street clothes, 'None of these things are horses, Joe. They'd kill that bunch of skates for their hides and hoofs up at Paris.' That was the day he'd won the Premio Commercio with Lantorna shooting her out of the field the last hundred meters like pulling a cork out of a bottle.

It was right after the Premio Commercio that we pulled out and left Italy. My old man and Holbrook and a fat wop in a straw hat that kept wiping his face with a handkerchief were having an argument at a table in the Galleria. They were all talking French and the two of them were after my old man about something. Finally he didn't say anything any more but just sat there and looked at Holbrook, and the two of them kept after him, first one talking and then the other, and the fat wop always butting in on Holbrook.

'You go out and buy me a *Sportsman,* will you, Joe?' my old man said, and handed me a couple of soldi without looking away from Holbrook.

So I went out of the Galleria and walked over to in front of the Scala and bought a paper, and came back and stood a little way away because I didn't want to butt in and my old man was sitting back in his chair looking down at his coffee and fooling with a spoon and Holbrook and the big wop were standing and the big wop was wiping his face and shaking his head. And I came up and my old man acted just as though the two of them weren't standing there and said, 'Want an ice, Joe?' Holbrook looked down at my old man and said slow and careful, 'You son of a bitch', and he and the fat wop went out through the tables.

My old man sat there and sort of smiled at me, but his face was white and he looked sick as hell and I was scared and felt sick inside because I knew something had happened and I didn't see how anybody could call my old man a son of a bitch, and get away with it. My old man opened up the *Sportsman* and studied the handicaps for a while and then he said, 'You got to take a lot of things in this world, Joe.' And three days later we left Milan for good on the Turin train for Paris, after an auction sale out in front of Turner's stables of everything we couldn't get into a trunk and a suit case.

We got into Paris early in the morning in a long, dirty station the old man told me was the Gare de Lyon. Paris was an awful big town after Milan. Seems like in Milan everybody is going somewhere and all the trams run somewhere and there ain't any sort of mix-up, but Paris is all balled up and they never do straighten it out. I got to like it, though, part of it, anyway, and say, it's got the best racecourses in the world. Seems as though that were the thing that keeps it all going and about the only thing you can figure on is that every day the buses will be going out to whatever track they're running at, going right out through everything to the track. I never really got to know Paris well, because I just came in about once or twice a week with the old man from Maisons and he always sat at the Café de la Paix on the Opéra side with the rest of the gang from Maisons and I guess that's one of the busiest parts of the town. But, say, it is funny that a big town like Paris wouldn't have a Galleria, isn't it?

Well, we went out to live at Maisons-Lafitte, where just about everybody lives except the gang at Chantilly, with a Mrs Meyers that runs a boarding house. Maisons is about the swellest place to live I've ever seen in all my life. The town ain't so much, but there's a lake and a swell forest that we used to go off bumming in all day, a couple of us kids, and my old man made me a sling shot and we got a lot of things with it but the best one was a magpie. Young Dick Atkinson shot a rabbit with it one day and we put it under a tree and were all sitting around and Dick had some cigarettes and all of a sudden the rabbit jumped up and beat it into the brush and we chased it but we couldn't find it. Gee, we had fun at Maisons. Mrs Meyers used to give me lunch in the morning and I'd be gone all day. I learned to talk French quick. It's an easy language.

As soon as we got to Maisons, my old man wrote to Milan for his license and was pretty worried till it came. He used to sit around the Café de Paris in Maisons with the gang, there were lots of guys he'd known when he rode up at Paris, before the war, lived at Maisons, and there's a lot of time to sit around because the work around a racing stable, for the jocks, that is, is all cleaned up by nine o'clock in the morning. They take the first batch of skins out to gallop them at 5.30 in the morning and they work the second lot at 8 o'clock. That means getting up early all right and going to bed early, too. If a jock's riding for somebody too, he can't go boozing around because the trainer always has an eye on him if he's a kid and if he ain't a kid he's always got an eye on himself. So mostly if a jock ain't working he sits around the Café de Paris with the gang and they can all sit around about two or three hours in front of some drink like a vermouth and seltz and they talk and tell stories and shoot pool and it's sort of like a club or the Galleria in Milan. Only it ain't really like the Galleria because there everybody is going by all the time and there's everybody around at the tables.

Well, my old man got his license all right. They sent it through to him without a word and he rode a couple of times. Amiens, up country and that sort of thing, but he didn't seem to get any engagement. Everybody liked him and whenever I'd come in to the Café in the forenoon I'd find somebody drinking with him because my old man wasn't tight like most of these jockeys that have got the first dollar they made riding at the World's Fair in St Louis in nineteen ought four. That's what my old man would say when he'd kid George Burns. But it seemed like everybody steered clear of giving my old man any mounts.

We went out to wherever they were running every day with the car from Maisons and that was the most fun of all. I was glad when the horses came back from Deauville and the summer. Even though it meant no more bumming in the woods, 'cause then we'd ride to Enghien or Tremblay or St Cloud and watch them from the trainers' and jockeys' stand. I sure learned about racing from going out with that gang and the fun of it was going every day.

I remember once out at St Cloud. It was a big two hundred thousand franc race with seven entries and War Cloud a big favorite. I went around to the paddock to see the horses with my old man and you never saw such horses. This War Cloud is a great big yellow horse that looks like just nothing but run. I never saw such a horse. He was being led around the paddocks with his head down and when he went by me I felt all hollow inside he was so beautiful. There never was such a wonderful, lean, running built horse. And he went around the paddock putting his feet just so and quiet and careful and moving easy like he knew just what he had to do and not jerking and standing up on his legs and getting wild eyed like you see these selling platers with a shot of dope in them. The crowd was so thick I couldn't see him again except just his legs going by and some yellow and my old man started out through the crowd and I followed him over to the jocks' dressing-room back in

186

the trees and there was a big crowd around there, too, but the man at the door in a derby nodded to my old man and we got in and everybody was sitting around and getting dressed and pulling shirts over their heads and pulling boots on and it all smelled hot and sweaty and linimenty and outside was the crowd looking in.

The old man went over and sat down beside George Gardner that was getting into his pants and said, 'What's the dope, George?' just in an ordinary tone of voice 'cause there ain't any use him feeling around because George either can tell him or he can't tell him.

'He won't win,' George says very low, leaning over and buttoning the bottoms of his pants.

'Who will?' my old man says, leaning over close so nobody can hear.

'Foxless,' George says, 'and if he does, save me a couple of tickets.'

My old man says something in a regular voice to George and George says, 'Don't ever bet on anything I tell you,' kidding like, and we beat it out and through all the crowd that was looking in, over to the 100 franc mutuel machine. But I knew something big was up because George is War Cloud's jockey. On the way he gets one of the yellow odds-sheets with the starting prices on and War Cloud is only paying 5 for 10, Cefisidote is next at 3 to 1 and fifth down the list this Foxless at 8 to 1. My old man bets five thousand on Foxless to win and puts on a thousand to place and we went around back of the grandstand to go up the stairs and get a place to watch the race.

We were jammed in tight and first a man in a long coat with a gray tall hat and a whip folded up in his hand came out and then one after another the horses, with the jocks up and a stable boy holding the bridle on each side and walking along, followed the old guy. That big yellow horse War Cloud came first. He didn't look so big when you first looked at him until you saw the length of his legs and the whole way he's built and the way he moves. Gosh, I never saw such a horse. George Gardner was riding him and they moved along slow, back of the old guy in the gray tall hat that walked along like he was the ring master in a circus. Back of War Cloud, moving along smooth and yellow in the sun, was a good looking black with a nice head with Tommy Archibald riding him; and after the black was a string of five more horses all moving along slow in a procession past the grandstand and the pesage. My old man said the black was Foxless and I took a good look at him and he was a nice-looking horse, all right, but nothing like War Cloud.

Everybody cheered War Cloud when he went by and he sure was one swell-looking horse. The procession of them went around on the other side past the pelouse and then back up to the near end of the course and the circus master had the stable boys turn them loose one after another so they could gallop by the stands on their way up to the post and let everybody have a good look at them. They weren't at the post hardly any time at all when the gong started and you could see them way off across the infield all in a bunch starting on the first swing like a lot of little toy horses. I was watching them through the glasses and War Cloud was running well back, with one of the bays making the pace. They swept down and around and came pounding past and War Cloud was way back when they passed us and this Foxless horse in front and going smooth. Gee, it's awful when they go by you and then you have to watch them go farther away and get smaller and smaller and then all bunched up on the turns and then coming around towards into the stretch and you feel like swearing and goddamming worse and worse. Finally they made the last turn and came into the straight away with this Foxless horse way out in front. Everybody was looking funny and saying 'War Cloud' in sort of a sick way and them pounding nearer down the stretch and then something came out of the pack right into my glasses like a horse-headed yellow streak and everybody began to yell 'War Cloud' as though they were crazy. War Cloud came on faster than I'd ever seen anything in my life and pulled up on Foxless that was going fast as any black horse could go with the jock flogging hell out of him with the gad and they were right dead neck and neck for a second but War Cloud seemed going about twice as fast with those great jumps and that head out – but it was while they were neck and neck that they passed the winning post and when the numbers went up in the slots the first one was 2 and that meant Foxless had won.

I felt all trembly and funny inside, and then we were all jammed in with the people going downstairs to stand in front of the board where they'd post what Foxless paid. Honest, watching the race I'd forgot how much my old man had bet on Foxless. I'd wanted War Cloud to win so damned bad. But now it was all over it was swell to know we had the winner.

'Wasn't it a swell race, Dad?' I said to him.

He looked at me sort of funny with his derby on the back of his head. 'George Gardner's a swell jockey, all right,' he said. 'It sure took a great jock to keep that War Cloud from winning.'

Of course I knew it was funny all the time. But my old man saying that right out like that sure took the kick all out of it for me and I didn't get the real kick back again ever, even when they posted the numbers upon the board and the bell rang to pay off and we saw that Foxless paid 67.50 for 10. All round people were saying, 'Poor War Cloud! Poor War Cloud!' And I thought, I wish I were a jockey and could have rode him instead of that son of a bitch. And that was funny, thinking of George Gardner as a son of a bitch because I'd always liked him and besides he'd given us the winner, but I guess that's what he is, all right.

My old man had a big lot of money after that race and he took to coming into Paris oftener. If they raced at Tremblay he'd have them drop him in town on their way back to Maisons, and he and I'd sit out in front of the Café de la Paix and watch the people go by. It's funny sitting there. There's streams of people going by and all sorts of guys come up and want to sell you things, and I loved to sit there with my old man. That was when we'd have the most fun. Guys would come by selling funny rabbits that jumped if you squeezed a bulb and they'd come up to us and my old man would kid with them. He could talk French just like English and all those kind of guys knew him 'cause you can always tell a jockey – and then we always sat at the same table and they got used to seeing us there. There were guys selling matrimonial papers and girls selling rubber eggs that when you squeezed them a rooster came out of them and one old wormy-looking guy that went by with post-cards of Paris, showing them to everybody, and, of course, nobody ever bought any, and then he would come back and show the under side of the pack and they would all be smutty post-cards and lots of people would dig down and buy them.

Gee, I remember the funny people that used to go by. Girls around supper time looking for somebody to take them out to eat and they'd speak to my old man and he'd make some joke at them in French and they'd pat me on the head and go on. Once there was an American woman sitting with her kid daughter at the next table to us and they were both eating ices and I kept looking at the girl and she was awfully good looking and I smiled at her and she smiled at me but that was all that ever came of it because I looked for her mother and her every day and I made up ways that I was going to speak to her and I wondered if I got to know her if her mother would let me take her out to Auteuil or Tremblay but I never saw either of them again. Anyway, I guess it wouldn't have been any good, anyway, because looking back on it I remember the way I thought out would be best to speak to her was to say, 'Pardon me, but perhaps I can give you a winner at Enghien today?' and, after all, maybe she would have thought I was a tout instead of really trying to give her a winner.

We'd sit at the Café de la Paix, my old man and me, and we had a big drag with the waiter because my old man drank whiskey and it cost five francs, and that meant a good tip when the saucers were counted up. My old man was drinking more than I'd ever seen him, but he wasn't riding at all now and besides he said that whiskey kept his weight down. But I noticed he was putting it on, all right, just the same. He'd busted away from his old gang out at Maisons and seemed to like just sitting around on the boulevard with me. But he was dropping money every day at the track. He'd feel sort of doleful after the last race, if he'd lost on the day, until we'd get to our table and he'd have his first whiskey and then he'd be fine.

He'd be reading the *Paris-Sport* and he'd look over at me and say, 'Where's your girl, Joe?' to kid me on account I had told him about the girl that day at the next table. And I'd get red, but I liked being kidded about her. It gave me a good feeling. 'Keep your eye peeled for her, Joe,' he'd say, 'she'll be back.'

He'd ask me questions about things and some of the things I'd say he'd laugh. And then he'd get started talking about things. About riding down in Egypt, or at St Moritz on the ice before my mother died, and about during the war when they had regular races down in the south of France without any purses, or betting or crowd or anything just to keep the breed up. Regular races with the jocks riding hell out of the horses. Gee, I could listen to my old man talk by the hour, especially when he'd had a couple or so of drinks. He'd tell me about when he was a boy in Kentucky and going coon hunting, and the old days in the States before everything went on the bum there. And he'd say, 'Joe, when we've got a decent stake, you're going back to the States and go to school.'

'What've I got to go back there to go to school for when everything's on the bum there?' I'd ask him.

'That's different,' he'd say and get the waiter over and pay the pile of saucers and we'd get a taxi to the Gare St Lazare and get on the train out to Maisons.

One day at Auteuil, after a selling steeplechase, my old man bought in the winner for 30,000 francs. He had to bid a little to get him but the stable let the horse go finally and my old man had his permit and his colors in a week. Gee, I felt proud when my old man was an owner. He fixed it up for stable space with Charles Drake and cut out coming in to Paris and started his running and sweating out again, and him and I were the whole stable gang. Our horse's name was Gilford, he was Irish bred and a nice, sweet jumper. My old man figured that training him and riding him, himself, he was a good investment. I was proud of everything and I thought Gilford was as good a horse as War Cloud. He was a good, solid jumper, a bay, with plenty of speed on the flat, if you asked him for it, and he was a nice-looking horse, too.

Gee, I was fond of him. The first time he started with my old man up, he finished third in a 2,500 metre hurdle race and when my old man got off him, all sweating and happy in the place stall, and went in to weigh, I felt as proud of him as though it was the first race he'd ever placed in. You see, when a guy ain't been riding for a long time, you can't make yourself really believe that he has ever rode. The whole thing was different now, 'cause down in Milan, even big races never seemed to make any difference to my old man, if he won he wasn't ever excited or anything, and now it was so I couldn't hardly sleep the night before a race and I knew my old man was excited, too, even if he didn't show it. Riding for yourself makes an awful difference.

Second time Gilford and my old man started, was a rainy Sunday at Auteuil, in the Prix du Marat, a 4500 meter steeplechase. As soon as he'd gone out I beat it up in the stand with the new glasses my old man had bought for me to watch them. They started way over at the far end of the course and there was some trouble at the barrier. Something with goggle blinders on was making a great fuss and rearing around and busted the barrier once, but I could see my old man in our black jacket, with a white cross and a black cap, sitting up on Gilford, and patting him with his hand. Then they were off in a jump and out of sight behind the trees and the gong going for dear life and the pari-mutuel wickets rattling down. Gosh, I was so excited, I was afraid to look at them, but I fixed the glasses on the place where they would come out back of the trees and then out they came with the old black jacket going third and they all sailing over the jump like birds. Then they went out of sight again and then they came pounding out and down the hill and all going nice and sweet and easy and taking the fence smooth in a bunch, and moving away from us all solid. Looked as though you could walk across on their backs they were all so bunched and going so smooth. Then they bellied over the big double Bullfinch and something came down. I couldn't see who it was, but in a minute the horse was up and galloping free and the field, all bunched still, sweeping around the long left turn into the straightaway. They jumped the stone wall and came jammed down the stretch towards the big water-jump right in front of the stands. I saw them coming and hollered at my old man as he went by, and he was leading by about a length and riding way out, and light as a monkey, and they were racing for the water-jump. They took off over the big hedge of the water-jump in a pack and then there was

192

a crash, and two horses pulled sideways out of it, and kept on going, and three others were piled up. I couldn't see my old man anywhere. One horse kneed himself up and the jock had hold of the bridle and mounted and went slamming on after the place money. The other horse was up and away by himself, jerking his head and galloping with the bridle rein hanging and the jock staggered over to one side of the track against the fence. Then Gilford rolled over to one side off my old man and got up and started to run on three legs with his off hoof dangling and there was my old man laying there on the grass flat out with his face up and blood all over the side of his head. I ran down the stand and bumped into a jam of people and got to the rail and a cop grabbed me and held me and two big stretcher-bearers were going out after my old man and around on the other side of the course I saw three horses, strung way out, coming out of the trees and taking the jump.

My old man was dead when they brought him in and while a doctor was listening to his heart with a thing plugged in his ears, I heard a shot up the track that meant they'd killed Gilford. I lay down beside my old man, when they carried the stretcher into the hospital room, and hung on to the stretcher and cried and cried, and he looked so white and gone and so awfully dead, and I couldn't help feeling that if my old man was dead maybe they didn't need to have shot Gilford. His hoof might have got well. I don't know. I loved my old man so much.

Then a couple of guys came in and one of them patted me on the back and then went over and looked at my old man and pulled a sheet off the cot and spread it over him; and the other was telephoning in French for them to send the ambulance to take him out to Maisons. And I couldn't stop crying, crying and choking, sort of, and George Gardner came in and sat down beside me on the floor and put his arm around me and says, 'Come on, Joe, old boy. Get up and we'll go out and wait for the ambulance.'

George and I went out to the gate and I was trying to stop bawling and George wiped off my face with his handkerchief and we were standing back a little ways while the crowd was going out of the gate and a couple of guys stopped near us while we were waiting for the crowd to get through the gate and one of them was counting a bunch of mutuel tickets and he said, 'Well, Butler got his, all right.'

The other guy said, 'I don't give a good goddam if he did, the crook. He had it coming to him on the stuff he's pulled.'

'I'll say he had,' said the other guy, and tore the bunch of tickets in two.

And George Gardner looked at me to see if I'd heard and I had all right and he said, 'Don't you listen to what those bums said, Joe. Your old man was one swell guy.'

But I don't know. Seems like when they get started they don't leave a guy nothing.

Chapter XIV

Maera lay still, his head on his arms, his face in the sand. He felt warm and sticky from the bleeding. Each time he felt the horn coming. Sometimes the bull only bumped him with his head. Once the horn went all the way through him and he felt it go into the sand. Someone had the bull by the tail. They were swearing at him and flopping the cape in his face. Then the bull was gone. Some men picked Maera up and started to run with him toward the barriers through the gate out the passage way around under the grandstand to the infirmary. They laid Maera down on a cot and one of the men went for the doctor. The doctor came running from the corral, where he had been sewing up picador horses. He had to stop and wash his hands. There was a great shouting going on in the grandstand overhead. Maera wanted to say something and found he could not talk. Maera felt everything getting larger and larger and then smaller and smaller. Then it got larger and larger and then smaller and smaller. Then everything commenced to run faster and faster as when they speed up a cinematograph film. Then he was dead.

Big Two-Hearted River: Part I

The train went on up the track out of sight, around one of the hills of burnt timber. Nick sat down on the bundle of canvas and bedding the baggage man had pitched out of the door of the baggage car. There was no town, nothing but the rails and the burned-over country. The thirteen saloons that had lined the one street of Seney had not left a trace. The foundations of the Mansion House hotel stuck up above the ground. The stone was chipped and split by the fire. It was all that was left of the town of Seney. Even the surface had been burned off the ground.

Nick looked at the burned-over stretch of hillside, where he had expected to find the scattered houses of the town and then walked down the railroad track to the bridge over the river. The river was there. It swirled against the log piles of the bridge. Nick looked down into the clear, brown water, colored from the pebbly bottom, and watched the trout keeping themselves steady in the current with wavering fins. As he watched them they changed their positions by quick angles, only to hold steady in the fast water again. Nick watched them a long time.

He watched them holding themselves with their noses into the current, many trout in deep, fast moving water, slightly distorted as he watched far down through the glassy convex surface of the pool, its surface pushing and swelling smooth against the resistance of the log-driven piles of the bridge. At the bottom of the pool were the big trout. Nick did not see them at first. Then he saw them at the bottom of the pool, big trout looking to hold themselves on the gravel bottom in a varying mist of gravel and sand, raised in spurts by the current.

Nick looked down into the pool from the bridge. It was a hot day. A kingfisher flew up the stream. It was a long time since Nick had looked into a stream and seen trout. They were very satisfactory. As the shadow of the kingfisher moved up the stream, a big trout shot upstream in a long angle, only his shadow marking the angle, then lost his shadow as he came through the surface of the water, caught the sun, and then, as he went back into the stream under the surface, his shadow seemed to float down the stream with the current, unresisting, to his post under the bridge where he tightened facing up into the current.

Nick's heart tightened as the trout moved. He felt all the old feeling.

He turned and looked down the stream. It stretched away, pebbly-bottomed with shallows and big boulders and a deep pool as it curved away around the foot of a bluff.

Nick walked back up the ties to where his pack lay in the cinders beside the railway track. He was happy. He adjusted the pack harness around the bundle, pulling straps tight, slung the pack on his back, got his arms through the shoulder straps and took some of the pull off his shoulders by leaning his forehead against the wide band of the tump-line. Still, it was too heavy. It was much too heavy. He had his leather rod-case in his hand and leaning forward to keep the weight of the pack high on his shoulders he walked along the road that paralleled the railway track, leaving the burned town behind in the heat, and then turned off around a hill with a high, fire-scarred hill on either side on to a road that went back into the country. He walked along the road feeling the ache from the pull of the heavy pack. The road climbed steadily. It was hard work walking up-hill. His muscles ached and the day was hot, but Nick felt happy. He felt he had left everything behind, the need for thinking, the need to write, other needs. It was all back of him.

From the time he had gotten down off the train and the baggage man had thrown his pack out of the open car door things had been different. Seney was burned, the country was burned over and changed, but it did not matter. It could not all be burned. He knew that. He hiked along the road, sweating in the sun, climbing to cross the range of hills that separated the railway from the pine plains.

The road ran on, dipping occasionally, but always climbing. Nick went on up. Finally the road after going parallel to the burnt hillside reached the top. Nick leaned back against a stump and slipped out of the pack harness. Ahead of him, as far as he could see, was the pine plain. The burned country stopped off at the left of the range of hills. On ahead islands of dark pine trees rose out of the plain. Far off to the left was the line of the river. Nick followed it with his eye and caught glints of the water in the sun.

There was nothing but the pine plain ahead of him, until the far blue hills that marked the Lake Superior height of land. He could hardly see them, faint and far away in the heat-light over the plain. If he looked too steadily they were gone. But if he only half-looked they were there, the far-off hills of the height of land.

Nick sat down against the charred stump and smoked a cigarette. His pack balanced on the top of the stump, harness holding ready, a hollow molded in it from his back. Nick sat smoking, looking out over the country. He did not need to get his map out. He knew where he was from the position of the river.

As he smoked, his legs stretched out in front of him, he noticed a grasshopper walk along the ground and up on to his woolen sock. The grasshopper was black. As he walked along the road, climbing, he had started many grasshoppers from the dust. They were all black. They were not the big grasshoppers with yellow and black or red and black wings whirring out from their black wing sheathing as they fly up. These were just ordinary hoppers, but all a sooty black in colour. Nick had wondered about them as he walked, without really thinking about them. Now, as he watched the black hopper that was nibbling at the wool of his sock with its fourway lip, he realized that they had all turned black from living in the burned-over land. He realized that the fire must have come the year before, but the grasshoppers were all black now. He wondered how long they would stay that way.

Carefully he reached his hand down and took hold of the

hopper by the wings. He turned him up, all his legs walking in the air, and looked at his jointed belly. Yes, it was black too, iridescent where the back and head were dusty.

'Go on, hopper,' Nick said, speaking out loud for the first time. 'Fly away somewhere.'

He tossed the grasshopper up into the air and watched him sail away to a charcoal stump across the road.

Nick stood up. He leaned his back against the weight of his pack where it rested upright on the stump and got his arms through the shoulder straps. He stood with the pack on his back on the brow of the hill looking out across the country, towards the distant river and then struck down the hillside away from the road. Underfoot the ground was good walking. Two hundred yards down the hillside the fire line stopped. Then it was sweet fern, growing ankle high, to walk through, and clumps of jackpines; a long undulating country with frequent rises and descents, sandy underfoot and the country alive again.

Nick kept his direction by the sun. He knew where he wanted to strike the river and he kept on through the pine plain, mounting small rises to see other rises ahead of him and sometimes from the top of a rise a great solid island of pines off to his right or his left. He broke off some sprigs of the heather sweet fern, and put them under his pack straps. The chafing crushed it and he smelled it as he walked.

He was tired and very hot, walking across the uneven, shadeless pine plain. At any time he knew he could strike the river by turning off to his left. It could not be more than a mile away. But he kept on toward the north to hit the river as far upstream as he could go in one day's walking.

For some time as he walked Nick had been in sight of one of the big islands of pine standing out above the rolling high ground he was crossing. He dipped down and then as he came slowly up to the crest of the ridge he turned and made towards the pine trees.

There was no underbrush in the island of pine trees. The trunks of the trees went straight up or slanted towards each other. The trunks were straight and brown without branches. The branches were high above. Some interlocked to make a solid shadow on the brown forest floor. Around the grove of trees was a bare space. It was brown and soft underfoot as Nick walked on it. This was the overlapping of the pine needle floor, extending out beyond the width of the high branches. The trees had grown tall and the branches moved high, leaving in the sun this bare space they had once covered with shadow. Sharp at the edge of this extension of the forest floor commenced the sweet fern.

Nick slipped off his pack and lay down in the shade. He lay on his back and looked up into the pine trees. His neck and back and the small of his back rested as he stretched. The earth felt good against his back. He looked up at the sky, through the branches, and then shut his eyes. He opened them and looked up again. There was a wind high up in the branches. He shut his eyes again and went to sleep.

Nick woke stiff and cramped. The sun was nearly down. His pack was heavy and the straps painful as he lifted it on. He leaned over with the pack on and picked up the leather rod-case and started out from the pine trees across the sweet fern swale, toward the river. He knew it could not be more than a mile.

He came down a hillside covered with stumps into a meadow. At the edge of the meadow flowed the river. Nick was glad to get to the river. He walked upstream through the meadow. His trousers were soaked with the dew as he walked. After the hot day, the dew had come quickly and heavily. The river made no sound. It was too fast and smooth. At the edge of the meadow, before he mounted to a piece of high ground to make camp, Nick looked down the river at the trout rising. They were rising to insects come from the swamp on the other side of the stream when the sun went down. The trout jumped out of the water to take them. While Nick walked through the little stretch of meadow alongside the stream, trout had jumped high out of the water. Now as he looked down the river, the insects must be settling on the surface for the trout were feeding steadily all down the stream. As far down the long stretch as he could see, the trout were rising, making circles all down the surface of the water, as though it were starting to rain.

The ground rose, wooded and sandy, to overlook the meadow, the stretch of river and the swamp. Nick dropped his pack and rod-case and looked for a level piece of ground. He was very hungry and he wanted to make his camp before he cooked. Between two jack-pines, the ground was quite level. He took the ax out of the pack and chopped out two projecting roots. That levelled a piece of ground large enough to sleep on. He smoothed out the sandy soil with his hand and pulled all the sweet fern bushes up by their roots. His hands smelled good from the sweet fern. He smoothed the uprooted earth. He did not want anything making lumps under the blankets. When he had the ground smooth, he spread his three blankets. One he folded double, next to the ground. The other two he spread on top.

With the ax he slit off a bright slab of pine from one of the stumps and split it into pegs for the tent. He wanted them long and solid to hold in the ground. With the tent unpacked and spread on the ground, the pack, leaning against a jack-pine, looked much smaller. Nick tied the rope that served the tent for a ridge-pole to the trunk of one of the pine trees and pulled the tent up off the ground with the other end of the rope and tied it to the other pine. The tent hung on the rope like a canvas blanket on a clothesline. Nick poked a pole he had cut up under the back peak of the canvas and then made it a tent by pegging out the sides. He pegged the sides out taut and drove the pegs deep, hitting them down into the ground with the flat of the axe until the rope loops were buried and the canvas was drum tight.

Across the open mouth of the tent Nick fixed cheesecloth to keep out mosquitoes. He crawled inside under the mosquito bar with various things from the pack to put at the head of the bed under the slant of the canvas. Inside the tent the light came through the brown canvas. It smelled pleasantly of canvas. Already there was something mysterious and home-like. Nick was happy as he crawled inside the tent. He had not been unhappy all day. This was different though. Now things were done. There had been this to do. Now it was done. It had been a hard trip. He was very tired. That was done. He had made his camp. He was settled. Nothing could touch him. It was a good place to camp. He was there, in the good place. He was in his home where he had made it. Now he was hungry.

He came out, crawling under the cheesecloth. It was quite dark outside. It was lighter in the tent.

Nick went over to the pack and found, with his fingers, a long nail in a paper sack of nails, in the bottom of the pack. He drove it into the pine tree, holding it close and hitting it gently with the flat of the axe. He hung the pack up on the nail. All his supplies were in the pack. They were off the ground and sheltered now.

Nick was hungry. He did not believe he had ever been hungrier. He opened and emptied a can of pork and beans and a can of spaghetti into the frying pan.

'I've got a right to eat this kind of stuff, if I'm willing to carry it,' Nick said. His voice sounded strange in the darkening woods. He did not speak again.

He started a fire with some chunks of pine he got with the axe from a stump. Over the fire he stuck a wire grill, pushing the four legs down into the ground with his boot. Nick put the frying pan on the grill over flames. He was hungrier. The beans and spaghetti warmed. Nick stirred them and mixed them together. They began to bubble, making little bubbles that rose with difficulty to the surface. There was a good smell. Nick got out a bottle of tomato ketchup and cut four slices of bread. The little bubbles were coming faster now. Nick sat down beside the fire and lifted the frying pan off. He poured about half the contents out into the tin plate. It spread slowly on the plate. Nick knew it was too hot. He poured on some tomato ketchup. He knew the beans and spaghetti were still too hot. He looked at the fire, then at the tent, he was not going to spoil it all by burning his tongue. For years he had never enjoyed fried bananas because he had never been able to wait for them to cool. His tongue was very sensitive. He was very hungry. Across the river in the swamp, in the almost dark, he saw a mist rising. He looked at the tent once more. All right. He took a full spoonful from the plate.

'Chrise,' Nick said, 'Geezus Chrise,' he said happily.

He ate the whole plateful before he remembered the bread. Nick finished the second plateful with the bread, mopping the plate shiny. He had not eaten since a cup of coffee and a ham sandwich in the station restaurant at St Ignace. It had been a very fine experience. He had been hungry before, but had not been able to satisfy it. He could have made camp hours before if he had wanted to. There were plenty of good places to camp on the river. But this was good.

Nick tucked two big chips of pine under the grill. The fire flared up. He had forgotten to get water for the coffee. Out of the pack he got a folding canvas bucket and walked down the hill, across the edge of the meadow, to the stream. The other bank was in the white mist. The grass was wet and cold as he knelt on the bank and dipped the canvas bucket into the stream. It bellied and pulled hard in the current. The water was ice cold. Nick rinsed the bucket and carried it full up to the camp. Up away from the stream it was not so cold.

Nick drove another big nail and hung up the bucket full of water. He dipped the coffee pot half full, put some more chips under the grill on to the fire and put the pot on. He could not remember which way he made coffee. He could remember an argument about it with Hopkins, but not which side he had taken. He decided to bring it to a boil. He remembered now that was Hopkins's way. He had once argued about everything with Hopkins. While he waited for the coffee to boil, he opened a small can of apricots. He liked to open cans. He emptied the can of apricots out into a tin cup. While he watched the coffee on the fire, he drank the juice syrup of the apricots, carefully at first to keep from spilling, then meditatively, sucking the apricots down. They were better than fresh apricots.

The coffee boiled as he watched. The lid came up and coffee and grounds ran down the side of the pot. Nick took it off the grill. It was a triumph for Hopkins. He put sugar in the empty apricot cup and poured some of the coffee out to cool. It was too hot to pour and he used his hat to hold the handle of the coffee pot. He would not let it steep in the pot at all. Not the first cup. It should be straight Hopkins all the way. Hop deserved that. He was a very serious coffee maker. He was the most serious man Nick had ever known. Not heavy, serious. That was a long time ago. Hopkins spoke without moving his lips. He had played polo. He made millions of dollars in Texas.

He had borrowed car fare to go to Chicago, when the wire came that his first big well had come in. He could have wired for money. That would have been too slow. They called Hop's girl the Blonde Venus. Hop did not mind because she was not his real girl. Hopkins said very confidently that none of them would make fun of his real girl. He was right. Hopkins went away when the telegram came. That was on the Black River. It took eight days for the telegram to reach him. Hopkins gave away his .22 calibre Colt automatic pistol to Nick. He gave his camera to Bill. It was to remember him always by. They were all going fishing again next summer. The Hop Head was rich. He would get a yacht and they would all cruise along the north shore of Lake Superior. He was excited but serious. They said good-bye and all felt bad. It broke up the trip. They never saw Hopkins again. That was a long time ago on the Black River.

Nick drank his coffee according to Hopkins. The coffee was bitter. Nick laughed. It made a good ending to the story. His mind was starting to work. He knew he could choke it because he was tired enough. He spilled the coffee out of the pot and shook the grounds loose into the fire. He lit a cigarette and went inside the tent. He took off his shoes and trousers, sitting on the blankets, rolled the shoes up inside the trousers for a pillow and got in between the blankets.

Out through the front of the tent he watched the glow of the fire, when the night wind blew on it. It was a quiet night. The swamp was perfectly quiet. Nick stretched under the blanket comfortably. A mosquito hummed close to his ear. Nick sat up and lit a match. The mosquito was on the canvas, over his head. Nick moved the match quickly up to it. The mosquito made a satisfactory hiss in the flame. The match went out. Nick lay down again under the blanket. He turned on his side and shut his eyes. He was sleepy. He felt sleep coming. He curled up under the blanket and went to sleep.

Chapter XV

They hanged Sam Cardinella at six o'clock in the morning in the corridor of the county jail. The corridor was high and narrow with tiers of cells on either side. All the cells were occupied. The prisoners had been brought in for the hanging. Five men sentenced to be hanged were in the five top cells. Three of the men to be hanged were negroes. They were very frightened. One of the white men sat on his cot with his head in his hands. The other lay flat on his cot with a blanket wrapped around his head.

They came out on to the gallows through a door in the wall. There were six or seven of them including two priests. They were carrying Sam Cardinella. He had been like that since about four o'clock in the morning.

While they were strapping his legs together two guards held him up and the two priests were whispering to him. 'Be a man, my son,' said one priest. When they came toward him with the cap to go over his head Sam Cardinella lost control of his sphincter muscles. The guards who had been holding him up dropped him. They were both disgusted. 'How about a chair, Will?' asked one of the guards. 'Better get one,' said a man in a derby hat.

When they all stepped back on the scaffolding back of the drop, which was very heavy, built of oak and steel and swung on ball bearings, Sam Cardinella was left sitting there strapped tight with the rope around his neck, the younger of the two priests kneeling beside the chair holding up a little crucifix. The priest skipped back on to the scaffolding just before the drop fell.

Big Two-Hearted River: Part II

In the morning the sun was up and the tent was starting to get hot. Nick crawled out under the mosquito netting stretched across the mouth of the tent, to look at the morning. The grass was wet on his hands as he came out. He held his trousers and his shoes in his hands. The sun was just up over the hill. There was the meadow, the river and the swamp. There were birch trees in the green of the swamp on the other side of the river.

The river was clear and smoothly fast in the early morning. Down about two hundred yards were three logs all the way across the stream. They made the water smooth and deep above them. As Nick watched, a mink crossed the river on the logs and went into the swamp. Nick was excited. He was excited by the early morning and the river. He was really too hurried to eat breakfast, but he knew he must. He built a little fire and put on the coffee pot.

While the water was heating in the pot he took an empty bottle and went down over the edge of the high ground to the meadow. The meadow was wet with dew and Nick wanted to catch grasshoppers for bait before the sun dried the grass. He found plenty of good grasshoppers. They were at the base of the grass stems. Sometimes they clung to a grass stem. They were cold and wet with the dew, and could not jump until the sun warmed them. Nick picked them up, taking only the medium-sized brown ones, and put them into the bottle. He turned over a log and just under the shelter of the edge were several hundred hoppers. It was a grasshopper lodging house. Nick put about fifty of the medium browns into the bottle.

While he was picking up the hoppers the others warmed in the sun and commenced to hop away. They flew when they hopped. At first they made one flight and stayed stiff when they landed, as though they were dead.

Nick knew that by the time he was through with breakfast they would be as lively as ever. Without dew in the grass it would take him all day to catch a bottle full of good grasshoppers and he would have to crush many of them, slamming at them with his hat. He washed his hands at the stream. He was excited to be near it. Then he walked up to the tent. The hopppers were already jumping stiffly in the grass. In the bottle, warmed by the sun, they were jumping in a mass. Nick put in a pine stick as a cork. It plugged the mouth of the bottle enough, so the hoppers could not get out and left plenty of air passage.

He had rolled the log back and knew he could get grasshoppers there every morning.

Nick laid the bottle full of jumping grasshoppers against a pine trunk. Rapidly he mixed some buckwheat flour with water and stirred it smooth, one cup of flour, one cup of water. He put a handful of coffee in the pot and dipped a lump of grease out of a can and slid it sputtering across the hot skillet. On the smoking skillet he poured smoothly the buckwheat batter. It spread like lava, the grease spitting sharply. Around the edges the buckwheat cake began to firm, then brown, then crisp. The surface was bubbling slowly to porousness. Nick pushed under the browned under surface with a fresh pine chip. He shook the skillet sideways and the cake was loose on the surface. I won't try to flop it, he thought. He slid the chip of clean wood all the way under the cake, and flopped it over on to its face. It spluttered in the pan.

When it was cooked Nick regreased the skillet. He used all the batter. It made another big flapjack and one smaller one.

Nick ate a big flapjack and a smaller one, covered with apple butter. He put apple butter on the third cake, folded it over twice, wrapped it in oiled paper and put it in his shirt pocket. He put the apple-butter jar back in the pack and cut bread for two sandwiches.

In the pack he found a big onion. He sliced it in two and peeled the silky outer skin. Then he cut one half into slices and made onion sandwiches. He wrapped them in oiled paper and buttoned them in the other pocket of his khaki shirt. He turned the skillet upside down on the grill, drank the coffee, sweetened and yellow brown with the condensed milk in it, and tidied up the camp. It was a good camp.

Nick took his fly rod out of the leather rod-case, jointed it, and shoved the rod-case back into the tent. He put on the reel and threaded the line through the guides. He had to hold it from hand to hand, as he threaded it, or it would slip back through its own weight. It was a heavy, double tapered fly line. Nick had paid eight dollars for it a long time ago. It was made heavy to lift back in the air and come forward flat and heavy and straight to make it possible to cast a fly which has no weight. Nick opened the aluminum leader box. The leaders were coiled between the damp flannel pads. Nick had wet the pads at the water cooler on the train up to St Ignace. In the damp pads the gut leaders had softened and Nick unrolled one and tied it by a loop at the end to a heavy fly line. He fastened a hook on the end of the leader. It was a small hook; very thin and springy.

Nick took it from his hook book, sitting with the rod across his lap. He tested the knot and the spring of the rod by pulling the line taut. It was a good feeling. He was careful not to let the hook bite into his finger.

He started down to the stream, holding his rod, the bottle of grasshoppers hung from his neck by a thong tied in half hitches around the neck of the bottle. His landing net hung by a hook from his belt. Over his shoulder was a long flour sack tied at each corner into an ear. The cord went over his shoulder. The sack flapped against his legs.

Nick felt awkward and professionally happy with all his equipment hanging from him. The grasshopper bottle swung against his chest. In his shirt the breast pockets bulged against him with the lunch and his fly book.

He stepped into the stream. It was a shock. His trousers clung tight to his legs. His shoes felt the gravel. The water was a rising cold shock.

Rushing, the current sucked against his legs. Where he stepped in, the water was over his knees. He waded with the current. The gravel slid under his shoes. He looked down at the swirl of water below each leg and tipped up the bottle to get a grasshopper.

The first grasshopper gave a jump in the neck of the bottle and went out into the water. He was sucked under in the whirl by Nick's right leg and came to the surface a little way down stream. He floated rapidly, kicking. In a quick circle, breaking the smooth surface of the water, he disappeared. A trout had taken him.

Another hopper poked his head out of the bottle. His antennae wavered. He was getting his front legs out of the bottle to jump. Nick took him by the head and held him while he threaded the slim hook under his chin, down through his thorax and into the last segments of his abdomen. The grasshopper took hold of the hook with his front feet, spitting tobacco juice on it. Nick dropped him into the water.

Holding the rod in his right hand he let out line against the pull of the grasshopper in the current. He stripped off line from the reel with his left hand and let it run free. He could see the hopper in the little waves of the current. It went out of sight.

There was a tug on the line. Nick pulled against the taut line. It was his first strike. Holding the now living rod across the current, he brought in the line with his left hand. The rod bent in jerks, the trout pumping against the current. Nick knew it was a small one. He lifted the rod straight up in the air. It bowed with the pull.

He saw the trout in the water jerking with his head and body against the shifting tangent of the line in the stream.

Nick took the line in his left hand and pulled the trout, thumping tiredly against the current, to the surface. His back was mottled with clear, water-over-gravel color, his side flashing in the sun. The rod under his right arm, Nick stooped, dipping his right hand into the current. He held the trout, never still, with his moist right hand, while he unhooked the barb from his mouth, then dropped him back into the stream.

He hung unsteadily in the current, then settled to the bottom beside a stone. Nick reached down his hand to touch him, his arm to the elbow under water. The trout was steady in the moving stream, resting on the gravel, beside a stone. As

212

Nick's fingers touched him, touched his smooth cool, underwater feeling he was gone, gone in a shadow across the bottom of the stream.

He's all right, Nick thought. He was only tired.

He had wet his hand before he touched the trout, so he would not disturb the delicate mucus that covered him. If a trout was touched with a dry hand, a white fungus attacked the unprotected spot. Years before when he had fished crowded streams, with fly fishermen ahead of him and behind him, Nick had again and again come on dead trout, furry with white fungus, drifted against a rock, or floating belly up in some pool. Nick did not like to fish with other men on the river. Unless they were of your party, they spoiled it.

He wallowed down the stream, above his knees in the current, through the fifty yards of shallow water above the pile of logs that crossed the stream. He did not rebait his hook and held it in his hand as he waded. He was certain he could catch small trout in the shallows, but he did not want them. There would be no big trout in the shallows this time of day.

Now the water deepened up his thighs sharply and coldly. Ahead was the smooth dammed-back flood of water above the logs. The water was smooth and dark; on the left, the lower edge of the meadow; on the right the swamp.

Nick leaned back against the current and took a hopper from the bottle. He threaded the hopper on the hook and spat on him for good luck. Then he pulled several yards of line from the reel and tossed the hopper out ahead on to the fast, dark water. It floated down towards the logs, then the weight of the line pulled the bait under the surface. Nick held the rod in his right hand, letting the line run out through his fingers.

There was a long tug. Nick struck and the rod came alive and dangerous, bent double, the line tightening, coming out of water, tightening, all in a heavy, dangerous, steady pull. Nick felt the moment when the leader would break if the strain increased and let the line go.

The reel ratcheted into a mechanical shriek as the line went out in a rush. Too fast. Nick could not check it, the line rushing out, the reel note rising as the line ran out.

213

With the core of the reel showing, his heart feeling stopped with the excitement, leaning back against the current that mounted icily his thighs, Nick thumbed the reel hard with his left hand. It was awkward getting his thumb inside the fly reel frame.

As he put on pressure the line tightened into sudden hardness and beyond the logs a huge trout went high out of the water. As he jumped, Nick lowered the tip of the rod. But he felt, as he dropped the tip to ease the strain, the moment when the strain was too great; the hardness too tight. Of course, the leader had broken. There was no mistaking the feeling when all spring left the line and it became dry and hard. Then it went slack.

His mouth dry, his heart down, Nick reeled in. He had never seen so big a trout. There was a heaviness, a power not to be held, and then the bulk of him, as he jumped. He looked as broad as a salmon.

Nick's hand was shaky. He reeled in slowly. The thrill had been too much. He felt, vaguely, a little sick, as though it would be better to sit down.

The leader had broken where the hook was tied to it. Nick took it in his hand. He thought of the trout somewhere on the bottom, holding himself steady over the gravel, far down below the light, under the logs, with the hook in his jaw. Nick knew the trout's teeth would cut through the snell of the hook. The hook would embed itself in his jaw. He'd bet the trout was angry. Anything that size would be angry. That was a trout. He had been solidly hooked. Solid as a rock. He felt like a rock, too, before he started off. By God, he was a big one. By God, he was the biggest one I ever heard of.

Nick climbed out on to the meadow and stood, water running down his trousers and out of his shoes, his shoes squelchy. He went over and sat on the logs. He did not want to rush his sensations any.

He wriggled his toes in the water in his shoes, and got out a cigarette from his breast pocket. He lit it and tossed the match into the fast water below the logs. A tiny trout rose at the match, as it swung around in the fast current. Nick laughed. He would finish the cigarette.

214

He sat on the logs, smoking, drying in the sun, the sun warm on his back, the river shallow ahead entering the woods, curving into the woods, shallows, light glittering, big water-smooth rocks, cedars along the bank and white birches, the logs warm in the sun, smooth to sit on, without bark, gray to the touch; slowly the feeling of disappointment left him. It went away slowly, the feeling of disappointment that came sharply after the thrill that made his shoulders ache. It was all right now. His rod lying out on the logs, Nick tied a new hook on the leader, pulling the gut tight until it grimped into itself in a hard knot.

He baited up, then picked up the rod and walked to the far end of the logs to get into the water, where it was not too deep. Under and beyond the logs was a deep pool. Nick walked around the shallow shelf near the swamp shore until he came out on the shallow bed of the stream.

On the left, where the meadow ended and the woods began, a great elm tree was uprooted. Gone over in a storm, it lay back into the woods, its roots clotted with dirt, grass growing in them, rising a solid bank beside the stream. The river cut to the edge of the uprooted tree. From where Nick stood he could see deep channels, like ruts, cut in the shallow bed of the stream by the flow of the current. Pebbly where he stood and pebbly and full of boulders beyond; where it curved near the tree roots, the bed of the stream was marly and between the ruts of deep water green weed fronds swung in the current.

Nick swung the rod back over his shoulder and forward, and the line, curving forward, laid the grasshopper down on one of the deep channels in the weeds. A trout struck and Nick hooked him.

Holding the rod far out toward the uprooted tree and sloshing backward in the current, Nick worked the trout, plunging, the rod bending alive, out of the danger of the weeds into the open river. Holding the rod, pumping alive against the current, Nick brought the trout in. He rushed, but always came, the spring of the rod yielding to the rushes, sometimes jerking under the water, but always bringing him in. Nick eased downstream with the rushes. The rod above his head he led the trout over the net, then lifted.

The trout hung heavy in the net, mottled trout back and silver sides in the meshes. Nick unhooked him; heavy sides, good to hold, big undershot jaw, and slipped him, heaving and big sliding, into the long sack that hung from his shoulders in the water.

Nick spread the mouth of the sack against the current and it filled, heavy with water. He held it up, the bottom in the stream, and the water poured out through the sides. Inside at the bottom was the big trout, alive in the water.

Nick moved downstream. The sack out ahead of him, sunk, heavy in the water, pulling from his shoulders.

It was getting hot, the sun hot on the back of his neck.

Nick had one good trout. He did not care about getting many trout. Now the stream was shallow and wide. There were trees along both banks. The trees of the left bank made short shadows on the current in the forenoon sun. Nick knew there were trout in each shadow. In the afternoon, after the sun had crossed toward the hills, the trout would be in the cool shadows on the other side of the stream.

The very biggest ones would lie up close to the bank. You could always pick them up there on the Black. When the sun was down they all moved out into the current. Just when the sun made the water blinding in the glare before it went down, you were liable to strike a big trout anywhere in the current. It was almost impossible to fish then, the surface of the water was blinding as a mirror in the sun. Of course, you could fish upstream, but in a stream like the Black, or this, you had to wallow against the current and in a deep place, the water piled up on you. It was no fun to fish upstream with this much current.

Nick moved along through the shallow stretch watching the banks for deep holes. A beech tree grew close beside the river, so that the branches hung down into the water. The stream went back under the leaves. There were always trout in a place like that.

Nick did not care about fishing that hole. He was sure he would get hooked in the branches.

It looked deep though. He dropped the grasshopper so the current took it under the water, back in under the overhanging branches. The line pulled hard and Nick struck. The trout threshed heavily, half out of water in the leaves and branches. The line was caught. Nick pulled hard and the trout was off. He reeled in and holding the reel in his hand, walked down the stream.

Ahead, close to the left bank, was a big log. Nick saw it was hollow; pointing up river the current entered it smoothly, only a little ripple spread each side of the log. The water was deepening. The top of the hollow log was gray and dry, it was partly in the shadow.

Nick took the cork out of the grasshopper bottle and a hopper clung to it. He picked him off, hooked him and tossed him out. He held the rod far out so the hopper on the water moved into the current flowing into the hollow log. Nick lowered the rod and the hopper floated in. There was a heavy strike. Nick swung the rod against the pull. It felt as though he were hooked into the log itself, except for the live feeling.

He tried to force the fish out into the current. It came, heavily.

The line went slack and Nick thought the trout was gone. Then he saw him, very near, in the current, shaking his head, trying to get the hook out. His mouth was clamped shut. He was fighting the hook in the clear flowing current. Looping in the line with his left hand, Nick swung the rod to make the line taut and tried to lead the trout toward the net, but he was gone, out of sight, the line pumping. Nick fought him against the current, letting him thump in the water against the spring of the rod. He shifted the rod to his left hand, worked the trout upstream, holding his weight, fighting on the rod, and then let him down into the net. He lifted him clear of the water, a heavy half circle in the net, the net dripping, unhooked him and slid him into the sack.

He spread the mouth of the sack and looked down in at the two big trout alive in the water.

Through the deepening water, Nick waded over to the hollow log. He took the sack off, over his head, the trout flopping as it came out of water, and hung it so the trout were deep in the water. Then he pulled himself up on the log and sat, the water from his trousers and boots running down into the stream. He laid his rod down, moved along to the shady end of the log and took the sandwiches out of his pocket. He dipped the sandwiches in the cold water. The current carried away the crumbs. He ate the sandwiches and dipped his hat full of water to drink, the water running out through his hat just ahead of his drinking.

It was cool in the shade, sitting on the log. He took a cigarette out and struck a match to light it. The match sunk into the gray wood, making a tiny furrow. Nick leaned over the side of the log, found a hard place and lit the match. He sat smoking and watching the river.

Ahead the river narrowed and went into a swamp. The river became smooth and deep and the swamp looked solid with cedar trees, their trunks close together, their branches solid. It would not be possible to walk through a swamp like that. The branches grew so low. You would have to keep almost level with the ground to move at all. You could not crash through the branches. That must be why the animals that lived in swamps were built the way they were, Nick thought.

He wished he had brought something to read. He felt like reading. He did not feel like going on into the swamp. He looked down the river. A big cedar slanted all the way across the stream. Beyond that the river went into the swamp.

Nick did not want to go in there now. He felt a reaction against deep wading with the water deepening up under his armpits, to hook big trout in places impossible to land them. In the swamp the banks were bare, the big cedars came together overhead, the sun did not come through, except in patches; in the fast deep water, in the half light, the fishing would be tragic. In the swamp fishing was a tragic adventure. Nick did not want it. He did not want to go down the stream any further today.

He took out his knife, opened it and stuck it in the log. Then he pulled up the sack, reached into it and brought out one of the trout. Holding him near the tail, hard to hold, alive, in his hand, he whacked him against the log. The trout quivered, rigid. Nick laid him on the log in the shade and broke the neck of the other fish the same way. He laid them side by side on the log. They were fine trout.

218

Nick cleaned them, slitting them from the vent to the tip of the jaw. All the insides and the gills and tongue came out in one piece. They were both males; long gray-white strips of milt, smooth and clean. All the insides clean and compact, coming out all together. Nick tossed the offal ashore for the minks to find.

He washed the trout in the stream. When he held them back up in the water they looked like live fish. Their color was not gone yet. He washed his hands and dried them on the log. Then he laid the trout on the sack spread out on the log, rolled them up in it, tied the bundle and put it in the landing net. His knife was still standing, blade stuck in the log. He cleaned it on the wood and put it in his pocket.

Nick stood up on the log, holding his rod, the landing net hanging heavy, then stepped into the water and splashed ashore. He climbed the bank and cut up into the woods, toward the high ground. He was going back to camp. He looked back. The river just showed through the trees. There were plenty of days coming when he could fish the swamp.

L'Envoi

The king was working in the garden. He seemed very glad to see me. We walked through the garden. 'This is the queen,' he said. She was clipping a rose bush. 'Oh, how do you do?' she said. We sat down at a table under a big tree and the king ordered whisky and soda. 'We have good whiskey anyway,' he said. The revolutionary committee, he told me, would not allow him to go outside the palace grounds. 'Plastiras is a very good man, I believe,' he said, 'but frightfully difficult. I think he did right, though, shooting those chaps. If Kerensky had shot a few men things might have been altogether different. Of course, the great thing in this sort of an affair is not to be shot oneself.'

It was very jolly. We talked for a long time. Like all Greeks he wanted to go to America.

The Undefeated

Manuel Garcia climbed the stairs to Don Miguel Retana's office. He set down his suitcase and knocked on the door. There was no answer. Manuel, standing in the hallway, felt there was some one in the room. He felt it through the door.

'Retana,' he said, listening.

There was no answer.

He's there, all right, Manuel thought.

'Retana,' he said and banged the door.

'Who's there?' said someone in the office.

'Me, Manolo,' Manuel said.

'What do you want?' asked the voice.

'I want to work,' Manuel said.

Something in the door clicked several times and it swung open. Manuel went in, carrying his suitcase.

A little man sat behind a desk at the far side of the room. Over his head was a bull's head, stuffed by a Madrid taxidermist; on the walls were framed photographs and bull-fight posters.

The little man sat looking at Manuel.

'I thought they'd killed you,' he said.

Manuel knocked with his knuckles on the desk. The little man sat looking at him across the desk.

'How many corridas you had this year?' Retana asked.

'One,' he answered.

'Just that one?' the little man asked.

'That's all.'

'I read about it in the papers,' Retana said. He leaned back in the chair and looked at Manuel.

Manuel looked up at the stuffed bull. He had seen it often before. He felt a certain family interest in it. It had killed his brother, the promising one, about nine years ago. Manuel remembered the day. There was a brass plate on the oak shield the bull's head was mounted on. Manuel could not read it, but he imagined it was in memory of his brother. Well, he had been a good kid.

The plate said: 'The Bull "Mariposa" of the Duke of Veragua, which accepted 9 varas for 7 caballos, and caused the death of Antonio Garcia, Novillero, April 27, 1909.'

Retana saw him looking at the stuffed bull's head.

'The lot the Duke sent me for Sunday will make a scandal,' he said. 'They're all bad in the legs. What do they say about them at the Café?'

'I don't know,' Manuel said. 'I just got in.'

'Yes,' Retana said. 'You still have your bag.'

He looked at Manuel, leaning back behind the big desk.

'Sit down,' he said. 'Take off your cap.'

Manuel sat down; his cap off, his face was changed. He looked pale, and his coleta pinned forward on his head, so that it would not show under the cap, gave him a strange look.

'You don't look well,' Retana said.

'I just got out of hospital,' Manuel said.

'I heard they'd cut your leg off,' Retana said.

'No,' said Manuel. 'It got all right.'

Retana leaned forward across the desk and pushed a wooden box of cigarettes toward Manuel.

'Have a cigarette,' he said.

'Thanks.'

Manuel lit it.

'Smoke?' he said, offering the match to Retana.

'No,' Retana waved his hand. 'I never smoke.'

Retana watched him smoking.

'Why don't you get a job and go to work?' he said.

'I don't want to work,' Manuel said. 'I am a bull-fighter.'

'There aren't any bull-fighters any more,' Retana said.

'I'm a bull-fighter,' Manuel said.

'Yes, while you're in there,' Retana said.

Manuel laughed.

Retana sat, saying nothing and looking at Manuel.

'I'll put you in a nocturnal if you want,' Retana offered.

'When?' Manuel asked.

'Tomorrow night.'

'I don't like to substitute for anybody,' Manuel said. That was the way they all got killed. That was the way Salvador got killed. He tapped his knuckles on the table.

'It's all I've got,' Retana said.

'Why don't you put me on next week?' Manuel suggested.

'You wouldn't draw,' Retana said. 'All they want is Litri and Rubito and La Torre. Those kids are good.'

'They'd come to see me get it,' Manuel said, hopefully.

'No, they wouldn't. They don't know who you are any more.'

'I've got a lot of stuff,' Manuel said.

'I'm offering to put you on tomorrow night,' Retana said. 'You can work with young Hernandez and kill two novillos after the Chariots.'

'Whose novillos?' Manuel asked.

'I don't know. Whatever stuff they've got in the corrals. What the veterinaries won't pass in the daytime.'

'I don't like to substitute,' Manuel said.

'You can take it or leave it,' Retana said. He leaned forward over the papers. He was no longer interested. The appeal that Manuel had made to him for a moment when he thought of the old days was gone. He would like to get him to substitute for Larita because he could get him cheaply. He could get others cheaply too. He would like to help him though. Still he had given him the chance. It was up to him.

'How much do I get?' Manuel asked. He was still playing with the idea of refusing. But he knew he could not refuse.

'Two hundred and fifty pesetas,' Retana said. He had thought of five hundred, but when he opened his mouth it said two hundred and fifty.

'You pay Villalta seven thousand,' Manuel said.

'You're not Villalta,' Retana said.

'I know it,' Manuel said.

'He draws it, Manolo,' Retana said in explanation.

'Sure,' said Manuel. He stood up. 'Give me three hundred, Retana.'

'All right,' Retana agreed. He reached in the drawer for a paper.

'Can I have fifty now?' Manuel asked.

'Sure,' said Retana. He took a fifty-peseta note out of his pocket-book and laid it, spread out flat, on the table.

Manuel picked it up and put it in his pocket.

'What about a cuadrilla?' he asked.

'There's the boys that always work for me nights,' Retana said. 'They're all right.'

'How about picadors?' Manuel asked.

'They're not much,' Retana admitted.

'I've got to have one good pic,' Manuel said.

'Get him then,' Retana said. 'Go and get him.'

'Not out of this,' Manuel said. 'I'm not paying for any cuadrilla out of sixty duros.'

Retana said nothing but looked at Manuel across the big desk.

'You know I've got to have one good pic,' Manuel said.

Retana said nothing but looked at Manuel from a long way off.

'It isn't right,' Manuel said.

Retana was still considering him, leaning back in his chair, considering him from a long way away.

'They're the regular pics,' he offered.

'I know,' Manuel said. 'I know your regular pics.'

Retana did not smile. Manuel knew it was over.

'All I want is an even break,' Manuel said reasoningly. 'When I go out there I want to be able to call my shots on the bull. It only takes one good picador.'

He was talking to a man who was no longer listening.

'If you want something extra,' Retana said, 'go and get it. There will be a regular cuadrilla out there. Bring as many of your own pics as you want. The charlotada is over by 10.30.'

'All right,' Manuel said. 'If that's the way you feel about it.'

'That's the way,' Retana said.

'I'll see you tomorrow night,' Manuel said.

'I'll be out there,' Retana said.

Manuel looked back. Retana was sitting forward looking at some papers. Manuel pulled the door tight until it clicked.

He went down the stairs and out of the door into the hot brightness of the street. It was very hot in the street and the light on the white buildings was sudden and hard on his eyes. He walked down the shady side of the steep street toward the Puerta del Sol. The shade felt solid and cool as running water. The heat came suddenly as he crossed the intersecting streets. Manuel saw no one he knew in all the people he passed.

Just before the Puerta del Sol he turned into a café.

It was quiet in the café. There were a few men sitting at tables against the wall. At one table four men played cards. Most of the men sat against the wall smoking, empty coffee-cups and liqueur-glasses before them on the tables. Manuel went through the long room to a small room in back. A man sat at a table in the corner asleep. Manuel sat down at one of the tables.

A waiter came in and stood beside Manuel's table.

'Have you seen Zurito?' Manuel asked him.

'He was in before lunch,' the waiter answered. 'He won't be back before five o'clock.'

'Bring me some coffee and milk and a shot of the ordinary,' Manuel said.

The waiter came back into the room carrying a tray with a big coffee-glass and a liqueur-glass on it. In his left hand he held a bottle of brandy. He swung these down to the table and a boy who had followed him poured coffee and milk into the glass from two shiny, spouted pots with long handles.

Manuel took off his cap and the waiter noticed his pigtail pinned forward on his head. He winked at the coffee-boy as he poured out the brandy into the little glass beside Manuel's coffee. The coffee-boy looked at Manuel's pale face curiously.

'You fighting here?' asked the waiter, corking up the bottle.

'Yes,' Manuel said. 'Tomorrow.'

The waiter stood there, holding the bottle on one hip.

'You in the Charlie Chaplins?' he asked.

The coffee-boy looked away, embarrassed.

'No. In the ordinary.'

'I thought they were going to have Chaves and Hernandez,' the waiter said.

227

'No. Me and another.'

Who? Chaves or Hernandez?'

'Hernandez, I think.'

'What's the matter with Chaves?'

'He got hurt.'

'Where did you hear that?'

'Retana.'

'Hey, Looie,' the waiter called to the next room, 'Chaves got cogida.'

Manuel had taken the wrapper off the lumps of sugar and dropped them into his coffee. He stirred it and drank it down, sweet, hot, and warming in his empty stomach. He drank off the brandy.

'Give me another shot of that,' he said to the waiter.

The waiter uncorked the bottle and poured the glass full, slopping another drink into the saucer. Another waiter had come up in front of the table. The coffee-boy was gone.

'Is Chaves hurt bad?' the second waiter asked Manuel.

'I don't know,' Manuel said, 'Retana didn't say.'

'A hell of a lot he cares,' the tall waiter said. Manuel had not seen him before. He must have just come up.

'If you stand in with Retana in this town, you're a made man,' the tall waiter said. 'If you aren't in with him, you might just as well go out and shoot yourself.'

'You said it,' the other waiter who had come in said. 'You said it then.'

'You're right I said it,' said the tall waiter. 'I know what I'm talking about when I talk about that bird.'

'Look what's he's done for Villalta,' the first waiter said.

'And that ain't all,' the tall waiter said. 'Look what he's done for Marcial Lalanda. Look what he's done for Nacional.'

'You said it, kid,' agreed the short waiter.

Manuel looked at them, standing talking in front of his table. He had drunk his second brandy. They had forgotten about him. They were not interested in him.

'Look at that bunch of camels,' the tall waiter went on. 'Did you ever see this Nacional II?'

'I seen him last Sunday didn't I?' the original waiter said.

'He's a giraffe,' the short waiter said.

'What did I tell you?' the tall waiter said. 'Those are Retana's boys.'

'Say, give me another shot of that,' Manuel said. He had poured the brandy the waiter had slopped over in the saucer into his glass and drank it while they were talking.

The original waiter poured his glass full mechanically, and the three of them went out of the room talking.

In the far corner the man was still asleep, snoring slightly on the intaking breath, his head back against the wall.

Manuel drank his brandy. He felt sleepy himself. It was too hot to go out into the town. Besides there was nothing to do. He wanted to see Zurito. He would go to sleep while he waited. He kicked his suitcase under the table to be sure it was there. Perhaps it would be better to put it back under the seat, against the wall. He leaned down and shoved it under. Then he leaned forward on the table and went to sleep.

When he woke there was some one sitting across the table from him. It was a big man with a heavy brown face like an Indian. He had been sitting there some time. He had waved the waiter away and sat reading the paper and occasionally looking down at Manuel, asleep, his head on the table. He read the paper laboriously, forming the words with his lips as he read. When it tired him he looked at Manuel. He sat heavily in the chair, his black Cordoba hat tipped forward.

Manuel sat up and looked at him.

'Hello, Zurito,' he said.

'Hello, kid,' the big man said.

'I've been asleep.' Manuel rubbed his forehead with the back of his fist.

'I thought maybe you were.'

'How's everything?'

'Good. How is everything with you?'

'Not so good.'

They were both silent. Zurito, the picador, looked at Manuel's white face. Manuel looked down at the picador's enormous hands folding the paper to put away in his pocket.

'I got a favor to ask you, Manos,' Manuel said.

Manosduros was Zurito's nickname. He never heard it

229

without thinking of his huge hands. He put them forward on the table self-consciously.

'Let's have a drink,' he said.

'Sure,' said Manuel.

The waiter came and went and came again. He went out of the room looking back at the two men at the table.

'What's the matter, Manolo?' Zurito set down his glass.

'Would you pic two bulls for me tomorrow night?' Manuel asked, looking up at Zurito across the table.

'No,' said Zurito. 'I'm not pic-ing.'

Manuel looked down at his glass. He had expected that answer; now he had it. Well, he had it.

'I'm sorry, Manolo, but I'm not pic-ing.' Zurito looked at his hands.

'That's all right,' Manuel said.

'I'm too old,' Zurito said.

'I just asked you,' Manuel said.

'Is it the nocturnal tomorrow?'

'That's it. I figured if I had just one good pic, I could get away with it.'

'How much are you getting?'

'Three hundred pesetas.'

'I get more than that for pic-ing.'

'I know,' said Manuel. 'I didn't have any right to ask you.'

'What do you keep on doing it for?' Zurito asked. 'Why don't you cut off your coleta, Manolo?'

'I don't know,' Manuel said.

'You're pretty near as old as I am,' Zurito said.

'I don't know,' Manuel said. 'I got to do it. If I can fix it so that I get an even break, that's all l want. I got to stick with it, Manos.'

'No, you don't.'

'Yes I do. I've tried keeping away from it.'

'I know how you feel. But it isn't right. You ought to get out and stay out.'

'I can't do it. Besides, I've been going good lately.'

Zurito looked at his face.

'You've been in the hospital.'

'But I was going great when I got hurt.'

230

Zurito said nothing. He tipped the cognac out of his saucer into his glass.

'The papers say they never saw a better faena,' Manuel said.

Zurito looked at him.

'You know when I get going I'm good,' Manuel said.

'You're too old,' the picador said.

'No,' said Manuel. 'You're ten years older than I am.'

'With me it's different.'

'I'm not too old,' Manuel said.

They sat silent, Manuel watching the picador's face.

'I was going great till I got hurt,' Manuel offered.

'You ought to have seen me, Manos,' Manuel said, reproachfully.

'I don't want to see you,' Zurito said. 'It makes me nervous.'

'You haven't seen me lately.'

'I've seen you plenty.'

Zurito looked at Manuel, avoiding his eyes.

'You ought to quit it, Manolo.'

'I can't,' Manuel said, 'I'm going good now, I tell you.'

Zurito leaned forward, his hands on the table.

'Listen. I'll pic for you and if you don't go big tomorrow night, you'll quit. See? Will you do that?'

'Sure.'

Zurito leaned back, relieved.

'You got to quit,' he said. 'No monkey business. You got to cut the coleta.'

'I won't have to quit,' Manuel said. 'You watch me. I've got the stuff.'

Zurito stood up. He felt tired from arguing.

'You got to quit,' he said. 'I'll cut your coleta myself.'

'No, you won't,' Manuel said. 'You won't have a chance.'

Zurito called the waiter.

'Come on,' said Zurito. 'Come on up to the house.'

Manuel reached under the seat for his suitcase. He was happy. He knew Zurito would pic for him. He was the best picador living. It was all simple now.

'Come on up to the house and we'll eat,' Zurito said.

Manuel stood in the patio de caballos waiting for the Charlie

Chaplins to be over. Zurito stood beside him. Where they stood it was dark. The high door that led into the bull ring was shut. Above them they heard a shout, then another shout of laughter. Then there was silence. Manuel liked the smell of the stables about the patio de caballos. It smelt good in the dark. There was another roar from the arena and then applause, prolonged applause, going on and on.

'You ever seen these fellows?' Zurito asked, big and looming beside Manuel in the dark.

'No,' Manuel said.

'They're pretty funny,' Zurito said. He smiled to himself in the dark.

The high, double, tight-fitting door into the bull-ring swung open and Manuel saw the ring in the hard light of the arc-lights, the plaza, dark all the way around, rising high; around the edge of the ring were running and bowing two men dressed like tramps, followed by a third in the uniform of a hotel bell-boy who stooped and picked up the hats and canes thrown down onto the sand and tossed them back up into the darkness.

The electric light went on in the patio.

'I'll climb onto one of those ponies while you collect the kids,' Zurito said.

Behind them came the jingle of the mules, coming out to go into the arena and be hitched onto the dead bull.

The members of the cuadrilla, who had been watching the burlesque from the runway between the barrera and the seats, came walking back and stood in a group talking, under the electric light in the patio. A good-looking lad in a silver-and-orange suit came up to Manuel and smiled.

'I'm Hernandez,' he said and put out his hand.

Manuel shook it.

'They're regular elephants we've got tonight,' the boy said cheerfully.

'They're big ones with horns,' Manuel agreed.

'You drew the worst lot,' the boy said.

'That's all right,' Manuel said. 'The bigger they are, the more meat for the poor.'

'Where did you get that one?' Hernandez grinned.

'That's an old one,' Manuel said. 'You line up your cuadrilla, so I can see what I've got.'

'You've got some good kids,' Hernandez said. He was very cheerful. He had been on twice before in nocturnals and was beginning to get a following in Madrid. He was happy the fight would start in a few minutes.

'Where are the pics?' Manuel asked.

'They're back in the corrals fighting about who gets the beautiful horses,' Hernandez grinned.

The mules came through the gate in a rush, the whips snapping, bells jangling and the young bull plowing a furrow of sand.

They formed up for the paseo as soon as the bull had gone through.

Manuel and Hernandez stood in front. The youths of the cuadrillas were behind, their heavy capes furled over their arms. In back, the four picadors, mounted, holding their steel-tipped push-poles erect in the half-dark of the corral.

'It's a wonder Retana wouldn't give us enough light to see the horses by,' one picador said.

'He knows we'll be happier if we don't get too good a look at these skins,' another pic answered.

'This thing I'm on barely keeps me off the ground,' the first picador said.

'Well, they're horses.'

'Sure, they're horses.'

They talked, sitting their gaunt horses in the dark.

Zurito said nothing. He had the only steady horse of the lot. He had tried him, wheeling him in the corrals and he responded to the bit and the spurs. He had taken the bandage off his right eye and cut the strings where they had tied his ears tight shut at the base. He was a good, solid horse, solid on his legs. That was all he needed. He intended to ride him all through the corrida. He had already, since he had mounted sitting in the half-dark in the big, quilted saddle, waiting for the paseo, pic-ed through the whole corrida in his mind. The other picadors went on talking on both sides of him. He did not hear them.

The two matadors stood together in front of their three

peones, their capes furled over their left arms in the same fashion. Manuel was thinking about the three lads in back of him. They were all three Madrilenos, like Hernandez, boys about nineteen. One of them, a gypsy, serious, aloof, and dark faced, he liked the look of. He turned.

'What's your name, kid?' he asked the gypsy.

'Fuentes,' the gypsy said.

'That's a good name,' Manuel said.

The gypsy smiled, showing his teeth.

'You take the bull and give him a little run when he comes out,' Manuel said.

'All right,' the gypsy said. His face was serious. He began to think about just what he would do.

'Here she goes,' Manuel said to Hernandez.

'All right. We'll go.'

Heads up, swinging with the music, their right arms swinging free, they stepped out, crossing the sanded arena under the arc-lights, the cuadrillas opening out behind, the picadors riding after, behind came the bull-ring servants and the jingling mules. The crowd applauded Hernandez as they marched across the arena. Arrogant, swinging, they looked straight ahead as they marched.

They bowed before the president, and the procession broke up into its component parts. The bull-fighters went over to the barrera and changed their heavy mantles for the light fighting capes. The mules went out. The picadors galloped jerkily around the ring, and two rode out the gate they had come in by. The servants swept the sand smooth.

Manuel drank a glass of water poured for him by one of Retana's deputies, who was acting as his manager and sword handler. Hernandez came over from speaking with his own manager.

'You got a good hand, kid,' Manuel complimented him.

'They like me,' Hernandez said happily.

'How did the paseo go?' Manuel asked Retana's man.

'Like a wedding,' said the handler. 'Fine. You came out like Joselito and Belmonte.'

Zurito rode by, a bulky equestrian statue. He wheeled his horse and faced him toward the toril on the far side of the ring where the bull would come out. It was strange under the arc-light. He pic-ed in the hot afternoon sun for big money. He didn't like this arc-light business. He wished they would get started.

Manuel went up to him.

'Pic him, Manos,' he said. 'Cut him down to size for me.'

'I'll pic him, kid,' Zurito spat on the sand. 'I'll make him jump out of the ring.'

'Lean on him, Manos,' Manuel said.

'I'll lean on him,' Zurito said. 'What's holding it up?'

'He's coming now,' Manuel said.

Zurito sat there, his feet in the box-stirrups, his great legs in the buckskin-covered armor gripping the horse, the reins in his left hand, the long pic held in his right hand, his broad hat well down over his eyes to shade them from the lights, watching the distant door of the toril. His horse's ears quivered. Zurito patted him with his left hand.

The red door of the toril swung back and for a moment Zurito looked into the empty passageway far across the arena. Then the bull came out in a rush, skidding on his four legs as he came out under the lights, then charging in a gallop, moving softly in a fast gallop, silent except as he woofed through wide nostrils as he charged, glad to be free after the dark pen.

In the first row of seats, slightly bored, leaning forward to write on the cement wall in front of his knees, the substitute bull-fight critic of *El Heraldo* scribbled: 'Campagnero, Negro, 42, came out at 90 miles an hour with plenty of gas –'

Manuel, leaning against the barrera, watching the bull, waved his hand and the gypsy ran out, trailing his cape. The bull, in full gallop, pivoted and charged the cape, his head down, his tail rising. The gypsy moved in a zigzag, and as he passed, the bull caught sight of him and abandoned the cape to charge the man. The gyp sprinted and vaulted the red fence of the barrera as the bull struck it with his horns. He tossed into it twice with his horns, banging into the wood blindly.

The critic of *El Heraldo* lit a cigarette and tossed the match at the bull, then wrote in his note-book, 'large and with enough horns to satisfy the cash customers, Campagnero showed a tendency to cut into the terrain of the bull-fighters.'

Manuel stepped out on the hard stand as the bull banged into the fence. Out of the corner of his eye he saw Zurito sitting the white horse close to the barrera, about a quarter of the way around the ring to the left. Manuel held the cape close in front of him, a fold in each hand, and shouted at the bull. 'Huh! Huh!' The bull turned, seemed to brace against the fence as he charged in a scramble, driving into the cape as Manuel side-stepped, pivoted on his heels with the charge of the bull, and swung the cape just ahead of the horns. At the end of the swing he was facing the bull again and held the cape at the same position close to his body, and pivoted again as the bull recharged. Each time, as he swung, the crowd shouted.

Four times he swung with the bull, lifting the cape so it billowed full, and each time bringing the bull around to charge again. Then, at the end of the fifth swing, he held the cape against his hip and pivoted, so the cape swung out like a ballet dancer's skirt and wound the bull around himself like a belt, to step clear, leaving the bull facing Zurito on the white horse, come up and planted firm, the horse facing the bull, its ears forward, its lips nervous, Zurito, his hat over his eyes, leaning forward, the long pole sticking out before and behind in a sharp angle under his right arm, held half-way down, the triangular iron point facing the bull.

El Heraldo's second-string critic, drawing on his cigarette, his eyes on the bull wrote: 'the veteran Manolo designed a series of acceptable veronicas, ending in a very Belmontistic recorte that earned applause from the regulars, and we entered the tercio of the cavalry.'

Zurito sat his horse, measuring the distance between the bull and the end of the pic. As he looked, the bull gathered himself together and charged, his eyes on the horse's chest. As he lowered his head to hook, Zurito sunk the point of the pic in the swelling hump of muscle above the bull's shoulder, leaning all his weight on the shaft, and with his left hand pulled the white horse into the air, front hoofs pawing, and swung him to the right as he pushed the bull under and through so the horns passed safely under the horse's belly and the horse came down,

236

quivering, the bull's tail brushing his chest as he charged the cape Hernandez offered him.

Hernandez ran sideways, taking the bull out and away with the cape, toward the other picador. He fixed him with a swing of the cape, squarely facing the horse and rider, and stepped back. As the bull saw the horse he charged. The picador's lance slid along his back, and as the shock of the charge lifted the horse, the picador was already half-way out of the saddle, lifting his right leg clear as he missed with the lance and falling to the left side to keep the horse between him and the bull. The horse, lifted and gored, crashed over with the bull driving into him, the picador gave a shove with his boots against the horse and lay clear, waiting to be lifted and hauled away and put on his feet.

Manuel let the bull drive into the fallen horse; he was in no hurry, the picador was safe; besides, it did a picador like that good to worry. He'd stay on longer next time. Lousy pics! He looked across the sand at Zurito a little way out from the barrera, his horse rigid, waiting.

'Huh!' he called to the bull, 'Tomar!' holding the cape in both hands so it would catch his eye. The bull detached himself from the horse and charged the cape, and Manuel, running sideways and holding the cape spread wide, stopped, swung on his heels, and brought the bull sharply around facing Zurito.

'Campagnero accepted a pair of varas for the death of one rosinante, with Hernandez and Manolo at the quites,' *El Heraldo's* critic wrote. 'He pressed on the iron and clearly showed he was no horse-lover. The veteran Zurito resurrected some of his old stuff with the pike-pole, notably the suerte –'

'Olé! Olé!' the man sitting beside him shouted. The shout was lost in the roar of the crowd, and he slapped the critic on the back. The critic looked up to see Zurito, directly below him, leaning far out over his horse, the length of the pic rising in a sharp angle under his armpit, holding the pic almost by the point, bearing down with all his weight, holding the bull off, the bull pushing and driving to get at the horse, and Zurito, far out, on top of him, holding him, holding him, and slowly pivoting the horse against the pressure, so that at last he was clear. Zurito felt the moment when the horse was clear and the bull could come past, and relaxed the absolute steel lock of his resistance, and the triangular steel point of the pic ripped in the bull's hump of shoulder muscle as he tore loose to find Hernandez's cape before his muzzle. He charged blindly into the cape and the boy took him out into the open arena.

Zurito sat patting his horse and looking at the bull charging the cape that Hernandez swung for him under the bright light while the crowd shouted.

'You see that one?' he said to Manuel.

'It was a wonder,' Manuel said.

'I got him that time,' Zurito said. 'Look at him now.'

At the conclusion of a closely turned pass of the cape the bull slid to his knees. He was up at once, but far out across the sand Manuel and Zurito saw the shine of the pumping flow of blood, smooth against the black of the bull's shoulder.

'I got him that time,' Zurito said.

'He's a good bull,' Manuel said.

'If they gave me another shot at him, I'd kill him,' Zurito said.

'They'll change the thirds on us,' Manuel said.

'Look at him now,' Zurito said.

'I got to go over there,' Manuel said, and started on a run for the other side of the ring, where the monos were leading a horse out by the bridle toward the bull, whacking him on the legs with rods and all, in a procession, trying to get him toward the bull, who stood, dropping his head, pawing, unable to make up his mind to charge.

Zurito, sitting his horse, walking him toward the scene, not missing any detail, scowled.

Finally the bull charged, the horse leaders ran for the barrera, the picador hit too far back, and the bull got under the horse, lifted him, threw him onto his back.

Zurito watched. The monos, in their red shirts, running out to drag the picador clear. The picador, now on his feet, swearing and flopping his arms. Manuel and Hernandez standing ready with their capes. And the bull, the great black bull, with a horse on his back, hooves dangling, the bridle caught in the horns. Black bull with a horse on his back, staggering short-legged, then arching his neck and lifting,

238

thrusting, charging to slide the horse off, horse sliding down. Then the bull into a lunging charge at the cape Manuel spread for him.

The bull was slower now, Manuel felt. He was bleeding badly. There was a sheen of blood all down his flank.

Manuel offered him the cape again. There he came, eyes open, ugly, watching the cape. Manuel stepped to the side and raised his arms, tightening the cape ahead of the bull for the veronica.

Now he was facing the bull. Yes, his head was going down a little. He was carrying it lower. That was Zurito.

Manuel flopped the cape; there he comes; he side-stepped and swung in another veronica. He's shooting awfully accurately, he thought. He's had enough fight, so he's watching now. He's hunting now. Got his eye on me. But I always give him the cape.

He shook the cape at the bull; there he comes; he sidestepped. Awful close that time. I don't want to work that close to him.

The edge of the cape was wet with blood where it had swept along the bull's back as he went by.

All right, here's the last one.

Manuel, facing the bull, having turned with him each charge, offered the cape with his two hands. The bull looked at him. Eyes watching, horns straight forward, the bull looked at him, watching.

'Huh!' Manuel said, 'Toro!' and leaning back, swung the cape forward. Here he comes. He side-stepped, swung the cape in back of him, and pivoted, so the bull followed a swirl of cape and then was left with nothing, fixed by the pass, dominated by the cape. Manuel swung the cape under his muzzle with one hand, to show the bull was fixed, and walked away.

There was no applause.

Manuel walked across the sand towards the barrera, while Zurito rode out of the ring. The trumpet had blown to change the act to the planting of the banderillos while Manuel had been working with the bull. He had not consciously noticed it. The monos were spreading canvas over the two dead horses and sprinkling sawdust around them.

Manuel came up to the barrera for a drink of water. Retana's man handed him the heavy porous jug.

Fuentes, the tall gypsy, was standing holding a pair of banderillos, holding them together, slim, red sticks, fish-hook points out. He looked at Manuel.

'Go on out there,' Manuel said.

The gypsy trotted out. Manuel set down the jug and watched. He wiped his face with his handkerchief.

The critic of *El Heraldo* reached for the bottle of warm champagne that stood between his feet, he took a drink, and finished his paragraph.

'– the aged Manolo rated no applause for a vulgar series of lances with the cape and we entered the third of the palings.'

Alone in the center of the ring the bull stood, still fixed. Fuentes, tall, flat-backed, walking towards him arrogantly, his arms spread out, the two slim, red sticks, one in each hand, held by the fingers, points straight forward. Fuentes walked forward. Back of him and to one side was a peon with a cape. The bull looked at him and was no longer fixed.

His eyes watched Fuentes, now standing still. Now he leaned back, calling to him. Fuentes twitched the two banderillos and the light on the steel points caught the bull's eye.

His tail went up and he charged.

He came straight, his eyes on the man. Fuentes stood still, leaning back, the banderillos pointing forward. As the bull lowered his head to hook, Fuentes leaned backward, his arms came together and rose, his two hands, touching, the banderillos two descending red lines, and leaning forward drove the points into the bull's shoulder, leaning far in over the bull's horns and pivoting on the two upright sticks, his legs tight together, his body, curving to one side to let the bull pass.

'Olé!' from the crowd.

The bull was hooking wildly, jumping like a trout, all four feet off the ground. The red shaft of the banderillos tossed as he jumped.

Manuel, standing at the barrera, noticed that he looked always to the right.

'Tell him to drop the next pair on the right,' he said to the kid who started to run out to Fuentes with the new banderillos.

A heavy hand fell on his shoulder. It was Zurito.

'How do you feel, kid?' he asked.

Manuel was watching the bull.

Zurito leaned forward on the barrera, leaning the weight of his body on his arms. Manuel turned to him.

'You're going good,' Zurito said.

Manuel shook his head. He had nothing to do now until the next third. The gypsy was very good with the banderillos. The bull would come to him in the next third in good shape. He was a good bull. It had all been easy up to now. The final stuff with the sword was all he worried over. He did not really worry. He did not even think about it. But standing there he had a heavy sense of apprehension. He looked out at the bull, planning his faena, his work with the red cloth that was to reduce the bull, to make him manageable.

The gypsy was walking out toward the bull again, walking heel-and-toe, insultingly, like a ballroom dancer, the red shafts of the banderillos, twitching with his walk. The bull watched him, not fixed now, hunting him, but waiting to get close enough so he could be sure of getting him, getting the horns into him.

As Fuentes walked forward the bull charged. Fuentes ran across the quarter of a circle as the bull charged and, as he passed running backwards, stopped, swung forward, rose on his toes, arms straight out, and sunk the banderillos straight down into the tight of the big shoulder muscles as the bull missed him.

The crowd were wild about it.

'That kid won't stay in this night stuff long,' Retana's man said to Zurito.

'He's good,' Zurito said.

'Watch him now.'

They watched.

Fuentes was standing with his back against the barrera. Two of the caudrilla were back of him, with their capes ready to flop over the fence to distract the bull.

The bull, with its tongue out, his barrel heaving, was

watching the gypsy. He thought he had him now. Back against the red planks. Only a short charge away. The bull watched him.

The gypsy bent back, drew back his arms, the banderillos pointed at the bull. He called to the bull, stamping one foot. The bull was suspicious. He wanted the man. No more barbs in the shoulder.

Fuentes walked a little closer to the bull. Bent back. Called again. Somebody in the crowd shouted a warning.

'He's too damn close,' Zurito said.

'Watch him,' Retana's man said.

Leaning back, inciting the bull with the banderillos, Fuentes jumped, both feet off the ground. As he jumped the bull's tail rose and he charged. Fuentes came down on his toes, arms straight out, whole body arching forward, and drove the shafts straight down as he swung his body clear of the right horn.

The bull crashed into the barrera where the flopping capes had attracted his eye as he lost the man.

The gypsy came running along the barrera toward Manuel, taking the applause of the crowd. His vest was ripped where he had not quite cleared the point of the horn. He was happy about it, showing it to the spectators. He made the tour of the ring. Zurito saw him go by, smiling, pointing at his vest. He smiled.

Somebody else was planting the last pair of banderillos. Nobody was paying any attention.

Retana's man tucked a baton inside the red cloth of a muleta, folded the cloth over it, and handed it over the barrera to Manuel. He reached in the leather sword-case, took out a sword, and holding it by its leather scabbard, reached it over the fence to Manuel. Manuel pulled the blade out by the red hilt and the scabbard fell limp.

He looked at Zurito. The big man saw he was sweating.

'Now you get him, kid,' Zurito said.

Manuel nodded

'He's in good shape,' Zurito said.

'Just like you want him,' Retana's man assured him.

Manuel nodded.

The trumpeter, up under the roof, blew for the final act, and

Manuel walked across the arena toward where, up in the dark boxes, the president must be.

In the front row of seats the substitute bull-fight critic of *El Heraldo* took a long drink of the warm champagne. He had decided it was not worth while to write a running story and would write up the corrida back in the office. What the hell was it anyway? Only a nocturnal. If he missed anything he would get it out of the morning papers. He took another drink of the champagne. He had a date at Maxim's at twelve. Who were these bull-fighters anyway? Kids and bums. A bunch of bums. He put his pad of paper in his pocket and looked over toward Manuel, standing very much alone in the ring, gesturing with his hat in a salute toward a box he could not see high up in the dark plaza. Out in the ring the bull stood quiet, looking at nothing.

'I dedicate this bull to you, Mr President, and to the public of Madrid, the most intelligent and generous of the world,' was what Manuel was saying. It was a formula. He said it all. It was a little long for nocturnal use.

He bowed at the dark, straightened, tossed his hat over his shoulder, and carrying the muleta in his left hand and the sword in his right, walked out toward the bull.

Manuel walked toward the bull. The bull looked at him; his eyes were quick. Manuel noticed the way the banderillos hung down on his left shoulder and the steady sheen of blood from Zurito's pic-ing. He noticed the way the bull's feet were. As he walked forward, holding the muleta in his left hand and the sword in his right, he watched the bull's feet. The bull could not charge without gathering his feet together. Now he stood square on them, dully.

Manuel walked toward him, watching his feet. This was all right. He could do this. He must work to get the bull's head down, so he could go in past the horns and kill him. He did not think about the sword, not about killing the bull. He thought about one thing at a time. The coming things oppressed him, though. Walking forward, watching the bull's feet, he saw successively his eyes, his wet muzzle and the wide, forward pointing spread of his horns. The bull had light circles about his eyes. His eyes watched Manuel. He felt he was going to get this little one with the white face.

243

Standing still now and spreading the red cloth of the muleta with the sword, pricking the point into the cloth so that the sword, now held in his left hand, spread the red flannel like the jib of a boat, Manuel noticed the points of the bull's horns. One of them was splintered from banging against the barrera. The other was sharp as a porcupine quill. Manuel noticed while spreading the muleta that the white base of the horn was stained red. While he noticed these things he did not lose sight of the bull's feet. The bull watched Manuel steadily.

He's on the defensive now, Manuel thought. He's reserving himself. I've got to bring him out of that and get his head down. Always get his head down. Zurito had his head down once, but he's come back. He'll bleed when I start him going and that will bring it down.

Holding the muleta, with the sword in his left hand widening it in front of him, he called to the bull.

The bull looked at him.

He leaned back insultingly and shook the wide-spread flannel.

The bull saw the muleta. It was a bright scarlet under the arc-light. The bull's legs tightened.

Here he comes. Whoosh! Manuel turned as the bull came and raised the muleta so that it passed over the bull's horns and swept down his broad back from head to tail. The bull had gone clean up in the air with the charge. Manuel had not moved.

At the end of the pass the bull turned like a cat coming around a corner and faced Manuel.

He was on the offensive again. His heaviness was gone. Manuel noted the fresh blood shining down the black shoulder and dripping down the bull's leg. He drew the sword out of the muleta and held it in his right hand. The muleta held low down in his left hand, leaning toward the left, he called to the bull. The bull's legs tightened, his eyes on the muleta. Here he comes, Manuel thought. Yuh!

He swung with the charge, sweeping the muleta ahead of the bull, his feet firm, the sword following the curve, a point of light under the arcs.

The bull recharged as the pase natural finished and Manuel

raised the muleta for a pase de pecho. Firmly planted, the bull came by his chest under the raised muleta. Manuel leaned his head back to avoid the clattering banderillo shafts. The hot, black bull body touched his chest as it passed.

Too damn close, Manuel thought. Zurito, leaning on the barrera, spoke rapidly to the gypsy, who trotted out toward Manuel with a cape. Zurito pulled his hat down low and looked out across the arena at Manuel.

Manuel was facing the bull again, the muleta held low and to the left. The bull's head was down as he watched the muleta.

'If it was Belmonte doing that stuff, they'd go crazy,' Retana's man said.

Zurito said nothing. He was watching Manuel out in the center of the arena.

'Where did the boss dig this fellow up?' Retana's man asked.

'Out of the hospital,' Zurito said.

'That's where he's going damn quick,' Retana's man said. Zurito turned on him.

'Knock on that,' he said, pointing to the barrera.

'I was just kidding, man,' Retana's man said.

'Knock on the wood.'

Retana's man leaned forward and knocked three times on the barrera.

'Watch the faena,' Zurito said.

Out in the center of the ring, under the lights, Manuel was kneeling, facing the bull, and as he raised the muleta in both hands the bull charged, tail up.

Manuel swung his body clear and, as the bull recharged, brought around the muleta in a half-circle that pulled the bull to his knees.

'Why, that one's a great bull-fighter,' Retana's man said.

'No, he's not,' said Zurito.

Manuel stood up and, the muleta in his left hand, the sword in his right, acknowledged the applause from the dark plaza.

The bull had humped himself up from his knees and stood waiting, his head hung low.

Zurito spoke to two of the other lads of the cuadrilla and they ran out to stand back of Manuel with their capes. There were four men back of him now. Hernandez had followed him since he first came out with the muleta. Fuentes stood watching, his cape held against his body, tall, in repose, watching lazy-eyed. Now the two came up. Hernandez motioned them to stand one at each side. Manuel stood alone, facing the bull.

Manuel waved back the men with the capes. Stepping back cautiously, they saw his face was white and sweating.

Didn't they know enough to keep back? Did they want to catch the bull's eye with the capes after he was fixed and ready? He had enough to worry about without that kind of thing.

The bull was standing, his four feet square, looking at the muleta. Manuel furled the muleta in his left hand. The bull's eyes watched it. His body was heavy on his feet. He carried his head low, but not too low.

Manuel lifted the muleta at him. The bull did not move. Only his eyes watched.

He's all lead, Manuel thought. He's all square. He's framed right. He'll take it.

He thought in bull-fight terms. Sometimes he had a thought and a particular piece of slang would not come into his mind and he could not realize the thought. His instincts and his knowledge worked automatically, and his brain worked slowly and in words. He knew all about bulls. He did not have to think about them. He just did the right thing. His eyes noted things and his body performed the necessary measures without thought. If he thought about it, he would be gone.

Now, facing the bull, he was conscious of many things at the same time. There were the horns, the one splintered, the other smoothly sharp, the need to profile himself towards the left horn, lance himself short and straight, lower the muleta so the bull would follow it, and, going in over the horns, put the sword all the way into a little spot about as big as a five-peseta piece straight in the back of the neck, between the sharp pitch of the bull's shoulders. He must do all this and must then come out from between the horns. He was conscious he must do all this, but his only thought was in words: 'Corto y derecho.'

'Corto y derecho,' he thought, furling the muleta. Short and straight. Corto y derecho, he drew the sword out of the muleta, profiled on the splintered left horn, dropped the muleta across his body, so his right hand with the sword on the level with his eye made the sign of the cross, and, rising on his toes, sighted along the dipping blade of the sword at the spot high up between the bull's shoulders.

Corto y derecho he launched himself on the bull.

There was a shock, and he felt himself go up in the air. He pushed on the sword as he went up and over, and it flew out of his hand. He hit the ground and the bull was on him. Manuel, lying on the ground, kicked at the bull's muzzle with his slippered feet. Kicking, kicking, the bull after him, missing him in his excitement, bumping him with his head, driving the horns into the sand. Kicking like a man keeping a ball in the air, Manuel kept the bull from getting a clean thrust at him.

Manuel felt the wind on his back from the capes flopping at the bull, and then the bull was gone, gone over him in a rush. Dark, as his belly went over. Not even stepped on.

Manuel stood up and picked up the muleta. Fuentes handed him the sword. It was bent where it had struck the shoulder-blade. Manuel straightened it on his knee and ran towards the bull, standing now beside one of the dead horses. As he ran, his jacket flopped where it had been ripped under his armpit.

'Get him out of there,' Manuel shouted to the gypsy. The bull had smelled the blood of the dead horse and ripped into the canvas-cover with his horns. He charged Fuentes's cape, with the canvas hanging from his splintered horn, and the crowd laughed. Out in the ring, he tossed his head to rid himself of the canvas. Hernandez, running up from behind him, grabbed the end of the canvas and neatly lifted it off the horn.

The bull followed it in a half-charge and stopped still. He was on the defensive again. Manuel was walking towards him with the sword and the muleta. Manuel swung the muleta before him. The bull would not charge.

Manuel profiled toward the bull, sighting along the dipping blade of the sword. The bull was motionless, seemingly dead on his feet, incapable of another charge.

Manuel rose to his toes, sighting along the steel, and charged.

Again there was the shock and he felt himself being borne back in a rush, to strike hard on the sand. There was no chance of kicking this time. The bull was on top of him. Manuel lay as though dead, his head on his arms, and the bull bumped him. Bumped his back, bumped his face in the sand. He felt the horn go into the sand between his folded arms. The bull hit him in the small of the back. His face drove into the sand. The horn drove through one of his sleeves and the bull ripped it off. Manuel was tossed clear and the bull followed the capes.

Manuel got up, found the sword and muleta, tried the point of the sword with his thumb, and ran towards the barrera for a new sword.

Retana's man handed him the sword over the edge of the barrera.

'Wipe off your face,' he said.

Manuel, running back again toward the bull, wiped his bloody face with his handkerchief. He had not seen Zurito. Where was Zurito?

The cuadrilla had stepped away from the bull and waited with their capes. The bull stood, heavy and dull again after the action.

Manuel walked toward him with the muleta. He stopped and shook it. The bull did not respond. He passed it right and left, left and right before the bull's muzzle. The bull's eyes watched it and turned with the swing, but he would not charge. He was waiting for Manuel.

Manuel was worried. There was nothing to do but go in. Corto y derecho. He profiled close to the bull, crossed the muleta in front of his body and charged. As he pushed in the sword, he jerked his body to the left to clear the horn. The bull passed him and the sword shot up in the air, twinkling under the arc-lights, to fall red-hilted on the sand.

Manuel ran over and picked it up. It was bent and he straightened it over his knee.

As he came running toward the bull, fixed again now, he passed Hernandez standing with his cape.

'He's all done,' the boy said encouragingly.

Manuel nodded, wiping his face. He put the bloody handkerchief in his pocket.

There was the bull. He was close to the barrera now. Damn him. Maybe he was all bone. Maybe there was not any place

248

for the sword to go in. The hell there wasn't! He'd show them.

He tried a pass with the muleta and the bull did not move. Manuel chopped the muleta back and forth in front of the bull. Nothing doing.

He furled the muleta, drew the sword out, profiled and drove in on the bull. He felt the sword buckle as he shoved it in, leaning his weight on it, and then it shot high in the air, end-over-ending into the crowd. Manuel jerked clear as the sword jumped.

The first cushions thrown down out of the dark missed him. Then one hit him in the face, his bloody face looking toward the crowd. They were coming down fast. Spotting the sand. Somebody threw an empty champagne-bottle from close range. It hit Manuel on the foot. He stood there watching the dark where the things were coming from. Then something whished through the air and struck by him. Manuel leaned over and picked it up. It was his sword. He straightened it over his knee and gestured with it to the crowd.

'Thank you,' he said. 'Thank you.'

Oh, the dirty bastards! Dirty bastards! Oh, the lousy, dirty bastards! He kicked into a cushion as he ran.

There was the bull. The same as ever. All right, you dirty, lousy bastard!

Manuel passed the muleta in front of the bull's black muzzle.

Nothing doing.

You won't! All right. He stepped close and jammed the sharp peak of the muleta into the bull's damp muzzle.

The bull was on him as he jumped back and as he tripped on a cushion he felt the horn go into him, into his side. He grabbed the horn with his two hands and rode backward, holding tight onto the place. The bull tossed him and he was clear. He lay still. It was all right. The bull was gone.

He got up coughing and feeling broken and gone. The dirty bastards!

'Give me the sword,' he shouted. 'Give me the stuff.'

Fuentes came up with the muleta and the sword.

Hernandez put his arm around him.

'Go on to the infirmary, man,' he said. 'Don't be a damn fool.'

'Get away from me,' Manuel said. 'Get to hell away from me.'

He twisted free. Hernandez shrugged his shoulders. Manuel ran toward the bull.

There was the bull standing, heavy, firmly planted.

All right, you bastard! Manuel drew the sword out of the muleta, sighted with the same movement, and flung himself onto the bull. He felt the sword go in all the way. Right up to the guard. Four fingers and his thumb into the bull. The blood was hot on his knuckles, and he was on top of the bull.

The bull lurched with him as he lay on, and seemed to sink; then he was standing clear. He looked at the bull going down slowly over on his side, then suddenly four feet in the air.

Then he gestured at the crowd, his hand warm from the bull blood.

All right, you bastards! he wanted to say something, but he started to cough. It was hot and choking. He looked down for the muleta. He must go over and salute the president. President hell! He was sitting down looking at something. It was the bull. His four feet up. Thick tongue out. Things crawling around on his belly and under his legs. Crawling where the hair was thin. Dead bull. To hell with the bull! To hell with them all! He started to get to his feet and commenced to cough. He sat down again, coughing. Somebody came and pushed him up.

They carried him across the ring to the infirmary, running with him across the sand, standing blocked at the gate as the mules came in, then around under the dark passageway, men grunting as they took him up the stairway, and then laid him down.

The doctor and two men in white were waiting for him. They laid him out on the table. They were cutting away his shirt. Manuel felt tired. His whole chest felt scalding inside. He started to cough and they held something to his mouth. Everybody was very busy.

There was an electric light in his eyes. He shut his eyes.

He heard someone coming very heavily up the stairs. Then he did not hear it. Then he heard a noise far off. That was the crowd. Well, somebody would have to kill his other bull. They had cut away all his shirt. The doctor smiled at him. There was Retana.

'Hello, Retana!' Manuel said. He could not hear his voice. Retana smiled at him and said something. Manuel could not hear it.

Zurito stood beside the table, bending over where the doctor was working. He was in his picador clothes, without his hat.

Zurito said something to him. Manuel could not hear it.

Zurito was speaking to Retana. One of the men in white smiled and handed Retana a pair of scissors. Retana gave them to Zurito. Zurito said something to Manuel. He could not hear it.

To hell with this operating-table. He'd been on plenty of operating-tables before. He was not going to die. There would be a priest if he was going to die.

Zurito was saying something to him. Holding up the scissors.

That was it. They were going to cut off his coleta. They were going to cut off his pigtail.

Manuel sat up on the operating-table. The doctor stepped back, angry. Some one grabbed him and held him.

'You couldn't do a thing like that, Manos,' he said.

He heard suddenly, clearly, Zurito's voice.

'That's all right,' Zurito said. 'I won't do it. I was joking.'

'I was going good,' Manuel said. 'I didn't have any luck. That was all.'

Manuel lay back. They had put something over his face. It was all familiar. He inhaled deeply. He felt very tired. He was very, very tired. They took the thing away from his face.

'I was going good,' Manuel said weakly. 'I was going great.'

Retana looked at Zurito and started for the door.

'I'll stay here with him,' Zurito said.

Retana shrugged his shoulders.

Manuel opened his eyes and looked at Zurito.

251

'Wasn't I going good, Manos?' he asked, for confirmation.

'Sure,' said Zurito. 'You were going great.'

The doctor's assistant put the cone over Manuel's face and he inhaled deeply. Zurito stood awkwardly, watching.

In Another Country

In the fall the war was always there, but we did not go to it any more. It was cold in the fall in Milan and the dark came very early. Then the electric lights came on, and it was pleasant along the streets looking in the windows. There was much game hanging outside the shops, and snow powdered in the fur of the foxes and the wind blew their tails. The deer hung stiff and heavy and empty, and small birds flew in the wind and the wind turned their feathers. It was a cold fall and the wind came down from the mountains.

We were all at the hospital every afternoon, and there were different ways of walking across the town through the dusk to the hospital. Two of the ways were alongside canals, but they were long. Always, though, you crossed a bridge across a canal to enter the hospital. There was a choice of three bridges. On one of them a woman sold roasted chestnuts. It was warm, standing in front of her charcoal fire, and the chestnuts were warm afterward in your pocket. The hospital was very old and very beautiful, and you entered through a gate and walked across a courtyard and out a gate on the other side. There were usually funerals starting from the courtyard. Beyond the old hospital were the new brick pavilions, and there we met every afternoon and were all very polite and interested in what was the matter, and sat in the machines that were to make so much difference.

The doctor came up to the machine where I was sitting and said: 'What did you like best to do before the war? Did you practise a sport?'

I said: 'Yes, football.'

'Good,' he said. 'You will be able to play football again better than ever.'

My knee did not bend and the leg dropped straight from the knee to the ankle without a calf, and the machine was to bend the knee and make it move as in riding a tricycle. But it did not bend yet, and instead the machine lurched when it came to the bending part. The doctor said: 'That will all pass. You are a fortunate young man. You will play football again like a champion.'

In the next machine was a major who had a little hand like a baby's. He winked at me when the doctor examined his hand, which was between two leather straps that bounced up and down and flapped the stiff fingers, and said: 'And will I too play football, captain-doctor?' He had been a very great fencer, and before the war the greatest fencer in Italy.

The doctor went to his office in a back room and brought a photograph which showed a hand that had been withered almost as small as the major's, before it had taken a machine course, and after was a little larger. The major held the photograph with his good hand and looked at it very carefully. 'A wound?' he asked.

'An industrial accident,' the doctor said.

'Very interesting, very interesting,' the major said, and handed it back to the doctor.

'You have confidence?'

'No,' said the major.

There were three boys who came each day who were about the same age I was. They were all three from Milan, and one of them was to be a lawyer, and one was to be a painter, and one had intended to be a soldier, and after we were finished with the machines, sometimes we walked back together to the Café Cova, which was next door to the Scala. We walked the short way through the communist quarter because we were four together. The people hated us because we were officers, and from a wine-shop someone called out, 'A basso gli ufficiali!' as we passed. Another boy who walked with us sometimes and made us five wore a black silk handkerchief across his face because he had no nose then and his face was to be rebuilt. He had gone out to the front from the military academy and been wounded within an hour after he had gone into the front line for the first time. They rebuilt his face, but he came from a very old family and they could never get the nose exactly right. He went to South America and worked in a bank. But this was a long time ago, and then we did not any of us know how it was going to be afterward. We only knew that there was always the war, but that we were not going to it any more.

We all had the same medals, except the boy with the black silk bandage across his face, and he had not been at the front long enough to get any medals. The tall boy with a very pale face who was to be a lawyer had been a lieutenant of Arditi and had three medals of the sort we each had only one of. He had lived a very long time with death and was a little detached. We were all a little detached, and there was nothing that held us together except that we met every afternoon at the hospital. Although, as we walked to the Cova through the tough part of town, walking in the dark, with light and singing coming out of the wine-shops, and sometimes having to walk into the street when the men and women would crowd together on the sidewalk so that we would have had to jostle them to get by, we felt held together by there being something that had happened that they, the people who disliked us, did not understand.

We ourselves all understood the Cova, where it was rich and warm and not too brightly lighted, and noisy and smoky at certain hours, and there were always girls at the tables and the illustrated papers on a rack on the wall. The girls at the Cova were very patriotic, and I found that the most patriotic people in Italy were the café girls – and I believe they are still patriotic.

The boys at first were very polite about my medals and asked me what I had done to get them. I showed them the papers, which were written in very beautiful language and full of *fratellanza* and *abnegazione,* but which really said, with the adjectives removed, that I had been given the medals because I was an American. After that their manner changed a little toward me, although I was their friend against outsiders. I was a friend, but I was never really one of them after they had read the citations, because it had been different with them and they had done very different things to get their medals. I had been wounded, it was true; but we all knew that being wounded, after all, was really an accident. I was never ashamed of the ribbons, though, and sometimes, after the cocktail hour, I would imagine myself having done all the things they had done to get their medals; but walking home at night through the empty streets with the cold wind and all the shops closed, trying to keep near the street lights, I knew that I would never have done such things, and I was very much afraid to die, and often lay in bed at night by myself, afraid to die and wondering how I would be when I went back to the front again.

The three with the medals were like hunting-hawks; and I was not a hawk, although I might seem a hawk to those who had never hunted; they, the three, knew better and so we drifted apart. But I stayed good friends with the boy who had been wounded his first day at the front, because he would never know how he would have turned out; so he could never be accepted either, and I liked him because I thought perhaps he would not have turned out to be a hawk either.

The major, who had been the great fencer, did not believe in bravery, and spent much time while we sat in the machines correcting my grammar. He had complimented me on how I spoke Italian, and we talked together very easily. One day I had said that Italian seemed such an easy language to me that I could not take a great interest in it; everything was so easy to say. 'Ah, yes,' the major said. 'Why, then, do you not take up the use of grammar?' So we took up the use of grammar, and soon Italian was such a difficult language that I was afraid to talk to him until I had the grammar straight in my mind.

The major came very regularly to the hospital. I do not think he ever missed a day, although I am sure he did not believe in the machines. There was a time when none of us believed in the machines, and one day the major said it was all nonsense. The machines were new then and it was we who were to prove them. It was an idiotic idea, he said, 'a theory, like any other.' I had not learned my grammar, and he said I was a stupid impossible disgrace, and he was a fool to have bothered with me. He was a small man and sat straight up in his chair with his right hand thrust into the machine and looked straight ahead at the wall while the straps thumped up and down with his fingers in them.

'What will you do when the war is over, if it is over?' he asked me. 'Speak grammatically!'

'I will go to the States.'

'Are you married?'

'No, but I hope to be.'

'The more of a fool you are,' he said. He seemed very angry. 'A man must not marry.'

'Why, Signor Maggiore?'

'Don't call me "Signor Maggiore".'

'Why must not a man marry?'

'He cannot marry. He cannot marry,' he said angrily. 'If he is to lose everything, he should not place himself in a position to lose that. He should not place himself in a position to lose. He should find things he cannot lose.'

He spoke very angrily and bitterly, and looked straight ahead while he talked.

'But why should he necessarily lose it?'

'He'll lose it,' the major said. He was looking at the wall. Then he looked down at the machine and jerked his little hand out from between the straps and slapped it hard against his thigh. 'He'll lose it,' he almost shouted. 'Don't argue with me!' Then he called to the attendant who ran the machines. 'Come and turn this damned thing off.'

He went back into the other room for the light treatment and the massage. Then I heard him ask the doctor if he might use his telephone and he shut the door. When he came back into the room, I was sitting in another machine. He was wearing his cape and had his cap on, and he came directly towards my machine and put his arm on my shoulder.

'I am so sorry,' he said, and patted me on the shoulder with his good hand. 'I would not be rude. My wife has just died. You must forgive me.'

'Oh –' I said, feeling sick for him. 'I am so sorry.'

He stood there biting his lower lip. 'It is very difficult,' he said. 'I cannot resign myself.'

He looked straight past me and out through the window. Then he began to cry. 'I am utterly unable to resign myself,' he

257

said and choked. And then crying, his head up looking at nothing, carrying himself straight and soldierly, with tears on both his cheeks and biting his lips, he walked past the machines and out of the door.

The doctor told me that the major's wife, who was very young and whom he had not married until he was definitely invalided out of the war, had died of pneumonia. She had been sick only a few days. No one expected her to die. The major did not come to the hospital for three days. Then he came at the usual hour, wearing a black band on the sleeve of his uniform. When he came back, there were large framed photographs around the wall, of all sorts of wounds before and after they had been cured by the machines. In front of the machine the major used were three photographs of hands like his that were completely restored. I do not know where the doctor got them. I always understood we were the first to use the machines. The photographs did not make much difference to the major because he only looked out of the window.

Hills Like White Elephants

The hills across the valley of the Ebro were long and white. On this side there was no shade and no trees and the station was between two lines of rails in the sun. Close against the side of the station there was the warm shadow of the building and a curtain, made of strings of bamboo beads, hung across the open door into the bar, to keep out flies. The American and the girl with him sat at a table in the shade, outside the building. It was very hot and the express from Barcelona would come in forty minutes. It stopped at this junction for two minutes and went on to Madrid.

'What should we drink?' the girl asked. She had taken off her hat and put it on the table.

'It's pretty hot,' the man said.

'Let's drink beer.'

'Dos cervezas,' the man said into the curtain.

'Big ones?' a woman asked from the doorway.

'Yes. Two big ones.'

The woman brought two glasses of beer and two felt pads. She put the felt pads and the beer glasses on the table and looked at the man and the girl. The girl was looking off at the line of hills. They were white in the sun and the country was brown and dry.

'They look like white elephants,' she said.

'I've never seen one.' The man drank his beer.

'No, you wouldn't have.'

'I might have,' the man said. 'Just because you say I wouldn't have doesn't prove anything.'

The girl looked at the bead curtain. 'They've painted something on it,' she said. 'What does it say?'

'Anis del Toro. It's a drink.'

'Could we try it?'

The man called 'Listen' through the curtain. The woman came out from the bar.

'Four reales.'

'He want two Anis del Toro.'

'With water?'

'Do you want it with water?'

'I don't know,' the girl said. 'Is it good with water?'

'It's all right.'

'You want them with water?' asked the woman.

'Yes, with water.'

'It tastes like licorice,' the girl said and put the glass down.

'That's the way with everything.'

'Yes,' said the girl. 'Everything tastes of licorice. Especially all the things you've waited so long for, like absinthe.'

'Oh, cut it out.'

'You started it,' the girl said. 'I was being amused. I was having a fine time.'

'Well, let's try and have a fine time.'

'All right. I was trying. I said the mountains looked like white elephants. Wasn't that bright?'

'That was bright.'

'I wanted to try this new drink. That's all we do, isn't it – look at things and try new drinks?'

'I guess so.'

The girl looked across at the hills.

'They're lovely hills,' she said. 'They don't really look like white elephants. I just meant the colouring of their skin through the trees.'

'Should we have another drink?'

'All right.'

The warm wind blew the bead curtain against the table.

'The beer's nice and cool,' the man said.

'It's lovely,' the girl said.

'It's really an awfully simple operation, Jig,' the man said. 'It's not really an operation at all.'

The girl looked at the ground the table legs rested on.

'I know you wouldn't mind it, Jig. It's really not anything. It's just to let the air in.'

The girl did not say anything.

'I'll go with you and I'll stay with you all the time. They just let the air in and then it's all perfectly natural.'

'Then what will we do afterward?'

'We'll be fine afterward. Just like we were before.'

'What makes you think so?'

'That's the only thing that bothers us. It's the only thing that's made us unhappy.'

The girl looked at the bead curtain, put her hand out and took hold of two of the strings of beads.

'And you think then we'll be all right and be happy.'

'I know we will. You don't have to be afraid. I've known lots of people that have done it.'

'So have I,' said the girl. 'And afterward they were all so happy.'

'Well,' the man said, 'if you don't want to you don't have to. I wouldn't have you do it if you didn't want to. But I know it's perfectly simple.'

'And you really want to?'

'I think it's the best thing to do. But I don't want you to do it if you don't really want to.'

'And if I do you'll be happy and things will be like they were and you'll love me?'

'I love you now. You know I love you.'

'I know. But if I do it, then it will be nice again if I say things are like white elephants, and you'll like it?'

'I'll love it. I love it now but I just can't think about it. You know how I get when I worry.'

'If I do it you won't ever worry?'

'I won't worry about that because it's perfectly simple.'

'Then I'll do it. Because I don't care about me.'

'What do you mean?'

'I don't care about me.'

'Well, I care about you.'

'Oh, yes. But I don't care about me. And I'll do it and then everything will be fine.'

'I don't want you to do it if you feel that way.'

The girl stood up and walked to the end of the station. Across, on the other side, were fields of grain and trees along the banks of the Ebro. Far away, beyond the river, were mountains. The shadow of a cloud moved across the field of grain and she saw the river through the trees.

'And we could have all this,' she said. 'And we could have everything and every day we make it more impossible.'

'What did you say?'

'I said we could have everything.'

'We can have everything.'

'No, we can't.'

'We can have the whole world.'

'No, we can't.'

'We can go everywhere.'

'No, we can't. It isn't ours any more.'

'It's ours.'

'No, it isn't. And once they take it away, you never get it back.'

'But they haven't taken it away.'

'We'll wait and see.'

'Come on back in the shade,' he said. 'You mustn't feel that way.'

'I don't feel any way,' the girl said. 'I just know things.'

'I don't want you to do anything that you don't want to do –'

'Nor that isn't good for me,' she said. 'I know. Could we have another beer?'

'All right. But you've got to realize –'

'I realize,' the girl said. 'Can't we maybe stop talking?'

They sat down at the table and the girl looked across at the hills on the dry side of the valley and the man looked at her and at the table.

'You've got to realize,' he said, 'that I don't want you to do it if you don't want to. I'm perfectly willing to go through with it if it means anything to you.'

'Doesn't it mean anything to you? We could get along.'

'Of course it does. But I don't want anybody but you. I don't want anyone else. And I know it's perfectly simple.'

'Yes, you know it's perfectly simple.'

'It's all right for you to say that, but I do know it.'

'Would you do something for me now?'

'I'd do anything for you.'

'Would you please please please please please please please stop talking?'

He did not say anything but looked at the bags against the wall of the station. There were labels on them from all the hotels where they had spent nights.

'But I don't want you to,' he said, 'I don't care anything about it.'

'I'll scream,' the girl said.

The woman came out through the curtains with two glasses of beer and put them down on the damp felt pads. 'The train comes in five minutes,' she said.

'What did she say?' asked the girl.

'That the train is coming in five minutes.'

The girl smiled brightly at the woman, to thank her.

'I'd better take the bags over to the other side of the station,' the man said. She smiled at him.

'All right. Then come back and we'll finish the beer.'

He picked up the two heavy bags and carried them around the station to the other tracks. Coming back, he walked through the barroom, where people waiting for the train were drinking. He drank an Anis at the bar and looked at the people. They were all waiting reasonably for the train. He went out through the bead curtain. She was sitting at the table and smiled at him.

'Do you feel better?' he asked.

'I feel fine,' she said. 'There's nothing wrong with me. I feel fine.'

The Killers

The door of Henry's lunch-room opened and two men came in. They sat down at the counter.

'What's yours?' George asked them.

'I don't know,' one of the men said. 'What do you want to eat, Al?'

'I don't know,' said Al. 'I don't know what I want to eat.'

Outside it was getting dark. The street-lights came on outside the window. The two men at the counter read the menu. From the other end of the counter Nick Adams watched them. He had been talking to George when they came in.

'I'll have a roast pork tenderloin with apple sauce and mashed potatoes,' the first man said.

'It isn't ready yet.'

'What the hell do you put it on the card for?'

'That's the dinner,' George explained. 'You can get that at six o'clock.'

George looked at the clock on the wall behind the counter.

'It's five o'clock.'

'The clock says twenty minutes past five,' the second man said.

'It's twenty minutes fast.'

'Oh, to hell with the clock,' the first man said. 'What have you got to eat?'

'I can give you any kind of sandwiches,' George said. 'You can have ham and eggs, bacon and eggs, liver and bacon, or a steak.'

'Give me chicken croquettes with green peas and cream sauce and mashed potatoes.'

'That's the dinner.'

'Everything we want's the dinner, eh? That's the way you work it.'

'I can give you ham and eggs, bacon and eggs, liver –'

'I'll take ham and eggs,' the man called Al said. He wore a derby hat and a black overcoat buttoned across the chest. His face was small and white and he had tight lips. He wore a silk muffler and gloves.

'Give me bacon and eggs,' said the other man. He was about the same size as Al. Their faces were different, but they were dressed like twins. Both wore overcoats too tight for them. They sat leaning forward, their elbows on the counter.

'Got anything to drink?' Al asked.

'Silver beer, bevo, ginger-ale,' George said.

'I mean you got anything to *drink?*'

'Just those I said.'

'This is a hot town,' said the other. 'What do they call it?'

'Summit.'

'Ever hear of it?' Al asked his friend.

'No,' said the friend.

'What do you do here nights?' Al asked.

'They eat the dinner,' his friend said. 'They all come here and eat the big dinner.'

'That's right,' George said.

'So you think that's right?' Al asked George.

'Sure.'

'You're a pretty bright boy, aren't you?'

'Sure,' said George.

'Well, you're not,' said the other little man. 'Is he, Al?'

'He's dumb,' said Al. He turned to Nick. 'What's your name?'

'Adams.'

'Another bright boy,' Al said. 'Ain't he a bright boy, Max?'

'The town's full of bright boys,' Max said.

George put the two platters, one of ham and eggs, the other of bacon and eggs, on the counter. He set down two side-dishes of fried potatoes and closed the wicket into the kitchen.

'Which is yours?' he asked Al.

'Don't you remember?'

'Ham and eggs.'

'Just a bright boy,' Max said. He leaned forward and took the ham and eggs. Both men ate with their gloves on. George watched them eat.

'What are *you* looking at?' Max looked at George.

'Nothing.'

'The hell you were. You were looking at me.'

'Maybe the boy meant it for a joke, Max,' Al said.

George laughed.

'*You* don't have to laugh,' Max said to him. '*You* don't have to laugh at all, see?'

'All right,' said George.

'So he thinks it's all right.' Max turned to Al. 'He thinks it's all right. That's a good one.'

'Oh, he's a thinker,' Al said. They went on eating.

'What's the bright boy's name down the counter?' Al asked Max.

'Hey, bright boy,' Max said to Nick. 'You go around on the other side of the counter with your boy friend.'

'What's the idea?' Nick asked.

'There isn't any idea.'

'You better go around, bright boy,' Al said. Nick went around behind the counter.

'What's the idea?' George asked.

'None of your damn business,' Al said. 'Who's out in the kitchen?'

'The nigger.'

'What do you mean the nigger?'

'The nigger that cooks.'

'Tell him to come in.'

'What's the idea?'

'Tell him to come in.'

'Where do you think you are?'

'We know damn well where we are,' the man called Max said. 'Do we look silly?'

'You talk silly,' Al said to him. 'What the hell do you argue with this kid for? Listen,' he said to George, 'tell the nigger to come out here.'

'What are you going to do to him?'

'Nothing. Use your head, bright boy. What would we do to

266

a nigger?'

George opened the slit that opened back into the kitchen. 'Sam,' he called. 'Come in here a minute.'

The door to the kitchen opened and the nigger came in. 'What was it?' he asked. The two men at the counter took a look at him.

'All right, nigger. You stand right there,' Al said.

Sam, the nigger, standing in his apron, looked at the two men sitting at the counter. 'Yes, sir,' he said. Al got down from his stool.

'I'm going back to the kitchen with the nigger and bright boy,' he said. 'Go on back to the kitchen, nigger. You go with him, bright boy.' The little man walked after Nick and Sam, the cook, back into the kitchen. The door shut after them. The man called Max sat at the counter opposite George. He didn't look at George but looked in the mirror that ran along back of the counter. Henry's had been made over from a saloon into a lunch-counter.

'Well, bright boy,' Max said, looking into the mirror, 'why don't you say something?'

'What's it all about?'

'Hey, Al,' Max called, 'bright boy wants to know what it's all about.'

'Why don't you tell him?' Al's voice came from the kitchen.

'What do you think it's all about?'

'I don't know.'

'What do you think?'

Max looked into the mirror all the time he was talking.

'I wouldn't say.'

'Hey, Al, bright boy says he wouldn't say what he thinks it's all about.'

'I can hear you, all right,' Al said from the kitchen. He had propped open the slit that dishes passed through into the kitchen with a catsup bottle. 'Listen, bright boy,' he said from the kitchen to George. 'Stand a little further along the bar. You move a little to the left, Max.' He was like a photographer arranging for a group picture.

'Talk to me, bright boy.' Max said. 'What do you think's going to happen?'

George did not say anything.

'I'll tell you,' Max said. 'We're going to kill a Swede. Do you know a big Swede named Ole Andreson?'

'Yes.'

'He comes here to eat every night, don't he?'

'Sometimes he comes here.'

'He comes here at six o'clock, don't he?'

'If he comes.'

'We know all that, bright boy,' Max said. 'Talk about something else. Ever go to the movies?'

'Once in a while.'

'You ought to go to the movies more. The movies are fine for a bright boy like you.'

'What are you going to kill Ole Andreson for? What did he ever do to you?'

'He never had a chance to do anything to us. He never even seen us.'

'And he's only going to see us once,' Al said from the kitchen.

'What are you going to kill him for, then?' George asked.

'We're killing him for a friend. Just to oblige a friend, bright boy.'

'Shut up,' said Al from the kitchen. 'You talk too goddam much.'

'Well, I got to keep bright boy amused. Don't I, bright boy?'

'You talk too damn much,' Al said. 'The nigger and my bright boy are amused by themselves. I got them tied up like a couple of girl friends in the convent.'

'I suppose you were in a convent.'

'You never know.'

'You were in a kosher convent. That's where you were.'

George looked up at the clock.

'If anybody comes in you tell them the cook is off, and if they keep after it, you tell them you'll go back and cook yourself. Do you get that, bright boy?'

'All right,' George said. 'What you going to do with us afterward?'

'That'll depend,' Max said. 'That's one of those things you never know at the time.'

George looked up at the clock. It was a quarter past six. The door from the street opened. A street-car motorman came in.

'Hello, George,' he said. 'Can I get supper?'

'Sam's gone out,' George said. 'He'll be back in about half an hour.'

'I'd better go up the street,' the motorman said. George looked at the clock. It was twenty minutes past six.

'That was nice, bright boy,' Max said. 'You're a regular little gentleman.'

'He knew I'd blow his head off,' Al said from the kitchen.

'No,' said Max. 'It ain't that. Bright boy is nice. He's a nice boy. I like him.'

At six fifty-five George said: 'He's not coming.'

Two other people had been in the lunch-room. Once George had gone out to the kitchen and made a ham-and-egg sandwich 'to go' that a man wanted to take with him. Inside the kitchen he saw Al, his derby hat tipped back, sitting on a stool beside the wicket with the muzzle of a sawed-off shotgun resting on the ledge. Nick and the cook were back to back in the corner, a towel tied in each of their mouths. George had cooked the sandwich, wrapped it up in oiled paper, put it in a bag, brought it in, and the man had paid for it and gone out.

'Bright boy can do everything,' Max said. 'He can cook and everything. You'd make some girl a nice wife, bright boy.'

'Yes?' George said. 'Your friend, Ole Andreson, isn't going to come.'

'We'll give him ten minutes,' Max said.

Max watched the mirror and the clock. The hands of the clock matched seven o'clock, and then five minutes past seven.

'Come on, Al,' said Max. 'We better go. He's not coming.'

'Better give him five minutes,' Al said from the kitchen.

In the five minutes a man came in, and George explained that the cook was sick.

'Why the hell don't you get another cook?' the man asked. 'Aren't you running a lunch-counter?' He went out.

'Come on, Al,' Max said.

'What about the two bright boys and the nigger?'

'They're all right.'

'You think so?'

'Sure. We're through with it.'

'I don't like it,' said Al. 'It's sloppy. You talk too much.'

'Oh, what the hell,' said Max. 'We got to keep amused, haven't we?'

'You talk too much, all the same,' Al said. He came out from the kitchen. The cut-off barrels of the shotgun made a slight bulge under the waist of his too tight-fitting overcoat. He straightened his coat with his gloved hands.

'So long, bright boy,' he said to George. 'You got a lot of luck.'

'That's the truth,' Max said. 'You ought to play the races, bright boy.'

The two of them went out the door. George watched them, through the window, pass under the arc-light and cross the street. In their tight overcoats and derby hats they looked like a vaudeville team. George went back through the swinging-door into the kitchen and untied Nick and the cook.

'I don't want any more of that,' said Sam, the cook. 'I don't want any more of that.'

Nick stood up. He had never had a towel in his mouth before.

'Say,' he said. 'What the hell?' He was trying to swagger it off.

'They were going to kill Ole Andreson,' George said. 'They were going to shoot him when he came in to eat.'

'Ole Andreson?'

'Sure.'

The cook felt the corners of his mouth with his thumbs.

'They all gone?' he asked.

'Yeah,' said George. 'They're gone now.'

'I don't like it,' said the cook. 'I don't like any of it at all.'

'Listen,' George said to Nick. 'You better go see Ole Andreson.'

'All right.'

'You better not have anything to do with it at all,' Sam, the cook, said. 'You better stay way out of it.'

'Don't go if you don't want to,' George said.

'Mixing up in this ain't going to get you anywhere,' the cook said. 'You stay out of it.'

'I'll go see him,' Nick said to George. 'Where does he live?'

The cook turned away.

'Little boys always know what they want to do,' he said.

'He lives up at Hirsch's rooming-house,' George said to Nick.

'I'll go up there.'

Outside the arc-light shone through the bare branches of a tree. Nick walked up the street beside the car-tracks and turned at the next arc-light down a side-street. Three houses up the street was Hirsch's rooming-house. Nick walked up the two steps and pushed the bell. A woman came to the door.

'Is Ole Andreson here?'

'Do you want to see him?'

'Yes, if he's in.'

Nick followed the woman up a flight of stairs and back to the end of the corridor. She knocked on the door.

'Who is it?'

'It's somebody to see you, Mr Andreson,' the woman said.

'It's Nick Adams.'

'Come in.'

Nick opened the door and went into the room. Ole Andreson was lying on the bed with all his clothes on. He had been a heavyweight prize-fighter and he was too long for the bed. He lay with his head on two pillows. He did not look at Nick.

'What was it?' he asked.

'I was up at Henry's,' Nick said, 'and two fellows came in and tied up me and the cook, and they said they were going to kill you.'

It sounded silly when he said it. Ole Andreson said nothing.

'They put us out in the kitchen,' Nick went on. 'They were going to shoot you when you came in to supper.'

Ole Andreson looked at the wall and did not say anything.

'George thought I better come and tell you about it.'

'There isn't anything I can do about it,' Ole Andreson said.

'I'll tell you what they were like.'

'I don't want to know what they were like,' Ole Andreson said. He looked at the wall. 'Thanks for coming to tell me about it.'

'That's all right.'

Nick looked at the big man lying on the bed.

'Don't you want me to go and see the police?'

'No,' Ole Andreson said. 'That wouldn't do any good.'

'Isn't there something I could do?'

'No. There ain't anything to do.'

'Maybe it was just a bluff.'

'No. It ain't just a bluff.'

Ole Andreson rolled over toward the wall.

'The only thing is,' he said, talking toward the wall, 'I just can't make up my mind to go out. I been in here all day.'

'Couldn't you get out of town?'

'No,' Ole Andreson said. 'I'm through with all that running around.'

He looked at the wall.

'There ain't anything to do now.'

'Couldn't you fix it up some way?'

'No. I got in wrong.' He talked in the same flat voice. 'There ain't anything to do. After a while I'll make up my mind to go out.'

'I better go back and see George,' Nick said.

'So long,' said Ole Andreson. He did not look toward Nick. 'Thanks for coming around.'

Nick went out. As he shut the door he saw Ole Andreson with all his clothes on, lying on the bed looking at the wall.

'He's been in his room all day,' the landlady said downstairs. 'I guess he don't feel well. I said to him: "Mr Andreson, you ought to go out and take a walk on a nice fall day like this," but he didn't feel like it.'

'He doesn't want to go out.'

'I'm sorry he don't feel well,' the woman said. 'He's an awfully nice man. He was in the ring, you know.'

'I know it.'

'You'd never know it except for the way his face is,' the woman said. They stood talking just inside the street door. 'He's just as gentle.'

'Well, good-night, Mrs Hirsch,' Nick said.

'I'm not Mrs Hirsch,' the woman said. 'She owns the place. I just look after it for her. I'm Mrs Bell.'

'Well, good-night, Mrs Bell,' Nick said.

'Good-night,' the woman said.

Nick walked up the dark street to the corner under the arc-light, and then along the car-tracks to Henry's eating-house. George was inside, back of the counter.

'Did you see Ole?'

'Yes,' said Nick. 'He's in his room and he won't go out.'

The cook opened the door from the kitchen when he heard Nick's voice.

'I don't even listen to it,' he said and shut the door.

'Did you tell him about it?' George asked.

'Sure. I told him, but he knows what it's all about.'

'What's he going to do?'

'Nothing.'

'They'll kill him.'

'I guess they will.'

'He must have got mixed up in something in Chicago.'

'I guess so,' said Nick.

'It's a hell of a thing.'

'It's an awful thing,' Nick said.

They did not say anything. George reached down for a towel and wiped the counter.

'I wonder what he did?' Nick said.

'Double-crossed somebody. That's what they kill them for.'

'I'm going to get out of this town,' Nick said.

'Yes,' said George. 'That's a good thing to do.'

'I can't stand to think about him waiting in the room and knowing he's going to get it. It's too damned awful.'

'Well,' said George, 'you better not think about it.'

Che Ti Dice La Patria?

The road of the pass was hard and smooth and not yet dusty in the early morning. Below were the hills with oak and chestnut trees, and far away below was the sea. On the other side were snowy mountains.

We came down from the pass through wooded country. There were bags of charcoal piled beside the road, and through the trees we saw charcoal-burners' huts. It was Sunday and the road, rising and falling, but always dropping away from the altitude of the pass, went through the scrub woods and through villages.

Outside the villages there were fields with vines. The fields were brown and the vines coarse and thick. The houses were white, and in the streets the men, in their Sunday clothes, were playing bowls. Against the walls of some of the houses there were pear trees, their branches candelabraed against the white walls. The pear trees had been sprayed, and the walls of the houses were stained a metallic blue-green by the spray vapor. There were small clearings around the villages where the vines grew, and then the woods.

In the village, twenty kilometers above Spezia, there was a crowd in the square, and a young man carrying a suitcase came up to the car and asked us to take him in to Spezia.

'There are only two places, and they are occupied,' I said. We had an old Ford coupé.

'I will ride on the outside.'

'You will be uncomfortable.'

'That makes nothing. I must go to Spezia.'

274

'Should we take him?' I asked Guy.

'He seems to be going anyway,' Guy said. The young man handed in a parcel through the window.

'Look after this,' he said. Two men tied his suitcase on the back of the car, above our suitcases. He shook hands with everyone, explained that to a Fascist and a man as used to travelling as himself there was no discomfort, and climbed up on the running-board on the left-hand side of the car, holding on inside, his right arm through the open window.

'You can start,' he said. The crowd waved. He waved with his free hand.

'What did he say?' Guy asked me.

'That we could start.'

'Isn't he nice?' Guy said.

The road followed a river. Across the river were mountains. The sun was taking the frost out of the grass. It was bright and cold and the air came through the open windshield.

'How do you think he likes it out there?' Guy was looking up the road. His view out of his side of the car was blocked by our guest. The young man projected from the side of the car like the figurehead of a ship. He had turned his coat collar up and pulled his hat down and his nose looked cold in the wind.

'Maybe he'll get enough of it,' Guy said. 'That's the side our bum tire's on.'

'Oh, he'd leave us if we blew out,' I said. 'He wouldn't get his travelling-clothes dirty.'

'Well, I don't mind him,' Guy said – 'except the way he leans out on the turns.'

The woods were gone; the road left the river to climb; the radiator was boiling, the young man looked annoyedly and suspiciously at the steam and the rusty water; the engine was grinding, with both Guy's feet on the first-speed pedal, up and up, back and forth and up, and finally, out level. The grinding stopped, and in the new quiet there was a great churning bubbling in the radiator. We were at the top of the last range above Spezia and the sea. The road descended with short, barely rounded turns. Our guest hung out on the turns and nearly pulled the top-heavy car over.

275

'You can't tell him not to,' I said to Guy. 'It's his sense of self-preservation.'

'The great Italian sense.'

'The greatest Italian sense.'

We came down around curves, through deep dust, and the dust powdering the olive trees. Spezia spread below along the sea. The road flattened outside the town. Our guest put his head in the window.

'I want to stop.'

'Stop it,' I said to Guy.

We slowed up, at the side of the road. The young man got down, went to the back of the car and untied the suitcase.

'I stop here, so you won't get into trouble carrying passengers,' he said. 'My package.'

I handed him the package. He reached in his pocket.

'How much do I owe you?'

'Nothing.'

'Why not?'

'I don't know,' I said.

'Then thanks,' the young man said, not 'thank you', or 'thank you very much,' or 'thank you a thousand times,' all of which you formerly said in Italy to a man when he handed you a time-table or explained about a direction. The young man uttered the lowest form of the word 'thanks' and looked after us suspiciously as Guy started the car. I waved my hand at him. He was too dignified to reply. We went on into Spezia.

'That's a young man that will go a long way in Italy,' I said to Guy.

'Well,' said Guy, 'he went twenty kilometers with us.'

A MEAL IN SPEZIA

We came into Spezia looking for a place to eat. The street was wide and the houses high and yellow. We followed the tram-track into the center of town. On the walls of the houses were stencilled eye-bugging portraits of Mussolini, with hand-painted 'vivas,' the double V in black paint with drippings of paint down the wall. Side-streets went down to the harbor. It was bright and the people were all out for Sunday. The stone paving had been sprinkled and there were damp stretches in the dust. We went close to the curb to avoid a tram.

'Let's eat somewhere simple,' Guy said.

We stopped opposite two restaurant signs. We were standing across the street and I was buying the papers. The two restaurants were side by side. A woman standing in the doorway of one smiled at us and we crossed the street and went in.

It was dark inside and at the back of the room three girls were sitting at a table with an old woman. Across from us, at another table, sat a sailor. He sat there neither eating nor drinking. Further back, a young man in a blue suit was writing at a table. His hair was pomaded and shining and he was very smartly dressed and clean-cut looking.

The light came through the doorway, and through the window where vegetables, fruit, steaks, and chops were arranged in a show-case. A girl came and took our order and another girl stood in the doorway. We noticed that she wore nothing under her house dress. The girl who took our order put her arm around Guy's neck while we were looking at the menu. There were three girls in all, and they all took turns going and standing in the doorway. The old woman at the table in the back of the room spoke to them and they sat down again with her.

There was no doorway leading from the room except into the kitchen. A curtain hung over it. The girl who had taken our order came in from the kitchen with spaghetti. She put it on the table and brought a bottle of red wine and sat down at the table.

'Well,' I said to Guy, 'you wanted to eat some place simple.'

'This isn't simple, this is complicated.'

'What do you say?' asked the girl. 'Are you Germans?'

'South Germans,' I said. 'The South Germans are a gentle, lovable people.'

'Don't understand,' she said.

'What's the mechanics of this place?' Guy asked. 'Do I have to let her put her arm around my neck?'

'Certainly,' I said. 'Mussolini has abolished the brothels. This is a restaurant.'

The girl wore a one-piece dress. She leaned forward against the table and put her hands on her breasts and smiled. She smiled better on one side than on the other and turned the good side toward us. The charm of the good side had been enhanced by some event which had smoothed the other side of her nose in, as warm wax can be smoothed. Her nose, however, did not look like warm wax. It was very cold and firmed, only smoothed in. 'You like me?' she asked Guy.

'He adores you,' I said. 'But he doesn't speak Italian.'

'Ich spreche Deutsch,' she said, and stroked Guy's hair.

'Speak to the lady in your native tongue, Guy.'

'Where do you come from?' asked the lady.

'Potsdam.'

'And you will stay here now for a little while?'

'In this so dear Spezia?' I asked.

'Tell her we have to go,' said Guy. 'Tell her we are very ill, and have no money.'

'My friend is a misogynist,' I said, 'an old German misogynist.'

'Tell him I love him.'

I told him.

'Will you shut your mouth and get us out of here?' Guy said. The lady had placed another arm around his neck. 'Tell him he is mine,' she said. I told him.

'Will you get us out of here?'

'You are quarrelling,' the lady said. 'You do not love one another.'

'We are Germans,' I said proudly, 'old South Germans.'

'Tell him he is a beautiful boy,' the lady said. Guy is thirty-eight and takes some pride in the fact that he is taken for a travelling salesman in France. 'You are a beautiful boy,' I said.

'Who says so?' Guy asked, 'you or her?'

'She does. I'm just your interpreter. Isn't that what you got me in on this trip for?'

'I'm glad it's her,' said Guy. 'I didn't want to have to leave you here too.'

'I don't know. Spezia's a lovely place.'

'Spezia,' the lady said. 'You are talking about Spezia.'

'Lovely place,' I said.

'It is my country,' she said. 'Spezia is my home and Italy is my country.'

'She says that Italy is her country.'

'Tell her it looks like her country,' Guy said.

'What have you for dessert?' I asked.

'Fruit,' she said. 'We have bananas.'

'Bananas are all right,' Guy said. 'They've got skins on.'

'Oh, he takes bananas,' the lady said. She embraced Guy.

'What does she say?' he asked, keeping his face out of the way.

'She is pleased because you take bananas.'

'Tell her I don't take bananas.'

'The Signor does not take bananas.'

'Ah,' said the lady, crestfallen, 'he doesn't take bananas.'

'Tell her I take a cold bath every morning,' Guy said.

'The Signor takes a cold bath every morning.'

'No understand,' the lady said.

Across from us, the property sailor had not moved. No one in the place paid any attention to him.

'We want the bill,' I said.

'Oh no. You must stay.'

'Listen,' the clean-cut young man said from the table where he was writing, 'let them go. These two are worth nothing.'

The lady took my hand. 'You won't stay? You won't ask him to stay?'

'We have to go,' I said. 'We have to get to Pisa, or if possible, Firenze, tonight. We can amuse ourselves in those cities at the end of the day. It is now the day. In the day we must cover distance.'

'To stay a little while is nice.'

'To travel is necessary during the light of day.'

'Listen,' the clean-cut young man said. 'Don't bother to talk with these two. I tell you they are worth nothing and I know.'

'Bring us the bill,' I said. She brought the bill from the old woman and went back and sat at the table. Another girl came in from the kitchen. She walked the length of the room and stood in the doorway.

'Don't bother with these two,' the clean-cut young man said in a wearied voice. 'Come and eat. They are worth nothing.'

We paid the bill and stood up. All the girls, the old woman, and the clean-cut young man sat down at table together. The property sailor sat with his head in his hands. No one had spoken to him all the time we were at lunch. The girl brought us our change that the old woman counted out for her and went back to her place at the table. We left a tip on the table and went out. When we were seated in the car ready to start, the girl came out and stood in the door. We started and I waved to her. She did not wave, but stood there looking after us.

AFTER THE RAIN

It was raining hard when we passed through the suburbs of Genoa and, even going very slowly behind the tram-cars and the motor trucks, liquid mud splashed on to the sidewalks, so that people stepped into doorways as they saw us coming. In San Pier d'Arena, the industrial suburb outside of Genoa, there is a wide street with two car-tracks and we drove down the centre to avoid sending the mud on the men going home from work. On our left was the Mediterranean. There was a big sea running and waves broke and the wind blew the spray against the car. A river-bed that, when we had passed, going into Italy, had been wide, stony and dry, was running brown and up to the banks. The brown water discoloured the sea and as the waves thinned and cleared in breaking, the light came through the yellow water and the crests, detached by the wind, blew across the road.

A big car passed us, going fast, and a sheet of muddy water rose up and over our wind-shield and radiator. The automatic wind-shield cleaner moved back and forth, spreading the film over the glass. We stopped and ate lunch at Sestri. There was no heat in the restaurant and we kept our hats and coats on. We could see the car outside, through the window. It was covered with mud and was stopped beside some boats that had been pulled up beyond the waves. In the restaurant you could see your breath.

The *pasta asciuta* was good; the wine tasted of alum, and we poured water into it. Afterward the waiter brought beefsteak and fried potatoes. A man and a woman sat at the far end of the restaurant. He was middle-aged and she was young and wore black. All during the meal she would blow out her breath in the cold damp air. The man would look at it and shake his head. They ate without talking and the man held her hand under the table. She was good-looking and they seemed very sad. They had a travelling-bag with them.

We had the papers and I read the account of the Shanghai fighting aloud to Guy. After the meal, he left with the waiter in search for a place which did not exist in the restaurant, and I cleaned off the wind-shield, the lights and the license plates with a rag. Guy came back and we backed the car out and started. The waiter had taken him across the road and into an old house. The people in the house were suspicious and the waiter had remained with Guy to see nothing was stolen.

'Although I don't know how, me not being a plumber, they expected me to steal anything,' Guy said.

As we came up on a headland beyond the town, the wind struck the car and nearly tipped it over.

'It's good it blows us away from the sea,' Guy said.

Well,' I said, 'they drowned Shelley somewhere along here.'

'That was down by Viareggio,' Guy said. 'Do you remember what we came to this country for?'

'Yes,' I said, 'but we didn't get it.'

'We'll be out of it tonight.'

'If we can get past Ventimiglia.'

'We'll see. I don't like to drive this coast at night.' It was early afternoon and the sun was out. Below, the sea was blue with whitecaps running toward Savona. Back, beyond the cape, the brown and blue water joined. Out ahead of us, a tramp steamer was going up the coast.

'Can you still see Genoa?' Guy asked.

'Oh, yes.'

'That next big cape ought to put it out of sight.'

'We'll see it a long time yet. I can still see Portofino Cape behind it.'

Finally we could not see Genoa. I looked back as we came out and there was only the sea, and below, in the bay, a line of beach with fishing-boats and above, on the side of the hill, a town and then capes far down the coast.

'It is gone now,' I said to Guy.

'Oh, it's been gone a long time now.'

'But we couldn't be sure till we got way out.'

There was a sign with a picture of an S-turn and Svolta Pericolosa. The road curved around the headland and the wind blew through the crack in the wind-shield. Below the cape was a flat stretch beside the sea. The wind had dried the mud and the wheels were beginning to lift dust. On the flat road we passed a Fascist riding a bicycle, a heavy revolver in a holster on his back. He held the middle of the road on his bicycle and we turned out for him. He looked up at us as we passed. Ahead there was a railway crossing, and as we came toward it the gates went down.

As we waited, the Fascist came up on his bicycle. The train went by and Guy started the engine.

'Wait,' the bicycle man shouted from behind the car. 'Your number's dirty.'

I got out with a rag. The number had been cleaned at lunch.

'You can read it,' I said.

'You think so?'

'Read it.'

'I cannot read it. It is dirty.'

I wiped it off with the rag.

'How's that?'

'Twenty-five lire.'

'What?' I said. 'You could have read it. It's only dirty from the state of the roads.'

'You don't like Italian roads?'

'They are dirty.'

'Fifty lire.' He spat in the road. 'Your car is dirty and you are dirty too.'

'Good. And give me a receipt with your name.'

He took out a receipt book, made in duplicate, and perforated, so one side could be given to the customer, and the other side filled in and kept as a stub. There was no carbon to record what the customer's ticket said.

'Give me fifty lire.'

282

He wrote in indelible pencil, tore out the slip and handed it to me. I read it.

'This is for twenty-five lire.'

'A mistake,' he said, and changed the twenty-five to fifty.

'And now the other side. Make it fifty in the part you keep.'

He smiled a beautiful Italian smile and wrote something on the receipt stub, holding it so I could not see.

'Go on,' he said, 'before your number gets dirty again.'

We drove for two hours after it was dark and slept in Menton that night. It seemed very cheerful and clean and sane and lovely. We had driven from Ventimiglia to Pisa and Florence, across the Romagna to Rimini, back through Forli, Imola, Bologna, Parma, Piacenza and Genoa, to Ventimiglia again. The whole trip had taken only ten days. Naturally, in such a short trip, we had no opportunity to see how things were with the country or the people.

Fifty Grand

'How are you going yourself, Jack?' I asked him.

'You seen this Walcott?' he says.

'Just in the gym.'

'Well,' Jack says, 'I'm going to need a lot of luck with that boy.'

'He can't hit you, Jack,' Soldier said.

'I wish to hell he couldn't.'

'He couldn't hit you with a handful of bird-shot.'

'Bird-shot'd be all right,' Jack says. 'I wouldn't mind bird-shot any.'

'He looks easy to hit,' I said.

'Sure,' Jack says, 'he ain't going to last long. He ain't going to last like you and me, Jerry. But right now he's got everything.'

'You'll left-hand him to death.'

'Maybe,' Jack says. 'Sure. I got a chance to.'

'Handle him like you handled Kid Lewis.'

'Kid Lewis,' Jack said. 'That kike!'

The three of us, Jack Brennan, Soldier Bartlett, and I were in Hanley's. There were a couple of broads sitting at the next table to us. They had been drinking.

'What do you mean, kike?' one of the broads says. 'What do you mean, kike, you big Irish bum?'

'Sure,' Jack says. 'That's it.'

'Kikes,' this broad goes on. 'They're always talking about kikes, these big Irishmen. What do you mean, kikes?'

'Come on. Let's get out of here.'

'Kikes,' this broad goes on. 'Whoever saw you ever buy a drink? Your wife sews your pockets up every morning. These Irishmen and their kikes! Ted Lewis could lick you too.'

'Sure,' Jack says. 'And you give away a lot of things free too, don't you?'

We went out. That was Jack. He could say what he wanted to when he wanted to say it.

Jack started training out at Danny Hogan's health farm over in Jersey. It was nice out there but Jack didn't like it much. He didn't like being away from his wife and the kids, and he was sore and grouchy most of the time. He liked me and we got along fine together; and he liked Hogan, but after a while Soldier Bartlett commenced to get on his nerves. A kidder gets to be an awful thing around a camp if his stuff goes sort of sour. Soldier was always kidding Jack, just sort of kidding him all the time. It wasn't very funny and it wasn't very good, and it began to get to Jack. It was sort of stuff like this. Jack would finish up with the weights and the bag and pull on the gloves.

'You want to work?' he'd say to Soldier.

'Sure. How you want me to work?' Soldier would ask. 'Want me to treat you rough like Walcott? Want me to knock you down a few times?'

'That's it,' Jack would say. He didn't like it any, though.

One morning we were all out on the road. We'd been out quite a way and now we were coming back. We'd go along fast for three minutes and then walk a minute, and then go fast for three minutes again. Jack wasn't ever what you would call a sprinter. He'd move around fast enough in the ring if he had to, but he wasn't any too fast on the road. All the time we were walking Soldier was kidding him. We came up the hill to the farmhouse.

'Well,' says Jack, 'you better go back to town, Soldier.'

'What do you mean?'

'You better go to town and stay there.'

'What's the matter?'

'I'm sick of hearing you talk.'

'Yes?' says Soldier.

'Yes,' says Jack.

285

'You'll be a damn sight sicker when Walcott gets through with you.'

'Sure,' says Jack, 'maybe I will. But I know I'm sick of you.'

So Soldier went off on the train to town that same morning. I went down with him to the train. He was good and sore.

'I was just kidding him,' he said. We were waiting on the platform. 'He can't pull that stuff with me, Jerry.'

'He's nervous and crabby,' I said. 'He's a good fellow, Soldier.'

'The hell he is. The hell he's ever been a good fellow.'

'Well,' I said, 'so long, Soldier.'

The train had come in. He climbed up with his bag.

'So long, Jerry,' he says. 'You be in town before the fight?'

'I don't think so.'

'See you then.'

He went in and the conductor swung up and the train went out. I rode back to the farm in the cart. Jack was on the porch writing a letter to his wife. The mail had come and I got the papers and went over on the other side of the porch and sat down to read. Hogan came out the door and walked over to me.

'Did he have a jam with Soldier?'

'Not a jam,' I said. 'He just told him to go back to town.'

'I could see it coming,' Hogan said. 'He never liked Soldier much.'

'No. He don't like many people.'

'He's a pretty cold one,' Hogan said.

'Well, he's always been fine to me.'

'Me too,' Hogan said. 'I got no kick on him. He's a cold one, though.'

Hogan went in through the screen door and I sat there on the porch and read the papers. It was just starting to get fall weather and it's nice country there in Jersey, up in the hills, and after I read the paper through I sat there and looked out at the country and the road down below against the woods with cars going along it, lifting the dust up. It was fine weather and pretty nice-looking country. Hogan came to the door and I said, 'Say, Hogan, haven't you got anything to shoot out here?'

'No,' Hogan said. 'Only sparrows.'

'Seen the paper?' I said to Hogan.

'What's in it?'

'Sande booted three of them in yesterday.'

'I got that on the telephone last night.'

'You follow them pretty close, Hogan?' I asked.

'Oh, I keep in touch with them,' Hogan said.

'How about Jack?' I said. 'Does he still play them?'

'Him?' said Hogan. 'Can you see him doing it?'

Just then Jack came around the corner with the letter in his hand. He's wearing a sweater and an old pair of pants and boxing shoes.

'Got a stamp, Hogan?' he asks.

'Give me the letter,' Hogan said. 'I'll mail it for you.'

'Say Jack,' I said, 'didn't you used to play the ponies?'

'Sure.'

'I knew you did. I knew I used to see you at Sheepshead.'

'What did you lay off them for?' Hogan asked.

'Lost money.'

Jack sat down on the porch by me. He leaned back against a post. He shut his eyes in the sun.

'Want a chair?' Hogan asked.

'No,' said Jack. 'This is fine.'

'It's a nice day,' I said. 'It's pretty nice out in the country.'

'I'd a damn sight rather be in town with the wife.'

'Well, you only got another week.'

'Yes,' Jack says. 'That's so.'

We sat there on the porch. Hogan was inside at the office.

'What do you think about the shape I'm in?' Jack asked me.

'Well, you can't tell,' I said. 'You got a week to get around into form.'

'Don't stall me.'

'Well,' I said, 'you're not right.'

'I'm not sleeping,' Jack said.

'You'll be all right in a couple of days.'

'No,' says Jack, 'I got the insomnia.'

'What's on your mind?'

'I miss the wife.'

'Have her come out.'

'No. I'm too old for that.'

'We'll take a long walk before you turn in and get you good and tired.'

'Tired!' Jack says. 'I'm tired all the time.'

He was that way all week. He wouldn't sleep at night and he'd get up in the morning feeling that way, you know, when you can't shut your hands.

'He's stale as poorhouse cake,' Hogan said. 'He's nothing.'

'I never seen Walcott,' I said.

'He'll kill him,' said Hogan. 'He'll tear him in two.'

'Well,' I said, 'everybody's got to get it sometime.'

'Not like this, though,' Hogan said. 'They'll think he never trained. It gives the farm a black eye.'

'You hear what the reporters said about him?'

'Didn't I! They said he was awful. They said they oughtn't to let him fight.'

'Well,' I said, 'they're always wrong, ain't they?'

'Yes,' said Hogan. 'But this time they're right.'

'What the hell do they know about whether a man's right or not?'

'Well,' said Hogan, 'they're not such fools.'

'All they did was pick Willard at Toledo. This Lardner he's so wise now, ask him about when he picked Willard at Toledo.'

'Aw, he wasn't out,' Hogan said. 'He only writes the big fights.'

'I don't care who they are,' I said. 'What the hell do they know? They can write maybe, but what the hell do they know?'

'You don't think Jack's in any shape, do you?' Hogan asked.

'No. He's through. All he needs is to have Corbett pick him to win for it to be all over.'

'Well, Corbett'll pick him,' Hogan says.

'Sure. He'll pick him.'

That night Jack didn't sleep any either. The next morning was the last day before the fight. After breakfast we were out on the porch again.

'What do you think about, Jack, when you can't sleep?' I said.

'Oh, I worry,' Jack says. 'I worry about property I got up in the Bronx, I worry about property I got in Florida. I worry

288

about the kids. I worry about the wife. Sometimes I think about fights. I think about that kike Ted Lewis and I get sore. I got some stocks and I worry about them. What the hell don't I think about?'

'Well,' I said, 'tomorrow night it'll all be over.'

'Sure,' said Jack. 'That always helps a lot, don't it? That just fixes everything all up, I suppose. Sure.'

He was sore all day. We didn't do any work. Jack just moved around a little to loosen up. He shadow-boxed a few rounds. He didn't even look good doing that. He skipped the rope a little while. He couldn't sweat.

'He'd be better not to do any work at all,' Hogan said. We were standing watching him skip rope. 'Don't he ever sweat at all any more?'

'He can't sweat.'

'Do you suppose he's got the con? He never had any trouble making weight, did he?'

'No, he hasn't got any con. He just hasn't got anything inside any more.'

'He ought to sweat,' said Hogan.

Jack came over, skipping the rope. He was skipping up and down in front of us, forward and back, crossing his arms every third time.

'Well,' he says. 'What are you buzzards talking about?'

'I don't think you ought to work out any more,' Hogan says. 'You'll be stale.'

'Wouldn't that be awful?' Jack says and skips away down the floor, slapping the rope hard.

That afternoon John Collins showed up out at the farm. Jack was up in his room. John came out in a car from town. He had a couple of friends with him. The car stopped and they all got out.

'Where's Jack?' John asked me.

'Up in his room, lying down.'

'Lying down?'

'Yes,' I said.

'How is he?'

I looked at the two fellows that were with John.

'They're friends of his,' John said.

'He's pretty bad,' I said.

'What's the matter with him?'

'He don't sleep.'

'Hell,' said John. 'That Irishman could never sleep.'

'He isn't right,' I said.

'Hell,' John said. 'He's never right. I've had him for ten years and he's never been right yet.'

The fellows who were with him laughed.

'I want you to shake hands with Mr Morgan and Mr Steinfelt,' John said. 'This is Mr Doyle. He's been training Jack.'

'Glad to meet you,' I said.

'Let's go up and see the boy,' the fellow called Morgan said.

'Let's have a look at him,' Steinfelt said.

We all went upstairs.

'Where's Hogan?' John asked.

'He's out in the barn with a couple of his customers,' I said.

'He got many people out here now?' John asked.

'Just two.'

'Pretty quiet, ain't it?' Morgan said.

'Yes,' I said. 'It's pretty quiet.'

We were outside Jack's room. John knocked on the door. There wasn't any answer.

'Maybe he's asleep,' I said.

'What the hell's he sleeping in the daytime for?'

John turned the handle and we all went in. Jack was lying asleep on the bed. He was face down and his face was in the pillow. Both his arms were around the pillow.

'Hey, Jack!' John said to him.

Jack's head moved a little on the pillow. 'Jack!' John says, leaning over him. Jack just dug a little deeper in the pillow. John touched him on the shoulder. Jack sat up and looked at us. He hadn't shaved and he was wearing an old sweater.

'Christ! Why can't you let me sleep?' he says to John.

'Don't be sore,' John says. 'I didn't mean to wake you up.'

'Oh no,' Jack says. 'Of course not.'

'You know Morgan and Steinfelt,' John said.

'Glad to see you,' Jack says.

'How do you feel, Jack,' Morgan asked him.

'Fine,' Jack says. 'How the hell would I feel?'

'You look fine,' Steinfelt says.

'Yes, don't I,' says Jack. 'Say,' he says to John. 'You're my manager. You get a big cut. Why the hell don't you come out here when the reporters was out! You want Jerry and me to talk to them?'

'I had Lew fighting in Philadelphia,' John said.

'What the hell's that to me?' Jack says. 'You're my manager. You get a big enough cut, don't you? You aren't making me any money in Philadelphia, are you? Why the hell aren't you out here when I ought to have you?'

'Hogan was here.'

'Hogan,' Jack says. 'Hogan's as dumb as I am.'

'Soldier Bartlett was out here working with you for a while, wasn't he?' Steinfelt said to change the subject.

'Yes, he was out here,' Jack says. 'He was out here all right.'

'Say, Jerry,' John said to me. 'Would you go and find Hogan and tell him we want to see him in about half an hour?'

'Sure,' I said.

'Why the hell can't he stick around?' Jack says. 'Stick around, Jerry.'

Morgan and Steinfelt looked at each other.

'Quiet down, Jack,' John said to him.

'I better go find Hogan,' I said.

'All right, if you want to go,' Jack says. 'None of these guys are going to send you away, though.'

'I'll go find Hogan,' I said.

Hogan was out in the gym in the barn. He had a couple of his health-farm patients with the gloves on. They neither one wanted to hit the other, for fear they would come back and hit him.

'That'll do,' Hogan said when he saw me come in. 'You can stop the slaughter. You gentlemen take a shower and Bruce will rub you down.'

They climbed out through the ropes and Hogan came over to me.

'John Collins is out with a couple of friends to see Jack,' I said.

'I saw them come up in the car.'

'Who are the two fellows with John?'

'They're what you call wise boys,' Hogan said. 'Don't you know them two?'

'No,' I said.

'That's Happy Steinfelt and Lew Morgan. They got a poolroom.'

'I been away a long time,' I said.

'Sure,' said Hogan. 'That Happy Steinfelt's a big operator.'

'I've heard his name,' I said.

'He's a pretty smooth boy,' Hogan said. 'They're a couple of sharpshooters.'

'Well,' I said. 'They want to see us in half an hour.'

'You mean they don't want to see us until a half an hour?'

'That's it.'

'Come on in the office,' Hogan said. 'To hell with those sharpshooters.'

After about thirty minutes or so Hogan and I went upstairs. We knocked on Jack's door. They were talking inside the room.

'Wait a minute,' somebody said.

'To hell with that stuff,' Hogan said. 'When you want me I'm down in the office.'

We heard the door unlock. Steinfelt opened it.

'Come on in, Hogan,' he says. 'We're all going to have a drink.'

'Well,' says Hogan. 'That's something.'

We went in. Jack was sitting on the bed. John and Morgan were sitting on a couple of chairs. Steinfelt was standing up.

'You're a pretty mysterious lot of boys,' Hogan said.

'Hello, Danny,' John says.

'Hello, Danny,' Morgan says and shakes hands.

Jack doesn't say anything. He just sits there on the bed. He ain't with the others. He's all by himself. He was wearing an old blue jersey and pants and had on boxing shoes. He needed a shave. Steinfelt and Morgan were dressers. John was quite a dresser too. Jack sat there looking Irish and tough.

Steinfelt brought out a bottle and Hogan brought in some glasses and everybody had a drink. Jack and I took one and the rest of them went on and had two or three each.

292

'Better save some for your ride back,' Hogan said.

'Don't you worry. We got plenty,' Morgan said.

Jack hadn't drunk anything since the one drink. He was standing up and looking at them. Morgan was sitting on the bed where Jack had sat.

'Have a drink, Jack,' John said and handed him the glass and the bottle.

'No,' Jack said, 'I never liked to go to these wakes.'

They all laughed. Jack didn't laugh.

They were all feeling pretty good when they left. Jack stood on the porch when they got into the car. They waved to him.

'So long,' Jack said.

We had supper. Jack didn't say anything all during the meal except, 'Will you pass me this?' or 'Will you pass me that?' The two health-farm patients ate at the same table with us. They were pretty nice fellows. After we finished eating we went out on the porch. It was dark early.

'Like to take a walk, Jerry?' Jack asked.

'Sure,' I said.

We put on our coats and started out. It was quite a way down to the main road and then we walked along the main road about a mile and a half. Cars kept going by and we would pull out to the side until they were past. Jack didn't say anything. After we had stepped out into the bushes to let a big car go by Jack said, 'To hell with this walking. Come on back to Hogan's.'

We went along a side road that cut up over the hill and cut across the fields back to Hogan's. We could see the lights of the house up on the hill. We came around to the front of the house and there standing in the doorway was Hogan.

'Have a good walk?' Hogan asked.

'Oh, fine,' Jack said. 'Listen, Hogan. Have you got any liquor?'

'Sure,' says Hogan. 'What's the idea?'

'Send it up to the room,' Jack says. 'I'm going to sleep tonight.'

'You're the doctor,' Hogan says.

'Come on up to the room, Jerry,' Jack says.

Upstairs Jack sat on the bed with his head in his hands.

'Ain't it a life?' Jack says.

Hogan brought in a quart of liquor and two glasses.

'Want some ginger ale?'

'What do you think I want to do, get sick?'

'I just asked you,' said Hogan.

'Have a drink?' said Jack.

'No, thanks,' said Hogan. He went out.

'How about you, Jerry?'

'I'll have one with you,' I said.

Jack poured out a couple of drinks. 'Now,' he said, 'I want to take it slow and easy.'

'Put some water in it,' I said.

'Yes,' Jack said. 'I guess that's better.'

We had a couple of drinks without saying anything. Jack started to pour me another.

'No,' I said, 'that's all I want.'

'All right,' Jack said. He poured himself out another big shot and put water in it. He was lighting up a little.

'That was a fine bunch out here this afternoon,' he said. 'They don't take any chances, those two.'

Then a little later, 'Well,' he says, 'they're right. What the hell's the good in taking chances?'

'Don't you want another, Jerry?' he said. 'Come on, drink along with me.'

'I don't need it, Jack,' I said. 'I feel all right.'

'Just have one more,' Jack said. It was softening him up.

'All right,' I said.

Jack poured one for me and another big one for himself.

'You know,' he said, 'I like liquor pretty well. If I hadn't been boxing I would have drunk quite a lot.'

'Sure,' I said.

'You know,' he said, 'I missed a lot, boxing.'

'You made plenty of money.'

'Sure, that's what I'm after. You know I miss a lot, Jerry.'

'How do you mean?'

'Well,' he says, 'like about the wife. And being away from home so much. It don't do my girls any good. "Who's your old man?" some of those society kids'll say to them. "My old man's Jack Brennan." That don't do them any good.'

'Hell,' I said, 'all that makes a difference is if they got dough.'

'Well,' says Jack, 'I got the dough for them all right.'

He poured out another drink. The bottle was about empty.

'Put some water in it,' I said. Jack poured in some water.

'You know,' he says, 'you ain't got any idea how I miss the wife.'

'Sure.'

'You ain't got any idea. You can't have an idea what it's like.'

'It ought to be better out in the country than in town.'

'With me now,' Jack said, 'it don't make any difference where I am. You can't have an idea what it's like.'

'Have another drink.'

'Am I getting soused? Do I talk funny?'

'You're coming on all right.'

'You can't have an idea what it's like. They ain't anybody can have an idea what it's like.'

'Except the wife,' I said.

'She knows,' Jack said. 'She knows all right. She knows. You bet she knows.'

'Put some water in that,' I said.

'Jerry,' says Jack, 'you can't have an idea what it gets to be like.'

He was good and drunk. He was looking at me steady. His eyes were sort of too steady.

'You'll sleep all right,' I said.

'Listen, Jerry,' Jack says. 'You want to make some money? Get some money down on Walcott.'

'Yes?'

'Listen, Jerry,' Jack put down the glass. 'I'm not drunk now, see? You know what I'm betting on him? Fifty grand.'

'That's a lot of dough.'

'Fifty grand,' Jack says, 'at two to one. I'll get twenty-five thousand bucks. Get some money on him, Jerry.'

'It sounds good,' I said.

'How can I beat him?' Jack says. 'It ain't crooked. How can I beat him? Why not make money on it?'

'Put some water in that,' I said.

'I'm through after this fight,' Jack says. 'I'm through with it. I got to take a beating. Why shouldn't I make money on it?'

'Sure.'

'I ain't slept for a week,' Jack says. 'All night I lay awake and worry my can off. I can't sleep, Jerry. You ain't got an idea what it's like when you can't sleep.'

'Sure.'

'I can't sleep. That's all. I just can't sleep. What's the use of taking care of yourself all these years when you can't sleep?'

'It's bad.'

'You ain't got an idea what it's like, Jerry, when you can't sleep.'

'Put some water in that,' I said.

Well, about eleven o'clock Jack passes out and I put him to bed. Finally he's so he can't keep from sleeping. I helped him get his clothes off and got him into bed.

'You'll sleep all right, Jack,' I said.

'Sure,' Jack says, 'I'll sleep now.'

'Good night, Jack,' I said.

'Good night, Jerry,' Jack says. 'You're the only friend I got.'

'Oh, hell,' I said.

'You're the only friend I got,' Jack says, 'them only friend I got.'

'Go to sleep,' I said.

'I'll sleep,' Jack says.

Downstairs Hogan was sitting at the desk in the office reading the papers. He looked up. 'Well, you get your boy friend to sleep?' he asks.

'He's off.'

'It's better for him than not sleeping,' Hogan said.

'Sure.'

'You'd have a hell of a time explaining that to these sport writers though,' Hogan said.

'Well, I'm going to bed myself,' I said.

'Good night,' said Hogan.

In the morning I came downstairs about eight o'clock and got some breakfast. Hogan had his two customers out in the barn doing exercises. I went out and watched them.

'One! Two! Three! Four!' Hogan was counting for them. 'Hello, Jerry,' he said. 'Is Jack up yet?'

'No. He's still sleeping.'

I went back to my room and packed up to go in to town. About nine-thirty I heard Jack getting up in the next room. When I heard him go downstairs I went down after him. Jack was sitting at the breakfast table. Hogan had come in and was standing beside the table.

'How do you feel, Jack?' I asked him.

'Not so bad.'

'Sleep well?' Hogan asked.

'I slept all right,' Jack said. 'I got a thick tongue but I ain't got a head.'

'Good,' said Hogan. 'That was good liquor.'

'Put it on the bill,' Jack says.

'What time you want to go into town?' Hogan asked.

'Before lunch,' Jack says. 'The eleven o'clock train.'

'Sit down, Jerry,' Jack said. Hogan went out.

I sat down at the table. Jack was eating a grapefruit. When he'd find a seed he'd spit it out in the spoon and dump it on the plate.

'I guess I was pretty stewed last night,' he started.

'You drank some liquor.'

'I guess I said a lot of fool things.'

'You weren't bad.'

'Where's Hogan?' he asked. He was through with the grapefruit.

'He's out in front in the office.'

'What did I say about betting on the fight?' Jack asked. He was holding the spoon and sort of poking at the grapefruit with it.

The girl came in with some ham and eggs and took away the grapefruit.

'Bring me another glass of milk,' Jack said to her. She went out.

'You said you had fifty grand on Walcott,' I said.

'That's right,' Jack said.

'That's a lot of money.'

'I don't feel too good about it,' Jack said.

'Something might happen.'

'No,' Jack said. 'He wants the title bad. They'll be shooting with him all right.'

'You can't ever tell.'

'No. He wants the title. It's worth a lot of money to him.'

'Fifty grand is a lot of money,' I said.

'It's business,' said Jack. 'I can't win. You know I can't win anyway.'

'As long as you're in there you got a chance.'

'No,' Jack says. 'I'm all through. It's just business.'

'How do you feel?'

'Pretty good,' Jack said. 'The sleep was what I needed.'

'You might go good.'

'I'll give them a good show,' Jack said.

After breakfast Jack called up his wife on the long-distance. He was inside the booth telephoning.

'That's the first time he's called her up since he's out here,' Hogan said.

'He writes her every day.'

'Sure,' Hogan says, 'a letter only costs two cents.'

Hogan said good-bye to us and Bruce, the nigger rubber, drove us down to the train in the cart.

'Good-bye, Mr Brennan,' Bruce said at the train, 'I sure hope you knock his can off.'

'So long,' Jack said. He gave Bruce two dollars. Bruce had worked on him a lot. He looked kind of disappointed. Jack saw me looking at Bruce holding the two dollars.

'It's all in the bill,' he said. 'Hogan charged me for the rubbing.'

On the train going into town Jack didn't talk. He sat in the corner of the seat with his ticket in his hat-band and looked out of the window. Once he turned and spoke to me.

'I told the wife I'd take a room at the Shelby tonight,' he said. 'It's just around the corner from the Garden. I can go up to the house tomorrow morning.'

'That's a good idea,' I said. 'Your wife ever see you fight, Jack?'

'No,' Jack says. 'She never seen me fight.'

I thought he must be figuring on taking an awful beating if

298

he doesn't want to go home afterwards. In town we took a taxi up to the Shelby. A boy came out and took our bags and we went in to the desk.

'How much are the rooms?' Jack asked.

'We only have double rooms,' the clerk says. 'I can give you a nice double room for ten dollars.'

'That's too steep.'

'I can give you a double room for seven dollars.'

'With a bath?'

'Certainly.'

'You might as well bunk with me, Jerry,' Jack says.

'Oh,' I said, 'I'll sleep down at my brother-in-law's.'

'I don't mean for you to pay it,' Jack says. 'I just want to get my money's worth.'

'Will you register, please?' the clerk says. He looked at the names. 'Number 238, Mister Brennan.'

We went up in the elevator. It was a nice big room with two beds and a door opening into a bath-room.

'This is pretty good,' Jack says.

The boy who brought us up pulled up the curtains and brought in our bags. Jack didn't make any move, so I gave the boy a quarter. We washed up and Jack said we better go out and get something to eat.

We ate lunch at Jimmy Hanky's place. Quite a lot of the boys were there. When we were about half through eating, John came in and sat down with us. Jack didn't talk much.

'How are you on the weight, Jack?' John asked him. Jack was putting away a pretty good lunch.

'I could make it with my clothes on,' Jack said. He never had to worry about taking off weight. He was a natural welterweight and he'd never gotten fat. He'd lost weight out at Hogan's.

'Well, that's one thing you never had to worry about,' John said.

'That's one thing,' Jack says.

We went around to the Garden to weigh in after lunch. The match was made at a hundred forty-seven pounds at three o'clock. Jack stepped on the scales with a towel around him. The bar didn't move. Walcott had just weighed and was standing with a lot of people around him.

'Let's see what you weigh, Jack,' Freedman, Walcott's manager said.

'All right, weigh *him* then,' Jack jerked his head toward Walcott.

'Drop the towel,' Freedman said.

'What do you make it?' Jack asked the fellows who were weighing.

'One hundred and forty-three pounds,' the fat man who was weighing said.

'You're down fine, Jack,' Freedman says.

'Weigh *him*,' Jack says.

Walcott came over. He was a blond with wide shoulders and arms like a heavyweight. He didn't have much legs. Jack stood about half a head taller than he did.

'Hello, Jack,' he said. His face was plenty marked up.

'Hello,' said Jack. 'How you feel?'

'Good,' Walcott says. He dropped the towel from around his waist and stood on the scales. He had the widest shoulders and back you ever saw.

'One hundred and forty-six pounds and twelve ounces.'

Walcott stepped off and grinned at Jack.

'Well,' John says to him, 'Jack's spotting you about four pounds.'

'More than that when I come in, kid,' Walcott says. 'I'm going to go and eat now.'

We went back and Jack got dressed. 'He's a pretty tough-looking boy,' Jack says to me.

'He looks as though he'd been hit plenty of times.'

'Oh, yes,' Jack says. 'He ain't hard to hit.'

'Where are you going?' John asked when Jack was dressed.

'Back to the hotel,' Jack says. 'You looked after everything?'

'Yes,' John says. 'It's all looked after.'

'I'm going to lie down a while,' Jack says.

'I'll come around for you about a quarter to seven and we'll go and eat.'

'All right.'

Up at the hotel Jack took off his shoes and his coat and lay down for a while. I wrote a letter. I looked over a couple of times and Jack wasn't sleeping. He was lying perfectly still but every once in a while his eyes would open. Finally he sits up.

'Want to play some cribbage, Jerry?' he says.

'Sure,' I said.

He went over to his suitcase and got out the cards and the cribbage board. We played cribbage and he won three dollars off me. John knocked at the door and came in.

'You want to play some cribbage, John?' Jack asked him.

John put his hat down on the table. It was all wet. His coat was wet too.

'Is it raining?' Jack asks.

'It's pouring,' John says. 'The taxi I had got tied up in the traffic and I got out and walked.'

'Come on, play some cribbage,' Jack says.

'You ought to go and eat.'

'No,' says Jack. 'I don't want to eat yet.'

So they played cribbage for about half an hour and Jack won a dollar and a half off him.

'Well, I suppose we got to go eat,' Jack says. He went to the window and looked out.

'Is it still raining?'

'Yes.'

'Let's eat in the hotel,' John says.

'All right,' Jack says, 'I'll play you once more to see who pays for the meal.'

After a little while Jack gets up and says, 'You buy the meal, John,' and we went downstairs and ate in the big dining-room.

After we ate we went upstairs and Jack played cribbage with John again and won two dollars and a half off him. Jack was feeling pretty good. John had a bag with him with all his stuff in it. Jack took off his shirt and collar and put on a jersey and a sweater, so he couldn't catch cold when he came out, and put his ring clothes and his bathrobe in a bag.

'You all ready?' John asks him. 'I'll call up and have them get a taxi.'

Pretty soon the telephone rang and they said the taxi was waiting.

We rode down in the elevator and went out through the lobby, and got in a taxi and rode around to the Garden. It was raining hard but there was a lot of people outside on the

301

streets. The Garden was sold out. As we came in on our way to the dressing-room I saw how full it was. It looked like half a mile down to the ring. It was all dark. Just the lights over the ring.

'It's a good thing, with this rain, they didn't try and pull this fight in the ball park,' John said.

'They got a good crowd,' Jack says.

'This is a fight that would draw a lot more than the Garden could hold.'

'You can't tell about the weather,' Jack says.

John came to the door of the dressing-room and poked his head in. Jack was sitting there with his bathrobe on, he had his arms folded and was looking at the floor. John had a couple of handlers with him. They looked over his shoulder. Jack looked up.

'Is he in?' he asked.

'He's just gone down,' John said.

We started down. Walcott was just getting into the ring. The crowd gave him a big hand. He climbed through between the ropes and put his two fists together and smiled, and shook them at the crowd, first at one side of the ring, then at the other, and then sat down. Jack got a good hand coming down through the crowd. Jack is Irish and the Irish always get a pretty good hand. An Irishman don't draw in New York like a Jew or an Italian but they always get a good hand. Jack climbed up and bent down to go through the ropes and Walcott came over from his corner and pushed the rope down for Jack to go through. The crowd thought that was wonderful. Walcott put his hand on Jack's shoulder and they stood there just for a second.

'So you're going to be one of these popular champions,' Jack says to him. 'Take your goddam hand off my shoulder.'

'Be yourself,' Walcott says.

This is all great for the crowd. How gentlemanly the boys are before the fight. How they wish each other luck.

Solly Freedman came over to our corner while Jack is bandaging his hands and John is over in Walcott's corner. Jack puts his thumb through the slit in the bandage and then wrapped his hands nice and smooth. I taped it around the wrist and twice across the knuckles.

'Hey,' Freedman says. 'Where do you get all that tape?'

'Feel of it,' Jack says. 'It's soft, ain't it? Don't be a hick.'

Freedman stands there all the time while Jack bandages the other hand and one of the boys that's going to handle him brings the gloves and I pull them on and work them around.

'Say, Freedman,' Jack asks, 'what nationality is this Walcott?'

'I don't know,' Solly says. 'He's some sort of a Dane.'

'He's a Bohemian,' the lad who brought the gloves said.

The referee called them out to the center of the ring and Jack walks out. Walcott comes out smiling. They met and the referee put his arm on each of their shoulders.

'Hello, popularity,' Jack says to Walcott.

'Be yourself.'

'What do you call yourself "Walcott" for?' Jack says. 'Didn't you know he was a nigger?'

'Listen –' says the referee, and he gives them the same old line. Once Walcott interrupts him. He grabs Jack's arms and says, 'Can I hit when he's got me like this?'

'Keep your hands off me,' Jack says. 'There ain't no moving-pictures of this.'

They went back to their corners. I lifted the bathrobe off Jack and he leaned on the ropes and flexed his knees a couple of times and scuffed his shoes in the rosin. The gong rang and Jack turned quick and went out. Walcott came toward him and they touched gloves and as soon as Walcott dropped his hands Jack jumped his left into his face twice. There wasn't anybody ever boxed better than Jack. Walcott was after him, going forward all the time with his chin on his chest. He's a hooker and he carries his hands pretty low. All he knows is to get in there and sock. But every time he gets in there close, Jack has the left hand in his face. It's just as though it's automatic. Jack just raises the left hand up and it's in Walcott's face. Three or four times Jack brings the right over but Walcott gets it on the shoulder or high up on the head. He's just like all these hookers. The only thing he's afraid of is another one of the same kind. He's covered everywhere you can hurt him. He don't care about a left-hand in his face.

After about four rounds Jack has him bleeding bad and his face all cut up, but every time Walcott's got in close he's socked so hard he's got two big red patches on both sides just below Jack's ribs. Every time he gets in close, Jack ties him up, then gets one hand loose and uppercuts him, but when Walcott gets his hands loose he socks Jack in the body so they can hear it outside in the street. He's a socker.

It goes along like that for three rounds more. They don't talk any. They're working all the time. We worked over Jack plenty too, in between the rounds. He don't look good at all but he never does much work in the ring. He don't move around much and that left-hand is just automatic. It's just like it was connected with Walcott's face and Jack just had to wish it in every time. Jack is always calm in close and he doesn't waste any juice. He knows everything about working in close too and he's getting away with a lot of stuff. While they were in our corner I watched him tie Walcott up, get his right hand loose, turn it and come up with an uppercut that got Walcott's nose with the heel of the glove. Walcott was bleeding bad and leaned his nose on Jack's shoulder so as to give Jack some of it too, and Jack sort of lifted his shoulder sharp and caught him against the nose, and then brought down the right hand and did the same thing again.

Walcott was sore as hell. By the time they'd gone five rounds he hated Jack's guts. Jack wasn't sore; that is, he wasn't any sorer than he always was. He certainly did used to make the fellows he fought hate boxing. That was why he hated Kid Lewis so. He never got the Kid's goat. Kid Lewis always had about three new dirty things Jack couldn't do. Jack was as safe as a church all the time he was in there, as long as he was strong. He certainly was treating Walcott rough. The funny thing was it looked as though Jack was an open classic boxer. That was because he had all that stuff too.

After the seventh round Jack says, 'My left's getting heavy.'

From then he started to take a beating. It didn't show at first. But instead of him running the fight it was Walcott was running it, instead of being safe all the time now he was in trouble. He couldn't keep him out with the left hand now. It looked as though it was the same as ever, only now instead of Walcott's punches just missing him they were just hitting him. He took an awful beating in the body.

'What's the round?' Jack asked.

'The eleventh.'

'I can't stay,' Jack says. 'My legs are going bad.'

Walcott had been just hitting him for a long time. It was like a baseball catcher pulls the ball and takes some of the shock off. From now on Walcott commenced to land solid. He certainly was a socking-machine. Jack was just trying to block everything now. It didn't show what an awful beating he was taking. In between the rounds I worked on his legs. The muscles would flutter under my hands all the time I was rubbing them. He was sick as hell.

'How's it go?' he asked John, turning around, his face all swollen.

'It's his fight.'

'I think I can last,' Jack says. 'I don't want this bohunk to stop me.'

It was going just the way he thought it would. He knew he couldn't beat Walcott. He wasn't strong any more. He was all right though. His money was all right and now he wanted to finish it off right to please himself. He didn't want to be knocked out.

The gong rang and we pushed him out. He went out slow. Walcott came right out after him. Jack put the left in his face and Walcott took it, came in under it and started working on Jack's body. Jack tried to tie him up and it was just like trying to hold onto a buzz-saw. Jack broke away from it and missed with the right. Walcott clipped him with a left-hook and Jack went down. He went down on his hands and knees and looked at us. The referee started counting. Jack was watching us and shaking his head. At eight John motioned to him. You couldn't hear on account of the crowd. Jack got up. The referee had been holding Walcott back with one arm while he counted.

When Jack was on his feet Walcott started toward him.

'Watch yourself, Jimmy,' I heard Solly Freedman yell to him.

Walcott came up to Jack looking at him. Jack stuck the left hand at him. Walcott just shook his head. He backed Jack up against the ropes, measured him and then hooked the left very light to the side of Jack's head and socked the right into the body as hard as he could sock, just as low as he could get it. He must have hit him five inches below the belt. I thought the eyes would come out of Jack's head. They stuck way out. His mouth come open.

The referee grabbed Walcott. Jack stepped forward. If he went down there went fifty thousand bucks. He walked as though all his insides were going to fall out.

'It wasn't low,' he said. 'It was an accident.'

The crowd were yelling so you couldn't hear anything.

'I'm all right,' Jack says. They were right in front of. The referee looks at John and then he shakes his head.

'Come on, you polak son-of-a-bitch,' Jack says to Walcott.

John was hanging onto the ropes. He had the towel ready to chuck in. Jack was standing just a little way out from the ropes. He took a step forward. I saw the sweat come out on his face like somebody had squeezed it and a big drop went down his nose.

'Come on and fight,' Jack says to Walcott.

The referee looked at John and waved Walcott on.

'Go in there, you slob,' he says.

Walcott went in. He didn't know what to do either. He never thought Jack could have stood it. Jack put the left in his face. There was such a hell of a lot of yelling going on. They were right in front of us. Walcott hit him twice. Jack's face was the worst thing I ever saw – the look on it! He was holding himself and all his body together and it all showed on his face. All the time he was thinking and holding his body in where it was busted.

Then he started to sock. His face looked awful all the time. He started to sock with his hands low down by his side, swinging at Walcott. Walcott covered up and Jack was swinging wild at Walcott's head. Then he swung the left and it hit Walcott in the groin and the right hit Walcott right bang where he'd hit Jack. Way below the belt. Walcott went down and grabbed himself there and rolled and twisted around.

The referee grabbed Jack and pushed him toward his corner. John jumps into the ring. There was all this yelling going on.

The referee was talking with the judges and then the announcer got into the ring with the megaphone and says, 'Walcott on a foul.'

The referee is talking to John and he says, 'What could I do? Jack wouldn't take the foul. Then when he's groggy he fouls him.'

'He'd lost it anyway,' John says.

Jack's sitting on the chair. I've got his gloves off and he's holding himself in down there with both hands. When he's got something supporting it his face doesn't look so bad.

'Go over and say you're sorry,' John says into his ear. 'It'll look good.'

Jack stands up and the sweat comes out all over his face. I put the bathrobe around him and he holds himself with one hand under the bathrobe and goes across the ring. They've picked Walcott up and they're working on him. There's a lot of people in Walcott's corner. Nobody speaks to Jack. He leans over Walcott.

'I'm sorry,' Jack says. 'I didn't mean to foul you.'

Walcott doesn't say anything. He looks too damned sick.

'Well, you're the champion now,' Jack says to him. 'I hope you get a hell of a lot of fun out of it.'

'Leave the kid alone,' Solly Freedman says.

'Hello, Solly,' Jack says. 'I'm sorry I fouled your boy.'

Freedman just looks at him.

Jack went to his corner walking that funny jerky way and we got him down through the ropes and through the reporters' tables and out down the aisle. A lot of people want to slap Jack on the back. He goes out through all that mob in his bathrobe to the dressing-room. It's a popular win for Walcott. That's the way the money was bet in the Garden.

Once we got inside the dressing-room Jack lay down and shut his eyes.

'We want to get to the hotel and get a doctor,' John says.

'I'm all busted inside,' Jack says.

'I'm sorry as hell, Jack,' John says.

'It's all right,' Jack says.

He lies there with his eyes shut.

'They certainly tried a nice double-cross,' John said.

'Your friends Morgan and Steinfelt,' Jack said. 'You got nice friends.'

He lies there, his eyes are open now. His face has still got that awful drawn look.

'It's funny how fast you can think when it means that much money,' Jack says.

'You're some boy, Jack,' John says.

'No,' Jack says. 'It was nothing.'

A Simple Enquiry

Outside, the snow was higher than the window. The sunlight came in through the window and shone on a map on the pineboard wall of the hut. The sun was high and the light came in over the top of the snow. A trench had been cut along the open side of the hut, and each clear day the sun, shining on the wall, reflected heat against the snow and widened the trench. It was late March. The major sat at a table against the wall. His adjutant sat at another table.

Around the major's eyes were two white circles where his snow-glasses had protected his face from the sun on the snow. The rest of his face had been burned and then tanned and then burned through the tan. His nose was swollen and there were edges of loose skin where blisters had been. While he worked at the papers he put the fingers of his left hand into a saucer of oil and then spread the oil over his face, touching it very gently with the tips of his fingers. He was very careful to drain his fingers on the edge of the saucer so there was only a film of oil on them, and after he had stroked his forehead and his cheeks, he stroked his nose very delicately between his fingers. When he had finished he stood up, took the saucer of oil and went into the small room of the hut where he slept. 'I'm going to take a little sleep,' he said to the adjutant. In that army an adjutant is not a commissioned officer. 'You will finish up.'

'Yes, signor maggiore,' the adjutant answered. He leaned back in his chair and yawned. He took a paper-covered book out of the pocket of his coat and opened it; then laid it down on the table and lit his pipe. He leaned forward on the table to read and puffed at his pipe. Then he closed the book and put it back in his pocket. He had too much paper-work to get through. He could not enjoy reading until it was done. Outside, the sun went behind a mountain and there was no more light on the wall of the hut. A soldier came in and put some pine branches, chopped into irregular lengths, into the stove. 'Be soft, Pinin,' the adjutant said to him. 'The major is sleeping.'

Pinin was the major's orderly. He was a dark-faced boy, and he fixed the stove, putting the pine wood in carefully, shut the door, and went into the back of the hut again. The adjutant went on with his papers.

'Tonani,' the major called.

'Signor maggiore?'

'Send Pinin in to me.'

'Pinin!' the adjutant called. Pinin came into the room. 'The major wants you,' the adjutant said.

Pinin walked across the main room of the hut towards the major's door. He knocked on the half-opened door. 'Signor maggiore?'

'Come in,' the adjutant heard the major say, 'and shut the door.'

Inside the room the major lay on his bunk. Pinin stood beside the bunk. The major lay with his head on the rucksack that he had stuffed with spare clothing to make a pillow. His long, burned, oiled face looked at Pinin. His hands lay on the blankets.

'You are nineteen?' he asked.

'Yes, signor maggiore.'

'You have ever been in love?'

'How do you mean, signor maggiore?'

'In love – with a girl?'

'I have been with girls.'

'I did not ask that. I asked if you had been in love – with a girl.'

'Yes, signor maggiore.'

'You are in love with this girl now? You don't write her. I read all your letters.'

'I am in love with her,' Pinin said, 'but I do not write her.'

310

'You are sure of this?'

'I am sure.'

'Tonani,' the major said in the same tone of voice, 'can you hear me talking?'

There was no answer from the next room.

'He can not hear,' the major said. 'And you are quite sure that you love a girl?'

'I am sure.'

'And,' the major looked at him quickly, 'that you are not corrupt?'

'I don't know what you mean, corrupt.'

'All right,' the major said. 'You needn't be superior.'

Pinin looked at the floor. The major looked at his brown face, down and up him, and at his hands. Then he went on, not smiling, 'And you don't really want –' the major paused. Pinin looked at the floor. 'That your great desire isn't really –' Pinin looked at the floor. The major leaned his head back on the rucksack and smiled. He was really relieved: life in the army was too complicated. 'You're a good boy,' he said. 'You're a good boy, Pinin. But don't be superior and be careful some one else doesn't come along and take you.'

Pinin stood still beside the bunk.

'Don't be afraid,' the major said. His hands were folded on the blankets. 'I won't touch you. You can go back to your platoon if you like. But you had better stay on as my servant. You've less chance of being killed.'

'Do you want anything of me, signor maggiore?'

'No,' the major said. 'Go on and get on with whatever you were doing. Leave the door open when you go out.'

Pinin went out, leaving the door open. The adjutant looked up at him as he walked awkwardly across the room and out the door. Pinin was flushed and moved differently than he had moved when he brought in the wood for the fire. The adjutant looked after him and smiled. Pinin came in with more wood for the stove. The major, lying on his bunk, looking at his cloth-covered helmet and his snow-glasses that hung from a nail on the wall, heard him walk across the floor. The little devil, he thought, I wonder if he lied to me.

Ten Indians

After one Fourth of July, Nick, driving home late from town in the big wagon with Joe Garner and his family, passed nine drunken Indians along the road. He remembered there were nine because Joe Garner, driving along in the dusk, pulled up the horses, jumped down into the road and dragged an Indian out of the wheel rut. The Indian had been asleep face down in the sand. Joe dragged him into bushes and got back up on the wagon-box.

'That makes nine of them,' Joe said, 'just between here and the edge of town.'

'Them Indians,' said Mrs Garner.

Nick was on the back seat with the two Garner boys. He was looking out from the back seat to see the Indian where Joe had dragged him alongside of the road.

'Was it Billy Tabeshaw?' Carl asked.

'No.'

'His pants looked mighty like Billy.'

'All Indians wear the same kind of pants.'

'I didn't see him at all,' Frank said. 'Pa was down into the road and back up again before I seen a thing. I thought he was killing a snake.'

'Plenty of Indians'll kill snakes tonight, I guess,' Joe Garner said.

'Them Indians,' said Mrs Garner.

They drove along. The road turned off from the main highway and went up into the hills. It was hard pulling for the horses and the boys got down and walked. The road was sandy.

Nick looked back from the top of the hill by the school house. He saw the lights of Petoskey and, off across Little Traverse Bay, the lights of Harbour Springs. They climbed back in the wagon again.

'They ought to put some gravel on that stretch,' Joe Garner said. The wagon went along the road through the woods. Joe and Mrs Garner sat close together on the front seat. Nick sat between the two boys. The road came out into a clearing.

'Right here was where Pa ran over the skunk.'

'It was further on.'

'It don't make no difference where it was,' Joe said without turning his head. 'One place is just as good as another to run over a skunk.'

'I saw two skunks last night,' Nick said.

'Where?'

'Down by the lake. They were looking for dead fish along the beach.'

'They were coons probably,' Carl said.

'They were skunks. I guess I know skunks.'

'You ought to,' Carl said. 'You got an Indian girl.'

'Stop talking that way, Carl,' said Mrs Garner.

'Well, they smell about the same.'

Joe Garner laughed.

'You stop laughing, Joe,' Mrs Garner said. 'I won't have Carl talk that way.'

'Have you got an Indian girl, Nickie?' Joe asked.

'No.'

'He has too, Pa,' Frank said. 'Prudence Mitchell's his girl.'

'She's not.'

'He goes to see her every day.'

'I don't.' Nick, sitting between the two boys in the dark felt hollow and happy inside himself to be teased about Prudence Mitchell. 'She ain't my girl,' he said.

'Listen to him,' said Carl. 'I see them together every day.'

'Carl can't get a girl,' his mother said, 'not even a squaw.'

Carl was quiet.

'Carl ain't no good with girls,' Frank said.

'You shut up.'

313

'You're all right, Carl,' Joe Garner said. 'Girls never got a man anywhere. Look at your pa.'

'Yes, that's what you would say,' Mrs Garner moved close to Joe as the wagon jolted. 'Well, you had plenty of girls in your time.'

'I'll bet Pa wouldn't ever have had a squaw for a girl.'

'Don't you think it,' Joe said. 'You better watch out to keep Prudie, Nick.'

His wife whispered to him and Joe laughed.

'What you laughing at?' asked Frank.

'Don't you say it, Garner,' his wife warned. Joe laughed again.

'Nickie can have Prudence,' Joe Garner said. 'I got a good girl.'

'That's the way to talk,' Mrs Garner said.

The horses were pulling heavily in the sand. Joe reached out in the dark with the whip.

'Come on, pull into it. You'll have to pull harder than this tomorrow.'

They trotted down the long hill, the wagon jolting. At the farmhouse everybody got down. Mrs Garner unlocked the door, went inside, and came out with a lamp in her hand. Carl and Nick unloaded the things from the back of the wagon. Frank sat on the front seat to drive to the barn and put up the horses. Nick went up the steps and opened the kitchen door. Mrs Garner was building a fire in the stove. She turned from pouring kerosene on the wood.

'Good-bye, Mrs Garner,' Nick said. 'Thanks for taking me.'

'Oh shucks, Nickie.'

'I had a wonderful time.'

'We like to have you. Won't you stay and eat some supper?'

'I better go. I think Dad probably waited for me.'

'Well, get along then. Send Carl up to the house, will you?'

'All right.'

'Good-night, Nickie.'

'Good-night, Mrs Garner.'

Nick went out the farmyard and down to the barn. Joe and Frank were milking.

'Good-night,' Nick said. 'I had a swell time.'

314

'Good-night, Nick,' Joe Garner called. 'Aren't you going to stay and eat?'

'No, I can't. Will you tell Carl his mother wants him?'

'All right. Good-night, Nickie.'

Nick walked barefoot along the path through the meadow below the barn. The path was smooth and the dew was cool on his bare feet. He climbed a fence at the end of the meadow, went down through a ravine, his feet wet in the swamp mud, and climbed up through the dry beech woods until he saw the lights of the cottage. He climbed over the fence and walked around to the front porch. Through the window he saw his father sitting by the table, reading in the light from the big lamp. Nick opened the door and went in.

'Well, Nickie,' his father said, 'was it a good day?'

'I had a swell time, Dad. It was a swell Fourth of July.'

'Are you hungry?'

'You bet.'

'What did you do with your shoes?'

'I left them in the wagon at Garner's.'

'Come on out to the kitchen.'

Nick's father went ahead with the lamp. He stopped and lifted the lid of the ice-box. Nick went on into the kitchen. His father brought out a piece of cold chicken on a plate and a pitcher of milk and put them on the table before Nick. He put down the lamp.

'There's some pie too,' he said. 'Will that hold you?'

'It's grand.'

His father sat down in a chair beside the oil-cloth-covered table. He made a big shadow on the kitchen wall.

'Who won the ball game?'

'Petoskey. Five to three.'

His father sat watching him eat and filled his glass from the milk-pitcher. Nick drank and wiped his mouth on his napkin. His father reached over to the shelf for the pie. He cut Nick a big piece. It was huckleberry pie.

'What did you do, Dad?'

'I went out fishing in the morning.'

'What did you get?'

'Only perch.'

His father sat watching Nick eat the pie.

'What did you do this afternoon?' Nick asked.

'I went for a walk up by the Indian camp.'

'Did you see anybody?'

'The Indians were all in town getting drunk.'

'Didn't you see anybody at all?'

'I saw your friend, Prudie.'

'Where was she?'

'She was in the woods with Frank Washburn. I ran onto them. They were having quite a time.'

His father was not looking at him.

'What were they doing?'

'I didn't stay to find out.'

'Tell me what they were doing.'

'I don't know,' his father said. 'I just heard them threshing around.'

'How did you know it was them?'

'I saw them.'

'I thought you said you didn't see them.'

'Oh, yes, I saw them.'

'Who was it with her?' Nick asked.

'Frank Washburn.'

'Were they – were they –'

'Were they what?'

'Were they happy?'

'I guess so.'

His father got up from the table and went out the kitchen screen door. When he came back Nick was looking at his plate. He had been crying.

'Have some more?' His father picked up the knife to cut the pie.

'No,' said Nick.

'You better have another piece.'

'No, I don't want any.'

His father cleared off the table.

'Where were they in the woods?' Nick asked.

'Up back of the camp.' Nick looked at his plate. His father said, 'You better go to bed, Nick.'

'All right.'

316

Nick went into his room, undressed, and got into bed. He heard his father moving around in the living room. Nick lay in the bed with his face in the pillow.

'My heart's broken,' he thought. 'If I feel this way my heart must be broken.'

After a while he heard his father blow out the lamp and go into his own room. He heard a wind come up in the trees outside and felt it come in cool through the screen. He lay for a long time with his face in the pillow, and after a while he forgot to think about Prudence and finally he went to sleep. When he awoke in the night he heard the wind in the hemlock tree outside the cottage and the waves of the lake coming in on the shore, and he went back to sleep. In the morning there was a big wind blowing and the waves were running high up on the beach and he was awake a long time before he remembered that his heart was broken.

A Canary For One

The train passed very quickly a long, red stone house with a garden and four thick palm-trees with tables under them in the shade. On the other side was the sea. Then there was a cutting through red stone and clay, and the sea was only occasionally and far below against rocks.

'I bought him in Palermo,' the American lady said. 'We only had an hour ashore and it was Sunday morning. The man wanted to be paid in dollars and I gave him a dollar and a half. He really sings very beautifully.'

It was very hot in the train and it was very hot in the *lit salon* compartment. There was no breeze came through the open window. The American lady pulled the window-blind down and there was no more sea, even occasionally. On the other side there was glass, then the corridor, then an open window, and outside the window were dusty trees and an oiled road and flat fields of grapes, with gray-stone hills behind them.

There was smoke from many tall chimneys – coming into Marseilles, and the train slowed down and followed one track through many others into the station. The train stayed twenty-five minutes in the station at Marseilles and the American lady bought a copy of *The Daily Mail* and a half-bottle of Evian water. She walked a little way along the station platform, but she stayed near the steps of the car because at Cannes, where it stopped for twelve minutes, the train had left with no signal of departure and she had gotten on only just in time. The American lady was a little deaf and she was afraid that perhaps signals of departure were given and that she did not hear them.

The train left the station in Marseilles and there was not only the switch-yards and the factory smoke but, looking back, the town of Marseilles and the harbor with stone hills behind it and the last of the sun on the water. As it was getting dark the train passed a farmhouse burning in a field. Motor-cars were stopped along the road and bedding and things from inside the farmhouse were spread in the field. Many people were watching the house burn. After it was dark the train was in Avignon. People got on and off. At the news-stand Frenchmen, returning to Paris, bought that day's French papers. On the station platform were negro soldiers. They wore brown uniforms and were tall and their faces shone, close under the electric light. Their faces were very black and they were too tall to stare. The train left Avignon station with the negroes standing there. A short white sergeant was with them.

Inside the *lit salon* compartment the porter had pulled down the three beds from inside the wall and prepared them for sleeping. In the night the American lady lay without sleeping because the train was a *rapide* and went very fast and she was afraid of the speed in the night. The American lady's bed was the one next to the window. The canary from Palermo, a cloth spread over his cage, was out of the draft in the corridor that went into the compartment wash room. There was a blue light outside the compartment, and all night the train went very fast and the American lady lay awake and waited for a wreck.

In the morning the train was near Paris, and after the American lady had come out from the wash-room, looking very wholesome and middle-aged and American in spite of not having slept, and had taken the cloth off the birdcage and hung the cage in the sun, she went back to the restaurant-car for breakfast. When she came back to the *lit salon* compartment again, the beds had been pushed back into the wall and made into seats, the canary was shaking his feathers in the sunlight that came through the open window, and the train was much nearer Paris.

'He loves the sun,' the American lady said. 'He'll sing now in a little while.'

The canary shook his feathers and pecked into them. 'I've

always loved birds,' the American lady said. 'I'm taking him home to my little girl. There – he's singing now.'

The canary chirped and the feathers on his throat stood out, and he dropped his bill and pecked into his feathers again. The train crossed a river and passed through a very carefully tended forest. The train passed through many outside of Paris towns. There were tram-cars in the towns and big advertisements for the Belle Jardinière and Dubonnet and Pernod on the walls toward the train. All that the train passed through looked as though it were for breakfast. For several minutes I had not listened to the American lady, who was talking to my wife.

'Is your husband American too?' asked the lady.

'Yes,' said my wife. 'We're both Americans.'

'I thought you were English.'

'Oh, no.'

'Perhaps that was because I wore braces,' I said. I had started to say suspenders and changed it to braces in the mouth, to keep my English character. The American lady did not hear. She was really quite deaf; she read lips, and I had not looked towards her. I had looked out of the window. She went on talking to my wife.

'I'm so glad you're Americans. American men make the best husbands,' the American lady was saying. 'That was why we left the Continent, you know. My daughter fell in love with a man in Vevey.' She stopped. 'They were simply madly in love.' She stopped again. 'I took her away, of course.'

'Did she get over it?' asked my wife.

'I don't think so,' said the American lady. 'She wouldn't eat anything and she wouldn't sleep at all. I've tried so very hard, but she doesn't seem to take an interest in anything. She doesn't care about things. I couldn't have her marrying a foreigner.' She paused. 'Some one, a very good friend, told me once, "No foreigner can make an American girl a good husband."'

'No,' said my wife, 'I suppose not.'

The American lady admired my wife's travelling-coat, and it turned out that the American lady had bought her own clothes for twenty years now from the same maison de couture in the Rue Saint Honoré. They had her measurements, and a vendeuse who knew her and her tastes picked the dresses out for her and they were sent to America. They came to the post-office near where she lived up-town in New York, and the duty was never exorbitant because they opened the dresses there in the post-office to appraise them and they were always very simple-looking and with no gold lace or ornaments that would make the dresses look expensive. Before the present vendeuse, named Thérèse, there had been another vendeuse, named Amélie. Altogether there had only been these two in the twenty years. It had always been the same couturier. Prices, however, had gone up. The exchange, though, equalized that. They had her daughter's measurements now too. She was grown up and there was not much chance of their changing now.

The train was now coming into Paris. The fortifications were levelled but grass had not grown. There were many cars standing on tracks – brown wooden restaurant-cars and brown wooden sleeping-cars that would go to Italy at five o'clock that night, if that train still left at five; the cars were marked Paris-Rome, and cars, with seats on the roofs, that went back and forth to the suburbs with, at certain hours, people in all the seats and on the roofs, if that were the way it were still done, and passing were the white walls and many windows of houses. Nothing had eaten any breakfast.

'Americans make the best husbands,' the American lady said to my wife. I was getting down the bags. 'American men are the only men in the world to marry.'

'How long ago did you leave Vevey?' asked my wife.

'Two years ago this fall. It's her, you know, that I'm taking the canary to.'

'Was the man your daughter was in love with a Swiss?'

'Yes' said the American lady. 'He was from a very good family in Vevey. He was going to be an engineer. They met there in Vevey. They used to go on long walks together.'

'I know Vevey,' said my wife. 'We were there on our honeymoon.'

'Were you really? That must have been lovely. I had no idea, of course, that she'd fall in love with him.'

'It was a very lovely place,' said my wife.

'It's such a fine old hotel,' said the American lady.

'Yes,' said my wife. 'We had a very fine room and in the fall the country was lovely.'

'Were you there in the fall?'

'Yes,' said my wife.

We were passing three cars that had been in a wreck. They were splintered open and the roofs sagged in.

'Look,' I said. 'There's been a wreck.'

The American lady looked and saw the last car. 'I was afraid of just that all night,' she said. 'I have terrific presentiments about things sometimes. I'll never travel on a *rapide* again at night. There must be other comfortable trains that don't go so fast.'

Then the train was in the dark of the Gare de Lyons, and then stopped and porters came up to the windows. I handed bags through the windows, and we were out on the dim longness of the platform, and the American lady put herself in charge of one of three men from Cook's who said: 'Just a moment, madame, and I'll look for your name.'

The porter brought a truck and piled on the baggage, and my wife said good-bye and I said good-bye to the American lady, whose name had been found by the man from Cook's on a typewritten page in a sheaf of typewritten pages which he replaced in his pocket.

We followed the porter with the truck down the long cement platform beside the train. At the end was a gate and a man took the tickets.

We were returning to Paris to set up separate residences.

An Alpine Idyll

It was hot coming down into the valley even in the early morning. The sun melted the snow from the skis we were carrying and dried the wood. It was spring in the valley but the sun was very hot. We came along the road into Galtur carrying our skis and rucksacks. As we passed the churchyard a burial was just over. I said, 'Grüss Gott,' to the priest as he walked past us coming out of the churchyard. The priest bowed.

'It's funny a priest never speaks to you,' John said.

'You'd think they'd like to say "Grüss Gott."'

'They never answer,' John said.

We stopped in the road and watched the sexton shovelling in the new earth. A peasant with a black beard and high leather boots stood beside the grave. The sexton stopped shovelling and straightened his back. The peasant in the high boots took the spade from the sexton and went on filling the grave – spreading the earth evenly as a man spreading manure in a garden. In the bright May morning the grave-filling looked unreal. I could not imagine any one being dead.

'Imagine being buried on a day like this,' I said to John.

'I wouldn't like it.'

'Well,' I said, 'we don't have to do it.'

We went on up the road past the houses of the town to the inn. We had been skiing in the Silvretta for a month, and it was good to be down in the valley. In the Silvretta the skiing had been all right, but it was spring skiing, the snow was good only in the early morning and again in the evening. The rest of the time it was spoiled by the sun. We were both tired of the sun.

You could not get away from the sun. The only shadows were made by rocks or by the hut that was built under the protection of a rock beside a glacier, and in the shade the sweat froze in your underclothing. You could not sit outside the hut without dark glasses. It was pleasant to be burned black but the sun had been very tiring. You could not rest in it. I was glad to be down away from the snow. It was too late in the spring to be up in the Silvretta. I was a little tired of skiing. We had stayed too long. I could taste the snow water we had been drinking melted off the tin roof of the hut. The taste was a part of the way I felt about skiing. I was glad there were other things beside skiing, and I was glad to be down, away from the unnatural high mountain spring, into this May morning in the valley.

The innkeeper sat on the porch of the inn, his chair tipped back against the wall. Beside him sat the cook.

'Ski-heil!' said the innkeeper.

'Heil!' we said and leaned the skis against the wall and took off our packs.

'How was it up above?' asked the innkeeper.

'Schön. A little too much sun.'

'Yes. There's too much sun this time of year.'

The cook sat on in his chair. The innkeeper went in with us and unlocked his office and brought out our mail. There was a bundle of letters and some papers.

'Let's get some beer,' John said.

'Good. We'll drink it inside.'

The proprietor brought two bottles and we drank them while we read the letters.

'We better have some more beer,' John said. A girl brought it this time. She smiled as she opened the bottles.

'Many letters,' she said.

'Yes. Many.'

'Prosit,' she said and went out, taking the empty bottles.

'I'd forgotten what beer tasted like.'

'I hadn't,' John said. 'Up in the hut I used to think about it a lot.'

'Well,' I said, 'we've got it now.'

'You oughtn't to ever do anything too long.'

'No. We were up there too long.'

'Too damn long,' John said. 'It's no good doing a thing too long.'

The sun came through the open window and shone through the beer bottles on the table. The bottles were half full. There was a little froth on the beer in the bottles, not much because it was very cold. It collared up when you poured it into the tall glasses. I looked out of the open window at the white road. The trees beside the road were dusty. Beyond was a green field and a stream. There were trees along the stream and a mill with a water wheel. Through the open side of the mill I saw a long log and a saw in it rising and falling. No one seemed to be tending it. There were four crows walking in the green field. One crow sat in a tree watching. Outside on the porch the cook got off his chair and passed into the hall that led back into the kitchen. Inside, the sunlight shone through the empty glasses on the table. John was leaning forward with his head on his arms.

Through the window I saw two men come up the front steps. They came into the drinking room. One was the bearded peasant in the high boots. The other was the sexton. They sat down at the table under the window. The girl came in and stood by their table. The peasant did not seem to see her. He sat with his hands on the table. He wore his old army clothes. There were patches on the elbows.

'What will it be?' asked the sexton. The peasant did not pay any attention.

'What will you drink?'

'Schnapps,' the peasant said.

'And a quarter litre of red wine,' the sexton told the girl.

The girl brought the drinks and the peasant drank the schnapps. He looked out of the window. The sexton watched him. John had his head forward on the table. He was asleep.

The innkeeper came in and went over to the table. He spoke in dialect and the sexton answered him. The peasant looked out of the window. The innkeeper went out of the room. The peasant stood up. He took a folded ten-thousand kronen note out of a leather pocket-book and unfolded it. The girl came up.

'Alles?' she asked.

'Alles,' he said.

'Let me buy the wine,' the sexton said.

'Alles,' the peasant repeated to the girl. She put her hand in the pocket of her apron, brought it out full of coins and counted out the change. The peasant went out the door. As soon as he was gone the innkeeper came into the room again and spoke to the sexton. He sat down at the table. They talked in dialect. The sexton was amused. The innkeeper was disgusted. The sexton stood up from the table. He was a little man with a mustache. He leaned out of the window and looked up the road.

'There he goes in,' he said.

'In the Löwen?'

'Ja.'

They talked again and then the innkeeper came over to our table. The innkeeper was a tall man and old. He looked at John asleep.

'He's pretty tired.'

'Yes, we were up early.'

'Will you want to eat soon?'

'Any time,' I said. 'What is there to eat?'

'Anything you want. The girl will bring the eating-card.'

The girl brought the menu. John woke up. The menu was written in ink on a card and the card slipped into a wooden paddle.

'There's the speise-karte,' I said to John. He looked at it. He was still sleepy.

'Won't you have a drink with us?' I asked the innkeeper.

He sat down. 'Those peasants are beasts,' said the innkeeper.

'We saw that one at a funeral coming into town.'

'That was his wife.'

'Oh.'

'He's a beast. All these peasants are beasts.'

'How do you mean?'

'You wouldn't believe it. You wouldn't believe what just happened about that one.'

'Tell me.'

'You wouldn't believe it.' The innkeeper spoke to the sexton. 'Franz, come over here.' The sexton came, bringing his little bottle of wine and his glass.

326

'The gentlemen are just come down from the Wiesbadener-hütte,' the innkeeper said. We shook hands.

'What will you drink?' I asked.

'Nothing,' Franz shook his finger.

'Another quarter liter?'

'All right.'

'Do you understand dialect?' the innkeeper asked.

'No.'

'What's it all about?' John asked.

'He's going to tell us about the peasant we saw filling the grave, coming into town.'

'I can't understand it, anyway,' John said. 'It goes too fast for me.'

'That peasant,' the innkeeper said, 'today he brought his wife in to be buried. She died last November.'

'December,' said the sexton.

'That makes nothing. She died last December then, and he notified the commune.'

'December eighteenth,' said the sexton.

'Anyway, he couldn't bring her over to be buried until the snow was gone.'

'He lives on the other side of the Paznaun,' said the sexton. 'But he belongs to this parish.'

'He couldn't bring her out at all?' I asked.

'No. He can only come, from where he lives, on skis until the snow melts. So today he brought her in to be buried and the priest, when he looked at her face, didn't want to bury her. You go on and tell it,' he said to the sexton. 'Speak German, not dialect.'

'It was very funny with the priest,' said the sexton. 'In the report to the commune she died of heart trouble. We knew she had heart trouble here. She used to faint in church sometimes. She did not come for a long time. She wasn't strong to climb. When the priest uncovered her face he asked Olz, "Did your wife suffer much?" "No" said Olz. "When I came in the house she was dead across the bed."

'The priest looked at her again. He didn't like it.

'"How did her face get that way?"

'"I don't know," Olz said.

327

' "You'd better find out," the priest said, and put the blanket back. Olz didn't say anything. The priest looked at him. Olz looked back at the priest. "You want to know?" '

' "I must know," the priest said.

'This is where it's good,' the innkeeper said. 'Listen to this. Go on, Franz.'

' "Well," said Olz, "when she died I made the report to the commune and I put her in the shed across the top of the big wood. When I started to use the big wood she was stiff and I put her up against the wall. Her mouth was open and when I came into the shed at night to cut up the wood, I hung the lantern from it."

' "Why did you do that?" asked the priest.

' "I don't know," said Olz.

' "Did you do that many times?"

' "Every time I went to work in the shed at night.'

' "It was very wrong," said the priest. "Did you love your wife?"

' "Ja, I loved her," Olz said. "I loved her fine." '

'Did you understand it all?' asked the innkeeper. 'You understand it all about his wife?'

'I heard it.'

'How about eating?' John asked.

'You order,' I said. 'Do you think it's true?' I asked the innkeeper.

'Sure it's true,' he said. 'These peasants are beasts.'

'Where did he go now?'

'He's gone to drink at my colleague's, the Löwen.'

'He didn't want to drink with me,' said the sexton.

'He didn't want to drink with me, after *he* knew about his wife,' said the innkeeper.

'Say,' said John. 'How about eating?'

'All right,' I said.

A Pursuit Race

William Campbell had been in a pursuit race with a burlesque show ever since Pittsburgh. In a pursuit race, in bicycle racing, riders start at equal intervals to ride after one another. They ride very fast because the race is usually limited to a short distance and if they slow their riding another rider who maintains his pace will make up the space that separates them equally at the start. As soon as a rider is caught and passed he is out of the race and must get down from his bicycle and leave the track. If none of the riders are caught the winner of the race is the one who has gained the most distance. In most pursuit races, if there are only two riders, one of the riders is caught inside of six miles. The burlesque show caught William Campbell at Kansas City.

William Campbell had hoped to hold a slight lead over the burlesque show until they reached the Pacific coast. As long as he preceded the burlesque show as advance man he was being paid. When the burlesque show caught up with him he was in bed. He was in bed when the manager of the burlesque troup came into his room and after the manager had gone out he decided that he might as well stay in bed. It was very cold in Kansas City and he was in no hurry to go out. He did not like Kansas City. He reached under the bed for a bottle and drank. It made his stomach feel better. Mr Turner, the manager of the burlesque show, had refused a drink.

William Campbell's interview with Mr Turner had been a little strange. Mr Turner had knocked on the door. Campbell had said: 'Come in!' When Mr Turner came into the room he

329

saw clothing on a chair, an open suitcase, the bottle on a chair beside the bed, and some one lying in the bed completely covered by the bed-clothes.

'Mister Campbell,' Mr Turner said.

'You can't fire me,' William Campbell said from underneath the covers. It was warm and white and close under the covers. 'You can't fire me because I've got down off my bicycle.'

'You're drunk,' Mr Turner said.

'Oh, yes,' William Campbell said, speaking directly against the sheet and feeling the texture with his lips.

'You're a fool,' Mr Turner said. He turned off the electric light. The light had been burning all night. It was now ten o'clock in the morning. 'You're a drunken fool. When did you get into this town?'

'I got into this town last night,' William Campbell said, speaking against the sheet. He found he liked to talk through a sheet. 'Did you ever talk through a sheet?'

'Don't try to be funny. You aren't funny.'

'I'm not being funny. I'm just talking through a sheet.'

'You're talking through a sheet all right.'

'You can go now, Mr Turner,' Campbell said. 'I don't work for you any more.'

'You know that anyway.'

'I know a lot,' William Campbell said. He pulled down the sheet and looked at Mr Turner. 'I know enough so I don't mind looking at you at all. Do you want to hear what I know?'

'No.'

'Good,' said William Campbell. 'Because really I don't know anything at all. I was just talking.' He pulled the sheet up over his face again. 'I love it under a sheet,' he said. Mr Turner stood beside the bed. He was a middle-aged man with a large stomach and a bald head and he had many things to do. 'You ought to stop off here, Billy, and take a cure,' he said. 'I'll fix it up if you want to do it.'

'I don't want to take a cure,' William Campbell said. 'I don't want to take a cure at all. I am perfectly happy. All my life I have been perfectly happy.'

'How long have you been this way?'

'What a question!' William Campbell breathed in and out through the sheet.

'How long have you been stewed, Billy?'

'Haven't I done my work?'

'Sure. I just asked you how long you've been stewed, Billy.'

'I don't know. But I've got my wolf back,' he touched the sheet with his tongue. 'I've had him for a week.'

'The hell you have.'

'Oh, yes. My dear wolf. Every time I take a drink he goes outside the room. He can't stand alcohol. The poor little fellow.' He moved his tongue round and round on the sheet. 'He's a lovely wolf. He's just like he always was.' William Campbell shut his eyes and took a deep breath.

'You got to take a cure, Bill,' Mr Turner said. 'You won't mind the Keeley. It isn't bad.'

'The Keeley,' William Campbell said. 'It isn't far from London.' He shut his eyes and opened them, moving the eyelashes against the sheet. 'I just love sheets,' he said. He looked at Mr Turner.

'Listen, you think I'm drunk.'

'You *are* drunk.'

'No, I'm not.'

'You're drunk and you've had D.T.'s.'

'No.' William Campbell held the sheet around his head. 'Dear sheet,' he said. He breathed against it gently. 'Pretty sheet. You love me, don't you, sheet? It's all in the price of the room. Just like in Japan. No,' he said. 'Listen Billy, dear Sliding Billy, I have a surprise for you. I'm not drunk. I'm hopped to the eyes.'

'No,' said Mr Turner.

'Take a look.' William Campbell carefully pulled the right sleeve of his pyjama jacket under the sheet, then shoved the right forearm out. 'Look at that.' On the forearm, from just above the wrist to the elbow, were small blue circles around tiny dark blue punctures. The circles almost touched one another. 'That's the new development,' William Campbell said. 'I drink a little now once in a while, just to drive the wolf out of the room.'

'They got a cure for that,' 'Sliding Billy' Turner said.

'No,' William Campbell said. 'They haven't got a cure for anything.'

'You can't just quit like that, Billy,' Turner said. He sat on the bed.

'Be careful of my sheet,' William Campbell said.

'You can't just quit at your age and take to pumping yourself full of that stuff just because you got in a jam.'

'There's a law against it. If that's what you mean.'

'No, I mean you got to fight it out.'

Billy Campbell caressed the sheet with his lips and his tongue. 'Dear sheet,' he said. 'I can kiss this sheet and see right through it at the same time.'

'Cut it out about the sheet. You can't just take to that stuff, Billy.'

William Campbell shut his eyes. He was beginning to feel a slight nausea. He knew that this nausea would increase steadily, without there ever being the relief of sickness, until something was done against it. It was at this point that he suggested that Mr Turner have a drink. Mr Turner declined. William Campbell took a drink from the bottle. It was a temporary measure. Mr Turner watched him. Mr Turner had been in this room much longer than he should have been, he had many things to do; although living in daily association with people who used drugs, he had a horror of drugs, and he was very fond of William Campbell; he did not wish to leave him. He was very sorry for him and he felt a cure might help. He knew there were good cures in Kansas City. But he had to go. He stood up.

'Listen Billy,' William Campbell said, 'I want to tell you something. You're called "Sliding Billy." That's because you can slide. I'm called just Billy. That's because I never could slide at all. I can't slide, Billy. I can't slide. It just catches. Every time I try it, it catches.' He shut his eyes. 'I can't slide, Billy. It's awful when you can't slide.'

'Yes,' said 'Sliding Billy' Turner.

'Yes, what?' William Campbell looked at him.

'You were saying.'

'No,' said William Campbell. 'I wasn't saying. It must have been a mistake.'

332

'You were saying about sliding.'

'No. It couldn't have been about sliding. But listen, Billy, and I'll tell you a secret. Stick to sheets, Billy. Keep away from women and horses and, and –' he stopped '– eagles, Billy. If you love horses you'll get horse-shit, and if you love eagles you'll get eagle-shit.' He stopped and put his head under the sheet.

'I got to go,' said 'Sliding Billy' Turner.

'If you love women you'll get a dose,' William Campbell said. 'If you love horses –'

'Yes, you said that.'

'Said what?'

'About horses and eagles.'

'Oh, yes. And if you love sheets.' He breathed on the sheet and stroked his nose against it. 'I don't know about sheets,' he said. 'I just started to love this sheet.'

'I have to go,' Mr Turner said. 'I got a lot to do.'

'That's all right,' William Campbell said. 'Everybody's got to go.'

'I better go.'

'All right, you go.'

'Are you all right, Billy?'

'I was never so happy in my life.'

'And you're all right?'

'I'm fine. You go along. I'll just lie here for a little while. Around noon I'll get up.'

But when Mr Turner came up to William Campbell's room at noon William Campbell was sleeping and as Mr Turner was a man who knew what things in life were very valuable he did not wake him.

Today is Friday

Three Roman soldiers are in a drinking-place at eleven o'clock at night. There are barrels around the wall. Behind the wooden counter is a Hebrew wine-seller. The three Roman soldiers are a little cock-eyed.

1st Roman Soldier – You tried the red?

2nd Soldier – No, I ain't tried it

1st Soldier – You better try it.

2nd Soldier – All right, George, we'll have a round of the red.

Hebrew Wine-seller – Here you are, gentlemen. You'll like that. [*He sets down an earthenware pitcher that he has filled from one of the casks.*] That's a nice little wine.

1st Soldier – Have a drink of it yourself. [*He turns to the third Roman soldier who is leaning on a barrel.*] What's the matter with you?

3rd Soldier – I got a gut-ache.

2nd Soldier – You've been drinking water.

1st Soldier – Try some of the red.

3rd Soldier – I can't drink the damn stuff. It makes my gut sour.

1st Soldier – You been out here too long.

3rd Soldier – Hell, don't I know it?

1st Soldier – Say, George, can't you give this gentleman something to fix up his stomach?

Hebrew Wine-seller – I got it right here.

[*The third soldier tastes the cup that the wine-seller has mixed for him.*]

3rd Soldier – Hey, what you put in that, camel chips?

Wine-seller – You drink that right down, Lootenant. That'll fix you up right.

3rd Soldier – Well, I couldn't feel any worse.

1st Soldier – Take a chance on it. George fixed me up fine the other day.

Hebrew Wine-seller – You were in bad shape, Lootenant. I know what fixes up a bad stomach.

[*The third Roman soldier drinks the cup down.*]

3rd Soldier –Jesus Christ [*He makes a face.*]

2nd Soldier – That false alarm!

1st Soldier – Oh, I don't know. He was pretty good in there today.

2nd Soldier – Why didn't he come down off the cross?

1st Soldier – He didn't want to come down off the cross. That's not his play.

2nd Soldier – Show me a guy that doesn't want to come down off the cross.

1st Soldier – Aw, hell, you don't know anything about it. Ask George there. Did he want to come down off the cross, George?

Wine-seller – I'll tell you, gentlemen, I wasn't out there. It's a thing I haven't taken any interest in.

2nd Soldier – Listen, I seen a lot of them – here and plenty of other places. Any time you show me one that doesn't want to get down off the cross when the time comes – when the time comes, I mean – I'll climb right up with him.

1st Soldier – I thought he was pretty good in there today.

3rd Soldier – He was all right.

2nd Soldier – You guys don't know what I'm talking about. I'm not saying whether he was good or not. What I mean is, when the time comes. When they first start nailing him, there isn't none of them wouldn't stop it if they could.

1st Soldier – Didn't you follow it, George?

Wine-seller – No, I didn't take any interest in it, Lootenant.

1st Soldier – I was surprised how he acted.

3rd Soldier – The part I don't like is the nailing them on. You know, that must get to you pretty bad.

2nd Soldier – It isn't that that's so bad, as when they first lift 'em up. [*He makes a lifting gesture with his two palms together.*] When the weight starts to pull on 'em. That's when it gets 'em.

3rd Soldier – It takes some of them pretty bad.

1st Soldier – Ain't I seen 'em? I seen plenty of them. I tell you, he was pretty good in there today.

[*The second Roman soldier smiles at the Hebrew wine-seller.*]

2nd Soldier – You're a regular Christer, big boy.

1st Soldier – Sure, go on and kid him. But listen while I tell you something. He was pretty good in there today.

2nd Soldier – What about some more wine?

[*The wine-seller looks up expectantly. The third soldier is sitting with his head down. He does not look well.*]

3rd Soldier – I don't wany any more.

2nd Soldier – Just for two, George.

[*The wine-seller puts out a pitcher of wine, a size smaller than the last one. He leans forward on the wooden counter.*]

1st Soldier – You see his girl?

2nd Soldier – Wasn't I standing right by her?

1st Soldier – She's a nice looker.

2nd Soldier – I knew her before he did. [*He winks at the wine-seller.*]

1st Soldier – I used to see her around the town.

2nd Soldier – She used to have a lot of stuff. He never brought *her* no good luck.

1st Soldier – Oh, he ain't lucky. But he looked pretty good to me in there today.

2nd Soldier – What became of his gang?

1st Soldier – Oh, they faded out. Just the women stuck by him.

2nd Soldier – They were a pretty yellow crowd. When they seen him go up there they didn't want any of it.

1st Soldier – The women stuck all right.

2nd Soldier – Sure they stuck all right.

1st Soldier – You see me slip the old spear into him?

2nd Soldier – You'll get into trouble doing that some day.

336

1st Soldier – It was the least I could do for him. I'll tell you he looked pretty good to me in there today.

Hebrew Wine-seller – Gentlemen, you know I got to close.

1st Soldier – We'll have one more round.

2nd Soldier – What's the use? This stuff don't get you anywhere. Come on, let's go.

1st Soldier – Just another round.

3rd Soldier – [*Getting up from the barrel*] – No, come on. Let's go. I feel like hell tonight.

1st Soldier – Just one more.

2nd Soldier – No, come on. We're going to go. Good night, George. Put it on the bill.

Hebrew Wine-seller – Good night, gentlemen. [*He looks a little worried.*] You couldn't let me have a little something on account, Lootenant?

2nd Soldier – What the hell, George! Wednesday's pay-day.

Wine-seller – It's all right, Lootenant. Good-night, gentlemen.

[*The three Roman soldiers go out the door into the street.*]
[*Outside in the street.*]

2nd Soldier – George is a kike just like all the rest of them.

1st Soldier – Oh, George is a nice fella.

2nd Soldier – Everybody's a nice fella to you tonight.

3rd Soldier – Come on, let's go up to the barracks. I feel like hell tonight.

2nd Soldier – You been out here too long.

3rd Soldier – No, it ain't just that. I feel like hell.

2nd Soldier – You been out here too long. That's all.

CURTAIN

Banal Story

So he ate an orange, slowly spitting out the seeds. Outside, the snow was turning to rain. Inside, the electric stove seemed to give no heat and rising from his writing-table, he sat down upon the stove. How good it felt! Here, at last, was life.

He reached for another orange. Far away in Paris, Mascart had knocked Danny Frush cuckoo in the second round. Far off in Mesopotamia, twenty-one feet of snow had fallen. Across the world in distant Australia, the English cricketers were sharpening up their wickets. *There* was Romance.

Patrons of the arts and letters have discovered The Forum, he read. It is the guide, philosopher, and friend of the thinking minority. Prize short-stories – will their authors write our best-sellers of tomorrow?

You will enjoy these warm, homespun, American tales, bits of real life on the open ranch, in crowded tenement or comfortable home, and all with a healthy undercurrent of humor.

I must read them, he thought.

He read on. Our children's children – what of them? Who of them? New means must be discovered to find room for us under the sun. Shall this be done by war or can it be done by peaceful methods?

Or will we all have to move to Canada?

Our deepest convictions – will Science upset them? Our civilization – is it inferior to older orders of things?

And meanwhile, in the far-off dripping jungles of Yucatan, sounded the chopping of the axes of the gum-choppers.

Do we want big men – or do we want them cultured? Take

338

Joyce. Take President Coolidge. What star must our college students aim at? There is Jack Britton. There is Doctor Henry Van Dyke. Can we reconcile the two? Take the case of Young Stribling.

And what of our daughters who must make their own Soundings? Nancy Hawthorne is obliged to make her own Soundings in the sea of life. Bravely and sensibly she faces the problems which come to every girl of eighteen.

It was a splendid booklet.

Are you a girl of eighteen? Take the case of Joan of Arc. Take the case of Bernard Shaw. Take the case of Betsy Ross.

Think of these things in 1925 – Was there a risqué page in Puritan history? Were there two sides to Pocahontas? Did she have a fourth dimension?

Are modern paintings – and poetry – Art? Yes and No. Take Picasso.

Have tramps codes of conduct? Send your mind adventuring.

There is Romance everywhere. *Forum* writers talk to the point, are possessed of humor and wit. But they do not try to be smart and are never long-winded.

Live the full life of the mind, exhilarated by new ideas, intoxicated by the Romance of the unusual. He laid down the booklet.

And meanwhile, stretched flat on a bed in a darkened room in his house in Triana, Manuel Garcia Maera lay with a tube in each lung, drowning with the pneumonia. All the papers in Andalucia devoted special supplements to his death, which had been expected for some days. Men and boys bought full length coloured pictures of him to remember him by, and lost the pictures they had of him in their memories by looking at the lithographs. Bull-fighters were very relieved he was dead, because he did always in the bull-ring the things they could only do sometimes. They all marched in the rain behind his coffin and there were one hundred and forty-seven bull-fighters followed him out to the cemetery, where they buried him in the tomb next to Joselito. After the funeral everyone sat in the cafés out of the rain, and many coloured pictures of Maera were sold to men who rolled them up and put them away in their pockets.

Now I Lay Me

That night we lay on the floor in the room and I listened to the silk-worms eating. The silk-worms fed in racks of mulberry leaves and all night you could hear them eating and a dropping sound in the leaves. I myself did not want to sleep because I had been living for a long time with the knowledge that if I ever shut my eyes in the dark and let myself go, my soul would go out of my body. I had been that way for a long time, ever since I had been blown up at night and felt it go out of me and go off and then come back. I tried never to think about it, but it had started to go since, in the nights, just at the moment of going off to sleep, and I could only stop it by a very great effort. So while now I am fairly sure that it would not really have gone out, yet then, that summer, I was unwilling to make the experiment.

I had different ways of occupying myself while I lay awake. I would think of a trout stream I had fished along when I was a boy and fish its whole length very carefully in my mind; fishing very carefully under all the logs, all the turns of the bank, the deep holes and the clear shallow stretches, sometimes catching trout and sometimes losing them. I would stop fishing at noon to eat my lunch; sometimes on a log over the stream; sometimes on a high bank under a tree, and I always ate my lunch very slowly and watched the stream below me while I ate. Often I ran out of bait because I would take only ten worms with me in a tobacco tin when I started. When I had used them all I had to find more worms, and sometimes it was very difficult digging in the bank of the stream where the cedar trees

340

kept out the sun and there was no grass but only the bare moist earth and often I could find no worms. Always though I found some kind of bait, but one time in the swamp I could find no bait at all and had to cut up one of the trout I had caught and use him for bait.

Sometimes I found insects in the swamp meadows, in the grass or under ferns, and used them. There were beetles and insects with legs like grass stems, and grubs in old rotten logs; white grubs with brown pinching heads that would not stay on the hook and emptied into nothing in the cold water, and wood ticks under logs where sometimes I found angle-worms that slipped into the ground as soon as the log was raised. Once I used a salamander from under an old log. The salamander was very small and neat and agile and a lovely colour. He had tiny feet that tried to hold on to the hook, and after that one time I never used a salamander, although I found them very often. Nor did I use crickets, because of the way they acted about the hook.

Sometimes the stream ran through an open meadow, and in the dry grass I would catch grasshoppers and use them for bait and sometimes I would catch grasshoppers and toss them into the stream and watch them float along swimming on the stream and circling on the surface as the current took them and then disappear as a trout rose. Sometimes I would fish four or five different streams in the night; starting as near as I could get to their source and fishing them down stream. When I had finished too quickly and the time did not go, I would fish the stream over again, starting where it emptied into the lake and fishing back up stream, trying for all the trout I had missed coming down. Some nights too I made up streams, and some of them were very exciting, and it was like being awake and dreaming. Some of those streams I still remember and think that I was fishing in them, and they are confused with streams I really know. I gave them all names and went to them on the train and sometimes walked for miles to get to them.

But some nights I could not fish, and on those nights I was cold-awake and said my prayers over and over and tried to pray for all the people I had ever known. That took up a great amount of time, for if you try to remember all the people you have ever known, going back to the earliest thing you remember – which was, with me, the attic of the house where I was born and my mother and father's wedding-cake in a tin box hanging from one of the rafters, and, in the attic, jars of snakes and other specimens that my father had collected as a boy and preserved in alcohol, the alcohol sunken in the jars so the backs of some of the snakes and specimens were exposed and had turned white – if you thought back that far, you remembered a great many people. If you prayed for all of them, saying a Hail Mary and an Our Father for each one, it took a long time and finally it would be light, and then you could go to sleep, if you were in a place where you could sleep in the daylight.

On those nights I tried to remember everything that had ever happened to me, starting with just before I went to the war and remembering back from one thing to another. I found I could only remember back to the attic in my grandfather's house. Then I would start there and remember this way again, until I reached the war.

I remember, after my grandfather died we moved away from that house and to a new house designed and built by my mother. Many things that were not to be moved were burned in the back-yard and I remember those jars from the attic being thrown in the fire, and how they popped in the heat and the fire flamed up from the alcohol. I remember the snakes burning in the fire in the back-yard. But there were no people in that, only things. I could not remember who burned the things even, and I would go on until I came to people and then stop and pray for them.

About the new house I remember how my mother was always cleaning things out and making a good clearance. One time when my father was away on a hunting trip she made a good thorough cleaning out in the basement and burnt everything that should not have been there. When my father came home and got down from his buggy and hitched the horse, the fire was still burning in the road beside the house. I went out to meet him. He handed me his shotgun and looked at the fire. 'What's this?' he asked.

'I've been cleaning out the basement, dear,' my mother said from the porch. She was standing there smiling, to meet him.

My father looked at the fire and kicked at something. Then he leaned over and picked something out of the ashes. 'Get a rake, Nick,' he said to me. I went to the basement and brought a rake and my father raked carefully in the ashes. He raked out stone axes and stone skinning knives and tools for making arrow-heads and pieces of pottery and many arrow-heads. They had all been blackened and chipped by the fire. My father raked them all out very carefully and spread them on the grass by the road. His shotgun in its leather case and his game-bag were on the grass where he had left them when he stepped down from the buggy.

'Take the gun and the bags in the house, Nick, and bring me a paper,' he said. My mother had gone inside the house. I took the shotgun, which was heavy to carry and banged against my legs, and the two game-bags and started toward the house. 'Take them one at a time,' my father said. 'Don't try to carry too much at once.' I put down the game-bags and took in the shotgun and brought out a newspaper from the pile in my father's office. My father spread all the blackened, chipped stone implements on the paper and then wrapped them up. 'The best arrow-heads went all to pieces,' he said. He walked into the house with the paper package and I stayed outside on the grass with the two game-bags. After a while I took them in. In remembering that, there were only two people, so I would pray for them both.

Some nights, though, I could not remember my prayers even. I could only get as far as 'On earth as it is in heaven' and then have to start all over and be absolutely unable to get past that. Then I would have to recognize that I could not remember and give up saying my prayers that night and try something else. So on some nights I would try to remember all the animals in the world by name and then the birds and then fishes and then countries and cities and then kinds of food and the names of all the streets I could remember in Chicago, and when I could not remember anything at all any more I would just listen. And I do not remember a night on which you could not hear things. If I could have a light I was not afraid to sleep, because I knew my soul would only go out of me if it were dark. So, of course, many nights I was where I could have a light and then I slept because I was nearly always tired and often very sleepy. And I am sure many times too that I slept without knowing it – but I never slept knowing it, and on this night I listened to the silk-worms. You can hear silk-worms eating very clearly in the night and I lay with my eyes open and listened to them.

There was only one other person in the room and he was awake too. I listened to him being awake, for a long time. He could not lie as quietly as I could because, perhaps, he had not had as much practice being awake. We were lying on blankets spread over straw and when he moved the straw was noisy, but the silk-worms were not frightened by any noise we made and ate on steadily. There were the noises of night seven kilometres behind the lines outside but they were different from the small noises inside the room in the dark. The other man in the room tried lying quietly. Then he moved again. I moved too, so he would know I was awake. He had lived ten years in Chicago. They had taken him for a soldier in nineteen fourteen when he had come back to visit his family, and they had given him me for an orderly because he spoke English. I heard him listening, so I moved again in the blankets.

'Can't you sleep, Signor Tenente?' he asked.

'No.'

'I can't sleep, either.'

'What's the matter?'

'I don't know. I can't sleep.'

'You feel all right?'

'Sure. I feel good. I just can't sleep.'

'You want to talk a while?' I asked.

'Sure. What can you talk about in this damn place?'

'This place is pretty good,' I said.

'Sure,' he said. 'It's all right.'

'Tell me about out in Chicago,' I said.

'Oh,' he said. 'I told you that once.'

'Tell me about how you got married.'

'I told you that.'

'Was the letter you got Monday – from her?'

'Sure. She writes me all the time. She's making good money with the place.'

'You'll have a nice place when you go back.'

'Sure. She runs it fine. She's making a lot of money.'

'Don't you think we'll wake them up, talking?' I asked.

'No. They can't hear. Anyway, they sleep like pigs. I'm different,' he said. 'I'm nervous.'

'Talk quiet,' I said. 'Want a smoke?'

We smoked skilfully in the dark.

'You don't smoke much, Signor Tenente.'

'No. I've just about cut it out.'

'Well,' he said, 'it don't do you any good and I suppose you get so you don't miss it. Did you ever hear a blind man won't smoke because he can't see the smoke coming out?'

'I don't believe it.'

'I think it's all bull, myself,' he said. 'I just heard it somewhere. You know how you hear things.'

We were both quiet and I listened to the silk-worms.

'You hear those damn silk-worms?' he asked. 'You can hear them chew.'

'It's funny,' I said.

'Say, Signor Tenente, is there something really the matter that you can't sleep? I never see you sleep. You haven't slept nights ever since I been with you.'

'I don't know, John,' I said. 'I got in pretty bad shape along early last spring and at night it bothers me.'

'Just like I am,' he said. 'I shouldn't have ever got in this war. I'm too nervous.'

'Maybe it will get better.'

'Say, Signor Tenente, what did you get in this war for, anyway?'

'I don't know, John. I wanted to, then.'

'Wanted to,' he said. 'That's a hell of a reason.'

'We oughtn't to talk out loud,' I said.

'They sleep just like pigs,' he said. 'They can't understand the English language, anyway. They don't know a damn thing. What are you going to do when it's all over and we go back to the States?'

'I'll get a job on a paper.'

'In Chicago?'

'Maybe.'

'Do you ever read what this fellow Brisbane writes? My wife cuts it out for me and sends it to me.'

'Sure.'

'Did you ever meet him?'

'No, but I've seen him.'

'I'd like to meet that fellow. He's a fine writer. My wife don't read English but she takes the paper just like when I was home and she cuts out the editorials and the sport page and sends them to me.'

'How are your kids?'

'They're fine. One of the girls is in the fourth grade now. You know, Signor Tenente, if I didn't have the kids I wouldn't be your orderly now. They'd have made me stay in the line all the time.'

'I'm glad you've got them.'

'So am I. They're fine kids but I want a boy. Three girls and no boy. That's a hell of a note.'

'Why don't you try and go to sleep?'

'No, I can't sleep now. I'm wide awake now, Signor Tenente. Say, I'm worried about you not sleeping though.'

'It'll be all right, John.'

'Imagine a young fellow like you not to sleep.'

'I'll get all right. It just takes a while.'

'You got to get all right. A man can't get along that don't sleep. Do you worry about anything? You got anything on your mind?'

'No, John, I don't think so.'

'You ought to get married, Signor Tenente. Then you wouldn't worry.'

'I don't know.'

'You ought to get married. Why don't you pick out some nice Italian girl with plenty of money? You could get any one you want. You're young and you got good decorations and you look nice. You been wounded a couple of times.'

'I can't talk the language well enough.'

'You talk it fine. To hell with talking the language. You don't have to talk to them. Marry them.'

'I'll think about it.'

'You know some girls, don't you?'

'Sure.'

'Well, you marry the one with the most money. Over here, the way they're brought up, they'll all make you a good wife.'

'I'll think about it.'

'Don't think about it, Signor Tenente. Do it.'

'All right.'

'A man ought to be married. You'll never regret it. Every man ought to be married.'

'All right,' I said. 'Let's try and sleep a while.'

'All right, Signor Tenente. I'll try it again. But you remember what I said.'

'I'll remember it,' I said. 'Now let's sleep a while, John.'

'All right,' he said. 'I hope you sleep, Signor Tenente.'

I heard him roll in his blankets on the straw and then he was very quiet and I listened to him breathing regularly. Then he started to snore. I listened to him snore for a long time and then I stopped listening to him snore and listened to the silk-worms eating. They ate steadily, making a dropping in the leaves. I knew a new thing to think about and lay in the dark with my eyes open and thought of all the girls I had ever known and what kind of wives they would make. It was a very interesting thing to think about and for a while it killed off trout fishing and interfered with my prayers. Finally, though, I went back to trout-fishing, because I found that I could remember all the streams and there was always something new about them, while the girls, after I had thought about them a few times, blurred and I could not call them into my mind and finally they all blurred and all became rather the same and I gave up thinking about them almost altogether. But I kept on with my prayers and I prayed very often for John in the nights and his class was removed from active service before the October offensive. I was glad he was not there, because he would have been a great worry to me. He came to the hospital in Milan to see me several months after and was very disappointed that I had not yet married, and I know he would feel very badly if he knew that, so far, I have never married. He was going back to America and he was very certain about marriage and knew it would fix up everything.

After The Storm

It wasn't about anything, something about making punch, and then we started fighting and I slipped and he had me down kneeling on my chest and choking me with both hands like he was trying to kill me and all the time I was trying to get the knife out of my pocket to cut him loose. Everybody was too drunk to pull him off me. He was choking me and hammering my head on the floor and I got the knife out and opened it up; and I cut the muscle right across his arm and he let go of me. He couldn't have held on if he wanted to. Then he rolled and hung onto the arm and started to cry and I said:

'What the hell you want to choke me for?'

I'd have killed him. I couldn't swallow for a week. He hurt my throat bad.

Well, I went out of there and there were plenty of them with him and some came out after me and I made to turn and was down by the docks and I met a fellow and he said somebody killed a man up the street. I said 'Who killed him?' and he said 'I don't know who killed him but he's dead all right,' and it was dark and there was water standing in the street and no lights and windows broke and boats all up in the town and trees blown down and everything all blown and I got a skiff and went out and found my boat where I had her inside of Mango Key and she was all right only she was full of water. So I bailed her out and pumped her out and there was a moon but plenty of clouds and still plenty rough and I took it down along; and when it was daylight I was off Eastern Harbor.

Brother, that was some storm. I was the first boat out and

you never saw water like that was. It was just as white as a lye barrel and coming from Eastern Harbor to Sou'west Key you couldn't recognize the shore. There was a big channel blown right out through the middle of the beach. Trees and all blown out and a channel cut through and all the water white as chalk and everything on it; branches and whole trees and dead birds, and all floating. Inside the keys were all the pelicans in the world and all kinds of birds flying. They must have gone inside there when they knew it was coming.

I lay at Sou'west Key a day and nobody came after me. I was the first boat out and I seen a spar floating and I knew there must be a wreck and I started out to look for her. I found her. She was a three-masted schooner and I could just see the stumps of her spars out of water. She was in too deep water and I didn't get anything off her. So I went on looking for something else. I had the start on all of them and I knew I ought to get whatever there was. I went on down over the sand-bars from where I left the three-masted schooner and I didn't find anything and I went on a long way. I was way out toward the quicksands and I didn't find anything so I went on. Then when I was in sight of the Rebecca Light I saw all kinds of birds making over something and I headed over for them to see what it was and there was a cloud of birds all right.

I could see something looked like a spar up out of the water and when I got over close the birds all went up in the air and stayed all around me. The water was clear out there and there was a spar of some kind sticking out just above the water and when I came up close to it I saw it was all dark under water like a long shadow and I came right over it and there under water was a liner, just lying there all underwater as big as the whole world. I drifted over her in the boat. She lay on her side and the stern was deep down. The port holes were all shut tight and I could see the glass shine in the water and the whole of her, the biggest boat I ever saw in my life laying there and I went along the whole length of her and then I went over and anchored and I had the skiff on the deck forward and I shoved it down into the water and sculled over the birds all around me.

I had a water glass like we use sponging and my hand shook so I could hardly hold it. All the port holes were shut that you could see going along over her but way down below near the bottom something must have been open because there were pieces of things floating out all the time. You couldn't tell what they were. Just pieces. That's what the birds were after. You never saw so many birds. They were all around me; crazy yelling.

I could see everything sharp and clear. I could see her rounded over and she looked a mile long under the water. She was lying on a clear white bank of sand and the spar was a sort of foremast or some sort of tackle that slanted out of the water the way she was laying on her side. Her bow wasn't very far under. I could stand on the letters of her name on her bow and my head was just out of water. But the nearest port hole was twelve feet down. I could just reach it with the grains pole and I tried to break it with that but I couldn't. The glass was too stout. So I sculled back to the boat and got a wrench and lashed it to the end of the grains pole and I couldn't break it. There I was looking down through the glass at that liner with everything in her and I was the first one to her and I couldn't get into her. She must have had five million dollars worth in her.

It made me shaky to think how much she must have in her. Inside the port hole that was closest I could see something but I couldn't make it out through water glass. I couldn't do any good with the grains pole and I took off my clothes and stood and took a couple of deep breaths and dove over off the stern with the wrench in my hand and swam down. I could hold on for a second to the edge of the port hole and I could see in and there was a woman inside with her hair floating all out. I could see her floating plain and I hit the glass twice with the wrench hard and I heard the noise clink in my ears but it wouldn't break and I had to come up.

I hung onto the dingy and got my breath and then I climbed in and took a couple of breaths and dove again. I swam down and took hold of the edge of the port hole with my fingers and held it and hit the glass as hard as I could with the wrench. I could see the woman floating in the water through the glass. Her hair was tied once close to her head and it floated all out in the water. I could see the rings on one of her hands. She was right up close to the port hole and I hit the glass twice and I didn't even crack it. When I came up I thought I wouldn't make it to the top before I'd have to breathe.

I went down once more and I cracked the glass, only cracked it, and when I came up my nose was bleeding and I stood on the bow of the liner with my bare feet on the letters of her name and my head just out and rested there and then I swam over to the skiff and pulled up into it and sat there waiting for my head to stop aching and looking down into the water glass, but I bled so I had to wash out the water glass. Then I lay back in the skiff and held my hand under my nose to stop it and I lay there with my head back looking up and there was a million birds above and all around.

When I quit bleeding I took another look through the glass and then I sculled over to the boat to try and find something heavier than the wrench but I couldn't find a thing; not even a sponge hook. I went back and the water was clearer all the time and you could see everything that floated out over the white bank of sand. I looked for sharks but there weren't any. You could have seen a shark a long way away. The water was so clear and the sand white. There was a grapple for an anchor on the skiff and I cut it off and went overboard and down with it. It carried me right down and past the port hole and I grabbed and couldn't hold anything and went on down and down, sliding along the curved side of her. I had to let go of the grapple. I heard it bump once and it seemed like a year before I came up through the top of the water. The skiff was floated away with the tide and I swam over to her with my nose bleeding in the water while I swam and I was plenty glad there weren't sharks; but I was tired.

My head felt cracked open and I lay in the skiff and rested and then I sculled back. It was getting along in the afternoon. I went down once more with the wrench and it didn't do any good. That wrench was too light. It wasn't any good diving unless you had a big hammer or something heavy enough to do good. Then I lashed the wrench to the grains pole again and I watched through the water glass and pounded on the glass and hammered until the wrench came off and I saw it in the glass, clear and sharp, going sliding down along her and then off and down to the quicksand and go in. Then I couldn't do a thing. The wrench was gone and I'd lost the grapple so I sculled back to the boat. I was too tired to get the skiff aboard and the sun was pretty low. The birds were all pulling out and leaving her and I headed for Sou'west Key towing the skiff and the birds going on ahead of me and behind me. I was plenty tired.

That night it came on to blow and it blew for a week. You couldn't get out to her. They come out from town and told me the fellow I'd had to cut was all right except for his arm and I went back to town and they put me under five hundred dollar bond. It came out all right because some of them, friends of mine, swore he was after me with an ax, but by the time we got back out to her the Greeks had blown her open and cleaned her out. They got the safe out with dynamite. Nobody ever knows how much they got. She carried gold and they got it all. They stripped her clean. I found her and I never got a nickel out of her.

It was a hell of a thing all right. They say she was just outside of Havana harbor when the hurricane hit and she couldn't get in or the owners wouldn't let the captain chance coming in; they say he wanted to try; so she had to go with it and in the dark they were running with it trying to go through the gulf between Rebecca and Tortugas when she struck on the quicksands. Maybe her rudder was carried away. Maybe they weren't even steering. But anyway they couldn't have known they were quicksands and when she struck the captain must have ordered them to open up the ballast tanks so she'd lay solid. But it was quicksand she'd hit and when they opened the tanks she went in stern first and then over on her beam ends. There were four hundred and fifty passengers and the crew on board of her and they must all have been aboard of her when I found her. They must have opened the tanks as soon as she struck and the minute she settled on it the quicksands took her down. Then her boilers must have burst and that must have been what made those pieces that came out. It was funny there weren't any sharks though. There wasn't a fish. I could have seen them on that clear white sand.

Plenty of fish now though; jewfish, the biggest kind. The

biggest part of her's under the sand now but they live inside of her; the biggest kind of jewfish. Some weigh three to four hundred pounds. Sometime we'll go out and get some. You can see the Rebecca light from where she is. They've got a buoy on her now. She's right at the end of the quicksand right at the edge of the gulf. She only missed going through by about a hundred yards. In the dark in the storm they just missed it; raining the way it was they couldn't have seen the Rebecca. Then they're not used to that sort of thing. The captain of a liner isn't used to scudding that way. They have a course and they tell me they set some sort of compass and it steers itself. They probably didn't know where they were when they ran with that blow but they came close to making it. Maybe they'd lost the rudder though. Anyway there wasn't another thing for them to hit till they'd get to Mexico once they were in that gulf. Must have been something though when they struck in that rain and wind and he told them to open her tanks. Nobody could have been on deck in that blow and rain. Everybody must have been below. They couldn't have lived on deck. There must have been some scenes inside all right because you know she settled fast. I saw the wrench go into the sand. The captain couldn't have known it was quicksand when she struck unless he knew these waters. He just knew it wasn't rock. He must have seen it all up in the bridge. He must have known what it was about when she settled. I wonder how fast she made it. I wonder if the mate was there with him. Do you think they stayed inside the bridge or do you think they took it outside? They never found any bodies. Not a one. Nobody floating. They float a long way with life belts too. They must have took it inside. Well, the Greeks got it all. Everything. They must have come fast all right. They picked her clean. First there was the birds, then me, then the Greeks, and even the birds got more out of her than I did.

A Clean, Well-Lighted Place

It was late and everyone had left the café except an old man who sat in the shadow the leaves of the tree made against the electric light. In the daytime the street was dusty, but at night the dew settled the dust and the old man liked to sit late because he was deaf and now at night it was quiet and he felt the difference. The two waiters inside the café knew that the old man was a little drunk, and while he was a good client they knew that if he became too drunk he would leave without paying, so they kept watch on him.

'Last week he tried to commit suicide,' one waiter said.

'Why?'

'He was in despair.'

'What about?'

'Nothing.'

'How do you know it was nothing?'

'He has plenty of money.'

They sat together at a table that was close against the wall near the door of the café and looked at the terrace where the tables were all empty except where the old man sat in the shadow of the leaves of the tree that moved slightly in the wind. A girl and a soldier went by in the street. The street light shone on the brass number on his collar. The girl wore no head covering and hurried beside him.

'The guard will pick him up,' one waiter said.

'What does it matter if he gets what he's after?'

'He had better get off the street now. The guard will get him. They went by five minutes ago.'

The old man sitting in the shadow rapped on his saucer

with his glass. The younger waiter went over to him.

'What do you want?'

The old man looked at him. 'Another brandy,' he said.

'You'll be drunk,' the waiter said. The old man looked at him. The waiter went away.

'He'll stay all night,' he said to his colleague. 'I'm sleepy now. I never get to bed before three o'clock. He should have killed himself last week.'

The waiter took the brandy bottle and another saucer from the counter inside the café and marched out to the old man's table. He put down the saucer and poured the glass full of brandy.

'You should have killed yourself last week,' he said to the deaf man. The old man motioned with his finger. 'A little more,' he said. The waiter poured on into the glass so that the brandy slopped over and ran down the stem into the top saucer of the pile. 'Thank you,' the old man said. The waiter took the bottle back inside the café. He sat down at the table with his colleague again.

'He's drunk now,' he said.

'He's drunk every night.'

'What did he want to kill himself for?'

'How should I know?'

'How did he do it?'

'He hung himself with a rope.'

'Who cut him down?'

'His niece.'

'Why did they do it?'

'Fear for his soul.'

'How much money has he got?'

'He's got plenty.'

'He must be eighty years old.'

'Anyway I should say he was eighty.'

'I wish he would go home. I never get to bed before three o'clock. What kind of hour is that to go to bed?'

'He stays up because he likes it.'

'He's lonely. I'm not lonely. I have a wife waiting in bed for me.'

'He had a wife once too.'

'A wife would be no good to him now.'

'You can't tell. He might be better with a wife.'

'His niece looks after him. You said she cut him down.'

'I know.'

'I wouldn't want to be that old. An old man is a nasty thing.'

'Not always. This old man is clean. He drinks without spilling. Even now, drunk. Look at him.'

'I don't want to look at him. I wish he would go home. He has no regard for those who must work.'

The old man looked from his glass across the square, then over at the waiters.

'Another brandy,' he said, pointing to his glass. The waiter who was in a hurry came over.

'Finished,' he said, speaking with that omission of syntax stupid people employ when talking to drunken people or foreigners. 'No more tonight. Close now.'

'Another,' said the old man.

'No. Finished.' The waiter wiped the edge of the table with a towel and shook his head.

The old man stood up, slowly counted the saucers, took a leather coin purse from his pocket and paid for the drinks, leaving half a peseta tip.

The waiter watched him go down the street, a very old man walking unsteadily but with dignity.

'Why didn't you let him stay and drink?' the unhurried waiter asked. They were putting up the shutters. 'It is not half-past two.'

'I want to go home to bed.'

'What is an hour?'

'More to me than to him.'

'An hour is the same.'

'You talk like an old man yourself. He can buy a bottle and drink at home.'

'It's not the same.'

'No, it is not,' agreed the waiter with a wife. He did not wish to be unjust. He was only in a hurry.

'And you? You have no fear of going home before your usual hour?'

'Are you trying to insult me?'

'No, hombre, only to make a joke.'

'No,' the waiter who was in a hurry said, rising from pulling down the metal shutters. 'I have confidence. I am all confidence.'

'You have youth, confidence, and a job,' the older waiter said. 'You have everything.'

'And what do you lack?'

'Everything but work.'

'You have everything I have.'

'No. I have never had confidence and I am not young.'

'Come on. Stop talking nonsense and lock up.'

'I am of those who like to stay late at the café,' the older waiter said. 'With all those who do not want to go to bed. With all those who need a light for the night.'

'I want to go home and into bed.'

'We are of two different kinds,' the older waiter said. He was now dressed to go home. 'It is not only a question of youth and confidence although those things are very beautiful. Each night I am reluctant to close up because there may be someone who needs the café.'

'Hombre, there are bodegas open all night long.'

'You do not understand. This is a clean and pleasant café. It is well lighted. The light is very good and also, now, there are shadows of the leaves.'

'Good-night,' said the younger waiter.

'Good-night,' the other said. Turning off the electric light he continued the conversation with himself. It is the light of course, but it is necessary that the place be clean and pleasant. You do not want music. Certainly you do not want music. Nor can you stand before a bar with dignity although that is all that is provided for these hours. What did he fear? It was not fear or dread. It was a nothing that he knew too well. It was all a nothing and a man was nothing too. It was only that and light was all it needed and a certain cleanness and order. Some lived in it and never felt it but he knew it all was nada y pues nada y nada y pues nada. Our nada who art in nada, nada be thy name thy kingdom nada thy will be nada in nada as it is in nada. Give us this nada our daily nada and nada us our nada as we nada our nadas and nada us not into nada but deliver us from nada;

357

pues nada. Hail nothing full of nothing, nothing is with thee. He smiled and stood before a bar with a shining steam pressure coffee machine.

'What's yours?' asked the barman.

'Nada.'

'Otro loco mas,' said the barman and turned away.

'A little cup,' said the waiter.

The barman poured it for him.

'The light is very bright and pleasant but the bar is unpolished,' the waiter said.

The barman looked at him but did not answer. It was too late at night for conversation.

'You want another copita?' the barman asked.

'No, thank you,' said the waiter and went out. He disliked bars and bodegas. A clean, well-lighted café was a very different thing. Now, without thinking further, he would go home to his room. He would lie in the bed and finally, with daylight, he would go to sleep. After all, he said to himself, it is probably only insomnia. Many must have it.

The Light of the World

When he saw us come in the door the bartender looked up and then reached over and put the glass covers on the two free-lunch bowls.

'Give me a beer,' I said. He drew it, cut the top off with the spatula and then held the glass in his hand. I put the nickel on the wood and he slid the beer toward me.

'What's yours?' he said to Tom.

'Beer.'

He drew that beer and cut it off and when he saw the money he pushed the beer across to Tom.

'What's the matter?' Tom asked.

The bartender didn't answer him. He just looked over our heads and said, 'What's yours?' to a man who'd come in.

'Rye,' the man said. The bartender put out the bottle and glass and a glass of water.

Tom reached over and took the glass off the free-lunch bowl. It was a bowl of pickled pigs' feet and there was a wooden thing that worked like a scissors, with two wooden forks at the end to pick them up with.

'No,' said the bartender and put the glass cover back on the bowl. Tom held the wooden scissors fork in his hand. 'Put it back,' said the bartender.

'You know where,' said Tom.

The bartender reached a hand forward under the bar, watching us both. I put fifty cents on the wood and he straightened up.

'What was yours?' he said.

'Beer,' I said, and before he drew the beer he uncovered both the bowls.

'Your goddam pig's feet stink,' Tom said, and spit what he had in his mouth on the floor. The bartender didn't say anything. The man who had drunk the rye paid and went out without looking back.

'You stink yourself,' the bartender said. 'All you punks stink.'

'He says we're punks,' Tommy said to me.

'Listen,' I said. 'Let's get out.'

'You punks clear the hell out of here,' the bartender said.

'I said we were going out,' I said. 'It wasn't your idea.'

'We'll be back,' Tommy said.

'No you won't,' the bartender told him.

'Tell him how wrong he is,' Tom turned to me.

'Come on,' I said.

Outside it was good and dark.

'What the hell kind of place is this?' Tommy said.

'I don't know,' I said. 'Let's go down to the station.'

We'd come in at that town at one end and we were going out the other. It smelled of hides and tan bark and the big piles of sawdust. It was getting dark as we came in, and now it was dark it was cold and the puddles of water in the road were freezing at the edges.

Down at the station there were five whores waiting for the train to come in, and six white men and four Indians. It was crowded and hot from the stove and full of stale smoke. As we came in nobody was talking and the ticket window was down.

'Shut the door, can't you!' somebody said.

I looked to see who said it. It was one of the white men. He wore stagged trousers and lumbermen's rubbers and a mackinaw shirt like the others, but he had no cap and his face was white and his hands were white and thin.

'Aren't you going to shut it?'

'Sure,' I said, and shut it.

'Thank you,' he said. One of the other men snickered.

'Ever interfere with a cook?' he said to me.

'No.'

'You can interfere with this one,' he looked at the cook. 'He

360

likes it.'

The cook looked away from him holding his lips tight together.

'He puts lemon juice on his hands,' the man said. 'He wouldn't get them in dishwater for anything. Look how white they are.'

One of the whores laughed out loud. She was the biggest whore I ever saw in my life and the biggest woman. And she had on one of those silk dresses that change colors. There were two other whores that were nearly as big but the big one must have weighed three hundred and fifty pounds. You couldn't believe she was real when you looked at her. All three had those changeable silk dresses. They sat side by side on the bench. They were huge. The other two were just ordinary looking whores, peroxide blondes.

'Look at his hands,' the man said and nodded his head at the cook. The whore laughed again and shook all over.

The cook turned and said to her quickly, 'You big disgusting mountain of flesh.'

She just kept on laughing and shaking.

'Oh, my Christ,' she said. She had a nice voice. 'Oh, my sweet Christ.'

The other two whores, the big ones, acted very quiet and placid as though they didn't have much sense, but they were big, nearly as big as the biggest one. They'd have both gone well over two hundred and fifty pounds. The other two were dignified.

Of the men, besides the cook and the one who talked, there were two other lumberjacks, one that listened, interested but bashful, and the other that seemed getting ready to say something, and two Swedes. Two Indians were sitting down at the end of the bench and one standing up against the wall.

The man who was getting ready to say something spoke to me very low, 'Must be like getting on top of a hay mow.'

I laughed and said it to Tommy.

'I swear to Christ I've never been anywhere like this,' he said. 'Look at the three of them.' Then the cook spoke up.

'How old are you boys?'

'I'm ninety-six and he's sixty-nine,' Tommy said.

361

'Ho! Ho! Ho!' the big whore shook with laughing. She had a really pretty voice. The other whores didn't smile.

'Oh, can't you be decent?' the cook said. 'I asked just to be friendly.'

'We're seventeen and nineteen,' I said.

'What's the matter with you?' Tommy turned to me.

'That's all right.'

'You can call me Alice,' the big whore said and then she began to shake again.

'Is that your name?' Tommy asked.

'Sure,' she said. 'Alice. Isn't it?' she turned to the man who sat by the cook.

'Alice. That's right.'

'That's the sort of name you'd have,' the cook said.

'It's my real name,' Alice said.

'What's the other girls' names?' Tom asked.

'Hazel and Ethel,' Alice said. Hazel and Ethel smiled. They weren't very bright.

'What's your name?' I said to one of the blondes.

'Frances,' she said.

'Frances what?'

'Frances Wilson. What's it to you?'

'What's yours?' I asked the other one.

'Oh, don't be fresh,' she said.

'He just wants us all to be friends,' the man who talked said. 'Don't you want to be friends?'

'No,' the peroxide one said. 'Not with you.'

'She's just a spitfire,' the man said. 'A regular little spitfire.'

The one blonde looked at the other and shook her head.

'Goddamned mossbacks,' she said.

Alice commenced to laugh again and to shake all over.

'There's nothing funny,' the cook said. 'You all laugh but there's nothing funny. You two young lads; where are you bound for?'

'Where are you going yourself?' Tom asked him.

'I want to go to Cadillac,' the cook said. 'Have you ever been there? My sister lives there.'

'He's a sister himself,' the man in the stagged trousers said.

'Can't you stop that sort of thing?' the cook asked. 'Can't

362

we speak decently?'

'Cadillac is where Steve Ketchel came from and where Ad Wolgast is from,' the shy man said.

'Steve Ketchel,' one of the blondes said in a high voice as though the name had pulled a trigger in her. 'His own father shot and killed him. Yes, by Christ, his own father. There aren't any more men like Steve Ketchel.'

'Wasn't his name Stanley Ketchel?' asked the cook.

'Oh, shut up,' said the blonde. 'What do you know about Steve? Stanley. He was no Stanley. Steve Ketchel was the finest and most beautiful man that ever lived. I never saw a man as clean and as white and as beautiful as Steve Ketchel. There never was a man like that. He moved just like a tiger and he was the finest, free est spender that ever lived.'

'Did you know him?' one of the men asked.

'Did I know him? Did I know him? Did I love him? You ask me that? I knew him like you know nobody in the world and I loved him like you love God. He was the greatest, finest, whitest, most beautiful man that ever lived, Steve Ketchel, and his own father shot him down like a dog.'

'Were you out on the coast with him?'

'No. I knew him before that. He was the only man I ever loved.'

Everyone was very respectful to the peroxide blonde, who said all this in a high stagey way, but Alice was beginning to shake again. I felt it sitting by her.

'You should have married him,' the cook said.

'I wouldn't hurt his career,' the peroxide blonde said. 'I wouldn't be a drawback to him. A wife wasn't what he needed. Oh, my God, what a man he was.'

'That was a fine way to look at it,' the cook said. 'Didn't Jack Johnson knock him out though?'

'It was a trick,' Peroxide said. 'That big dinge took him by surprise. He'd just knocked Jack Johnson down, the big black bastard. That nigger beat him by a fluke.'

The ticket window went up and the three Indians went over to it.

'Steve knocked him down,' Peroxide said. 'He turned to smile at me.'

'I thought you said you weren't on the coast,' someone said.

'I went out just for that fight. Steve turned to smile at me and that black son of a bitch from hell jumped up and hit him by surprise. Steve could lick a hundred like that black bastard.'

'He was a great fighter,' the lumberjack said.

'I hope to God he was,' Peroxide said. 'I hope to God they don't have fighters like that now. He was like a god, he was. So white and clean and beautiful and smooth and fast and like a tiger or like lightning.'

'I saw him in the moving pictures of the fight,' Tom said. We were all very moved. Alice was shaking all over and I looked and saw she was crying. The Indians had gone outside on the platform.

'He was more than any husband could ever be,' Peroxide said. 'We were married in the eyes of God and I belong to him right now and always will and all of me is his. I don't care about my body. They can take my body. My soul belongs to Steve Ketchel. By God, he was a man.'

Everybody felt terribly. It was sad and embarrassing. Then Alice, who was still shaking, spoke. 'You're a dirty liar,' she said in that low voice. 'You never laid Steve Ketchel in your life and you know it.'

'How can you say that?' Peroxide said proudly.

'I say it because it's true,' Alice said. 'I'm the only one here that ever knew Steve Ketchel and I come from Mancelona and I knew him there and it's true and you know it's true and God can strike me dead if it isn't true.'

'He can strike me too,' Peroxide said.

'This is true, true, true, and you know it. Not just made up and I know exactly what he said to me.'

'What did he say?' Peroxide asked, complacently.

Alice was crying so she could hardly speak from shaking so. 'He said, "You're a lovely piece, Alice." That's exactly what he said.'

'It's a lie,' Peroxide said.

'It's true,' Alice said. 'That's truly what he said.'

'It's a lie,' Peroxide said proudly.

'No, it's true, true, true, to Jesus and Mary true.'

'Steve couldn't have said that. It wasn't the way he talked,' Peroxide said happily.

'It's true,' said Alice in her nice voice. 'And it doesn't make any difference to me whether you believe it or not.' She wasn't crying any more and she was calm.

'It would be impossible for Steve to have said that,' Peroxide declared.

'He said it,' Alice said and smiled. 'And I remember when he said it and I *was* a lovely piece then exactly as he said, and right now I'm a better piece than you, you dried up old hotwater bottle.'

'You can't insult me,' said Peroxide. 'You big mountain of pus. I have my memories.'

'No,' Alice said in that sweet lovely voice, 'you haven't got any real memories except having your tubes out and when you started C. and M. Everything else you just read in the papers. I'm clean and you know it, and men like me, even though I'm big, and you know it, and I never lie and you know it.'

'Leave me with my memories,' Peroxide said. 'With my true, wonderful memories.'

Alice looked at her and then at us and her face lost that hurt look and she smiled and she had the prettiest face I ever saw. She had a pretty face and a nice smooth skin and a lovely voice and she was nice all right and really friendly. But my God she was big. She was big as three women. Tom saw me looking at her and said, 'Come on. Let's go.'

'Good-bye,' said Alice. She certainly had a nice voice.

'Good-bye,' I said.

'Which way are you boys going?' asked the cook.

'The other way from you,' Tom told him.

God Rest You Merry, Gentlemen

In those days the distances were all very different, the dirt blew off the hills that now have been cut down, and Kansas City was very like Constantinople. You may not believe this. No one believes this; but it is true. On this afternoon it was snowing and inside an automobile dealer's show window, lighted against the early dark, there was a racing motor car finished entirely in silver with Dans Argent lettered on the hood. This I believed to mean the silver dance or the silver dancer, and, slightly puzzled which it meant but happy in the sight of the car and pleased by my knowledge of a foreign language, I went along the street in the snow. I was walking from the Woolf Brother's saloon where, on Christmas and Thanksgiving Day, a free turkey dinner was served, toward the city hospital which was on a high hill that overlooked the smoke, the buildings and the streets of the town. In the reception room of the hospital were the two ambulance surgeons Doc Fischer and Doctor Wilcox, sitting, the one before a desk, the other in a chair against the wall.

Doc Fischer was thin, sand-blond, with a thin mouth, amused eyes and gambler's hands. Doctor Wilcox was short, dark and carried an indexed book, *The Young Doctor's Friend and Guide,* which, being consulted on any given subject, told symptoms and treatment. It was also cross-indexed so that being consulted on symptoms it gave diagnoses. Doc Fischer had suggested that any future editions should be further cross-indexed so that if consulted as to the treatments being given, it would reveal ailments and symptoms. 'As an aid to memory,' he said.

Doctor Wilcox was very sensitive about this book but could not get along without it. It was bound in limp leather and fitted his coat pocket and he had bought it at the advice of one of his professors who had said, 'Wilcox, you have no business being a physician and I have done everything in my power to prevent you from being certified as one. Since you are now a member of this learned profession I advise you, in the name of humanity, to obtain a copy of *The Young Doctor's Friend and Guide,* and use it, Doctor Wilcox. Learn to use it.'

Doctor Wilcox had said nothing but he had bought the leather-bound guide that same day.

'Well, Horace,' Doc Fischer said as I came in the receiving room which smelt of cigarettes, iodoform, carbolic and an overheated radiator.

'Gentlemen,' I said.

'What news along the rialto?' Doc Fischer asked. He affected a certain extravagance of speech which seemed to me to be of the utmost elegance.

'The free turkey at Woolf's,' I answered.

'You partook?'

'Copiously.'

'Many of the confrères present?'

'All of them. The whole staff.'

'Much Yuletide cheer?'

'Not much.'

'Doctor Wilcox here has partaken slightly,' Doc Fischer said. Doctor Wilcox looked up at him, then at me.

'Want a drink?' he asked.

'No, thanks,' I said.

'That's all right,' Doctor Wilcox said.

'Horace,' Doc Fischer said, 'you don't mind me calling you Horace, do you?'

'No.'

'Good old Horace. We've had an extremely interesting case.'

'I'll say,' said Doctor Wilcox.

'You know the lad who was in here yesterday?'

'Which one?'

'The lad who sought eunuch-hood.'

367

'Yes.' I had been there when he came in. He was a boy about sixteen. He came in with no hat on and was very excited and frightened but determined. He was curly haired and well built and his lips were prominent.

'What's the matter with you, son?' Doctor Wilcox asked him.

'I want to be castrated,' the boy said.

'Why?' Doc Fischer asked.

'I've prayed and I've done everything and nothing helps.'

'Helps what?'

'That awful lust.'

'What awful lust?'

'The way I get. The way I can't stop getting. I pray all night about it.'

'Just what happens?' Doc Fischer asked.

The boy told him. 'Listen, boy,' Doc Fischer said. 'There's nothing wrong with you. That's the way you're supposed to be. There's nothing wrong with that.'

'It is wrong,' said the boy. 'It's a sin against purity. It's a sin against our Lord and Saviour.'

'No,' said Doc Fischer. 'It's a natural thing. It's the way you are supposed to be and later on you will think you are very fortunate.'

'Oh, you don't understand,' the boy said.

'Listen,' Doc Fischer said and he told the boy certain things.

'No. I won't listen. You can't make me listen.'

'Please listen,' Doc Fischer said.

'You're just a goddamned fool,' Doctor Wilcox said to the boy.

'Then you won't do it?' the boy asked.

'Do what?'

'Castrate me.'

'Listen,' Doc Fischer said. 'No one will castrate you. There is nothing wrong with your body. You have a fine body and you must not think about that. If you are religious remember that what you complain of is no sinful state but the means of consummating a sacrament.'

'I can't stop it happening,' the boy said. 'I pray all night and I pray in the daytime. It is a sin, a constant sin against purity.'

368

'Oh, go and –' Doctor Wilcox said.

'When you talk like that I don't hear you,' the boy said with dignity to Doctor Wilcox. 'Won't you please do it?' he asked Doc Fischer.

'No,' said Doc Fischer. 'I've told you, boy.'

'Get him out of here,' Doctor Wilcox said.

'I'll get out,' the boy said. 'Don't touch me. I'll get out.'

That was about five o'clock on the day before.

'So what happened?' I asked.

'So at one o'clock this morning,' Doc Fischer said, 'we receive the youth self-mutilated with a razor.'

'Castrated?'

'No,' said Doc Fischer. 'He didn't know what castrate meant.'

'He may die,' Doctor Wilcox said.

'Why?'

'Loss of blood.'

'The good physican here, Doctor Wilcox, my colleague, was on call and he was unable to find this emergency listed in his book.'

'The hell with you talking that way,' Doctor Wilcox said.

'I only mean it in the friendliest way, Doctor,' Doc Fischer said, looking at his hands, at his hands that had, with his willingness to oblige and his lack of respect for Federal statutes made him his trouble. 'Horace here will bear me out that I only speak of it in the very friendliest way. It was an amputation the young man performed, Horace.'

'Well, I wish you wouldn't ride me about it,' Doctor Wilcox said. 'There isn't any need to ride me.'

'Ride you, Doctor, on the day, the very anniversary, of our Saviour's birth?'

'*Our Saviour*? Ain't you a Jew?' Doctor Wilcox said.

'So I am. So I am. It always is slipping my mind. I've never given it any proper importance. So good of you to remind me. *Your* Saviour. That's right. *Your* Saviour, undoubtedly *your* Saviour – and the ride for Palm Sunday.'

'You're too damned smart,' Doctor Wilcox said.

'An excellent diagnosis, Doctor. I was always too damned smart. Too damned smart on the coast certainly. Avoid it,

369

Horace. You haven't much tendency but sometimes I see a gleam. But what a diagnosis – and without the book.'

'The hell with you,' Doctor Wilcox said.

'All in good time, Doctor,' Doc Fischer said. 'All in good time. If there is such a place I shall certainly visit it. I have even had a very small look into it. No more than a peek, really. I looked away almost at once. And do you know what the young man said, Horace, when the good Doctor here brought him in? He said, "Oh, I asked you to do it. I asked you so many times to do it."'

'On Christmas Day, too,' Doctor Wilcox said.

'The significance of the particular day is not important,' Doc Fischer said.

'Maybe not to you,' said Doctor Wilcox.

'You hear him, Horace?' Doc Fischer said. 'You hear him? Having discovered my vulnerable point, my achilles tendon so to speak, the doctor pursues his advantage.'

'You're too damned smart,' Doctor Wilcox said.

The Sea Change

'All right,' said the man. 'What about it?'

'No,' said the girl, 'I can't.'

'You mean you won't.'

'I can't,' the girl said. 'That's all that I mean.'

'You mean that you won't.'

'All right,' said the girl. 'You have it your own way.'

'I don't have it my own way. I wish to God I did.'

'You did for a long time,' the girl said.

It was early, and there was no one in the café except the barman and these two who sat together at a table in the corner. It was the end of the summer and they were both tanned, so that they looked out of place in Paris. The girl wore a tweed suit, her skin was a smooth golden brown, her blonde hair was cut short and grew beautifully away from her forehead. The man looked at her.

'I'll kill her,' he said.

'Please don't,' the girl said. She had very fine hands and the man looked at them. They were slim and brown and very beautiful.

'I will. I swear to God I will.'

'It won't make you happy.'

'Couldn't you have gotten into something else? Couldn't you have gotten into some other jam?'

'It seems not,' the girl said. 'What are you going to do about it?'

'I told you.'

'No; I mean really.'

371

'I don't know,' he said. She looked at him and put out her hand. 'Poor old Phil,' she said. He looked at her hands, but he did not touch her hand with his.

'No, thanks,' he said.

'It doesn't do any good to say I'm sorry?'

'No.'

'Nor to tell you how it is?'

'I'd rather not hear.'

'I love you very much.'

'Yes, this proves it.'

'I'm sorry,' she said, 'if you don't understand.'

'I understand. That's the trouble. I understand.'

'You do,' she said. 'That makes it worse, of course.'

'Sure,' he said, looking at her. 'I'll understand all the time. All day and all night. Especially at night. I'll understand. You don't have to worry about that.'

'I'm sorry,' she said.

'If it was a man –'

'Don't say that. It wouldn't be a man. You know that. Don't you trust me?'

'That's funny,' he said. 'Trust you. That's really funny.'

'I'm sorry,' she said. 'That's all I seem to say. But when we do understand each other there's no use to pretend we don't.'

'No,' he said. 'I suppose not.'

'I'll come back if you want me.'

'No. I don't want you.'

Then they did not say anything for a while.

'You don't believe I love you, do you?' the girl asked.

'Let's not talk rot,' the man said.

'Don't you really believe I love you?'

'Why don't you prove it?'

'You didn't use to be that way. You never asked me to prove anything. That isn't polite.'

'You're a funny girl.'

'You're not. You're a fine man and it breaks my heart to go off and leave you –'

'You have to, of course.'

'Yes, she said, I have to and you know it.'

He did not say anything and she looked at him and put her

372

hand out again. The barman was at the far end of the bar. His face was white and so was his jacket. He knew these two and thought them a handsome young couple. He had seen many handsome young couples break up and new couples form that were never so handsome long. He was not thinking about this, but about a horse. In half an hour he could send across the street to find if the horse had won.

'Couldn't you just be good to me and let me go?' the girl asked.

'What do you think I'm going to do?'

Two people came in the door and went up to the bar.

'Yes, sir,' the barman took the orders.

'You can't forgive me? When you know about it?' the girl asked.

'No.'

'You don't think things we've had and done should make any difference in understanding?'

' "Vice is a monster of such fearful mien," ' the young man said bitterly, ' "that to be something or other needs but to be seen. Then we something, something, then embrace." ' He could not remember the words. 'I can't quote,' he said.

'Let's not say vice,' she said. 'That's not very polite.'

'Perversion,' he said.

'James,' one of the clients addressed the barman, 'you're looking very well.'

'You're looking very well yourself,' the barman said.

'Old James,' the other client said. 'You're fatter, James.'

'It's terrible,' the barman said, 'the way I put it on.'

'Don't neglect to insert the brandy, James,' the first client said.

'No, sir,' said the barman. 'Trust me.'

The two at the bar looked over at the two at the table, then looked back at the bar again. Toward the barman was the comfortable direction.

'I'd like it better if you didn't use words like that,' the girl said. 'There's no necessity to use a word like that.'

'What do you want me to call it?'

'You don't have to call it. You don't have to put any name to it.'

'That's the name for it.'

'No,' she said. 'We're made up of all sorts of things. You've known that. You've used it well enough.'

'You don't have to say that again.'

'Because that explains it to you.'

'All right,' he said. 'All right.'

'You mean all wrong. I know. It's all wrong. But I'll come back. I told you I'd come. I'll come back right away.'

'No, you won't.'

'I'll come back.'

'No, you won't. Not to me.'

'You'll see.'

'Yes,' he said. 'That's the hell of it. You probably will.'

'Of course I will.'

'Go on, then.'

'Really?' She could not believe him, but her voice was happy.

'Go on,' his voice sounded strange to him. He was looking at her, at the way her mouth went and the curve of her cheek bones, at her eyes and at the way her hair grew on her forehead and at the edge of her ear and at her neck.

'Not really. Oh, you're too sweet,' she said. 'You're too good to me.'

'And when you come back tell me all about it.' His voice sounded very strange. He did not recognize it. She looked at him quickly. He was settled into something.

'You want me to go?' she asked seriously.

'Yes,' he said seriously. 'Right away.' His voice was not the same, and his mouth was very dry. 'Now,' he said.

She stood up and went out quickly. She did not look back at him. He watched her go. He was not the same-looking man as he had been before he had told her to go. He got up from the table, picked up the two checks and went over to the bar with them.

'I'm a different man, James,' he said to the barman. 'You see in me quite a different man.'

'Yes, sir?' said James.

'Vice,' said the brown young man, 'is a very strange thing, James.' He looked out the door. He saw her going down the street. As he looked in the glass, he saw he was really quite a different-looking man. The other two at the bar moved down to make room for him.

'You're right there, sir,' James said.

The other two moved down a little more, so that he could be quite comfortable. The young man saw himself in the mirror behind the bar. 'I said I was a different man, James,' he said. Looking into the mirror he saw that this was quite true.

'You look very well, sir,' James said. 'You must have had a very good summer.'

A Way You'll Never Be

The attack had gone across the field, been held up by machine-gun fire from the sunken road and from the group of farm houses, encountered no resistance in the town, and reached the bank of the river. Coming along the road on a bicycle, getting off to push the machine when the surface of the road became too broken, Nicholas Adams saw what had happened by the position of the dead.

They lay alone or in clumps in the high grass of the field and along the road, their pockets out, and over them were flies and around each body or group of bodies were the scattered papers.

In the grass and the grain, beside the road, and in some places scattered over the road, there was much material: a field kitchen, it must have come over when things were going well; many of the calf-skin-covered haversacks, stick bombs, helmets, rifles, sometimes one butt-up, the bayonet stuck in the dirt, they had dug quite a little at the last; stick bombs, helmets, rifles, entrenching tools, ammunition boxes, star-shell pistols, their shells scattered about, medical kits, gas masks, empty gas-mask cans, a squat, tripoded machine gun in a nest of empty shells, full belts protruding from the boxes, the water-cooling can empty and on its side, the breech block gone, the crew in odd positions, and around them, in the grass, more of the typical papers.

There were mass prayer books, group postcards showing the machine-gun unit standing in ranked and ruddy cheerfulness as in a football picture for a college annual; now they were humped and swollen in the grass; propaganda postcards showing a soldier in Austrian uniform bending a woman backward over a bed; the figures were impressionistically drawn; very attractively depicted and had nothing in common with actual rape in which the woman's skirts are pulled over her head to smother her, one comrade sometimes sitting upon the head. There were many of these inciting cards which had evidently been issued just before the offensive. Now they were scattered with the smutty postcards, photographic; the small photographs of village girls by village photographers, the occasional pictures of children, and the letters, letters, letters. There was always much paper about the dead and the débris of this attack was no exception.

These were new dead and no one had bothered with anything but their pockets. Our own dead, or what he thought of, still, as our own dead, were surprisingly few, Nick noticed. Their coats had been opened too and their pockets were out, and they showed, by their positions, the manner and the skill of the attack. The hot weather had swollen them all alike regardless of nationality.

The town had evidently been defended, at the last, from the line of the sunken road and there had been few or no Austrians to fall back into it. There were only three bodies in the street and they looked to have been killed running. The houses of the town were broken by the shelling and the street had much rubble of plaster and mortar and there were broken beams, broken tiles, and many holes, some of them yellow edged from the mustard gas. There were many pieces of shell, and shrapnel balls were scattered in the rubble. There was no one in the town at all.

Nick Adams had seen no one since he had left Fornaci, although, riding along the road through the over-foliaged country, he had seen guns hidden under screens of mulberry leaves to the left of the road, noticing them by the heat-waves in the air above the eaves where the sun hit the metal. Now he went on through the town, surprised to find it deserted, and came out on the low road beneath the bank of the river. Leaving the town there was a bare open space where the road slanted down and he could see the placid reach of the river and the low curve of the opposite bank and the whitened, sun-baked mud where the Austrians had dug. It was all very lush and over-green since he had seen it last and becoming historical had made no change in this, the lower river.

The battalion was along the bank to the left. There was a series of holes in the top of the bank with a few men in them. Nick noticed where the machine-guns were posted and the signal rockets in their racks. The men in the holes in the side of the bank were sleeping. No one challenged. He went on and as he came around a turn in the mud bank a young second lieutenant with a stubble of beard and red-rimmed, very bloodshot eyes pointed a pistol at him.

'Who are you?'

Nick told him.

'How do I know this?'

Nick showed him the tessera with photograph and identification and the seal of the third army. He took hold of it.

'I will keep this.'

'You will not,' Nick said. 'Give me back the card and put your gun away. There. In the holster.'

'How am I to know who you are?'

'The tessera tells you.'

'And if the tessera is false? Give me that card.'

'Don't be a fool,' Nick said cheerfully. 'Take me to your company commander.'

'I should send you to battalion headquarters.'

'All right,' said Nick. 'Listen, do you know the Captain Paravicini? The tall one with the small moustache who was an architect and speaks English?'

'You know him?'

'A little.'

'What company does he command?'

'The second.'

'He is commanding the battalion.'

'Good,' said Nick. He was relieved to know that Para was all right. 'Let us go to the battalion.'

As Nick had left the edge of the town three shrapnel had burst high and to the right over one of the wrecked houses and since then there had been no shelling. But the face of this

378

officer looked like the face of a man during a bombardment. There was the same tightness and the voice did not sound natural. His pistol made Nick nervous.

'Put it away,' he said. 'There's the whole river between them and you.'

'If I thought you were a spy I would shoot you now,' the second lieutenant said.

'Come on,' said Nick. 'Let us go to the battalion.' This officer made him very nervous.

The Captain Paravicini, acting major, thinner and more English-looking than ever, rose when Nick saluted from behind the table in the dugout that was battalion headquarters.

'Hello,' he said. 'I didn't know you. What are you doing in that uniform?'

'They've put me in it.'

'I am very glad to see you, Nicolo.'

'Right. You look well. How was the show?'

'We made a very fine attack. Truly. A very fine attack. I will show you. Look.'

He showed on the map how the attack had gone.

'I came from Fornaci,' Nick said. 'I could see how it had been. It was very good.'

'It was extraordinary. Altogether extraordinary. Are you attached to the regiment?'

'No. I am supposed to move around and let them see the uniform.'

'How odd.'

'If they see one American uniform that is supposed to make them believe others are coming.'

'But how will they know it is an American uniform?'

'You will tell them.'

'Oh. Yes, I see. I will send a corporal with you to show you about and you will make a tour of the lines.'

'Like a bloody politician,' Nick said.

'You would be much more distinguished in civilian clothes. They are what is really distinguished.'

'With a homburg hat,' said Nick.

'Or with a very furry fedora.'

'I'm supposed to have my pockets full of cigarettes and

379

postal cards and such things,' Nick said. 'I should have a musette full of chocolate. These I should distribute with a kind word and a pat on the back. But there weren't any cigarettes and postcards and no chocolate. So they said to circulate around anyway.'

'I'm sure your appearance will be very heartening to the troops.'

'I wish you wouldn't,' Nick said. 'I feel badly enough about it as it is. In principle, I would have brought you a bottle of brandy.'

'In principle,' Para said and smiled, for the first time, showing yellowed teeth. 'Such a beautiful expression. Would you like some Grappa?'

'No, thank you,' Nick said.

'It hasn't any ether in it.'

'I can taste that still,' Nick remembered suddenly and completely.

'You know I never knew you were drunk until you started talking coming back in the camions.'

'I was stinking in every attack,' Nick said.

'I can't do it,' Para said. 'I took it in the first show, the very first show, and it only made me very upset and then frightfully thirsty.'

'You don't need it.'

'You're much braver in an attack than I am.'

'No,' Nick said. 'I know how I am and I prefer to get stinking. I'm not ashamed of it.'

'I've never seen you drunk.'

'No?' said Nick. 'Never? Not when we rode from Mestre to Portogrande that night and I wanted to go to sleep and used the bicycle for a blanket and pulled it up under my chin?'

'That wasn't in the lines.'

'Let's not talk about how I am,' Nick said. 'It's a subject I know too much about to want to think about it any more.'

'You might as well stay here a while,' Paravicini said. 'You can take a nap if you like. They didn't do much to this in the bombardment. It's too hot to go out yet.'

'I suppose there is no hurry.'

'How are you really?'

'I'm fine. I'm perfectly all right.'

'No. I mean really.'

'I'm all right. I can't sleep without a light of some sort. That's all I have now.'

'I said it should have been trepanned. I'm no doctor but I know that.'

'Well, they thought it was better to have it absorb, and that's what I got. What's the matter? I don't seem crazy to you, do I?'

'You seem in top-hole shape.'

'It's a hell of a nuisance once they've had you certified as nutty,' Nick said. 'No one ever has any confidence in you again.'

'I would take a nap, Nicolo,' Paravicini said. 'This isn't battalion headquarters as we used to know it. We're just waiting to be pulled out. You oughtn't to go out in the heat now – it's silly. Use that bunk.'

'I might just lie down,' Nick said.

Nick lay on the bunk. He was very disappointed that he felt this way and more disappointed, even, that it was so obvious to Captain Paravicini. This was not as large a dugout as the one where that platoon of the class of 1899, just out at the front, got hysterics during the bombardment before the attack, and Para had had him walk them two at a time outside to show them nothing would happen, he wearing his own chin strap tight across his mouth to keep his lips quiet. Knowing they could not hold it when they took it. Knowing it was all a bloody balls – If he can't stop crying, break his nose to give him something else to think about. I'd shoot one but it's too late now. They'd all be worse. Break his nose. They've put it back to five-twenty. We've only got four minutes more. Break that other silly bugger's nose and kick his silly arse out of here. Do you think they'll go over? If they don't, shoot two and try to scoop the others out some way. Keep behind them, sergeant. It's no use to walk ahead and find there's nothing coming behind you. Bail them out as you go. What a bloody balls. All right. That's right. Then, looking at the watch, in that quiet tone, that valuable quiet tone, 'Savoia'. Making it cold, no time to get it, he couldn't find his own after the cave-in, one whole end had caved in; it was that started them; making it cold up that slope the only time he hadn't done it stinking. And after they came back the teleferica house burned, it seemed, and some of the wounded got down four days later and some did not get down, but we went up and we went back and we came down – we always came down. And there was Gaby Deslys, oddly enough, with feathers on; you called me baby doll a year ago tadada you said that I was rather nice to know tadada with feathers on, with feathers off, the great Gaby, and my name's Harry Pilcer, too, we used to step out of the far side of the taxis when it got steep going up the hill and he could see that hill every night when he dreamed with Sacré Cœur, blown white, like a soap bubble. Sometimes his girl was there and sometimes she was with someone else and he could not understand that, but those were the nights the river ran so much wider and stiller than it should and outside of Fossalta there was a low house painted yellow with willows all around it and a low stable and there was a canal, and he had been there a thousand times and never seen it, but there it was every night as plain as the hill, only it frightened him. That house meant more than anything and every night he had it. That was what he needed but it frightened him especially when the boat lay there quietly in the willows on the canal, but the banks weren't like this river. It was all lower, as it was at Portogrande, where they had seen them come wallowing across the flooded ground holding the rifles high until they fell with them in the water. Who ordered that one? If it didn't get so damned mixed up he could follow it all right. That was why he noticed everything in such detail to keep it all straight so he would know just where he was, but suddenly it confused without reason as now, he lying in a bunk at battalion headquarters, with Para commanding a battalion and he in a bloody American uniform. He sat up and looked around; they all watching him. Para was gone out. He lay down again.

The Paris part came earlier and he was not frightened of it except when she had gone off with someone else and the fear that they might take the same driver twice. That was what frightened him about that. Never about the front. He never dreamed about the front now any more but what frightened him so that he could not get rid of it was that long yellow house and the different width of the river. Now he was back here at the river, he had gone through that same town, and there was no house. Nor was the river that way. Then where did he go each night and what was the peril, and why would he wake, soaking wet, more frightened than he had ever been in a bombardment, because of a house and a long stable and a canal?

He sat up, swung his legs carefully down; they stiffened any time they were out straight for long; returned the stares of the adjutant, the signallers and the two runners by the door and put on his cloth-covered trench helmet.

'I regret the absence of the chocolate, the postal-cards and cigarettes,' he said. 'I am, however, wearing the uniform.'

'The major is coming back at once,' the adjutant said. In that army the adjutant is not a commissioned officer.

'The uniform is not very correct,' Nick told them. 'But it gives you the idea. There will be several millions of Americans here shortly.'

'Do you think they will send Americans down here?' asked the adjutant.

'Oh, absolutely. Americans twice as large as myself, healthy, with clean hearts, sleep at night, never been wounded, never been blown up, never had their heads caved in, never been scared, don't drink, faithful to the girls they left behind them, many of them never had crabs, wonderful chaps. You'll see.'

'Are you an Italian?' asked the adjutant.

'No, American. Look at the uniform. Spagnolini made it but it's not quite correct.'

'A North or South American?'

'North,' said Nick. He felt it coming on now. He would quiet down.

'But you speak Italian.'

'Why not? Do you mind if I speak Italian? Haven't I a right to speak Italian?'

'You have Italian medals.'

'Just the ribbons and the papers. The medals come later. Or you give them to people to keep and the people go away; or they are lost with your baggage. You can purchase others in Milan. It is the papers that are of importance. You must not feel badly about them. You will have some yourself if you stay at the front long enough.'

'I am a veteran of the Iritrea campaign,' said the adjutant stiffly. 'I fought in Tripoli.'

'It's quite something to have met you,' Nick put out his hand. 'Those must have been trying days. I noticed the ribbons. Were you, by any chance, on the Carso?'

'I have just been called up for this war. My class was too old.'

'At one time I was under the age limit,' Nick said. 'But now I am reformed out of the war.'

'But why are you here now?'

'I am demonstrating the American uniform,' Nick said. 'Don't you think it is very significant? It is a little tight in the collar but soon you will see untold millions wearing this uniform swarming like locusts. The grasshopper, you know, what we call the grasshopper in American, is really a locust. The true grasshopper is small and green and comparatively feeble. You must not, however, make a confusion with the seven-year locust or cicada which emits a peculiar sustained sound which at the moment I cannot recall. I try to recall it but I cannot. I can almost hear it and then it is quite gone. You will pardon me if I break off our conversation?'

'See if you can find the major,' the adjutant said to one of the two runners. 'I can see you have been wounded,' he said to Nick.

'In various places,' Nick said. 'If you are interested in scars I can show you some very interesting ones but I would rather talk about grasshoppers. What we call grasshoppers that is; and what are, really, locusts. These insects at one time played a very important part in my life. It might interest you and you can look at the uniform while I am talking.'

The adjutant made a motion with his hand to the second runner who went out.

'Fix your eyes on the uniform. Spagnolini made it, you know. You might as well look, too,' Nick said to the signallers,

'I really have no rank. We're under the American consul. It's perfectly all right for you to look. You can stare, if you like. I will tell you about the American locust. We always preferred one that we called the medium-brown. They last the best in the water and fish prefer them. The larger ones that fly making a noise somewhat similar to that produced by a rattlesnake rattling his rattlers, a very dry sound, have vivid colored wings, some are bright red, others yellow barred with black, but their wings go to pieces in the water and they make a very blowsy bait, while the medium-brown is a plump, compact, succulent hopper than I can recommend as far as one may well recommend something you gentlemen will probably never encounter. But I must insist that you will never gather a sufficient supply of the insects for a day's fishing by pursuing them with your hands or trying to hit them with a bat. That is sheer nonsense and a useless waste of time. I repeat, gentlemen, that you will get nowhere at it. The correct procedure, and one which should be taught all young officers at every small-arms course if I had anything to say about it, and who knows but what I will have, is the employment of a seine or net made of common mosquito netting. Two officers holding this length of netting at alternate ends, or let us say one at each end, stoop, hold the bottom extremity of the net in one hand and the top extremity in the other and run into the wind. The hoppers, flying with the wind, fly against the length of netting and are imprisoned in its folds. It is no trick at all to catch a very great quantity indeed, and no officer, in my opinion, should be without a length of mosquito netting suitable for the improvisation of one of these grasshopper seines. I hope I have made myself clear, gentlemen. Are there any questions? If there is anything in the course you do not understand please ask questions. Speak up. None? Then I would like to close on this note. In the words of that great soldier and gentleman, Sir Henry Wilson: Gentlemen, either you must govern or you must be governed. Let me repeat it. Gentlemen, there is one thing I would like to have you remember. One thing I would like you to take with you as you leave this room. Gentlemen, either you must govern – or you must be governed. That is all, gentlemen. Good-day.'

He removed his cloth-covered helmet, put it on again and, stooping, went out the low entrance of the dugout. Para, accompanied by the two runners, was coming down the line of the sunken road. It was very hot in the sun and Nick removed the helmet.

'There ought to be a system for wetting these things,' he said. 'I shall wet this one in the river.' He started up the bank.

'Nicolo,' Paravicini called. 'Nicolo. Where are you going?'

'I don't really have to go.' Nick came down the slope, holding the helmet in his hands. 'They're a damned nuisance wet or dry. Do you wear yours all the time?'

'All the time,' said Para. 'It's making me bald. Come inside.' Inside Para told him to sit down.

'You know they're absolutely no damned good,' Nick said. 'I remember when they were a comfort when we first had them, but I've seen them full of brains too many times.'

'Nicolo,' Para said. 'I think you should go back. I think it would be better if you didn't come up to the line until you have had those supplies. There's nothing here for you to do. If you move around, even with something worth giving away, the men will group and that invites shelling. I won't have it.'

'I know it's silly,' Nick said. 'It wasn't my idea. I heard the brigade was here so I thought I would see you or someone else I knew. I could have gone to Zenzon or to San Dona. I'd like to go to San Dona to see the bridge again.'

'I won't have you circulating around to no purpose,' Captain Paravicini said.

'All right,' said Nick. He felt it coming on again.

'You understand?'

'Of course,' said Nick. He was trying to hold it in.

'Anything of that sort should be done at night.'

'Naturally,' said Nick. He knew he could not stop it now.

'You see, I am commanding the battalion,' Para said.

'And why shouldn't you be?' Nick said. Here it came. 'You can read and write, can't you?'

'Yes,' said Para gently.

'The trouble is you have a damned small battalion to command. As soon as it gets to strength again they'll give you back your company. Why don't they bury the dead? I've seen them now. I don't care about seeing them again. They can bury them any time as far as I'm concerned and it would be much better for you. You'll all get bloody sick.'

'Where did you leave your bicycle?'

'Inside the last house.'

'Do you think it will be all right?'

'Don't worry,' Nick said. 'I'll go in a little while.'

'Lie down a little while, Nicolo.'

'All right.'

He shut his eyes, and in place of the man with the beard who looked at him over the sights of the rifle, quite calmly before squeezing off, the white flash and club-like impact, on his knees, hot-sweet choking, coughing it on to the rock while they went past him, he saw a long yellow house with a low stable and the river much wider than it was and stiller. 'Christ,' he said, 'I might as well go.'

He stood up.

'I'm going, Para,' he said. 'I'll ride back now in the afternoon. If any supplies have come I'll bring them down tonight. If not I'll come at night when I have something to bring.'

'It is still hot to ride,' Captain Paravicini said.

'You don't need to worry,' Nick said. 'I'm all right now for quite a while. I had one then but it was easy. They're getting much better. I can tell when I'm going to have one because I talk so much.'

'I'll send a runner with you.'

'I'd rather you didn't. I know the way.'

'You'll be back soon?'

'Absolutely.'

'Let me send –'

'No,' said Nick. 'As a mark of confidence.'

'Well, ciaou then.'

'Ciaou,' said Nick. He started back along the sunken road toward where he had left his bicycle. In the afternoon the road would be shady once he had passed the canal. Beyond that there were trees on both sides that had not been shelled at all. It was on that stretch that, marching, they had once passed the Terza Savoia cavalry regiment riding in the snow with their lances. The horses' breath made plumes in the cold air. No, that was somewhere else. Where was that?

'I'd better get to that damned bicycle,' Nick said to himself. 'I don't want to lose the way to Fornaci.'

The Mother Of A Queen

When his father died he was only a kid and his manager buried him perpetually. That is, so he would have the plot permanently. But when his mother died his manager thought they might not always be so hot on each other. They were sweethearts; sure he's a queen, didn't you know that, of course he is. So he just buried her for five years.

Well, when he came back to Mexico from Spain he got the first notice. It said it was the first notice that the five years were up and would he make arrangements for the continuing of his mother's grave. It was only twenty dollars for perpetual. I had the cash box then and I said let me attend to it, Paco. But he said no, he would look after it. He'd look after it right away. It was his mother and he wanted to do it himself.

Then in a week he got the second notice. I read it to him and I said I thought he had looked after it.

No, he said, he hadn't.

'Let me do it,' I said. 'It's right here in the cash box.'

No, he said. Nobody could tell him what to do. He'd do it himself when he got around to it. 'What's the sense in spending money sooner than necessary?'

'All right,' I said, 'but see you look after it.' At this time he had a contract for six fights at four thousand pesos a fight besides his benefit fight. He made over fifteen thousand dollars there in the capital alone. He was just tight, that's all.

The third notice came in another week and I read it to him. It said that if he did not make the payment by the following Saturday his mother's grave would be opened and her remains

389

dumped on the common boneheap. He said he would go attend to it that afternoon when he went to town.

'Why not have me do it?' I asked him.

'Keep out of my business,' he said. 'It's my business and I'm going to do it.'

'All right, if that's the way you feel about it,' I said. 'Do your own business.'

He got the money out of the cash box, although then he always carried a hundred or more pesos with him all the time, and he said he would look after it. He went out with the money and of course I thought he had attended to it.

A week later the notice came that they had no response to the final warning and so his mother's body had been dumped on the boneheap; on the public boneheap.

'Jesus Christ,' I said to him, 'you said you'd pay that and you took the money out of the cash box to do it and now what's happened to your mother? My God, think of it! The public boneheap and your own mother. Why didn't you let me look after it? I would have sent it when the first notice came.'

'It's none of your business. It's *my* mother.'

'It's none of *my* business, yes, but it was *your* business. What kind of blood is it in a man that will let that be done to his mother? You don't deserve to have a mother.'

'It is my mother,' he said. 'Now she is so much dearer to me. Now I don't have to think of her buried in one place and be sad. Now she is all about me in the air, like the birds and the flowers. Now she will always be with me.'

'Jesus Christ,' I said, 'what kind of blood have you anyway? I don't want you to even speak to me.'

'She is all around me,' he said. 'Now I will never be sad.'

At the time he was spending all kinds of money around women trying to make himself seem a man and fool people, but it didn't have any effect on people that knew anything about him. He owed me over six hundred pesos and he wouldn't pay me. 'Why do you want it now?' he'd say. 'Don't you trust me? Aren't we friends?'

'It isn't friends or trusting you. It's that I paid the accounts out of my money while you were away and now I need the money back and you have it to pay me.'

'I haven't got it.'

'You have it,' I said. 'It's in the cash box now and you can pay me.'

'I need that money for something,' he said. 'You don't know all the needs I have for money.'

'I stayed here all the time you were in Spain and you authorized me to pay these things as they came up, all these things of the house, and you didn't send any money while you were gone and I paid over six hundred pesos in my own money and now I need it and you can pay me.'

'I'll pay you soon,' he said. 'Right now I need the money badly.'

'For what?'

'For my own business.'

'Why don't you pay me some on account?'

'I can't,' he said. 'I need that money too badly. But I will pay you.'

He had fought only twice in Spain, they couldn't stand him there, they saw through him quick enough, and he had seven new fighting suits made and this is the kind of thing he was: he had them packed so badly that four of them were ruined by sea water on the trip back and he couldn't even wear them.

'My God,' I said to him, 'you go to Spain. You stay there the whole season and only fight two times. You spend all the money you took with you on suits and then have them spoiled by salt water so you can't wear them. That is the kind of season you have and then you talk to me about running your own business. Why don't you pay me the money you owe me so I can leave?'

'I want you here,' he said, 'and I will pay you. But now I need the money.'

'You need it too badly to pay for your own mother's grave to keep your mother buried. Don't you?' I said.

'I am happy about what has happened to my mother,' he said. 'You cannot understand.'

'Thank Christ I can't,' I said. 'You pay me what you owe me or I will take it out of the cash box.'

'I will keep the cash box myself,' he said.

'No, you won't,' I said.

That very afternoon he came to me with a punk, some fellow from his own town who was broke, and said, 'Here is a paesano who needs money to go home because his mother is very sick.' This fellow was just a punk, you understand, a nobody he'd never seen before, but from his home town, and he wanted to be the big generous matador with a fellow townsman.

'Give him fifty pesos from the cash box,' he told me.

'You just told me you had no money to pay me,' I said. 'And now you want to give fifty pesos to this punk.'

'He is a fellow townsman,' he said, 'and he is in distress.'

'You bitch,' I said. I gave him the key of the cash box. 'Get it yourself. I'm going to town.'

'Don't be angry,' he said. 'I'm going to pay you.'

I got the car out to go to town. It was his car but he knew I drove it better than he did. Everything he did I could do better. He knew it. He couldn't even read and write. I was going to see somebody and see what I could do about making him pay me. He came out and said, 'I'm coming with you and I'm going to pay you. We are good friends. There is no need to quarrel.'

We drove into the city and I was driving. Just before we came into the town he pulled out twenty pesos.

'Here's the money,' he said.

'You motherless bitch,' I said to him and told him what he could do with the money. 'You give fifty pesos to that punk and then offer me twenty when you owe me six hundred. I wouldn't take a nickel from you. You know what you can do with it.'

I got out of the car without a peso in my pocket and I didn't know where I was going to sleep that night. Later I went out with a friend and got my things from his place. I never spoke to him again until this year. I met him walking with three friends in the evening on the way to the Callao cinema in the Gran Via in Madrid. He put his hand out to me.

'Hello Roger, old friend,' he said to me. 'How are you? People say you are talking against me. That you say all sorts of unjust things about me.'

'All I say is you never had a mother,' I said to him. That's the worst thing you can say to insult a man in Spanish.

'That's true,' he said. 'My poor mother died when I was so young it seems as though I never had a mother. It's very sad.'

There's a queen for you. You can't touch them. Nothing can touch them. They spend money on themselves or for vanity, but they never pay. Try to get one to pay. I told him what I thought of him right there on the Gran Via, in front of three friends, but he speaks to me now when I meet him as though we were friends. What kind of blood is it that makes a man like that?

One Reader Writes

She sat at the table in her bedroom with a newspaper folded open before her and only stopping to look out of the window at the snow which was falling and melting on the roof as it fell. She wrote this letter, writing it steadily with no necessity to cross out or rewrite anything.

Roanoke, Virginia
February 6, 1933

Dear Doctor –

May I write you for some very important advice – I have a decision to make and don't know just whom to trust most I dare not ask my parents – and so I come to you – and only because I need not see you, can I confide in you even. Now here is the situation – I married a man in US service in 1929 and that same year he was sent to China, Shanghai – he staid three years – and came home – he was discharged from the service some few months ago – and went to his mother's home in Helena, Arkansas. He wrote for me to come home – I went, and found he is taking a course of injections and I naturally ask, and found he is being treated for I don't know how to spell the word but it sound like this 'sifilus' – Do you know what I mean – now tell me will it ever be safe for me to live with him again – I did not come in close contact with him at any time since his return from China. He assures me he will be OK after the doctor finishes with him – Do you think it right – I often heard my Father say one could well wish themselves dead if once they became a victim of that malady – I believe my Father but want to believe my Husband most – Please, please tell me what to

do – I have a daughter born while her Father was in China –
   Thanking you and trusting wholly in your advice I am

and signed her name.

   Maybe he can tell me what's right to do, she said to herself.
Maybe he can tell me. In the picture in the paper he looks like
he'd know. He looks smart, all right. Every day he tells somebody what to do. He ought to know. I want to do whatever is
right. It's such a long time though. It's a long time. And it's
been a long time. My Christ, it's been a long time. He had to
go wherever they sent him, I know, but I don't know what he
had to get it for. Oh, I wish to Christ he wouldn't have got it.
I don't care what he did to get it. But I wish to Christ he
hadn't ever got it. It does seem like he didn't have to have got
it. I don't know what to do. I wish to Christ he hadn't got any
kind of malady. I don't know why he had to get a malady.

Homage To Switzerland

PART I

PORTRAIT OF MR WHEELER IN MONTREUX

Inside the station café it was warm and light. The wood of the
tables shone from wiping and there were baskets of pretzels in
glazed paper sacks. The chairs were carved, but the seats were
worn and comfortable. There was a carved wooden clock on
the wall and a bar at the far end of the room. Outside the
window it was snowing.

Two of the station porters sat drinking new wine at the table
under the clock. Another porter came in and said the Simplon-
Orient Express was an hour late at Saint Maurice. He went out.
The waitress came over to Mr Wheeler's table.

'The Express is an hour late, sir,' she said. 'Can I bring you
some coffee?'

'If you think it won't keep me awake.'

'Please?' asked the waitress.

'Bring me some,' said Mr Wheeler.

'Thank you.'

She brought the coffee from the kitchen and Mr Wheeler
looked out the window at the snow falling in the light from the
station platform.

'Do you speak other languages besides English?' he asked
the waitress.

'Oh, yes, sir. I speak German and French and the dialects.'

'Would you like a drink of something?'

'Oh, no, sir. It is not permitted to drink in the café with the clients.'

'You won't take a cigar?'

'Oh, no, sir, I don't smoke, sir.'

'That is all right,' said Mr Wheeler. He looked out of the window again, drank the coffee, and lit a cigarette.

'Fräulein,' he called. The waitress came over.

'What would you like, sir?'

'You,' he said.

'You must not joke me like that.'

'I'm not joking.'

'Then you must not say it.'

'I haven't time to argue,' Mr Wheeler said. 'The train comes in forty minutes. If you'll go upstairs with me I'll give you a hundred francs.'

'You should not say such things, sir. I will ask the porter to speak with you.'

'I don't want a porter,' Mr Wheeler said. 'Nor a policeman nor one of those boys that sell cigarettes. I want you.'

'If you talk like that you must go out. You cannot stay here and talk like that.'

'Why don't you go away, then? If you go away I can't talk to you.'

The waitress went away. Mr Wheeler watched to see if she spoke to the porters. She did not.

'Mademoiselle!' he called. The waitress came over. 'Bring me a bottle of Sion, please.'

'Yes, sir.'

Mr Wheeler watched her go out, then come in with the wine and bring it to his table. He looked toward the clock.

'I'll give you two hundred francs,' he said.

'Please do not say such things.'

'Two hundred francs is a great deal of money.'

'You will not say such things!' the waitress said. She was losing her English. Mr Wheeler looked at her interestedly.

'Two hundred francs.'

'You are hateful.'

'Why don't you go away then? I can't talk to you if you're not here.'

The waitress left the table and went over to the bar. Mr Wheeler drank the wine and smiled to himself for some time.

'Mademoiselle,' he called. The waitress pretended not to hear him. 'Mademoiselle,' he called again. The waitress came over.

'You wish something?'

'Very much. I'll give you three hundred francs.'

'You are hateful.'

'Three hundred francs Swiss.'

She went away and Mr Wheeler looked after her. A porter opened the door. He was the one who had Mr Wheeler's bags in his charge.

'The train is coming, sir,' he said in French. Mr Wheeler stood up.

'Mademoiselle,' he called. The waitress came toward the table. 'How much is the wine?'

'Seven francs.'

Mr Wheeler counted out eight francs and left them on the table. He put on his coat and followed the porter onto the platform where the snow was falling.

'Au revoir, Mademoiselle,' he said. The waitress watched him go. He's ugly, she thought, ugly and hateful. Three hundred francs for a thing that is nothing to do. How many times have I done that for nothing. And no place to go here. If he had sense he would know there was no place. No time and no place to go. Three hundred francs to do that. What people those Americans.

Standing on the cement platform beside his bags, looking down the rails toward the headlight of the train coming through the snow, Mr Wheeler was thinking that it was very inexpensive sport. He had only spent, actually, aside from the dinner, seven francs for a bottle of wine and a franc for the tip. Seventy-five centimes would have been better. He would have felt better now if the tip had been seventy-five centimes. One franc Swiss is five francs French. Mr Wheeler was headed for Paris. He was very careful about money and did not care for women. He had been in that station before and he knew there was no upstairs to go to. Mr Wheeler never took chances.

PART II

MR JOHNSON TALKS ABOUT IT AT VEVEY

Inside the station café it was warm and light; the tables were shiny from wiping and on some there were red and white striped table cloths; and there were blue and white striped table cloths on the others and on all of them baskets with pretzels in glazed paper sacks. The chairs were carved but the wood seats were worn and comfortable. There was a clock on the wall, a zinc bar at the far end of the room, and outside the window it was snowing. Two of the station porters sat drinking new wine at the table under the clock.

Another porter came in and said the Simplon-Orient Express was an hour late at Saint-Maurice. The waitress came over to Mr Johnson's table.

'The Express is an hour late, sir,' she said. 'Can I bring you some coffee?'

'If it's not too much trouble.'

'Please?' asked the waitress.

'I'll take some.'

'Thank you.'

She brought the coffee from the kitchen and Mr Johnson looked out the window at the snow falling in the light from the station platform.

'Do you speak other languages besides English?' he asked the waitress.

'Oh, yes, I speak German and French and the dialects.'

'Would you like a drink of something?'

'Oh, no, sir it is not permitted to drink in the café with the clients.'

'Have a cigar?'

'Oh, no, sir,' she laughed. 'I don't smoke, sir.'

'Neither do I,' said Johnson. 'It's a dirty habit.'

The waitress went away and Johnson lit a cigarette and drank the coffee. The clock on the wall marked a quarter to ten. His watch was a little fast The train was due at ten-thirty – an hour late meant eleven-thirty. Johnson called to the waitress.

'Signorina!'

'What would you like, sir?'

'You wouldn't like to play with me?' Johnson asked. The waitress blushed.

'No, sir.'

'I don't mean anything violent. You wouldn't like to make up a party and see the night life of Vevey? Bring a girl friend if you like.'

'I must work,' the waitress said. 'I have my duty here.'

'I know,' said Johnson. 'But couldn't you get a substitute? They used to do that in the Civil War.'

'Oh, no, sir. I must be here myself in the person.'

'Where did you learn your English?'

'At the Berlitz school, sir.'

'Tell me about it,' Johnson said. 'Were the Berlitz undergraduates a wild lot? What about all this necking and petting? Were there many smoothies? Did you ever run into Scott Fitzgerald?'

'Please?'

'I mean were your college days the happiest days of your life? What sort of team did Berlitz have last fall?'

'You are joking, sir?'

'Only feebly,' said Johnson. 'You're an awfully good girl. And you don't want to play with me?'

'Oh, no, sir,' said the waitress. 'Would you like me to bring you something?'

'Yes,' said Johnson. 'Would you bring me the wine list?'

'Yes, sir.'

Johnson walked over with the wine list to the table where the three porters sat. They looked up at him. They were old men.

'Wollen Sie trinken?' he asked. One of them nodded and smiled.

'Oui, monsieur.'

'You speak French?'

'Oui, monsieur.'

'What shall we drink? Connais vous des champagnes?'

'Non, monsieur.'

'Faut les connaître,' said Johnson. 'Fräulein,' he called the waitress. 'We will drink champagne.'

'Which champagne would you prefer, sir?'

'The best,' said Johnson. 'Laquelle est le best?' he asked the porters.

'Le meilleur?' asked the porter who had spoken first.

'By all means.'

The porter took out a pair of gold-rimmed glasses from his coat pocket and looked over the list. He ran his finger down the four typewritten names and prices.

'Sportsman,' he said. 'Sportsman is the best.'

'You agree, gentlemen?' Johnson asked the other porters. The one porter nodded. The other said in French, 'I don't know them personally but I've often heard speak of Sportsman. It's good.'

'A bottle of Sportsman,' Johnson said to the waitress. He looked at the price on the wine card: eleven francs Swiss. 'Make it two Sportsmen. Do you mind if I sit here with you?' he asked the porter who had suggested Sportsman.

'Sit down. Put yourself here, please.' The porter smiled at him. He was folding his spectacles and putting them away in their case. 'Is it the gentleman's birthday?'

'No,' said Johnson. 'It's not a fête. My wife has decided to divorce me.'

'So,' said the porter. 'I hope not.' The other porter shook his head. The third porter seemed a little deaf.

'It is doubtless a common experience,' said Johnson, 'like the first visit to the dentist or the first time a girl is unwell, but I have been upset.'

'It is understandable,' said the oldest porter. 'I understand it.'

'None of you gentlemen is divorced?' Johnson asked. He had stopped clowning with the language and was speaking good French now and had been for some time.

'No,' said the porter who had ordered Sportsman. 'They don't divorce much here. There are gentlemen who are divorced but not many.'

'With us,' said Johnson, 'it's different. Practically everyone is divorced.'

'That's true,' the porter confirmed. 'I've read it in the paper.'

'I myself am somewhat in retard,' Johnson went on. 'This is the first time I have been divorced. I am thirty-five.'

'Mais vous êtes encore jeune,' said the porter. He explained to the two others. 'Monsieur n'a que trente-cinq ans.' The other porters nodded. 'He's very young,' said one.

'And it is really the first time you've been divorced?' asked the porter.

'Absolutely,' said Johnson. 'Please open the wine, mademoiselle.'

'And it is very expensive?'

'Ten thousand francs.'

'Swiss money?'

'No, French money.'

'Oh, yes. Two thousand francs Swiss. All the same it's not cheap.'

'No.'

'And why does one do it?'

'One is asked to.'

'But why do they ask that?'

'To marry someone else.'

'But it's idiotic.'

'I agree with you,' said Johnson. The waitress filled the four glasses. They all raised them.

'Prosit,' said Johnson.

'A votre santé, monsieur,' said the porter. The other two porters said 'Salut.' The champagne tasted like sweet pink cider.

'Is it a system always to respond in a different language in Switzerland?' Johnson asked.

'No,' said the porter. 'French is more cultivated. Besides, this is la Suisse Romande.'

'But you speak German?'

'Yes. Where I come from they speak German.'

'I see,' said Johnson, 'and you say you have never been divorced?'

'No. It would be too expensive. Besides I have never married.'

'Ah,' said Johnson. 'And these other gentlemen?'

'They are married.'

'You like being married?' Johnson asked one of the porters.

'What?'

'You like the married state?'

'Oui. C'est normale.'

'Exactly,' said Johnson. 'Et vous, monsieur?'

'Ça va,' said the other porter.

'Pour moi,' said Johnson, 'ça ne va pas.'

'Monsieur is going to divorce,' the first porter explained.

'Oh,' said the second porter.

'Ah ha,' the third porter said.

'Well,' said Johnson, 'the subject seems to be exhausted. You're not interested in my troubles,' he addressed the first porter.

'But, yes,' said the porter.

'Well, let's talk about something else.'

'As you wish.'

'What can we talk about?'

'You do the sport?'

'No,' said Johnson. 'My wife does though.'

'What do you do for amusement?'

'I am a writer.'

'Does that make much money?'

'No. But later on when you get known it does.'

'It is interesting.'

'No,' said Johnson, 'it is not interesting. I am sorry, gentlemen, but I have to leave you. Will you please drink the other bottle?'

'But the train does not come for three-quarters of an hour.'

'I know,' said Johnson. The waitress came and he paid for the wine and his dinner.

'You're going out, sir?' she asked.

'Yes,' said Johnson, 'just for a little walk. I'll leave my bags here.'

He put on his muffler, his coat, and his hat. Outside the snow was falling heavily. He looked back through the window at the three porters sitting at the table. The waitress was filling their glasses from the last wine of the opened bottle. She took the unopened bottle back to the bar. That makes them three francs something apiece, Johnson thought. He turned and walked down the platform. Inside the café he had thought that talking about it would blunt it; but it had not blunted it; it had only made him feel nasty.

PART III

THE SON OF A FELLOW MEMBER AT TERRITET

In the station café at Territet it was a little too warm; the lights were bright and the tables shiny from polishing. There were baskets with pretzels in glazed paper sacks on the tables and cardboard pads for the beer glasses in order that the moist glasses would not make rings on the wood. The chairs were carved but the wooden seats were worn and quite comfortable. There was a clock on the wall, a bar at the far end of the room, and outside the window it was snowing. There was an old man drinking coffee at a table under the clock and reading the evening paper. A porter came in and said the Simplon-Orient Express was an hour late at Saint Maurice. The waitress came over to Mr Harris's table. Mr Harris had just finished dinner.

'The Express is an hour late, sir. Can I bring you some coffee?'

'If you like.'

'Please?' asked the waitress.

'All right,' said Mr Harris.

'Thank you, sir,' said the waitress.

She brought the coffee from the kitchen and Mr Harris put sugar in it, crunched the lumps with his spoon, and looked out the window at the snow falling in the light from the station platform.

'Do you speak other languages besides English?' he asked the waitress.

'Oh, yes, sir. I speak German and French and the dialects.'

'Which do you like best?'

'They are all very much the same, sir. I can't say I like one better than another.'

'Would you like a drink of something or a coffee?'

'Oh, no, sir, it is not permitted to drink in the café with the clients.'

'You wouldn't like a cigar?'

'Oh, no, sir,' she laughed. 'I don't smoke, sir.'

'Neither do I,' said Harris, 'I don't agree with David Belasco.'

'Please?'

'Belasco. David Belasco. You can always tell him because he has his collar on backwards. But I don't agree with him. Then, too, he's dead now.'

'Will you excuse me, sir?' asked the waitress.

'Absolutely,' said Harris. He sat forward in the chair and looked out of the window. Across the room the old man had folded his paper. He looked at Mr Harris and then picked up his coffee cup and saucer and walked to Harris's table.

'I beg your pardon if I intrude,' he said in English, 'but it has just occurred to me that you might be a member of the National Geographic Society.'

'Please sit down,' Harris said. The gentleman sat down.

'Won't you have another coffee or a liqueur?'

'Thank you,' said the gentleman.

'Won't you have a kirsch with me?'

'Perhaps. But you must have it with me.'

'No, I insist.' Harris called the waitress. The old gentleman took out from an inside pocket of his coat a leather pocket-book. He took off a wide rubber band and drew out several papers, selected one, and handed it to Harris.

'That is my certificate of membership,' he said. 'Do you know Frederick J. Roussel in America?'

'I'm afraid I don't.'

'I believe he is very prominent.'

'Where does he come from? Do you know what part of the States?'

'From Washington, of course. Isn't that the headquarters of the Society?'

'I believe it is.'

'You believe it is. Aren't you sure?'

'I've been away a long time,' Harris said.

'You're not a member, then?'

405

'No. But my father is. He's been a member for a great many years.'

'Then he should know Frederick J. Roussel. He is one of the officers of the society. You will observe that it is by Mr Roussel that I was nominated for membership.'

'I'm awfully glad.'

'I am sorry you are not a member. But you could obtain nomination through your father?'

'I think so,' said Harris. 'I must when I go back.'

'I would advise you to,' said the gentleman. 'You see the magazine, of course?'

'Absolutely.'

'Have you seen the number with the coloured plates of the North American fauna?'

'Yes. I have it in Paris.'

'And the number containing the panorama of the volcanoes of Alaska?'

'That was a wonder.'

'I enjoyed very much, too, the wild animal photographs of George Shiras three.'

'They were damned fine.'

'I beg your pardon?'

'They were excellent. That fellow Shiras –'

'You call him that fellow?'

'We're old friends,' said Harris.

'I see. You know George Shiras three. He must be very interesting.'

'He is. He's the most interesting man I know.'

'And do you know George Shiras two? Is he interesting too?'

'Oh, he's not so interesting.'

'I should imagine he would be very interesting.'

'You know, a funny thing. He's not so interesting. I've often wondered why.'

'H'm,' said the gentleman. 'I should have thought anyone in that family would be interesting.'

'Do you remember the panorama of the Sahara Desert?' Harris asked.

'The Sahara Desert? That was nearly fifteen years ago.'

'That's right. That was one of my father's favorites.'

'He doesn't prefer the newer numbers?'

'He probably does. But he was very fond of the Sahara panorama.'

'It was excellent. But to me its artistic value far exceeded its scientific interest.'

'I don't know,' said Harris. 'The wind blowing all that sand and that Arab with his camel kneeling toward Mecca.'

'As I recall, the Arab was standing holding the camel.'

'You're quite right,' said Harris. 'I was thinking of Colonel Lawrence's book.'

'Lawrence's book deals with Arabia, I believe.'

'Absolutely,' said Harris. 'It was the Arab reminded me of it.'

'He must be a very interesting young man.'

'I believe he is.'

'Do you know what he is doing now?'

'He's in the Royal Air Force.'

'And why does he do that?'

'He likes it.'

'Do you know if he belongs to the National Geographic Society?'

'I wonder if he does.'

'He would make a very good member. He is the sort of person they want as a member. I would be very happy to nominate him if you think they would like to have him.'

'I think they would.'

'I have nominated a scientist from Vevey and a colleague of mine from Lausanne and they were both elected. I believe they would be very pleased if I nominated Colonel Lawrence.'

'It's a splendid idea,' said Harris. 'Do you come here to the café often?'

'I come here for coffee after dinner.'

'Are you in the University?'

'I am not active any longer.'

'I'm just waiting for the train,' said Harris. 'I'm going up to Paris and sail from Havre for the States.'

'I have never been to America. But I would like to go very much. Perhaps I shall attend a meeting of the society some time. I would be very happy to meet your father.'

'I'm sure he would have liked to meet you but he died last year. Shot himself, oddly enough.'

'I am very truly sorry. I am sure his loss was a blow to science as well as to his family.'

'Science took it awfully well.'

'This is my card,' Harris said. 'His initials were E.J. instead of E.D. I know he would have liked to know you.'

'It would have been a great pleasure.' The gentleman took out a card from the pocketbook and gave it to Harris. It read:

DR SIGISMUND WYER, PH.D.

Member of the National Geographic
Society, Washington, D.C., U.S.A.

'I will keep it very carefully,' Harris said.

A Day's Wait

He came into the room to shut the windows while we were still in bed and I saw he looked ill. He was shivering, his face was white, and he walked slowly as though it ached to move.

'What's the matter, Schatz?'

'I've got a headache.'

'You better go back to bed.'

'No I'm all right.'

'You go to bed. I'll see you when I'm dressed.'

But when I came downstairs he was dressed, sitting by the fire, looking a very sick and miserable boy of nine years. When I put my hand on his forehead I knew he had a fever.

'You go up to bed,' I said, 'you're sick.'

'I'm all right,' he said.

When the doctor came he took the boy's temperature.

'What is it?' I asked him.

'One hundred and two.'

Downstairs, the doctor left three different medicines in different coloured capsules with instructions for giving them. One was to bring down the fever, another a purgative, the third to overcome an acid condition. The germs of influenza can only exist in an acid condition, he explained. He seemed to know all about influenza and said there was nothing to worry about if the fever did not go over one hundred and four degrees. This was a light epidemic of flu and there was no danger if you avoided pneumonia.

Back in the room I wrote the boy's temperature down and made a note of the time to give the various capsules.

'Do you want me to read to you?'

'All right. If you want to,' said the boy. His face was very white and there were dark areas under his eyes. He lay still in the bed and seemed very detached from what was going on.

I read aloud from Howard Pyle's *Book of Pirates;* but I could see he was not following what I was reading.

'How do you feel, Schatz?' I asked him.

'Just the same, so far,' he said.

I sat at the foot of the bed and read to myself while I waited for it to be time to give another capsule. It would have been natural for him to go to sleep, but when I looked up he was looking at the foot of the bed, looking very strangely.

'Why don't you try to go to sleep? I'll wake you up for the medicine.'

'I'd rather stay awake.'

After a while he said to me, 'You don't have to stay in here with me, Papa, if it bothers you.'

'It doesn't bother me.'

'No, I mean you don't have to stay if it's going to bother you.'

I thought perhaps he was a little lightheaded and after giving him the prescribed capsules at eleven o'clock I went out for a while.

It was a bright, cold day, the ground covered with a sleet that had frozen so that it seemed as if all the bare trees, the bushes, the cut brush and all the grass and the bare ground had been varnished with ice. I took the young Irish setter for a little walk up the road and along a frozen creek, but it was difficult to stand or walk on the glassy surface and the red dog slipped and slithered and I fell twice, hard, once dropping my gun and having it slide away over the ice.

We flushed a covey of quail under a high clay bank with overhanging brush and I killed two as they went out of sight over the top of the bank. Some of the covey lit in trees, but most of them scattered into brush piles and it was necessary to jump on the ice-coated mounds of brush several times before they would flush. Coming out while you were poised

unsteadily on the icy springy brush they made difficult
shooting and I killed two, missed five, and started back pleased
to have found a covey close to the house and happy there were
so many left to find on another day.

At the house they said the boy had refused to let anyone
come into the room.

'You can't come in,' he said. 'You mustn't get what I have.'

I went up to him and found him in exactly the position I had
left him, white-faced but with the tops of his cheeks flushed by
the fever, staring still, as he had stared, at the foot of the bed.

I took his temperature.

'What is it?'

'Something like a hundred,' I said. It was one hundred and
two and four tenths.

'It was a hundred and two,' he said.

'Who said so?'

'The doctor.'

'Your temperature is all right,' I said. 'It's nothing to worry
about.'

'I don't worry,' he said, 'but I can't keep from thinking.'

'Don't think,' I said. 'Just take it easy.'

'I'm taking it easy,' he said and looked straight ahead. He
was evidently holding tight on to himself about something.

'Take this with water.'

'Do you think it will do any good?'

'Of course it will.'

I sat down and opened the *Pirate* book and commenced to
read, but I could see he was not following, so I stopped.

'About what time do you think I'm going to die?' he asked.

'What?'

'About how long will it be before I die?'

'You aren't going to die. What's the matter with you?'

'Oh, yes, I am. I heard him say a hundred and two.'

'People don't die with a fever of one hundred and two.
That's a silly way to talk.'

'I know they do. At school in France the boys told me you
can't live with forty-four degrees. I've got a hundred and two.'

He had been waiting to die all day, ever since nine o'clock in
the morning.

411

'You poor Schatz,' I said. 'Poor old Schatz. It's like miles and kilometers. You aren't going to die. That's a different thermometer. On that thermometer thirty-seven is normal. On this kind it's ninety-eight.'

'Are you sure?'

'Absolutely,' I said. 'It's like miles and kilometers. You know, like how many kilometers we make when we do seventy miles in the car?'

'Oh,' he said.

But his gaze at the foot of the bed relaxed slowly. The hold over himself relaxed too, finally, and the next day it was very slack and he cried very easily at little things that were of no importance.

A Natural History Of The Dead

It has always seemed to me that the war has been omitted as a field for the observation of the naturalist. We have charming and sound accounts of the flora and fauna of Patagonia by the late W.H. Hudson, the Reverend Gilbert White has written most interestingly of the Hoopoe on its occasional and not at all common visits to Selborne, and Bishop Stanley has given us a valuable, although popular, *Familiar History of Birds*. Can we not hope to furnish the reader with a few rational and interesting facts about the dead? I hope so.

When that persevering traveller, Mungo Park, was at one period of his course fainting in the vast wilderness of an African desert, naked and alone, considering his days as numbered and nothing appearing to remain for him to do but to lie down and die, a small moss-flower of extraordinary beauty caught his eye. 'Though the whole plant,' says he, 'was no larger than one of my fingers, I could not contemplate the delicate confirmation of its roots, leaves and capsules without admiration. Can that Being who planted, watered and brought to perfection, in this obscure part of the world, a thing which appears of so small importance, look with unconcern upon the situation and suffering of creatures formed after his own image? Surely not. Reflections like these would not allow me to despair; I started up and, disregarding both hunger and fatigue, travelled forward, assured that relief was at hand; and I was not disappointed.'

With a disposition to wonder and adore in like manner, as Bishop Stanley says, can any branch of Natural History be studied without increasing the faith, love and hope which we also, every one of us, need in our journey through the wilderness of life? Let us therefore see what inspiration we may derive from the dead.

In war the dead are usually the male of the human species although this does not hold true with animals, and I have frequently seen dead mares among the horses. An interesting aspect of war, too, is that it is only there that the naturalist has an opportunity to observe the dead of mules. In twenty years of observation in civil life I had never seen a dead mule and had begun to entertain doubts as to whether these animals were really mortal. On rare occasions I had seen what I took to be dead mules, but on close approach these always proved to be living creatures who seemed to be dead through their quality of complete repose. But in war these animals succumb in much the same manner as the more common and less hardy horse.

Most of those mules that I saw dead were along mountain roads or lying at the foot of steep declivities whence they had been pushed to rid the road of their encumbrance. They seemed a fitting enough sight in the mountains where one was accustomed to their presence and looked less incongruous there than they did later, at Smyrna, where the Greeks broke the legs of all their baggage animals and pushed them off the quay into the shallow water to drown. The numbers of broken-legged mules and horses drowning in the shallow water called for a Goya to depict them. Although, speaking literally, one can hardly say that they called for a Goya since there has only been one Goya, long dead, and it is extremely doubtful if these animals were they able to call, would call for pictorial representation of their plight but, more likely, would if they were articulate, call for some one to alleviate their condition.

Regarding the sex of the dead it is a fact that one becomes so accustomed to the sight of all the dead being men that the sight of a dead woman is quite shocking. I first saw inversion of the usual sex of the dead after the explosion of a munition factory which had been situated in the countryside near Milan, Italy. We drove to the scene of the disaster in trucks along poplar-shaded roads, bordered with ditches containing much minute animal life, which I could not clearly observe because

414

of the great clouds of dust raised by the trucks. Arriving where
the munition plant had been, some of us were put to patrolling
about those large stocks of munitions which for some reason
had not exploded, while others were put at extinguishing a fire
which had gotten into the grass of an adjacent field; which task
being concluded, we were ordered to search the immediate
vicinity and surrounding fields for bodies. We found and
carried to an improvised mortuary a good number of these
and, I must admit, frankly, the shock it was to find that these
dead were women rather than men. In those days women had
not yet commenced to wear their hair cut short, as they did
later for several years in Europe and America, and the most disturbing thing, perhaps because it was the most unaccustomed,
was the presence and, even more disturbing, the occasional
absence of this long hair. I remember that after we had
searched quite thoroughly for the complete dead we collected
fragments. Many of these were detached from a heavy, barbed-
wire fence which had surrounded the position of the factory
and from the still existent portions of which we picked many of
these detached bits which illustrated only too well the
tremendous energy of high explosive. Many fragments we
found a considerable distance away in the fields, they being
carried farther by their own weight.

On our return to Milan I recall one or two of us discussing
the occurrence and agreeing that the quality of unreality and
the fact that there were no wounded did much to rob the
disaster of a horror which might have been much greater. Also
the fact that it had been so immediate and that the dead were
in consequence still as little unpleasant as possible to carry and
deal with made it quite removed from the usual battlefield
experience. The pleasant, though dusty, ride through the
beautiful Lombard countryside also was a compensation for
the unpleasantness of the duty and on our return, while we
exchanged impressions, we all agreed that it was indeed
fortunate that the fire which broke out just before we arrived
had been brought under control as rapidly as it had and before
it had attained any of the seemingly huge stocks of unexploded
munitions. We agreed too that the picking up of the fragments
had been an extraordinary business; it being amazing that the

human body should be blown into pieces which exploded along no anatomical lines, but rather divided as capriciously as the fragmentation in the burst of a high explosive shell.

A naturalist, to obtain accuracy of observation, may confine himself in his observations to one limited period and I will take first that following the Austrian offensive of June, 1918, in Italy as one in which the dead were present in their greatest numbers, a withdrawal having been forced and an advance later made to recover the ground lost so that the positions after the battle were the same as before except for the presence of the dead. Until the dead are buried they change somewhat in appearance each day. The colour changes in Caucasian races from white to yellow, to yellow-green, to black. If left long enough in the heat the flesh comes to resemble coal-tar, especially where it has been broken or torn, and it has quite a visible tarlike iridescence. The dead grow larger each day until sometimes they become quite too big for their uniforms, filling these until they seem blown tight enough to burst. The individual members may increase in girth to an unbelievable extent and faces fill as taut and globular as balloons. The surprising thing, next to their progressive corpulence, is the amount of paper that is scattered about the dead. The ultimate position, before there is any question of burial, depends on the location of the pockets in the uniform. In the Austrian army these pockets were in the back of the breeches and the dead, after a short time, all consequently lay on their faces, the two hip pockets pulled out and scattered around them in the grass, all those papers their pockets had contained. The head, the flies, the indicative positions of the bodies in the grass, and the amount of paper scattered are the impressions one retains. The smell of a battlefield in hot weather one cannot recall. You can remember that there was such a smell, but nothing ever happens to you to bring it back. It is unlike the smell of a regiment, which may come to you suddenly while riding in the street car and you will look across and see the man who has brought it to you. But the other thing is gone as completely as when you have been in love; you remember things that happened, but the sensation cannot be recalled.

One wonders what the persevering traveller, Mungo Park,

would have seen on a battlefield in hot weather to restore his confidence. There were always poppies in the wheat in the end of June and in July, and the mulberry trees were in full leaf and one could see the heat waves rise from the barrels of the guns where the sun struck them through the screens of leaves; the earth was turned a bright yellow at the edge of holes where mustard gas shells had been and the average broken house is finer to see than one that has been shelled, but few travellers would take a good full breath of that early summer air and have any such thoughts as Mungo Park about those formed in His own image.

The first thing that you find about the dead was that, hit badly enough, they died like animals. Some quickly from a little wound you would not think would kill a rabbit. They die from little wounds as rabbits die sometimes from three or four small grains of shot that hardly seem to break the skin. Others would die like cats; a skull broken in and iron in the brain, they lie alive two days like cats that crawl into the coal bin with a bullet in the brain and will not die until you cut their heads off. Maybe cats do not die then, they say they have nine lives, I do not know, but most men die like animals, not men. I'd never seen a natural death, so called, and so I blamed it on the war and like the persevering traveller, Mungo Park, knew that there was something else, that always absent something else, and then I saw one.

The only natural death I've ever seen, outside of loss of blood, which isn't bad, was death from Spanish influenza. In this you drown in mucus, choking, and how you know the patient's dead is: at the end he turns to be a little child again, though with his manly force, and fills the sheets as full as any diaper with one vast, final, yellow cataract that flows and dribbles on after he's gone. So now I want to see the death of any self-called Humanist[1] because a persevering traveller like Mungo Park or me lives on and maybe yet will live to see the actual death of members of this literary sect and watch the

[1] The reader's indulgence is requested for this mention of an extinct phenomenon. The reference, like all references to fashion, dates the story but it is retained because of its mild historical interest and because its omission would spoil the rhythm.

noble exits that they make. In my musings as a naturalist it has occurred to me that while decorum is an excellent thing some must be indecorous if the race is to be carried on since the position prescribed for procreation is indecorous, highly indecorous, and it occurred to me that perhaps that is what these people are, or were: the children of decorous cohabitation. But regardless of how they started I hope to see the finish of a few, and speculate how worms will try that long preserved sterility; with their quaint pamphlets gone to bust and into foot-notes all their lust.

While it is, perhaps, legitimate to deal with these self-designated citizens in a natural history of the dead, even though the designation may mean nothing by the time this work is published, yet it is unfair to the other dead, who were not dead in their youth of choice, who owned no magazines, many of whom had doubtless never even read a review, that one has seen in the hot weather with a half-pint of maggots working where their mouths have been. It was not always hot weather for the dead, much of the time it was the rain that washed them clean when they lay in it and made the earth soft when they were buried in it and sometimes then kept on until the earth was mud and washed them out and you had to bury them again. Or in the winter in the mountains you had to put them in the snow and when the snow melted in the spring some one else had to bury them. They had beautiful burying grounds in the mountains, war in the mountains is the most beautiful of all war, and in one of them, at a place called Pocol, they buried a general who was shot through the head by a sniper. This is where those writers are mistaken who write books called *Generals Die in Bed*, because this general died in a trench dug in snow, high in the mountains, wearing an Alpini hat with an eagle feather in it and a hole in front you couldn't put your little finger in and a hole in back you could put your fist in, if it were a small fist and you wanted to put it there, and much blood in the snow. He was a damned fine general, and so was General von Behr who commanded the Bavarian Alpenkorps troops in the battle of Caporetto and was killed in his staff car by the Italian rearguard as he drove into Udine ahead of his troups, and the titles of all such books should be

418

Generals Usually Die in Bed, if we are to have any sort of accuracy in such things.

In the mountains too, sometimes, the snow fell on the dead outside the dressing station on the side that was protected by the mountain from any shelling. They carried them into a cave that had been dug into the mountainside before the earth froze. It was in this cave that a man whose head was broken as a flower-pot may be broken, although it was all held together by membranes and a skillfully applied bandage now soaked and hardened, with the structure of his brain disturbed by a piece of broken steel in it, lay a day, a night, and a day. The stretcher-bearers asked the doctor to go in and have a look at him. They saw him each time they made a trip and even when they did not look at him they heard him breathing. The doctor's eyes were red and the lids swollen, almost shut from tear gas. He looked at the man twice, once in daylight, once with a flashlight. That too would have made a good etching for Goya, the visit with the flashlight, I mean. After looking at him the second time the doctor believed the stretcher bearers when they said the soldier was still alive.

'What do you want me to do about it?' he asked.

There was nothing they wanted done. But after a while they asked permission to carry him out and lay him with the badly wounded.

'No. No. No!' said the doctor, who was busy. 'What's the matter? Are you afraid of him?'

'We don't like to hear him in there with the dead.'

'Don't listen to him. If you take him out of there you will have to carry him right back in.'

'We wouldn't mind that, Captain Doctor.'

'No,' said the doctor. 'No. Didn't you hear me say no?'

'Why don't you give him an overdose of morphine?' asked an artillery officer who was waiting to have a wound in his arm dressed.

'Do you think that is the only use I have for morphine? Would you like me to have to operate without morphine? You have a pistol, go out and shoot him yourself.'

'He's been shot already,' said the officer. 'If some of you doctors were shot you'd be different.'

'Thank you very much,' said the doctor waving a forceps in the air. 'Thank you a thousand times. What about these eyes?' He pointed the forceps at them. 'How would you like these?'

'Tear gas. We call it lucky if it's tear gas.'

'Because you leave the line,' said the doctor. 'Because you come running here with your tear gas to be evacuated. You rub onions in your eyes.'

'You are beside yourself. I do not notice your insults. You are crazy.'

The stretcher-bearers came in.

'Captain Doctor,' one of them said.

'Get out of here!' said the doctor.

They went out.

'I will shoot the poor fellow,' the artillery officer said. 'I am a humane man. I will not let him suffer.'

'Shoot him then,' said the doctor. 'Shoot him. Assume the responsibility. I will make a report. Wounded shot by lieutenant of artillery in first curing post. Shoot him. Go ahead, shoot him.'

'You are not a human being.'

'My business is to care for the wounded, not to kill them. That is for gentlemen of the artillery.'

'Why don't you care for him then?'

'I have done so. I have done all that can be done.'

'Why don't you send him down on the cable railway?'

'Who are you to ask me questions? Are you my superior officer? Are you in command of this dressing post? Do me the courtesy to answer.'

The lieutenant of artillery said nothing. The others in the room were all soldiers and there were no other officers present.

'Answer me,' said the doctor holding a needle up in his forceps. 'Give me a response.'

'F— yourself,' said the artillery officer.

'So,' said the doctor. 'So, you said that. All right. All right. We shall see.'

The lieutenant of artillery stood up and walked toward him.

'F— yourself,' he said. 'F— yourself. F— your mother. F— your sister . . .'

The doctor tossed the saucer full of iodine in his face. As he

420

came towards him, blinded, the lieutenant fumbled for his pistol. The doctor skipped quickly behind him, tripped him and, as he fell to the floor, kicked him several times and picked up the pistol in his rubber gloves. The lieutenant sat on the floor holding his good hand to his eyes.

'I'll kill you!' he said. 'I'll kill you as soon as I can see.'

'I am the boss,' said the doctor. 'All is forgiven since you know I am the boss. You cannot kill me because I have your pistol. Sergeant! Adjutant! Adjutant!'

'The adjutant is at the cable railway,' said the sergeant.

'Wipe out this officer's eyes with alcohol and water. He has got iodine in them. Bring me the basin to wash my hands. I will take this officer next.'

'You won't touch me.'

'Hold him tight. He is a little delirious.'

One of the stretcher-bearers came in.

'Captain Doctor.'

'What do you want?'

'The man in the dead-house —'

'Get out of here.'

'Is dead, Captain Doctor. I thought you would be glad to know.'

'See, my poor lieutenant? We dispute about nothing. In time of war we dispute about nothing.'

'F— you,' said the lieutenant of artillery. He still could not see. 'You've blinded me.'

'It is nothing,' said the doctor. 'Your eyes will be all right. It is nothing. A dispute about nothing.'

'Ayee! Ayee! Ayee!' suddenly screamed the lieutenant. 'You have blinded me! You have blinded me!'

'Hold him tight,' said the doctor. 'He is in much pain. Hold him very tight.'

Wine of Wyoming

It was a hot afternoon in Wyoming; the mountains were a long way away and you could see snow on their tops, but they made no shadow, and in the valley the grain-fields were yellow, the road was dusty with cars passing, and all the small wooden houses at the edge of town were baking in the sun. There was a tree made shade over Fontan's back porch and I sat there at the table and Madame Fontan brought up cold beer from the cellar. A motor-car turned off the main road and came up the side road, and stopped beside the house. Two men got out and came in through the gate. I put the bottles under the table. Madame Fontan stood up.

'Where's Sam?' one of the men asked at the screen door.

'He ain't here. He's at the mines.'

'You got some beer?'

'No. Ain't got any beer. That's a last bottle. All gone.'

'What's he drinking?'

'That's a last bottle. All gone.'

'Go on, give us some beer. You know me.'

'Ain't got any beer. That's a last bottle. All gone.'

'Come on, let's go some place where we can get some real beer,' one of them said, and they went out to the car. One of them walked unsteadily. The motor-car jerked in starting, whirled on the road, and went on and away.

'Put the beer on the table,' Madame Fontan said. 'What's the matter, yes, all right. What's the matter? Don't drink off the floor.'

'I didn't know who they were,' I said.

'They're drunk,' she said. 'That's what makes the trouble. Then they go somewhere else and say they got it here. Maybe they don't even remember.' She spoke French, but it was only French occasionally, and there were many English words and some English constructions.

'Where's Fontan?'

'Il fait de la vendange. Oh, my God, il est crazy pour le vin.'

'But you like the beer?'

'Oui, j'aime la bière, mais Fontan, il est crazy pour le vin.'

She was a plump old woman with a lovely ruddy complexion and white hair. She was very clean and the house was very clean and neat. She came from Lens.

'Where did you eat?'

'At the hotel.'

'Mangez ici. Il ne faut pas manger a l'hôtel ou au restaurant. Mangez ici!'

'I don't want to make you trouble. And besides they eat all right at the hotel.'

'I never eat at the hotel. Maybe they eat all right there. Only once in my life I ate at a restaurant in America. You know what they gave me? They gave me pork that was raw!'

'Really?'

'I don't lie to you. It was pork that wasn't cooked! Et mon fils il est marié avec une américaine et tout le temps il a mangé les *beans* en *can*.'

'How long has he been married?'

'Oh, my God, I don't know. His wife weighs two hundred twenty-five pounds. She don't work. She don't cook. She gives him beans en can.'

'What does she do?'

'All the time she reads. Rien que des books. Tout le temps elle stay in the bed and read books. Already she can't have another baby she's too fat. There ain't any room.'

'What's the matter with her?'

'She reads books all the time. He's a good boy. He works hard. He worked in the mines; now he works on a ranch. He never worked on a ranch before, and the man that owns the ranch said to Fontan that he never saw anybody work better on

423

that ranch than that boy. Then he comes home and she feeds him nothing.'

'Why doesn't he get a divorce?'

'He ain't got no money to get a divorce. Besides, il est *crazy* pour elle.'

'Is she beautiful?'

'He thinks so. When he brought her home I thought I would die. He's such a good boy and works hard all the time and never run around or make any trouble. Then he goes away to work in the oil-fields and brings home this Indienne that weighs right then one hundred eighty-five pounds.'

'Elle est Indienne?'

'She's Indian all right. My God, yes. All the time she says sonofabitch goddam. She don't work.'

'Where is she now?'

'Au show.'

'Where's that?'

'*Au show. Moving* pictures. All she does is read and go to the show.'

'Have you got any more beer?'

'My God, yes. Sure. You come and eat with us tonight.'

'All right. What should I bring?'

'Don't bring anything. Nothing at all. Maybe Fontan will have some of the wine.'

That night I had dinner at Fontan's. We ate in the dining-room and there was a clean tablecloth. We tried the new wine. It was very light and clear and good, and still tasted of the grapes. At the table there were Fontan and Madame and the little boy, André.

'What did you do today?' Fontan asked. He was an old man with small mine-tired body, a drooping gray mustache, and bright eyes, and was from the Centre near Saint-Etienne.

'I worked on my book.'

'Were your books all right?' asked Madame.

'He means he writes a book like a writer. Un roman,' Fontan explained.

'Pa, can I go to the show?' André asked.

'Sure,' said Fontan. André turned to me.

424

'How old do you think I am? Do you think I look fourteen years old?' He was a thin little boy, but his face looked sixteen.

'Yes. You look fourteen.'

'When I go to the show I crouch down like this and try to look small.' His voice was very high and breaking. 'If I give them a quarter they keep it all but if I give them only fifteen cents they let me in all right.'

'I only give you fifteen cents, then,' said Fontan.

'No. Give me the whole quarter. I'll get it changed on the way.'

'Il faut revenir tout de suite après le show,' Madame Fontan said.

'I come right back.' André went out the door. The night was cooling outside. He left the door open and a cool breeze came in.

'Mangez!' said Madame Fontan. 'You haven't eaten anything.' I had eaten two helpings of chicken and French fried potatoes, three ears of sweet corn, some sliced cucumbers, and two helpings of salad.

'Perhaps he wants some kek,' Fontan said.

'I should have gotten some kek for him,' Madame Fontan said. 'Mangez du fromage. Mangez du crimcheez. Vous n'avez rien mangé. I ought to have gotten kek. Americans always eat kek.'

'Mais j'ai rudement bien mangé.'

'Mangez! Vous n'avez rien mangé. Eat it all. We don't save anything. Eat it all up.'

'Eat some more salad,' Fontan said.

'I'll get some more beer,' Madame Fontan said. 'If you work all day in a book-factory you get hungry.'

'Elle ne comprend pas que vous êtes écrivain,' Fontan said. He was a delicate old man who used the slang and knew the popular songs of his period of military service in the end of the 1890's. 'He writes the books himself,' he explained to Madame.

'You write the books yourself?' Madame asked.

'Sometimes.'

'Oh!' she said. 'Oh! You write them yourself. Oh! Well, you

425

get hungry if you do that too. Mangez! Je vais chercher de la bière.'

We heard her walking on the stairs to the cellar. Fontan smiled at me. He was very tolerant of people who had not his experience and worldly knowledge.

When André came home after the show we were still sitting in the kitchen and were talking about hunting.

'Labor day we all went to Clear Creek,' Madame said. 'Oh my God, you ought to have been there all right. We all went in the truck. Tout le monde est allé dans le truck. Nous sommes partis le dimanche. C'est le truck de Charley.'

'On a mangé, on a bu du vin, de la bière, et il y avait aussi un français qui a apporté de l'absinthe,' Fontan said. 'Un français de la Californie!'

'My God, nous avons chanté. There's a farmer comes to see what's the matter, and we give him something to drink, and he stayed with us a while. There was some Italians come too and they want to stay with us too. We sung a song about the Italians and they don't understand it. They didn't know we didn't want them, but we didn't have nothing to do with them, and after a while they went away.'

'How many fish did you catch?'

'Très peu. We went to fish a little while, but then we came back to sing again. Nous avons chanté, vous savez.'

'In the night,' said Madame, 'toutes les femmes dorment dans le truck. Les hommes à côté du feu. In the night I hear Fontan come to get some more wine, and I tell him, Fontan, my God, leave some for tomorrow. Tomorrow they won't have anything to drink, and then they'll be sorry.'

'Mais nous avons tout bu,' Fontan said. 'Et le lendemain it ne reste rien.'

'What did you do?'

'Noun avons pêché sérieusement.'

'Good trout, all right, too. My god, yes. All the same; half pound one ounce.'

'How big?'

'Half-pound one ounce. Just right to eat. All the same size; half-pound one ounce.'

'How do you like America?' Fontan asked me.

'It's my country, you see. So I like it, because it's my country. Mais on ne mange pas très bien. D'antan, oui. Mais maintenant, no.'

'No,' said Madame. 'On ne mange pas bien.' She shook her head. 'Et aussi, il y a trop de Polack. Quand j'étais petite ma mère m'a dit, "vous mangez comme les Polacks." Je n'ai jamais compris ce que c'est qu'un Polack. Mais maintenant en Amérique je comprends. Il y a trop de Polack. Et, my God, ils sont sales, les Polacks.'

'It is fine for hunting and fishing,' I said.

'Oui. Ça, c'est le meilleur. La chasse et la pêche,' Fontan said. 'Qu'est-ce que vous avez comme fusil?'

'A twelve-gauge pump.'

'Il est bon, le pump,' Fontan nodded his head.

'Je veux aller à la chasse moi-même, André said in his high little boy's voice.

'Tu ne peux pas,' Fontan said. He turned to me.

'Ils sont des sauvages, les boys, vous savez. Ils sont des sauvages. Ils veulent shooter les uns les autres.'

'Je veux aller tout seul,' André said, very shrill and excited.

'You can't go,' Madame Fontan said. 'You are too young.'

'Je veux aller tout seul,' André said shrilly. 'Je veux shooter les rats d'eau.'

'What are rats d'eau?' I asked.

'You don't know them? Sure you know them. What they call the muskrats.'

André had brought the twenty-two-calibre rifle out from the cupboard and was holding it in his hands under the light.

'Ils sont des sauvages,' Fontan explained. 'Ils veulent shooter les uns les autres.'

'Je veux aller tout seul,' André shrilled. He looked desperately along the barrel of the gun. 'Je veux shooter les rats d'eau. Je connais beaucoup de rats d'eau.'

'Give me the gun,' Fontan said. He explained again to me. 'They're savages. They would shoot one another.'

André held tight on to the gun.

'On peut looker. On ne fait pas de mal. On peut looker.'

'Il est crazy pour le shooting,' Madame Fontan said. 'Mais il est trop jeune.'

André put the twenty-two-calibre rifle back in the cupboard.

'When I'm bigger I'll shoot the muskrats and the jack-rabbits too,' he said in English. 'One time I went out with papa and he shot a jack-rabbit just a little bit and I shot it and hit it.'

'C'est vrai,' Fontan nodded. 'Il a tué un jack.'

'But he hit it first,' André said. 'I want to go all by myself and shoot all by myself. Next year I can do it.' He went over in a corner and sat down to read a book. I had picked it up when we came into the kitchen to sit after supper. It was a library book – *Frank on a Gunboat*.

'Il aime les books,' Madame Fontan said. 'But it's better than to run around at night with the other boys and steal things.'

'Books are all right,' Fontan said. 'Monsieur il fait les books.'

'Yes, that's so, all right. But too many books are bad,' Madame Fontan said. 'Ici, c'est une maladie, les books. C'est comme les churches. Ici il y a trop de churches. En France il y a seulement les catholiques et le protestant – et très peu de protestants. Mais ici rien que de churches. Quand j'étais venue ici je disais, oh, my God, what are all the churches?'

'C'est vrai,' Fontan said. 'Il y a trop de churches.'

'The other day,' Madame Fontan said, 'there was a little French girl here with her mother, the cousin of Fontan, and she said to me, "En Amérique il ne faut pas être catholique. It's not good to be catholique. The Americans don't like you to be catholique. It's like the dry law." I said to her, "What you going to be? Heh? It's better to be catholique if you're catholique." But she said, "No, it isn't any good to be catholique in America." But I think it's better to be catholique if you are. Ce n'est pas bon de changer sa religion. My God, no.'

'You go to the mass here?'

'No. I don't go in America, only sometimes in a long while. Mais je reste catholique. It's no good to change the religion.'

'On dit que Schmidt est catholique,' Fontan said.

'On dit, mais on ne sait jamais,' Madame Fontan said. 'I don't think Schmidt is catholique. There's not many catholique in America.'

'We are catholique,' I said.

'Sure, but you live in France,' Madame Fontan said. 'Je ne crois pas que Schmidt est catholique. Did he ever live in France?'

'Les Polacks sont catholiques,' Fontan said.

'That's true,' Madame Fontan said. 'They go to church, then they fight with knives all the way home and kill each other all day Sunday. But they're not real catholiques. They're Polack catholiques.'

'All catholiques are the same,' Fontan said. 'One catholique is like another.'

'I don't believe Schmidt is catholique,' Madame Fontan said. 'That's awful funny if he's catholique. Moi, je ne crois pas.'

'Il est catholique,' I said.

'Schmidt is catholique,' Madame Fontan mused. 'I wouldn't have believed it. My God, it est catholique.'

'Marie, va chercher de la bière, Fontan said. 'Monsieur a soif – moi aussi.'

'Yes, all right,' Madame Fontan said from the next room. She went downstairs and we heard the stairs creaking. André sat reading in the corner. Fontan and I sat at the table, and he poured the beer from the last bottle into our two glasses, leaving a little in the bottom.

'C'est un bon pays pour la chasse,' Fontan said. 'J'aime beaucoup shooter les canards.'

'Mais il y a très bonne chasse aussi en France,' I said.

'C'est vrai,' Fontan said. 'Nous avons beaucoup de gibier là-bas.'

Madame Fontan came up the stairs with the beer bottles in her hands. 'Il est catholique,' she said. 'My God, Schmidt est catholique.'

'You think he'll be the President?' Fontan asked. 'No,' I said.

The next afternoon I drove out to Fontan's, through the shade of the town, then along the dusty road, turning up the side road and leaving the car beside the fence. It was another hot day. Madame Fontan came to the back door. She looked like Mrs Santa Claus, clean and rosy-faced and white-haired, and waddling when she walked.

'My God, hello,' she said. 'It's hot, my God.' She went back into the house to get some beer. I sat on the back porch and looked through the screen and the leaves of the tree at the heat and, away off, the mountains. There were furrowed brown mountains, and above them three peaks and a glacier with snow that you could see through the trees. The snow looked very white and pure and unreal. Madame Fontan came out and put down the bottles on the table.

'What you see out there?'

'The snow.'

'C'est joli, la neige.'

'Have a glass, too.'

'All right.'

She sat down on a chair beside me. 'Schmidt,' she said. 'If he's the President, you think we get the wine and beer all right?'

'Sure,' I said. 'Trust Schmidt.'

'Already we paid seven hundred fifty-dollars in fines when they arrested Fontan. Twice the police arrested us and once the governments. All the money we made all the time Fontan worked in the mines and I did washing. We paid it all. They put Fontan in jail. Il n'a jamais fait de mal à personne.'

'He's a good man,' I said. 'It's a crime.'

'We don't charge too much money. The wine one dollar a litre. The beer ten cents a bottle. We never sell the beer before it's good. Lots of places they sell the beer right away when they make it, and then it gives everybody a headache. What's the matter with that? They put Fontan in jail and they take seven hundred fifty-five dollars.'

'It's wicked,' I said. 'Where is Fontan?'

'He stays with the wine. He has to watch it now to catch it just right,' she smiled. She did not think about the money any more. 'Vous savez, il est crazy pour le vin. Last night he brought a little bit home with him, what you drank, and a little bit of the new. The last new. It ain't ready yet, but he drank a little bit, and this morning he put a little bit in his coffee. Dans son café vous savez! Il est crazy pour le vin! Il est comme ça. Son pays est comme ça. Where I live in the north they don't drink any wine. Everybody drinks beer. By

430

where we lived there was a big brewery right near us. When I was a little girl I didn't like the smell of the hops in the carts. Nor in the fields. Je n'aime pas les houblons. No, my God, not a bit. The man that owns the brewery said to me and my sister to go to the brewery and drink the beer, and then we'd like the hops. That's true. Then we liked them all right. He had them give us the beer. We liked them all right then. But Fontan, il est crazy pour le vin. One time he killed a jack-rabbit and he wanted me to cook it with a sauce with wine, make a black sauce with wine and butter and mushrooms and onion and everything in it, for the jack. My God, I make the sauce all right, and he eat it all and said, "La sauce est meilleure que le jack." Dans son pays c'est comme ça. Il y a beaucoup de gibier et de vin. Moi, j'aime les pommes de terre, le saucisson, et la bière, C'est bon, la bière, C'est très bon pour la santé.'

'It's good,' I said. 'It and wine too.'

'You're like Fontan. But there was a thing here that I never saw. I don't think you've ever seen it either. There were Americans came here and they put whiskey in the beer.'

'No,' I said.

'Oui, My God, yes, that's true. Et aussi une femme qui a vomis sur la table!'

'Comment?'

'C'est vrai. Elle a vomis sur la table. Et après elle a vomis dans ses shoes. And afterwards they came back and say they want to come again and have another party the next Saturday, and I say no, my God, no! When they came I locked the door.'

'They're bad when they're drunk.'

'In the winter-time when the boys go to the dance they come in the cars and wait outside and say to Fontan, "Hey, Sam, sell us a bottle wine," or they buy the beer, and then they take the moonshine out of their pockets in a bottle and pour it in the beer and drink it. My God, that's the first time I ever saw that in my life. They put whiskey in the beer. My God, I don't understand *that!*'

'They want to get sick, so they'll know they're drunk.'

'One time a fellow comes here came to me and said he wanted me to cook them a big supper and they drink one two bottles of wine, and their girls come too, and then they go to the dance. All right I said. So I made a big supper, and when they come already they drank a lot. Then they put whiskey in the wine. My God, yes. I said to Fontan, "On va être malade!" "Oui," il dit. Then these girls were sick, nice girls too, all-right girls. They were sick right at the table. Fontan tried to take them by the arm and show them where they could be sick all right in the cabinet, but the fellows said no, they were all right right there at the table.'

Fontan had come in. 'When they come again I locked the door. "No," I said. "Not for hundred fifty dollars." My God, no.'

'There is a word for such people when they do like that, in French,' Fontan said. He stood looking very old and tired from the heat.

'What?'

'Cochon,' he said delicately, hesitating to use such a strong word. 'They were like the cochon. C'est un mot très fort,' he apologized, 'mais vomir sur la table –' he shook his head sadly.

'Cochons,' I said. 'That's what they are – cochons. Salauds.'

The grossness of the words was distasteful to Fontan. He was glad to speak of something else.

'Il y a des gens très gentils, très sensibles, qui viennent aussi,' he said. 'There are officers from the fort. Very nice men. Good fellas. Everybody that was ever in France they want to come and drink wine. They like wine all right.'

'There was one man,' Madame Fontan said, 'and his wife never lets him get out. So he tells her he's tired, and goes to bed, and when she goes to the show he comes straight down here, sometimes in his pajamas just with a coat over them. "Maria, some beer," he says, "for God's sake." He sits in his pajamas and drinks the beer, and then he goes up to the fort and gets back in bed before his wife comes home from the show.'

'C'est un original,' Fontan said, 'mais vraiment gentil. He's a nice fella.'

'My God, yes, nice fella all right,' Madame Fontan said. 'He's always in bed when his wife gets back from the show.'

'I have to go away tomorrow,' I said. 'To the Crow Reservation. We go there for the opening of the prairie-chicken season.'

'Yes? You come back here before you go away. You come back here all right?'

'Absolutely.'

'Then the wine will be done,' Fontan said. 'We'll drink a bottle together.'

'Three bottles,' Madame Fontan said.

'I'll be back,' I said.

'We count on you,' Fontan said.

'Good night,' I said.

We got in early in the afternoon from the shooting-trip. We had been up that morning since five o'clock. The day before we had had good shooting, but that morning we had not seen a prairie-chicken. Riding in the open car, we were very hot and we stopped to eat our lunch out of the sun, under a tree beside the road. The sun was high and the patch of shade was very small. We ate sandwiches and crackers with sandwich filling on them, and were thirsty and tired, and glad when we finally were out and on the main road back to town. We came up behind a prairie-dog town and stopped the car to shoot at the prairie-dogs with the pistol. We shot two, but then stopped, because the bullets that missed glanced off the rocks and the dirt, and sung off across the fields, and beyond the fields there were some trees along a watercourse, with a house, and we didn't want to get in trouble from stray bullets going toward the house. So we drove on, and finally were on the road coming down-hill toward the outlying houses of the town. Across the plain we could see the mountains. They were blue that day, and the snow on the high mountains shone like glass. The summer was ending, but the new snow had not yet come to stay on the high mountains; there was only the old sun-melted snow and ice, and from a long way away it shone very brightly.

We wanted something cool and some shade. We were sunburned and our lips blistered from the sun and alkali dust. We turned up the side road to Fontan's, stopped the car outside the house and went in. It was cool inside the dining-room. Madame Fontan was alone.

'Only two bottles beer,' she said. 'It's all gone. The new is no good yet.'

I gave her some birds. 'That's good,' she said. 'All right. Thanks. That's good.' She went out to put the birds away where it was cooler. When we finished the beer I stood up. 'We have to go,' I said.

'You come back tonight all right? Fontan he's going to have the wine.'

'We'll come back before we go away.'

'You go away?'

'Yes. We have to leave in the morning.'

'That's too bad you go away. You come tonight. Fontan will have the wine. We'll make a fête before you go.'

'We'll come before we go.'

But that afternoon there were telegrams to send, the car to be gone over – a tire had been cut by a stone and needed vulcanizing – and, without the car, I walked into the town, doing things that had to be done before we could go. When it was supper-time I was too tired to go out. We did not want a foreign language. All we wanted was to go early to bed.

As I lay in bed before I went to sleep, with all the things of the summer piled around ready to be packed, the windows open and the air coming in cool from the mountains, I thought it was a shame not to have gone to Fontan's – but in a little while I was asleep. The next day we were busy all morning packing and ending the summer. We had lunch and were ready to start by two o'clock.

'We must go and say good-bye to the Fontans,' I said.

'Yes, we must.'

'I'm afraid they expected us last night.'

'I suppose we could have gone.'

'I wish we'd gone.'

We said good-bye to the man at the desk at the hotel, and to Larry and our other friends in the town, and then drove out to Fontan's. Both Monsieur and Madame were there. They were glad to see us. Fontan looked old and tired.

'We thought you would come last night,' Madame Fontan

said. 'Fontan had three bottles of wine. When you did not come he drank it all up.'

'We can only stay a minute,' I said. 'We just came to say good-bye. We wanted to come last night. We intended to come, but we were too tired after the trip.'

'Go get some wine,' Fontan said.

'There is no wine. You drank it all up.'

Fontan looked very upset.

'I'll go get some,' he said. 'I'll just be gone a few minutes. I drank it up last night. We had it for you.'

'I knew you were tired. "My God," I said, "they're too tired all right to come." ' Madame Fontan said. 'Go get some wine, Fontan.'

'I'll take you in the car,' I said.

'All right,' Fontan said. 'That way we'll go faster.'

We drove down the road in the motor-car and turned up a side road about a mile away.

'You'll like that wine,' Fontan said. 'It's come out well. You can drink it for supper tonight.'

We stopped in front of a frame house. Fontan knocked on the door. There was no answer. We went around to the back. The back door was locked too. There were empty tin cans around the back door. We looked in the window. There was nobody inside. The kitchen was dirty and sloppy, but all the doors and windows were tight shut.

'That son of a bitch. Where is she gone out?' Fontan said. He was desperate.

'I know where I can get a key,' he said. 'You stay here.' I watched him go down to the next house down the road, knock on the door, talk to the woman who came out, and finally come back. He had a key. We tried the front door and the back, but it wouldn't work.

'That son of a bitch,' Fontan said. 'She's gone away somewhere.'

Looking through the window I could see where the wine was stored. Close to the window you could smell the inside of the house. It smelled sweet and sickish like an Indian house. Suddenly Fontan took a loose board and commenced digging at the earth beside the back door.

'I can get in,' he said. 'Son of a bitch, I can get in.'

There was a man in the back yard of the next house doing something to one of the front wheels of an old Ford.

'You better not,' I said. 'That man will see you. He's watching.'

Fontan straightened up. 'We'll try the key once more,' he said. We tried the key and it did not work. It turned half-way in either direction.

'We can't get in,' I said. 'We better go back.'

'I'll dig up the back,' Fontan offered.

'No, I wouldn't let you take the chance.'

'I'll do it.'

'No,' I said. 'That man would see. Then they would seize it.'

We went out to the car and drove back to Fontan's, stopping on the way to leave the key. Fontan did not say anything but swear in English. He was incoherent and crushed. We went in the house.

'That son of a bitch!' he said. 'We couldn't get the wine. My own wine that I made.'

All the happiness went from Madame Fontan's face. Fontan sat down in a corner with his head in his hands.

'We must go,' I said. 'It doesn't make any difference about the wine. You drink to us when we're gone.'

'Where did that crazy go?' Madame Fontan asked.

'I don't know,' Fontan said. 'I don't know where she go. Now you go away without any wine.'

'That's all right,' I said.

'That's not good,' Madame Fontan said. She shook her head.

'We have to go,' I said. 'Good-bye and good luck. Thank you for the fine times.'

Fontan shook his head. He was disgraced. Madame Fontan looked sad.

'Don't feel bad about the wine,' I said.

'He wanted you to drink his wine,' Madam Fontan said. 'You can come back next year?'

'No. Maybe the year after.'

'You see?' Fontan said to her.

'Good-bye,' I said. 'Don't think about the wine. Drink some

for us when we're gone.' Fontan shook his head. He did not smile. He knew when he was ruined.

'That son of a bitch,' Fontan said to himself.

'Last night he had three bottles,' Madame Fontan said to comfort him, he shook his head.

'Good-bye,' he said.

Madame Fontan had tears in her eyes.

'Good-bye,' she said. She felt badly for Fontan.

'Good-bye,' we said. We all felt very badly. They stood in the doorway and we got in, and I started the motor. We waved. They stood together sadly on the porch. Fontan looked very old, and Madame Fontan looked sad. She waved to us and Fontan went in the house. We turned up the road.

'They felt so badly. Fontan felt terribly.'

'We ought to have gone last night.'

'Yes, we ought to have.'

We were through the town and out on the smooth road beyond, with the stubble of grain-fields on each side and the mountains off to the right. It looked like Spain, but it was Wyoming.

'I hope they have a lot of good luck.'

'They won't,' I said, 'and Schmidt won't be President either.'

The cement road stopped. The road was gravelled now and we left the plain and started up between two foot-hills; the road in a curve and commencing to climb. The soil of the hills was red, the sage grew in gray clumps, and as the road rose we could see across the hills and away across the plain of the valley to the mountains. They were farther away now and they looked more like Spain than ever. The road curved and climbed again, and ahead there were some grouse dusting in the road. They flew as we came toward them, their wings beating fast, then sailing in long slants, and lit on the hillside below.

'They are so big and lovely. They're bigger than European partridges.'

'It's a fine country for la chasse, Fontan says.'

'And when the chasse is gone?'

'They'll be dead then.'

'The boy won't.'

'There's nothing to prove he won't be,' I said.
'We ought to have gone last night.'
'Oh, yes,' I said. 'We ought to have gone.'

The Gambler, The Nun, And The Radio

They brought them in around midnight and then, all night long, every one along the corridor heard the Russian.

'Where is he shot?' Mr Frazer asked the night nurse.

'In the thigh, I think.'

'What about the other one?'

'Oh, he's going to die, I'm afraid.'

'Where is he shot?'

'Twice in the abdomen. They only found one of the bullets.'

They were both beet workers, a Mexican and a Russian, and they were sitting drinking coffee in an all-night restaurant when some one came in the door and started shooting at the Mexican. The Russian crawled under a table and was hit, finally, by a stray shot fired at the Mexican as he lay on the floor with two bullets in his abdomen. That was what the paper said.

The Mexican told the police he had no idea who shot him. He believed it to be an accident.

'An accident that he fired eight shots at you and hit you twice, there?'

'Sí, señor,' said the Mexican, who was named Cayetano Ruiz.

'An accident that he hit me at all, the cabron,' he said to the interpreter.

'What does he say?' asked the detective sergeant, looking across the bed at the interpreter.

'He says it was an accident.'

'Tell him to tell the truth, that he is going to die,' the detective said.

'Na,' said Cayetano. 'But tell him that I feel very sick and would prefer not to talk so much.'

'He says that he is telling the truth,' the interpreter said. Then, speaking confidently, to the detective, 'He don't know who shot him. They shot him in the back.'

'Yes,' said the detective. 'I understand that, but why did the bullets all go in the front?'

'Maybe he is spinning around,' said the interpreter.

'Listen,' said the detective shaking his finger almost at Cayetano's nose, which projected, waxen yellow, from his dead-man's face in which his eyes were alive as a hawk's. 'I don't give a damn who shot you, but I've got to clear this thing up. Don't you want the man who shot you to be punished? Tell him that,' he said to the interpreter.

'He says to tell who shot you.'

'Mandarlo al carajo,' said Cayetano, who was very tired.

'He says he never saw the fellow at all,' the interpreter said. 'I tell you straight they shot him in the back.'

'Ask him who shot the Russian.'

'Poor Russian,' said Cayetano. 'He was on the floor with his head enveloped in his arms. He started to give cries when they shoot him and he is giving cries ever since. Poor Russian.'

'He says some fellow that he doesn't know. Maybe the same fellow that shot him.'

'Listen,' the detective said. 'This isn't Chicago. You're not a gangster. You don't have to act like a moving picture. It's all right to tell who shot you. Anybody would tell who shot them. That's all right to do. Suppose you don't tell me who he is and he shoots somebody else. Suppose he shoots a woman or a child. You can't let him get away with that. You tell him,' he said to Mr Frazer. 'I don't trust that damn interpreter.'

'I am very reliable,' the interpreter said. Cayetano looked at Mr Frazer.

'Listen, amigo,' said Mr Frazer. 'The policeman says that we are not in Chicago but in Halley, Montana. You are not a bandit and this has nothing to do with the cinema.'

'I believe him,' said Cayetano softly. 'Ya lo creo.'

'One can, with honor, denounce one's assailant. Every one

440

does it here, he says. He says what happens if after shooting you, this man shoots a woman or a child?'

'I am not married,' Cayetano said.

'He says any woman, any child.'

'The man is not crazy,' Cayetano said.

'He says you should denounce him,' Mr Frazer finished.

'Thank you,' Cayetano said. 'You are of the great translators. I speak English, but badly. I understand it all right. How did you break your leg?'

'A fall off a horse.'

'What bad luck. I am very sorry. Does it hurt much?'

'Not now. At first, yes.'

'Listen, amigo,' Cayetano began, 'I am very weak. You will pardon me. Also I have much pain; enough pain. It is very possible that I die. Please get this policeman out of here because I am very tired.' He made as though to roll to one side; then held himself still.

'I told him everything exactly as you said and he said to tell you truly, that he doesn't know who shot him and that he is very weak and wishes you would question him later on,' Mr Frazer said.

'He'll probably be dead later on.'

'That's quite possible.'

'That's why I want to question him now.'

'Somebody shot him in the back, I tell you,' the interpreter said.

'Oh, for Chrisake,' the detective sergeant said, and put his notebook in his pocket.

Outside in the corridor the detective sergeant stood with the interpreter beside Mr Frazer's wheeled chair.

'I suppose you think somebody shot him in the back too?'

'Yes,' Frazer said. 'Somebody shot him in the back. What's it to you?'

'Don't get sore,' the sergeant said. 'I wish I could talk spick.'

'Why don't you learn?'

'You don't have to get sore. I don't get any fun out of asking that spick questions. If I could talk spick it would be different.'

441

'You don't need to talk Spanish,' the interpreter said. 'I am a very reliable interpreter.'

'Oh, for Chrisake,' the sergeant said. 'Well, so long. I'll come up and see you.'

'Thanks. I'm always in.'

'I guess you are all right. That was bad luck all right. Plenty bad luck.'

'It's coming along good now since he spliced the bone.'

'Yes, but it's a long time. A long, long time.'

'Don't let anybody shoot you in the back.'

'That's right,' he said. 'That's right. Well, I'm glad you're not sore.'

'So long,' said Mr Frazer.

Mr Frazer did not see Cayetano again for a long time, but each morning Sister Cecilia brought news of him. He was so uncomplaining she said and he was very bad now. He had peritonitis and they thought he could not live. Poor Cayetano, she said. He had such beautiful hands and such a fine face and he never complains. The odor, now, was really terrific. He would point toward his nose with one finger and smile and shake his head, she said. He felt badly about the odor. It embarrassed him, Sister Cecilia said. Oh, he was such a fine patient. He always smiled. He wouldn't go to confession to Father but he promised to say his prayers, and not a Mexican had been to see him since he had been brought in. The Russian was going out at the end of the week. I could never feel anything about the Russian, Sister Cecilia said. Poor fellow, he suffered too. It was a greased bullet and dirty and the wound infected, but he made so much noise and then I always like the bad ones. That Cayetano, he's a bad one. Oh, he must really be a bad one, a thoroughly bad one, he's so fine and delicately made and he's never done any work with his hands. He's not a beet worker. I know he's not a beet worker. His hands are so smooth and not a callous on them. I know he's a bad one of some sort. I'm going down and pray for him now. Poor Cayetano, he's having a dreadful time and he doesn't make a sound. What did they have to shoot him for? Oh, that poor

442

Cayetano! I'm going right down and pray for him.

She went right down and prayed for him.

In that hospital a radio did not work very well until it was dusk. They said it was because there was so much ore in the ground or something about the mountains, but anyway it did not work well at all until it began to get dark outside; but all night it worked beautifully and when one station stopped you could go farther west and pick up another. The last one that you could get was Seattle, Washington, and due to the difference in time, when they signed off at four o'clock in the morning it was five o'clock in the morning in the hospital; and at six o'clock you could get the morning revellers in Minneapolis. That was on account of the difference in time, too, and Mr Frazer used to like to think of the morning revellers arriving at the studio and picture how they would look getting off a street car before daylight in the morning carrying their instruments. Maybe that was wrong and they kept their instruments at the place they revelled, but he always pictured them with their instruments. He had never been in Minneapolis and believed he probably would never go there, but he knew what it looked like that early in the morning.

Out of the window of the hospital you could see a field with tumbleweed coming out of the snow, and a bare clay butte. One morning the doctor wanted to show Mr Frazer two pheasants that were out there in the snow, and pulling the bed toward the window, the reading light fell off the iron bedstead and hit Mr Frazer on the head. This does not sound so funny now but it was funny then. Every one was looking out the window, and the doctor, who was a most excellent doctor, was pointing at the pheasants and pulling the bed toward the window, and then, just as in a comic section, Mr Frazer was knocked out by the leaded base of the lamp hitting the top of his head. It seemed the antithesis of healing or whatever people were in the hospital for, and every one thought it was very funny, as a joke on Mr Frazer and on the doctor. Everything is much simpler in a hospital, including the jokes.

From the other window, if the bed was turned, you could see the town, with a little smoke over it, and the Dawson mountains looking like real mountains with the winter snow on them. Those were the two views since the wheeled chair had proved to be premature. It is really best to be in bed if you are in a hospital; since two views, with time to observe them, from a room the temperature of which you can control, are much better than any number of views seen for a few minutes from hot, empty rooms that are waiting for some one else, or just abandoned, which you are wheeled in and out of. If you stay long enough in a room the view, whatever it is, acquires a great value and becomes very important and you would not change it, not even by a different angle. Just as, with the radio, there are certain things that you become fond of, and you welcome them and resent the new things. The best tunes they had that winter were 'Sing Something Simple,' 'Singsong Girl,' and 'Little White Lies.' No other tunes were as satisfactory, Mr Frazer felt. 'Betty Co-ed' was a good tune too, but the parody of the words which came unavoidably into Mr Frazer's mind, grew so steadily and increasingly obscene that there being no one to appreciate it, he finally abandoned it and let the song go back to football.

About nine o'clock in the morning they would start using the X-ray machine, and then the radio, which, by then, was only getting Hailey, became useless. Many people in Hailey who owned radios protested about the hospital's X-ray machine which ruined their morning reception, but there was never any action taken, although many felt it was a shame the hospital could not use their machine at a time when people were not using their radios.

About the time when it became necessary to turn off the radio Sister Cecilia came in.

'How's Cayetano, Sister Cecilia?' Mr Frazer asked.

'Oh, he's very bad.'

'Is he out of his head?'

'No, but I'm afraid he's going to die.'

'How are you?'

'I'm very worried about him, and do you know that absolutely no one has come to see him? He could die just like a dog for all those Mexicans care. They're really dreadful.'

'Do you want to come up and hear the game this afternoon?'

'Oh, no,' she said. 'I'd be too excited. I'll be in the chapel praying.'

'We ought to be able to hear it pretty well,' Mr Frazer said. 'They're playing out on the coast and the difference in time will bring it late enough so we can get it all right.'

'Oh, no. I couldn't do it. The world series nearly finished me. When the Athletics were at bat I was praying right out loud: "Oh, Lord, direct their batting eyes! Oh, Lord, may he hit one! Oh, Lord, may he hit safely!" Then when they filled the bases in the third game, you remember, it was too much for me. "Oh, Lord, may he hit it out of the lot! Oh, Lord, may he drive it clean over the fence!" Then you know when the Cardinals would come to bat it was simply dreadful. "Oh, Lord, may they not see it! Oh, Lord, don't let them even catch a glimpse of it! Oh, Lord, may they fan!" And this game is even worse. It's Notre Dame. Our Lady. No, I'll be in the chapel. For Our Lady. They're playing for Our Lady. I wish you'd write something sometime for Our Lady. You could do it. You know you could do it, Mr Frazer.'

'I don't know anything about her that I could write. It's mostly been written already,' Mr Frazer said. 'You wouldn't like the way I write. She wouldn't care for it either.'

'You'll write about her sometime,' Sister said. 'I know you will. You must write about Our Lady.'

'You'd better come up and hear the game.'

'It would be too much for me. No, I'll be in the chapel doing what I can.'

That afternoon they had been playing about five minutes when a probationer came into the room and said, 'Sister Cecilia wants to know how the game is going?'

'Tell her they have a touchdown already.'

In a little while the probationer came into the room again.

'Tell her they're playing them off their feet,' Mr Frazer said.

A little later he rang the bell for the nurse who was on floor duty. 'Would you mind going down to the chapel or sending word down to Sister Cecilia that Notre Dame has them fourteen to nothing at the end of the first quarter and that it's all right. She can stop praying.'

In a few minutes Sister Cecilia came into the room. She was very excited. 'What does fourteen to nothing mean? I don't know anything about this game. That's a nice safe lead in baseball. But I don't know anything about football. It may not mean a thing. I'm going right back down to the chapel and pray until it's finished.'

'They have them beaten,' Frazer said. 'I promise you. Stay and listen with me.'

'No. No. No. No. No. No. No,' she said. 'I'm going right down to the chapel to pray.'

Mr Frazer sent down word whenever Notre Dame scored, and finally, when it had been dark a long time, the final result.

'How's Sister Cecilia?'

'They're all at chapel,' she said.

The next morning Sister Cecilia came in. She was very pleased and confident.

'I knew they couldn't beat Our Lady,' she said. 'They couldn't. Cayetano's better too. He's much better. He's going to have visitors. He can't see them yet, but they are going to come and that will make him feel better and know he's not forgotten by his own people. I went down and saw that O'Brien boy at Police Headquarters and told him that he's got to send some Mexicans up to see poor Cayetano. He's going to send some this afternoon. Then that poor man will feel better. It's wicked the way no one has come to see him.'

That afternoon about five o'clock three Mexicans came into the room.

'Can one?' asked the biggest one, who had very thick lips and was quite fat.

'Why not?' Mr Frazer answered. 'Sit down, gentlemen. Will you take something?'

'Many thanks,' said the big one.

'Thanks,' said the darkest and smallest one.

'Thanks, no,' said the thin one. 'It mounts to my head.'

He tapped his head.

The nurse brought some glasses. 'Please give them the bottle,' Frazer said. 'It is from Red Lodge,' he explained.

'That of Red Lodge is the best,' said the big one. 'Much better than that of Big Timber.'

'Clearly,' said the smallest one, 'and costs more too.'

'In Red Lodge it is of all prices,' said the big one.

'How many tubes has the radio?' asked the one who did not drink.

'Seven.'

'Very beautiful,' he said. 'What does it cost?'

'I don't know,' Mr Frazer said. 'It is rented.'

'You gentlemen are friends of Cayetano?'

'No,' said the big one. 'We are friends of he who wounded him.'

'We were sent here by the police,' the smallest one said.

'We have a little place,' the big one said. 'He and I,' indicating the one who did not drink. 'He has a little place too,' indicating the small dark one. 'The police tell us we have to come – so we come.'

'I am very happy you have come.'

'Equally,' said the big one.

'Will you have another little cup?'

'Why not?' said the big one.

'With your permission,' said the smallest one.

'Not me,' said the thin one. 'It mounts to my head.'

'It is very good,' said the smallest one.

'Why not try some,' Mr Frazer asked the thin one. 'Let a little mount to your head.'

'Afterwards comes the headache,' said the thin one.

'Could you not send friends of Cayetano to see him?' Frazer asked.

'He has no friends.'

'Every man has friends.'

'This one, no.'

'What does he do?'

'He is a card-player.'

'Is he good?'

'I believe it.'

'From me,' said the smallest one, 'he won one hundred and eighty dollars. Now there is no longer one hundred and eighty dollars in the world.'

'From me,' said the thin one, 'he won two hundred and eleven dollars. Fix yourself on that figure.'

447

'I never played with him,' said the fat one.

'He must be very rich,' Mr Frazer suggested.

'He is poorer than we,' said the little Mexican. 'He has no more than the shirt on his back.'

'And that shirt is of little value now,' Mr Frazer said. 'Perforated as it is.'

'Clearly.'

'The one who wounded him was a card-player?'

'No, a beet worker. He has had to leave town.'

'Fix yourself on this,' said the smallest one. 'He was the best guitar player ever in this town. The finest.'

'What a shame.'

'I believe it,' said the biggest one. 'How could he touch the guitar?'

'There are no good guitar players left?'

'Not the shadow of a guitar player.'

'There is an accordion player who is worth something,' the thin man said.

'There are a few who touch various instruments,' the big one said. 'You like music?'

'How would I not?'

'We will come one night with music? You think the sister would allow it? She seems very amiable.'

'I am sure she would permit it when Cayetano is able to hear it.'

'Is she a little crazy?' asked the thin one.

'Who?'

'That sister.'

'No,' Mr Frazer said. 'She is a fine woman of great intelligence and sympathy.'

'I distrust all priests, monks, and sisters,' said the thin one.

'He had bad experiences when a boy,' the smallest one said.

'I was acolyte,' the thin one said proudly. 'Now I believe in nothing. Neither do I go to mass.'

'Why? Does it mount to your head?'

'No,' said the thin one. 'It is alcohol that mounts to my head. Religion is the opium of the poor.'

'I thought marijuana was the opium of the poor,' Frazer said.

'Did you ever smoke opium?' the big one asked.

'No.'

'Nor I,' he said. 'It seems it is very bad. One commences and cannot stop. It is a vice.'

'Like religion,' said the thin one.

'This one,' said the smallest Mexican, 'is very strong against religion.'

'It is necessary to be strong against something,' Mr Frazer said politely.

'I respect those who have faith even though they are ignorant,' the thin one said.

'Good,' said Mr Frazer.

'What can we bring you?' asked the big Mexican. 'Do you lack for anything?'

'I would be glad to buy some beer if there is good beer.'

'We will bring beer.'

'Another copita before you go?'

'It is very good.'

'We are robbing you.'

'I can't take it. It goes to my head. Then I have a bad headache and sick at the stomach.'

'Good-bye, gentlemen.'

'Good-bye and thanks.'

They went out and there was supper and then the radio, turned to be as quiet as possible and still be heard, and the stations finally signing off in this order: Denver, Salt Lake City, Los Angeles, and Seattle. Mr Frazer received no picture of Denver from the radio. He could see Denver from the *Denver Post*, and correct the picture from *The Rocky Mountain News*. Nor did he ever have any feel of Salt Lake City or Los Angeles from what he heard from those places. All he felt about Salt Lake City was that it was clean, but dull, and there were too many ballrooms mentioned in too many big hotels for him to see Los Angeles. He could not feel it for the ballrooms. But Seattle he came to know very well, the taxicab company with the big white cabs (each cab equipped with radio itself) he rode in every night out to the roadhouse on the Canadian side where he followed the course of parties by the musical selections they phoned for. He lived in Seattle from two o'clock on, each night, hearing the pieces that all the different people asked for, and it was as real as Minneapolis, where the revellers left their beds each morning to make that trip down to the studio. Mr Frazer grew very fond of Seattle, Washington.

The Mexicans came and brought beer but it was not good beer. Mr Frazer saw them but he did not feel like talking, and when they went he knew they would not come again. His nerves had become tricky and he disliked seeing people while he was in this condition. His nerves went bad at the end of five weeks, and while he was pleased they lasted that long yet he resented being forced to make the same experiment when he already knew the answer. Mr Frazer had been through this all before. The only thing which was new to him was the radio. He played it all night long, turned so low he could barely hear it, and he was learning to listen to it without thinking.

Sister Cecilia came into the room about ten o'clock in the morning on that day and brought the mail. She was very handsome, and Mr Frazer liked to see her and to hear her talk, but the mail, supposedly coming from a different world, was more important. However, there was nothing in the mail of any interest.

'You look *so* much better,' she said. 'You'll be leaving us soon.'

'Yes,' Mr Frazer said. 'You look very happy this morning.'

'Oh, I am. This morning I feel as though I might be a saint.'

Mr Frazer was a little taken aback at this.

'Yes,' Sister Cecilia went on. 'That's what I want to be. A saint. Ever since I was a little girl I've wanted to be a saint. When I was a girl I thought if I renounced the world and went into the convent I would be a saint. That was what I wanted to be and that was what I thought I had to do to be one. I expected I would be a saint. I was absolutely sure I would be one. For just a moment I thought I was one. I was so happy and it seemed so simple and easy. When I awoke in the morning I expected I would be a saint, but I wasn't. I have never been one. I want so to be one. All I want is to be a saint.

That is all I've ever wanted. And this morning I feel as though I might be one. Oh, I hope I will get to be one.'

'You'll be one. Everybody gets what they want. That's what they always tell me.'

'I don't know now. When I was a girl it seemed so simple. I knew I would be a saint. Only I believed it took time when I found it did not happen suddenly. Now it seems almost impossible.'

'I'd say you had a good chance.'

'Do you really think so? No, I don't want just to be encouraged. Don't just encourage me. I want to be a saint. I want so to be a saint.'

'Of course you'll be a saint,' Mr Frazer said.

'No, probably I won't be. But, oh, if I could only be a saint! I'd be perfectly happy.'

'You're three to one to be a saint.'

'No, don't encourage me. But, oh, if I could only be a saint! If I could only be a saint.'

'How's your friend Cayetano?'

'He's going to get well but he's paralyzed. One of the bullets hit the big nerve that goes down through his thigh and that leg is paralyzed. They only found it out when he got well enough so that he could move.'

'Maybe the nerve will regenerate.'

'I'm praying that it will,' Sister Cecilia said. 'You ought to see him.'

'I don't feel like seeing anybody.'

'You know you'd like to see him. They could wheel him in here.'

'All right.'

They wheeled him in, thin, his skin transparent, his hair black, and needing to be cut, his eyes very laughing, his teeth bad when he smiled.

'Hola, amigo! Que tal?'

'As you see,' said Mr Frazer. 'And thou?'

'Alive and with the leg paralyzed.'

'Bad,' Mr Frazer said. 'But the nerve can regenerate and be as good as new.'

451

'So they tell me.'

'What about the pain?'

'Not now. For a while I was crazy with it in the belly. I thought the pain alone would kill me.'

Sister Cecilia was observing them happily.

'She tells me you never made a sound,' Mr Frazer said.

'So many people in the ward,' the Mexican said deprecatingly. 'What class of pain do you have?'

'Big enough. Clearly not as bad as yours. When the nurse goes out I cry an hour, two hours. It rests me. My nerves are bad now.'

'You have the radio. If I had a private room and a radio I would be crying and yelling all night long.'

'I doubt it.'

'Hombre, si. It's very healthy. But you cannot do it with so many people.'

'At least,' Mr Frazer said, 'the hands are still good. They tell me you make your living with the hands.'

'And the head,' he said, tapping his forehead. 'But the head isn't worth as much.'

'Three of your countrymen were here.'

'Sent by the police to see me.'

'They brought some beer.'

'It probably was bad.'

'It was bad.'

'Tonight, sent by the police, they come to serenade me.' He laughed, then tapped his stomach. 'I cannot laugh yet. As musicians they are fatal.'

'And the one who shot you?'

'Another fool. I won thirty-eight dollars from him at cards. That is not to kill about.'

'The three told me you win much money.'

'And am poorer than the birds.'

'How?'

'I am a poor idealist. I am the victim of illusions.' He laughed, then grinned and tapped his stomach. 'I am a professional gambler but I like to gamble. To really gamble. Little gambling is all crooked. For real gambling you need luck. I have no luck.'

452

'Never?'

'Never. I am completely without luck. Look, this cabron who shoots me just now. Can he shoot? No. The first shot he fires into nothing. The second is intercepted by the poor Russian. That would seem to be luck. What happens? He shoots me twice in the belly. He is a lucky man. I have no luck. He could not hit a horse if he were holding the stirrup. All luck.'

'I thought he shot you first and the Russian after.'

'No, the Russian first, me after. The paper was mistaken.'

'Why didn't you shoot him?'

'I never carry a gun. With my luck, if I carried a gun I would be hanged ten times a year. I am a cheap card player, only that.' He stopped, then continued. 'When I make a sum of money I gamble and when I gamble I lose. I have passed at dice for three thousand dollars and crapped out for the six. With good dice. More than once.'

'Why continue?'

'If I live long enough the luck will change. I have had bad luck now for fifteen years. If I ever get any good luck I will be rich.' He grinned. 'I am a good gambler, really I would enjoy being rich.'

'Do you have bad luck with all games?'

'With everything and with women.' He smiled again, showing his bad teeth.

'Truly?'

'Truly.'

'And what is there to do?'

'Continue, slowly, and wait for luck to change.'

'But with women?'

'No gambler has luck with women. He is too concentrated. He works nights. When he should be with the woman. No man who works nights can hold a woman if the woman is worth anything.'

'You are a philosopher.'

'No, hombre. A gambler of the small towns. One small town, then another, another, then a big town, then start over again.'

'Then shot in the belly.'

'The first time,' he said. 'That has only happened once.'

'I tire you talking?' Mr Frazer suggested.

'No,' he said. 'I must tire you.'

'And the leg?'

'I have no great use for the leg. I am all right with the leg or not. I will be able to circulate.'

'I wish you luck, truly, and with all my heart,' Mr Frazer said.

'Equally,' he said. 'And that the pain stops.'

'It will not last, certainly. It is passing. It is of no importance.'

'That it passes quickly.'

'Equally.'

That night the Mexicans played the accordion and the other instruments in the ward and it was cheerful and the noise of the inhalation and exhalation of the accordion, and of the bells, the traps, and the drum came down the corridor. In that ward there was a rodeo rider who had come out of the chutes on Midnight on a hot dusty afternoon with the big crowd watching, and now, with a broken back, was going to learn to work in leather and to cane chairs when he got well enough to leave the hospital. There was a carpenter who had fallen with a scaffolding and broken both ankles and both wrists. He had lit like a cat but without a cat's resiliency. They could fix him up so that he could work again but it would take a long time. There was a boy from a farm, about sixteen years old, with a broken leg that had been badly set and was to be rebroken. There was Cayetano Ruiz, a small-town gambler with a paralyzed leg. Down the corridor Mr Frazer could hear them all laughing and merry with the music made by the Mexicans who had been sent by the police. The Mexicans were having a good time. They came in, very excited, to see Mr Frazer and wanted to know if there was anything he wanted them to play, and they came twice more to play at night of their own accord.

The last time they played Mr Frazer lay in his room with the door open and listened to the noisy, bad music and could not keep from thinking. When they wanted to know what he wished played, he asked for the Cucaracha, which has the sinister lightness and deftness of so many of the tunes men have gone to die to. They played noisily and with emotion. The tune was better than most of such tunes, to Mr Frazer's mind, but the effect was all the same.

In spite of this introduction of emotion, Mr Frazer went on thinking. Usually he avoided thinking all he could, except when he was writing, but now he was thinking about those who were playing and what the little one had said.

Religion is the opium of the people. He believed that, that dyspeptic little joint-keeper. Yes, and music is the opium of the people. Old mount-to-the-head hadn't thought of that. And now economics is the opium of the people; along with patriotism the opium of the people in Italy and Germany. What about sexual intercourse; was that an opium of the people? Of some of the people. Of some of the best of the people. But drink was a sovereign opium of the people, oh, an excellent opium. Although some prefer the radio, another opium of the people, a cheap one he had just been using. Along with these went gambling, an opium of the people if there ever was one; one of the oldest. Ambition was another, an opium of the people, along with a belief in any new form of government. What you wanted was the minimum of government, always less government. Liberty, what we believed in, now the name of a MacFadden publication. We believed in that although they had not found a new name for it yet. But what was the real one? What was the real, the actual, opium of the people? He knew it very well. It was gone just a little way around the corner in that well-lighted part of his mind that was there after two or more drinks in the evening; that he knew was there (it was not really there of course). What was it? He knew very well. What was it? Of course; bread was the opium of the people. Would he remember that and would it make sense in the daylight? Bread is the opium of the people.

'Listen,' Mr Frazer said to the nurse when she came. 'Get that little thin Mexican in here, will you, please?'

'How do you like it?' the Mexican said at the door.

'Very much.'

'It is a historic tune,' the Mexican said. 'It is the tune of the real revolution.'

'Listen,' said Mr Frazer. 'Why should the people be operated on without anaesthetic?'

'I do not understand.'

'Why are not all the opiums of the people good? What do you want to do with the people?'

'They should be rescued from ignorance.'

'Don't talk nonsense. Education is an opium of the people. You ought to know that. You've had a little.'

'You do not believe in education?'

'No,' said Mr Frazer. 'In knowledge, yes.'

'I do not follow you.'

'Many times I do not follow myself with pleasure.'

'You want to hear the Cucaracha another time?' asked the Mexican worriedly.

'Yes,' said Mr Frazer. 'Play the Cucaracha another time. It's better than the radio.'

Revolution, Mr Frazer thought, is no opium. Revolution is a catharsis; an ecstasy which can only be prolonged by tyranny. The opiums are for before and for after. He was thinking well, a little too well.

They would go now in a little while, he thought, and they would take the Cucaracha with them. Then he would have a little spot of the giant killer and play the radio, you could play the radio so that you could hardly hear it.

Fathers And Sons

There had been a sign to detour in the center of the main street of this town, but cars had obviously gone through, so, believing it was some repair which had been completed, Nicholas Adams drove on through the town along the empty, brick-paved street, stopped by traffic lights that flashed on and off on this traffic-less Sunday, and would be gone next year when the payments on the system were not met; on under the heavy trees of the small town that are a part of your heart if it is your town and you have walked under them, but that are only too heavy, that shut out the sun and that dampen the houses for a stranger; out past the last house and onto the highway that rose and fell straight away ahead with banks of red dirt sliced cleanly away and the second-growth timber on both sides. It was not his country but it was the middle of fall and all of this country was good to drive through and to see. The cotton was picked and in the clearings there were patches of corn, some cut with streaks of red sorghum, and, driving easily, his son asleep on the seat by his side, the day's run made, knowing the town he would reach for the night, Nick noticed which corn fields had soy beans or peas in them, how the thickets and the cut-over lay, where the cabins and houses were in relation to the fields and the thickets; hunting the country in his mind as he went by; sizing up each clearing as to feed and cover and figuring where you would find a covey and which way they would fly.

In shooting quail you must not get between them and their habitual cover, once the dogs have found them, or when they flush they will come pouring at you, some rising steep, some skipping by your ears, whirring into a size you have never seen them in the air as they pass, the only way being to turn and take them over your shoulder as they go, before they set their wings and angle down into the thicket. Hunting this country for quail as his father had taught him, Nicholas Adams started thinking about his father. When he first thought about him it was always the eyes. The big frame, the quick movements, the wide shoulders, the hooked, hawk nose, the beard that covered the weak chin, you never thought about – it was always the eyes. They were protected in his head by the formation of the brows; set deep as though a special protection had been devised for some very valuable instrument. They saw much farther and much quicker than the human eye sees and they were the great gift his father had. His father saw as a big-horn ram or as an eagle sees, literally.

He would be standing with his father on one shore of the lake, his own eyes were very good then, and his father would say, 'They've run up the flag.' Nick could not see the flag or the flag pole. 'There,' his father would say, 'it's your sister Dorothy. She's got the flag up and she's walking out onto the dock.'

Nick would look across the lake and he could see the long wooded shore-line, the higher timber behind, the point that guarded the bay, the clear hills of the farm and the white of their cottage in the trees but he could not see any flag pole, or any dock, only the white of the beach and the curve of the shore.

'Can you see the sheep on the hillside toward the point?'

'Yes.'

They were a whitish patch on the gray-green of the hill.

'I can count them,' his father said.

Like all men with a faculty that surpasses human require-ments, his father was very nervous. Then, too, he was sentimental, and, like most sentimental people, he was both cruel and abused. Also, he had much bad luck, and it was not all of his own. He had died in a trap that he had helped only a little to set, and they had all betrayed him in their various ways before he died. All sentimental people are betrayed so many times. Nick could not write about him yet, although he would later, but the quail country made him remember him as he was when Nick was a boy and he was very grateful to him for two things: fishing and shooting. His father was as sound on those two things as he was unsound on sex, for instance, and Nick was glad that it had been that way; for some one has to give you your first gun or the opportunity to get it and use it, and you have to live where there is game or fish if you are to learn about them, and now, at thirty-eight, he loved to fish and to shoot exactly as much as when he first had gone with his father. It was a passion that had never slackened and he was very grateful to his father for bringing him to know it.

While for the other, that his father was not sound about, all the equipment you will ever have is provided and each man learns all there is for him to know about it without advice; and it makes no difference where you live. He remembered very clearly the only two pieces of information his father had given him about that. Once when they were out shooting together Nick shot a red squirrel out of a hemlock tree. The squirrel fell, wounded, and when Nick picked him up bit the boy clean through the ball of the thumb.

'The dirty little bugger,' Nick said and smacked the squirrel's head against the tree. 'Look how he bit me.'

His father looked and said, 'Suck it out clean and put some iodine on when you get home.'

'The little bugger,' Nick said.

'Do you know what a bugger is?' his father asked him.

'We call anything a bugger,' Nick said.

'A bugger is a man who has intercourse with animals.'

'Why?' Nick said.

'I don't know,' his father said. 'But it is a heinous crime.'

Nick's imagination was both stirred and horrified by this and he thought of various animals but none seemed attractive or practical and that was the sum total of direct sexual knowledge bequeathed him by his father except on one other subject. One morning he read in the paper that Enrico Caruso had been arrested for mashing.

'What is mashing?'

'It is one of the most heinous of crimes,' his father answered.

Nick's imagination pictured the great tenor doing something strange, bizarre, and heinous with a potato masher to a beautiful lady who looked like the pictures of Anna Held on the inside of cigar boxes. He resolved, with considerable horror, that when he was old enough he would trying mashing at least once.

His father had summed up the whole matter by stating that masturbation produced blindness, insanity, and death, while a man who went with prostitutes would contract hideous venereal diseases and that the thing to do was to keep your hands off of people. On the other hand his father had the finest pair of eyes he had ever seen and Nick had loved him very much and for a long time. Now, knowing how it had all been, even remembering the earliest times before things had gone badly was not good remembering. If he wrote it he could get rid of it. He had gotten rid of many things by writing them. But it was still too early for that. There were still too many people. So he decided to think of something else. There was nothing to do about his father and he had thought it all through many times. The handsome job the undertaker had done on his father's face had not blurred in his mind and all the rest of it was quite clear, including the responsibilities. He had complimented the undertaker. The undertaker had been both proud and smugly pleased. But it was not the undertaker that had given him that last face. The undertaker had only made certain dashingly executed repairs of doubtful artistic merit. The face had been making itself and being made for a long time. It had modelled fast in the last three years. It was a good story but there were still too many people alive for him to write it.

Nick's own education in those earlier matters had been acquired in the hemlock woods behind the Indian camp. This was reached by a trail which ran from the cottage through the woods to the farm and then by a road which wound through the slashings to the camp. Now if he could still feel all of that trail with bare feet. First there was the pine-needle loam through the hemlock woods behind the cottage where the fallen logs crumbled into wood dust and long splintered pieces of wood hung like javelins in the tree that had been struck by lightning. You crossed the creek on a log and if you stepped off

460

there was the black muck of the swamp. You climbed a fence out of the woods and the trail was hard in the sun across the field with cropped grass and sheep sorrel and mullen growing and to the left the quaky bog of the creek bottom where the killdeer plover fed. The spring house was in that creek. Below the barn, there was fresh warm manure and the other older manure that was caked dry on top. Then there was another fence and the hard, hot trail from the barn to the house and the hot sandy road that ran down to the woods, crossing the creek, on a bridge this time, where the cat-tails grew that you soaked in kerosene to make jack-lights with for spearing fish at night.

Then the main road went off to the left, skirting the woods on the wide clay and shale road, cool under the trees, and broadened for them to skid out the hemlock bark the Indians cut. The hemlock bark was piled in long rows of stacks, roofed over with more bark, like houses, and the peeled logs lay huge and yellow where the trees had been felled. They left the logs in the woods to rot, they did not even clear away or burn the tops. It was only the bark they wanted for the tannery at Boyne City; hauling it across the lake on the ice in winter, and each year there was less forest and more open, hot, shadeless, weed-grown slashing.

But there was still much forest then, virgin forest where the trees grew high before there were any branches and you walked on the brown, clean, springy-needled ground with no undergrowth and it was cool on the hottest days and they three lay against the trunk of a hemlock wider than two beds are long, with the breeze high in the tops and the cool light that came in patches, and Billy said:

'You want Trudy again?'

'You want to?'

'Uh Huh.'

'Come on.'

'No, here.'

'But Billy –'

'I no mind Billy. He my brother.'

Then afterwards they sat, the three of them, listening for a black squirrel that was in the top branches where they could not see him. They were waiting for him to bark again because when he barked he would jerk his tail and Nick would shoot where he saw any movement. His father gave him only three cartridges a day to hunt with and he had a single-barrel twenty-gauge shotgun with a very long barrel.

'Son of a bitch never move,' Billy said.

'You shoot, Nickie. Scare him. We see him jump. Shoot him again,' Trudy said. It was a long speech for her.

'I've only got two shells,' Nick said.

'Son of a bitch,' said Billy.

They sat against the tree and were quiet. Nick was feeling hollow and happy.

'Eddie says he going to come some night sleep in bed with your sister Dorothy.'

'What?'

'He said.'

Trudy nodded.

'That's all he want to do,' she said. Eddie was their older half-brother. He was seventeen.

'If Eddie Gilby ever comes at night and even speaks to Dorothy you know what I'd do to him? I'd kill him like this.' Nick cocked the gun and hardly taking aim pulled the trigger, blowing a hole as big as your hand in the head or belly of that half-breed bastard Eddie Gilby. 'Like that. I'd kill him like that.'

'He better not come then,' Trudy said. She put her hand in Nick's pocket.

'He better watch out plenty,' said Billy.

'He's big bluff,' Trudy was exploring with her hand in Nick's pocket. 'But don't you kill him. You get plenty trouble.'

'I'd kill him like that,' Nick said. Eddie Gilby lay on the ground with his chest shot away. Nick put his foot on him proudly.

'I'd scalp him,' he said happily.

'No,' said Trudy. 'That's dirty.'

'I'd scalp him and send it to his mother.'

'His mother dead,' Trudy said. 'Don't you kill him, Nickie. Don't you kill him for me.'

'After I scalped him I'd throw him to the dogs.'

Billy was very depressed. 'He better watch out,' he said gloomily.

'They'd tear him to pieces,' Nick said, pleased with the picture. Then, having scalped the half-breed renegade and standing watching the dogs tear him, his face unchanged, he fell backward against the tree, held tight around the neck, Trudy holding, choking him, and crying. 'No kill him! No kill him! No kill him! No. No. No. Nickie. Nickie. Nickie!'

'What's the matter with you?'

'No kill him.'

'I got to kill him.'

'He's just a big bluff.'

'All right,' Nickie said. 'I won't kill him unless he comes around the house. Let go of me.'

'That's good,' Trudy said. 'You want to do anything now? I feel good now.'

'If Billy goes away.' Nick had killed Eddie Gilby, then pardoned him his life, and he was a man now.

'You go, Billy. You hang around all the time. Go on.'

'Son a bitch,' Billy said. 'I get tired this. What we come? Hunt or what?'

'You can take the gun. There's one shell.'

'All right. I get a big black one all right.'

'I'll holler,' Nick said.

Then, later, it was a long time after and Billy was still away.

'You think we make a baby?' Trudy folded her brown legs together happily and rubbed against him. Something inside Nick had gone a long way away.

'I don't think so,' he said.

'Make plenty baby what the hell.'

They heard Billy shoot.

'I wonder if he got one.'

'Don't care,' said Trudy.

Billy came through the trees. He had the gun over his shoulder and he held a black squirrel by the front paws.

'Look,' he said. 'Bigger than a cat. You all through?'

'Where'd you get him?'

'Over there. Saw him jump first.'

463

'Got to go home,' Nick said.

'No,' said Trudy.

'I got to get there for supper.'

'All right.'

'Want to hunt tomorrow?'

'All right.'

'You can have the squirrel.'

'All right.'

'Come out after supper?'

'No.'

'How you feel?'

'Good.'

'All right.'

'Give me a kiss on the face,' said Trudy.

Now, as he rode along the highway in the car and it was getting dark, Nick was all through thinking about his father. The end of the day never made him think of him. The end of the day had always belonged to Nick alone and he never felt right unless he was alone at it. His father came back to him in the fall of the year, or in the early spring when there had been jacksnipe on the prairie, or when he saw shocks of corn, or when he saw a lake, or if he ever saw a horse and buggy, or when he saw, or heard, wild geese, or in a duck blind; remembering the time an eagle dropped through the whirling snow to strike a canvas-covered decoy, rising, his wings beating, the talons caught in the canvas. His father was with him, suddenly, in deserted orchards and in new-plowed fields, in thickets, on small hills, or when going through dead grass, whenever splitting wood or hauling water, by grist mills, cider mills and dams and always with open fires. The towns he lived in were not towns his father knew. After he was fifteen he had shared nothing with him.

His father had frost in his beard in cold weather and in hot weather he sweated very much. He liked to work in the sun on the farm because he did not have to and he loved manual work, which Nick did not. Nick loved his father but hated the smell of him and once when he had to wear a suit of his father's underwear that had gotten too small for his father it made him feel sick and he took it off and put it under two stones in the creek and said that he had lost it. He had told his father how it was when his father had made him put it on but his father had said it was freshly washed. It had been, too. When Nick had asked him to smell of it his father sniffed at it indignantly and said that it was clean and fresh. When Nick came home from fishing without it and said he lost it he was whipped for lying.

Afterwards he had sat inside the woodshed with the door open, his shotgun loaded and cocked, looking across at his father sitting on the screen porch reading the paper, and thought, 'I can blow him to hell. I can kill him.' Finally he felt his anger go out of him and he felt a little sick about it being the gun that his father had given him. Then he had gone to the Indian camp, walking there in the dark, to get rid of the smell. There was only one person in his family that he liked the smell of; one sister. All the others he avoided all contact with. That sense blunted when he started to smoke. It was a good thing. It was good for a bird dog but it did not help a man.

'What was it like, Papa, when you were a little boy and used to hunt with the Indians?'

'I don't know,' Nick was startled. He had not even noticed the boy was awake. He looked at him sitting beside him on the seat. He had felt quite alone but this boy had been with him. He wondered for how long. 'We used to go all day to hunt black squirrels,' he said. 'My father only gave me three shells a day because he said that would teach me to hunt and it wasn't good for a boy to go banging around. I went with a boy named Billy Gilby and his sister Trudy. We used to go out nearly every day all one summer.'

'Those are funny names for Indians.'

'Yes, aren't they,' Nick said.

'But tell me what they were like.'

'They were Ojibways,' Nick said. 'And they were very nice.'

'But what were they like to be with?'

'It's hard to say,' Nick Adams said. Could you say she did first what no one has ever done better and mention plump brown legs, flat belly, hard little breasts, well holding arms, quick searching tongue, the flat eyes, the good taste of mouth, then uncomfortably, tightly, sweetly, moistly, lovely, tightly, achingly, fully, finally, unendingly, never-endingly, never-to-

465

endingly, suddenly ended, the great bird flown like an owl in the twilight, only it daylight in the woods and hemlock needles stuck against your belly. So that when you go in a place where Indians have lived you smell them gone and all the empty pain killer bottles and the flies that buzz do not kill the sweetgrass smell, the smoke smell and that other like a fresh cased marten skin. Nor any jokes about them nor old squaws take that away. Nor the sick sweet smell they get to have. Nor what they did finally. It wasn't how it ended. They all ended the same. Long time ago good. Now no good.

And about the other. When you have shot one bird flying you have shot all birds flying. They are all different and they fly in different ways but the sensation is the same and the last one is as good as the first. He could thank his father for that.

'You might not like them,' Nick said to the boy. 'But I think you would.'

'And my grandfather lived with them too when he was a boy, didn't he?'

'Yes. When I asked him what they were like he said that he had many friends among them.'

'Will I ever live with them?'

'I don't know,' Nick said. 'That's up to you.'

'How old will I be when I get a shotgun and can hunt by myself?'

'Twelve years old if I see you are careful.'

'I wish I was twelve now.'

'You will be, soon enough.'

'What was my grandfather like? I can't remember him except that he gave me an air rifle and an American flag when I came over from France that time. What was he like?'

'He's hard to describe. He was a great hunter and fisherman and he had wonderful eyes.'

'Was he greater than you?'

'He was a much better shot and his father was a great wing shot too.'

'I'll bet he wasn't better than you.'

'Oh, yes he was. He shot very quickly and beautifully. I'd rather see him shoot than any man I ever knew. He was always

466

very disappointed in the way I shot.'

'Why do we never go to pray at the tomb of my grandfather?'

'We live in a different part of the country. It's a long way from here.'

'In France that wouldn't make any difference. In France we'd go. I think I ought to go to pray at the tomb of my grandfather.'

'Sometime we'll go.'

'I hope we won't live somewhere so that I can never go to pray at your tomb when you are dead.'

'We'll have to arrange it.'

'Don't you think we might all be buried at a convenient place? We could all be buried in France. That would be fine.'

'I don't want to be buried in France,' Nick said.

'Well, then, we'll have to get some convenient place in America. Couldn't we all be buried out at the ranch?'

'That's an idea.'

'Then I could stop and pray at the tomb of my grandfather on the way to the ranch.'

'You're awfully practical.'

'Well, I don't feel good never to have even visted the tomb of my grandfather.'

'We'll have to go,' Nick said. 'I can see we'll have to go.'

True at First Light

Ernest Hemingway

Written when Hemingway returned from his 1953 safari in Africa, and edited by his son Patrick, *True at First Light* is a rich blend of autobiography and fiction, a breathtaking final work from one of the twentieth century's most beloved and important writers.

The book opens on the day Hemingway's close friend Pop, a legendary hunter, leaves him in charge of the camp. Tensions have heightened among the various tribes and news arrives of a potential attack on the hunters, forcing Hemingway not only to take up his new role as a leader, but, equally important, to assist his wife Mary in pursuing the great lion she is determined to kill before Christmas. Passionately detailing the African landscape, the excitement of the chase, and the heartfelt relationships with his African neighbours, Hemingway weaves a tale that is rich in laughter, beauty and insight.

'Captures the beauty of the African landscape and the thrill of the hunt, in true Hemingway style'
Red

'This is writing of a high order; sympathetic, luminous, hypnotic, humane'
Caledonia

arrow books

A Farewell to Arms

Ernest Hemingway

In 1918 Ernest Hemingway enlisted to fight in the 'war to end all wars'. He volunteered for ambulance service in Italy, was wounded and twice decorated. Out of his experiences came *A Farewell To Arms.*

In an unforgettable depiction of war, Hemingway recreates the fear, the comradeship, the courage of his young American volunteers, and the men and women he encounters along the way with conviction and brutal honesty. A love story of immense drama and uncompromising passion *A Farewell To Arms* is a testament to Hemingway's unique and unflinching views of the world and the people around him.

'A novel of great power'
Times Literary Supplement

'Hard, almost metallic, glittering, blinding by the reflections of its hard surface, utterly free of sentimentality'
Arnold Bennett

'A most beautiful, moving and humane book'
Vita Sackville-West

arrow books

ALSO AVAILABLE IN ARROW

The Old Man and the Sea
Ernest Hemingway

'The best short story Hemingway has written . . . no page of this beautiful master-work could have been done better or differently'
Sunday Times

Set in the Gulf Stream off the coast of Havana, Hemingway's magnificent fable is the story of an old man, a young boy and a giant fish. In a perfectly crafted story, which won for Hemingway the Nobel Prize for Literature, is a unique and timeless vision of the beauty and grief of man's challenge to the elements in which he lives.

'It is unsurpassed in Hemingway's oeuvre. Every word tells and there is not a word too many'
Anthony Burgess

'A quite wonderful example of narrative art. The writing is as taut, and at the same time as lithe and cunningly played out, as the line on which the old man plays the fish'
Guardian

arrow books

THE POWER OF READING

Visit the Random House website and get connected with information on all our books and authors

EXTRACTS from our recently published books and selected backlist titles

COMPETITIONS AND PRIZE DRAWS Win signed books, audiobooks and more

AUTHOR EVENTS Find out which of our authors are on tour and where you can meet them

LATEST NEWS on bestsellers, awards and new publications

MINISITES with exclusive special features dedicated to our authors and their titles

READING GROUPS Reading guides, special features and all the information you need for your reading group

LISTEN to extracts from the latest audiobook publications

WATCH video clips of interviews and readings with our authors

RANDOM HOUSE INFORMATION including advice for writers, job vacancies and all your general queries answered

Come home to Random House

www.rbooks.co.uk